Too Close to Home

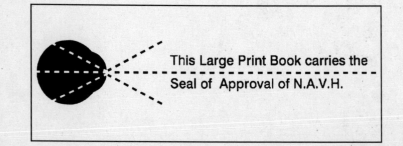

WOMEN OF JUSTICE, BOOK 1

Too Close to Home

Lynette Eason

THORNDIKE PRESS

A part of Gale, Cengage Learning

GALE
CENGAGE Learning·

Detroit • New York • San Francisco • New Haven, Conn • Waterville, Maine • London

GALE
CENGAGE Learning™

LIBRARY OF CONGRESS CATALOGING-IN-PUBLICATION DATA

Eason, Lynette.
    Too close to home / By Lynette Eason.
        p. cm. — (Thorndike Press large print Christian fiction)
    (Women of justice ; bk. 1)
    ISBN-13: 978-1-4104-3669-6 (hardcover)
    ISBN-10: 1-4104-3669-1 (hardcover)
    1. United States. Federal Bureau of Investigation—Fiction. 2. Criminal investigation—Technological innovations—Fiction. 3. Large type books. I. Title.
    PS3605.A79T66 2011
    813'.6—dc22   2011001247

Published in 2011 by arrangement with Revell Books, a division of Baker Publishing Group.

Printed in Mexico
1 2 3 4 5 6 7 15 14 13 12 11

Dedicated to Jack,
Lauryn, and Will Eason —
I love you to pieces.

1

"Wake up, partner," the voice rumbled in his ear as Connor Wolfe's sleep-drugged mind struggled to keep up. "We've found another body. In a dumpster behind the BI-LO off East Main."

He shifted the phone and glanced at the clock.

The number 2:08 glared at him. Great. Just the way he wanted to start his Monday morning.

"Be right there." He hung up and closed his eyes for a brief moment before gathering the energy to swing his feet to the floor. Two hours of sleep. Well, he'd gone with less. However, at the age of forty-two, he seemed to feel the lack a lot more than he did ten years ago. Shaking his head to fling off the fog of interrupted sleep, he headed for the shower, wondering if he should wake up Jenna, his sixteen-year-old daughter, or just hope she slept through the rest of the night.

He settled on leaving her a note. Fifteen minutes later, hair still damp, he directed his unmarked Ford toward the crime scene. His partner, Andrew West, would meet him there.

First a cop, then a homicide detective with SLED, the South Carolina Law Enforcement Division, Connor had seen a lot in relation to crime, but this case had him by the throat and wouldn't let go. Six disappearances and now three dead bodies — and very limited evidence. The first girl disappeared sixteen months ago. When the second victim disappeared two months later, speculation ran rampant. Were the vanishings related?

Then the third girl, Leslie Sanders, disappeared five weeks after that, and SLED had taken over the case. Connor had been the lead detective assigned to it, not only because it was his hometown, but because he'd also requested it. He had a lot of contacts — and he hoped he'd be able to spend more time with Jenna if they were living in the same city for an extended period of time. Since accepting the position as a detective for SLED in Columbia a year ago, Connor had lived there and Jenna had stayed behind with her grandparents against Connor's better judgment. But he had to make a living, and SLED operatives were required to live within a fifty-mile radius of the state's capital. However, as long as he was working the case, he could reside in the city where the investigation took place. And be near Jenna so he could work on repairing a relationship he was afraid was beyond help.

On the plus side, he'd been paired up with Andrew West, a new detective working his first case with SLED, but Connor's closest friend for many years. A man he considered the brother he'd never had. The match had been perfect.

Connor knew in his gut the girls' deaths were connected — he just couldn't prove it. The first two crime scenes didn't even connect the two girls except for one thing. They'd both had a baby.

If this third dead girl showed evidence of giving birth, Connor would know without a doubt they had a serial killer on their hands. He hoped he was wrong.

Was pretty sure he wasn't.

It was why he and Andrew had been called in on this case. Sheriff Chesterfield usually hesitated about calling in outside help, but was professional enough to admit he needed their help and resources.

Dead girls and terrified parents. Not a pretty combination. Add gullible kids who thought bad things only happened to other people, and he had a potentially explosive situation on his hands. The attorney general's office and the governor demanded answers he didn't have, the media wouldn't let it go, and the mayor had resorted to threats.

Unfortunately, Connor had no idea what to tell them.

And very little to show. A fiber here, a hair there, but nothing that matched up with anything or anyone in the criminal database. Witnesses whose stories conflicted left them with nothing solid. And even the similarities in the witnesses' stories hadn't panned out. The killer was so good it was terrifying.

And then there was Jenna.

Connor's angry sixteen-year-old daughter defied him at every opportunity. When her mother died four years ago in a car wreck, it turned his little family's world upside down — and dropped him and his daughter into the midst of a battle of the wills.

Flashing lights and a yellow tape barrier ahead demanded his attention. Right now, he had another murder to solve — and at least three more missing girls to find.

Connor wheeled to a stop and hopped out of the vehicle. Even in the wee hours of the morning, a small crowd had formed to gawk at the sight of a crime scene. Quiet murmurs and speculation filled the air as yellow crime scene tape flapped in the occasional gust.

He pushed his way through and flashed his badge to the uniformed officer on the other side of the tape. "Detective Connor Wolfe."

The man handed Connor a paper suit and booties for Connor to don in order to protect the crime scene, then wrote Connor's name, badge number, and time of arrival down in the logbook. Connor ducked under and paused for a moment to get a feel for the place. A light breeze held the smells from the various fast-food restaurants, cigarette smoke — and the unmistakable odor of a dead body.

Crime scene investigators worked the area. Serena Hopkins, the medical examiner, hunched awkwardly over the side of the dumpster. She looked up and saluted Connor when he approached, then went back to her scrutiny of the body that lay very near the top. She spoke with her back to him. "Hey there, Connor. Good thing she was discovered when she was. The truck comes first thing in the morning to empty this particular bin. I'll be finished in a minute and you can come up and have a look."

"Thanks, Serena." He shook his head as he did every time he saw the woman in action. Tall, willowy, with straight as a stick, raven-colored hair and ice blue eyes, she was runway model perfect — with a mind so quick Connor finally quit trying to match wits with her.

Never in a million years would he have picked this job for her, but after getting to know her and working with her over the past year, he couldn't see her doing anything else.

Connor walked closer. The stench in the air grew stronger.

Jake Hollister, thirty-five years old with gray-streaked blond hair, efficiently led the crime scene unit. He knelt easily, examining the asphalt about six feet away from the dumpster. Connor had worked with him in the past. From their first case together, he'd quickly grown to respect and appreciate Jake as a professional who took his job seriously. They often met at the gym for a game of one-on-one basketball.

Connor stuffed his hands in the front pockets of his jeans. "Hey, Jake. Is it Leslie Sanders?"

Jake looked up and nodded, his eyes shadowed. "Yep."

"Found anything in common with the other two?"

Jake bagged something that might be evidence, tagged it, and tossed it in his collections bag. He stood to face Connor, his frustration obvious. "I found a folded piece of paper, but it's so ratty, I'm afraid it'll fall apart if I do anything with it here. The lab might be able to figure out what it is. Other than that, there's nothing much on the surface. I'll know more later today." He sighed and used the back of his wrist to rub his nose. "The only thing that tells me these three murders are linked is the gender and age of the victims — and my gut. According to Serena, this one was shot. They've all died differently, but when we get her back to the morgue, I'll bet Serena'll find she's recently had a baby."

"You know, Jake, this guy is really starting to get under my skin."

"Yeah, join the club."

"We've been working every medical facility within a thirty-mile radius and nothing. Not a sign these pregnant girls have ever seen a doctor. I don't get it."

His phone rang. Frowning, he pulled it out of the clip to check out the caller ID.

Jenna? He gave Jake a sign to hang on and stepped away to answer. "Jenna, are you all right?"

"Dad? Dad? Where are you?"

"I'm at a crime scene, honey. I left you a note on the counter. Are you okay?"

Sniffling. "Yeah, yeah, I'm okay. I didn't see your note. I . . . um . . . woke up to go to the bathroom and you weren't in your bed and it . . . I didn't know . . ." A frustrated sigh echoed in his ear. "I had to make sure you were okay. When are you coming home?"

"I'll be there as soon as I can."

"Why do you have to be a cop? Why can't you have a nice boring, safe job?" she whined.

Frustration had him shoving a hand through his slowly drying hair. "Jenna, darling, I can't get into this right now." He glanced at Jake who shot him a sympathetic look.

"Right. Sorry I bothered you."

"Jenna —"

She'd already hung up.

Connor sighed and scrubbed the stubble on his chin. Guilt pressed hard on his chest. He knew he let work consume him. At first it was to escape the pain of losing Julia, the wife he'd loved — yet seemed to battle with

14

incessantly.

But now, if he were honest with himself, work was his escape from the stress of constant fighting with a stubborn sixteen-year-old.

When he'd gotten assigned to this case, he leased an apartment so he wouldn't have to disturb his parents with his crazy hours, and he'd hoped Jenna could stay with him as often as possible. But those crazy hours meant that Jenna ended up staying more with her grandparents than with him, simply so she would have more stability in her life — especially during the school year.

This last week had been a little slower than usual, and Connor was trying to spend some quality time with Jenna. Like last night he'd picked her up from a friend's house and taken her out to eat. She'd come to the apartment and fallen asleep watching a movie.

Unfortunately, it looked like Jenna wouldn't be spending any more nights with him. Instead, she was going to have to go back to her grandparents' for a while. A fact she'd fight him on, but if she couldn't handle waking up and finding him gone . . .

And she shouldn't have to handle it. It wasn't fair to her.

But not much was these days. Poor Jenna.

He sighed and, not for the first time, wished he'd never become a cop. Then again, if he wasn't a cop, he didn't know who he would be.

In the confines of his pocket, Connor balled his hand into a fist, resisting the urge to hit something. Slipping the phone back in his clip, he said to Jake, "Guess I'll have to talk to her tomorrow . . . er . . . later today." And call his parents in the morning. He turned to the dumpster. "Hey, Serena, can I come up now?"

Serena shoved herself back from the edge of the bin with a grunt. "Sure, Connor, I think I've got everything I need. Harley got the pictures so I'm sure he'll be emailing them to you." She looked down into the dumpster, a sad look crossing her face before she could clear it. "I guess she's yours for now. After we get her to the morgue, I'll be able to tell you a lot more."

Serena made her way down the strategically placed stepladder and allowed Connor to replace her. He climbed up and peered over the edge. The smell assaulted him and he turned his head away for a moment. She'd been here for at least a day, although, in the steamy, southern, September heat, it was hard for him to tell exactly how long. And she could have been dead somewhere else for a period of time before landing here. He'd leave that speculation to Serena.

Leslie had disappeared a little over a year ago. Now this.

Dear God, why?

It was the only thought he'd allow to pass through his mind before professionalism took over. "Blonde, eighteen years old. A hundred pounds or so." Ignoring the stench, Connor spoke into his voice-activated recorder to register the details. Later, he would write out the transcript to study.

Jake grunted.

Connor continued his assessment. "Face up, arms above her head, gunshot wound to the chest. Fully dressed, jewelry on both hands, bracelets, earrings. Miniskirt and sandals. Cuts and bruises on both knees."

He turned and looked down at Jake. "Who found her?"

"Guy over there in the car."

Connor's gaze followed Jake's pointing finger. "Homeless and looking for something to eat?"

"Yep. Guy's crazy as a loon. Kept saying something about the black monster who was going to eat him."

"Black monster?"

Jake shrugged. "Like I said, he's nuts."

"Let's see if there are any cameras around

17

here that might have caught something," he said, and motioned to the guy who worked with Serena. Johnny St. James, late fifties, gray hair, and a potbelly. One of the nicest guys Connor knew. After all this guy had seen on his job, he still managed to enjoy living.

Johnny arrived, gurney in tow, and Connor shook hands with him. "Good to see you again, Johnny. Sorry it has to be this way."

Johnny nodded and stepped over to the dumpster. "Yeah, me too. Crying shame. Where are the parents of these kids anyway?"

"Wish I knew, John."

Guilt stabbed him again as he thought about Jenna. Parents, himself included, had to work and couldn't keep an eye on a teenager 24/7. Still . . .

Connor walked over to greet the detective standing beside the police car. "Hey there, partner. Heck of a way to start a Monday. You get any sleep?"

Andrew heaved a long-suffering sigh. "About two hours."

"Yeah, me too. How's Angie?"

"Mad."

"Whew. That's not good."

"Tell me about it." Andrew slapped a

manila folder on the hood of the car. "Here are the photos from the other two crime scenes. Wanna take a look?"

"Yeah, I guess."

Pulling the photos from the folder, Andrew spread them out. Connor separated the pictures, his gut twisting at the sight of the ugly deaths these girls had suffered.

Again he thought about Jenna. Just the thought of her ending up like those girls.

He shuddered. Somehow he had to figure out a way to be there for her more.

"All right, let's talk through it." Andrew pointed to Amanda Sheridan. "Sixteen years old, strangled, had a baby."

Connor tag teamed with Andrew, bouncing facts and ideas off of each other helped keep everything straight in his mind — and helped solve more than one case. "She was found in a ditch off the side of I-85 approximately two days after she was killed. Scared that poor trucker to death."

"Bet he'll use rest areas from now on."

Shoving his hands in his pockets, Connor ignored the sweat running down his back and looked over at the dumpster. "The second girl, Bethany Whitehouse, she was drowned."

"Yeah, the marks around her neck show the guy held her with her back facing him.

Thumbs pressed against the back of her neck."

"No prints, though. He wore gloves."

"Uh huh. Couldn't make it easy for us."

Connor stepped away, then walked back and looked at the pictures once more. "I don't get it. What's the connection? There's got to be something to link these girls and we're not seeing it — I mean besides the baby angle. This dumpster is in a really busy area, fully visible to passing traffic. The side of the road, also in plain sight. But the girl who drowned washed up on a man-made beach at Lake Bowen twenty miles out of town."

Andrew rubbed his eyes. "If there's a link, it's subtle."

"Or something we just haven't even come across yet." Connor gathered the photos back and stuffed them in the folder. They called out to him, demanding justice. "Go make nice with Angie and I'll see you in the morning."

"It *is* morning, but I got you. She's just gotten over being mad at me from the last time I had to get up and leave. Now, I get to start all over again." He slapped Connor on the back. "No, Angie can wait. You go handle the parents, I'll hang around here and see what else I can come up with."

20

Angie and Andrew had been married less than three months. They were both still adjusting to life as a couple — and all the job entailed. Thirty-two-year-old Andrew had been a detective for six months. Angie might act mad, but Connor knew how much she loved the guy. Connor wasn't worried about his friend's marriage.

Right now, he dreaded telling Leslie Sanders's parents that their daughter would never come home again. He practiced his speech all the way to the morgue.

From behind the yellow tape, The Agent watched them work. He watched the man snap pictures of the crowd as he'd known he would. They would study those pictures later, comparing them to the other two scenes with the crowds. But they wouldn't notice him. He didn't stand out. And he never looked the same. So he didn't try to turn from the photographer, but he never looked directly at the camera either.

They'd found Leslie faster than he'd thought they would, but that was all right. She'd served her purpose and The Agent had done his job.

He'd disposed of the body.

The man, obviously a cop, climbed up to

look over the bin. He looked sad . . . then angry.

The Agent shook his head, wanted to explain that there was no need for sorrow or anger. Leslie would live on. She'd done something not many people did in their lives. Leslie had provided extreme joy and pleasure to those who deserved it — and he'd assisted in that.

And been well compensated for it too, he thought smugly.

Yes, it would all be fine. Leslie would be buried and he could move on to the next girl. His fingers itched and he wondered how he should kill the next one. Experimenting with different ways to kill them was interesting — and disgusting too. *Drowning was the way to go. Simple, no mess. Yeah. Drowning.* The cops would try to figure out why the girls died by different methods, but there really wasn't anything to figure out.

It had been hard killing the first one. Strangling her, watching the life seep from her eyes. He'd thrown up afterward. The second one he'd drowned so he couldn't see her soul drain, or the fixed empty stare. That had been better. The crazy thing was, he hadn't killed Leslie. Boss had done that. Shot her in the chest. Very messy. It turned The Agent's stomach and he knew he could never shoot one of the girls. A cop? Yeah, he could shoot a cop. But the girls, yes, he'd probably just drown them from now on.

He scanned the scene again. For a moment he chilled at the expression on the tall cop's face. This man might cause him some trouble.

The Agent shrugged it off. No, he was too careful, too skilled, too smart. He had his purpose. To fulfill Boss's orders. To carry out the plan.

And live well because of it.

Oh yes, the money was definitely important. Lots and lots of delicious money.

Soon he'd have enough and be one of the deserving ones. Equal to those who'd benefited from Leslie and the other girls' great sacrifice. A sacrifice that brought infinite joy and smiles. Yes, soon he would smile like that too.

It was as simple as that.

2

Jenna Wolfe stared at her geometry teacher, Mr. Alexander, and tried to paste a look on her face that said, "This is fascinating stuff."

In truth, she was bored silly — and sleepy. Finding her dad gone last night had creeped her out. Sure, she was sixteen, almost seventeen, and often stayed by herself, but she didn't like waking up to an empty house. Regret cramped her. She shouldn't have called her dad and acted like a whiny baby. Now she was stuck staying at her grandparents'. She wanted her dad home — with her, all night long.

Jenna sighed, shifted in her seat, and tried to focus on the math, but really, who cared about the Pythagorean theorem?

Jenna had more serious things to deal with right now. Like how to get Bradley Fox to notice her. Frankly, Jenna thought the two of them would make the perfect couple.

"The Fox and the Wolfe." It was just too

cool — and would make the most romantic love story in the history of Stanton High School.

Jenna knew she was pretty; everyone told her so. She also saw it every morning when she looked in the mirror. A flawless complexion, curly dark hair, and wide blue eyes.

Unfortunately, she was also shy when it came to boys she liked. Shy and socially inept. The fact caused her immense frustration, because she could have incredibly intelligent conversations in her daydreams or on the computer, but when it came to actually doing it in real life, she totally froze up.

"Psst. Jenna."

Jenna cut her eyes to her best friend, Patty Thomas, who sat in the desk directly next to hers. Jenna raised a brow and silently mouthed, "What?"

Patty held up a folded piece of paper in front of her geometry book so the teacher wouldn't be able to see what she was doing if he happened to turn from the board. She subtly waved it.

Jenna stuck her hand out and palmed it with a practiced move. Hiding it under her desk, she opened it and read "Party this Friday at Janet's. BYOB!"

Jenna sighed. BYOB as in "bring your own

bottle" . . . of beer, wine, a cooler, whatever. Where would she get her hands on some this time? She'd worked so hard to become one of the "in" crowd, but lately, the partying and drinking were beginning to wear thin. So were the lies she constantly had to tell — and remember.

She simply looked up and nodded.

Patty tossed her chestnut-colored hair and grinned, green eyes snapping. She mouthed, "Cool."

Jenna watched Patty turn her attention back to Mr. Alexander. The irony didn't escape Jenna. She shook her head and blinked her eyes, forcing them open. Patty could sleep through class and still ace every test she took. Unfortunately, Jenna couldn't do that.

She had to study for every A she got. Lately, though, she couldn't stay motivated, no matter how hard she tried. It was September and five weeks into the school year. Her four-and-a-half week interims had not been great. Not terrible, but definitely not great either. Her dad didn't even know about those grades. He would, however, ask to see her report card. That gave her roughly four weeks to get her grades back up.

Right now, though, the only thing that really interested her was Bradley Fox and the new friend she'd met on the internet, 2COOL2BLV — Too cool to believe.

Now there was someone she could trust. Oh, she knew that she should be careful, that there were some real psychos out there just looking for some gullible young thing to take advantage of, but 2COOL wasn't like that. He was incredibly sweet and always knew the right thing to say. And besides, Jenna was smarter than the average teen.

After all, her dad was "supercop."

Jenna smirked. When her dad had finally decided to let her get online by herself, she had been fully "in-serviced" on the hazards of the internet — and the creeps who prowl it. He was so paranoid it was ridiculous.

She knew how to take care of herself. 2COOL had proven himself; lived up to his name. After all, she'd been talking to him online for two months now. If he was some perv, he'd have made his move by now, right? A thrill shot through her. She couldn't wait to get home to talk to him. At least he was around when she needed him.

Connor knew that if he didn't get some real sleep soon, his body was going to override his brain and simply shut itself down.

But this case haunted him and he knew

that even if he went home this minute, he wouldn't sleep. Fortunately, he kept a change of clothing, a toothbrush, and a razor in his locker at the office. He'd shave in the bathroom, change clothes, grab a strong cup of coffee, and keep working. And check on Jenna. He'd missed breakfast with her this morning. Again. But at least he'd managed to arrange for her to stay with his parents for the next little while.

"Hey, partner, how'd it go?" Andrew entered the locker room and slapped him on the back.

Connor didn't have to ask Andrew what he was asking about. Andrew hadn't gone with him to break the news to Leslie's family; he'd stayed at the crime scene with the investigators, questioning witnesses and coming up empty.

"Her parents took it hard, of course. Apparently she was a straight A student, member of the cheerleading squad, debate team, and wanted to go to medical school. She scored a perfect 1600 on her SATs at the end of her junior year. She would have been a freshman in college this year."

"Wow, ouch. You tell them she'd had a baby?"

"Nope, and they didn't mention anything about the possibility of her being pregnant.

Didn't even have a boyfriend when she disappeared a little over a year ago. And according to Serena, the baby was born pretty recently, so she would have gotten pregnant after her disappearance. Anyway, that's one fact we're keeping to ourselves."

"Good idea. Maybe someone will trip up and say something about it."

"Yeah." Connor rubbed the stubble on his chin. "You know, Andrew, I just don't get it. These kids that are disappearing, they're not the kids with parents who don't care. They're not throwaway kids or street kids or even runaways. All six who have disappeared are from middle- to upper-class families. Families with money. What do you make of that?"

"Coincidence?"

Connor shrugged. "Maybe, but I don't buy it. There's got to be a connection somewhere. All six have access to money, but there's been no kind of ransom demand. Weird. But if you look at all the evidence, the information we've gathered, they're not girls who found out they were pregnant and decided to run away. At least it doesn't seem like it. But what's the link?"

"The first girl, Amanda Sheridan. She was sixteen years old, blonde, blue eyes."

"Right."

"The second girl. Bethany Whitehouse. Brown hair, fair skin, brown eyes."

"Polar opposites. The only thing they have in common is their age and they're Caucasian. They went to rival high schools."

"The third girl, the one we just found. Leslie Sanders, eighteen, green eyes, blonde hair, Caucasian."

Connor shook his head. "Then the guy went off the mark and snatched Sydney Carter, who has red hair, fair skin, and freckles."

"But still a teen. He isn't going by how they look, like hair color or skin color. There's something else. It's possible it's the age factor. They're easy to access, innocent, trusting, or if they're suspicious at first, he's charming enough to put them at ease."

"The next two girls, Veronica Batson and Julienna Harris. They're both black."

"It's enough to make me crazy. The girls aren't taken for ransom. They're all pretty, attractive girls. Human trafficking? Sex trade? Then when they get pregnant, they're no longer useful? But where are the babies? Sold on the black market? I may be grabbing at straws, but it's because I don't have anything else to grab."

Connor slammed the locker and walked over to the sink to splash cold water on his face. In the mirror, Connor watched Andrew nod, then pinch the bridge of his nose for a brief moment.

"I don't know," his partner muttered, "it hurts my head after a while to think about it, and yet I find I can't think of much anything else. Angie's ready to join the force just to be able to see me once in a while. And I'm about ready to let her. You talk to Jenna this morning?"

Connor winced. "No, not yet." He glanced at his watch. 8:15. Too late. "She's at school already. Her grandmother would have dropped her off about twenty minutes ago."

"Don't let this case kill your relationship with her, Connor."

"I don't plan to."

"Did you make it to church this weekend?"

Connor shot Andrew a look that was half irritated, half amused. "You ask me that every Monday morning. What? You think the answer's going to change?"

"God's in the miracle business," Andrew drawled and shrugged. "You never know."

"Well, it'll take more than a miracle to get me in church," Connor muttered under his breath — just loud enough for Andrew to catch it.

"You know, Jenna might benefit from going to church. Angie and I would be glad to have her come with us even if you're not interested."

"Aw, man, are you going to start beating on that dead horse again? You know how I feel about church."

"Okay, if not church, what about God? Do you really want Jenna thinking it's all right to ignore God?"

Connor slapped a hand against the sink. "No, I don't want her thinking that, Andrew, but what do I tell her, how do I make her go to church when I don't even know what I believe about God?"

Andrew blew out a sigh. "I don't know, partner, but you've got to do something. Jenna's not a little girl anymore, and she's going to follow in your spiritual footsteps. It's your job as her dad to guide her —"

Connor held up a hand. "Enough." He shot his friend a glare and bit his tongue against the desire to tell Andrew in no uncertain terms to back off.

And Andrew could read body language pretty well. He walked over and gave Connor another slap on the back before heading for the door. "I'm going home for a couple of hours of sleep — and to reassure Angie she's still married to me. I guess I won't even bother suggesting you head home."

Connor grimaced. "Thanks, partner."

Andrew shook his head and left without another word.

After Connor finished in the bathroom, he headed for his desk.

An officer stopped him. "Hey, Connor?"

"Yeah?"

"You know that piece of paper from the dead girl's pocket? Jake's got something for you."

Fatigue momentarily forgotten, Connor's senses leapt into alert mode. "What?"

"Don't know, I was just told to pass the message on if I saw you before you checked your messages." The young officer nodded toward the blinking red light on Connor's phone.

"Thanks."

Connor closed the distance to his desk and reached for his handset. Ignoring the message light, he dialed Jake's extension.

"Jake Hollister."

"What'd you find on Leslie Sanders?"

"Hey, Connor. I'm fine, thanks so much for asking. And how's your morning going?"

"Sorry, man."

" 'S all right. I'm just messing with you." Jake became all business. "Yeah, we found a piece of paper with an Instant Message conversation between the screen names TIME4FUN and SEASANDS4EVR. Gimme your fax number so I don't have to look it up and I'll send you a copy. The elevator's broken again and I'm not walking over there."

Connor rattled off the number, thanked the man, and hung up. He grabbed his coffee and headed to stake out the fax machine, still wondering what he was going to do about Jenna.

3

Samantha Cash loved her job as a computer forensics expert with the FBI. And hated it. As an agent, she got to be in the field occasionally, so she made sure she kept her skills honed with drills and practice; as a computer expert, she also got called on to catch the criminals by using her intellect.

Chasing bad guys gave her a thrill no roller-coaster ride could match. Yet knowing what they'd done to their victims made her sick, and the fact that she was a necessary entity in a world gone mad grieved her. However, each time she assisted in putting one of the bad guys away behind bars, a measure of peace returned to her soul. If only she could find the one —

Don't go there, Sam. She dragged her weary body out of the car and waved at the driver, her friend and sometimes partner, Tom Jackson. "Thanks for the ride. See you next time."

"That was good work, Sam. You're a genius."

Sam heard the fatigue in his deep voice and it matched her own. She could only manage a weak smile as she studied his good-looking features. Tall, with bright green eyes and a strong chin. She felt sibling affection for him, but knew he had the females after him wherever he went. Not for the first time, she wondered why she didn't feel anything romantic for the guy. Ignoring her internal questions, she nodded. "Yeah, you too."

Concern pulled his blond brows down. "Get some rest."

"That's the plan. My beeper's off for the next twelve hours." Speaking of which — Sam reached down and flicked the button that would shut off the palm-sized device. "Bye, Tom. Be careful driving home. You're as worn out as I am."

"I'll be careful. I gotta get to my other job."

Tom was former FBI. An ex-agent who'd decided he liked marching to his own drummer instead of following someone else's beat. Now, he hired out his skills to the highest bidder. Because of his previous work with the FBI, he often still worked for them, just as contract labor. He also teamed up with Sam when the need arose. As far as partners went, Tom was a good one.

"No way," she protested. "You need rest, my friend."

"Got bills to pay."

"Ugh, don't I know it. All right, see you later."

He drove off and Sam turned to trudge up the three steps to her first-floor apartment. Turning the key in the lock, she shoved open the door and stepped into the silent cavern that she called "home." Four white walls, a fireplace, and the musty smell of closed-up space greeted her.

Since she rarely spent any time here, she didn't bother to keep anything living that might expire during one of her many absences, and much to her mother's chagrin, decorating didn't rate high on her priority list.

She never had anyone over as the only people she could really call friends were co-workers — and when they were together, they were working. Sam merely used the apartment to crash and grab the occasional meal — and sometimes veg out in front of the television before moving on to the next crime.

She glanced at the clock on the wall over her fireplace and groaned.

Four in the morning. Was it Monday or Tuesday? Maybe it was Wednesday. No, definitely early Monday morning — she'd missed church again yesterday. Why couldn't the bad guys keep normal hours? She sighed at the silly thought. Exhausted to the point of being physically sick, she knew it was time for some sleep.

Sam ignored the blinking light on her answering machine, glanced at the caller ID box, and grimaced. Her mother. Not up to twenty questions, she didn't even bother listening to the message.

Walking past the efficiency kitchen on her right, she headed straight down the short hallway to her bedroom located at the end.

Sam kicked off her sandals and fell across the queen-sized mattress. Her body appreciated the soft comfort; unfortunately, her brain refused to power down. Images from the past fourteen hours clicked and whirred through her mind.

Knowing better than to fight it, Sam let herself process it. At two o'clock yesterday afternoon, she had received a call about a parent who discovered several days ago that his twelve-year-old son had been chatting online with a possible predator. The father asked his son about it, and the boy admitted that he was friends with the person who went by SK8BRDR as his screen name.

Then his son had failed to show up for supper.

The father, desperate to figure out where his child was, had gone online and found one email detailing a meeting between SK8BRDR and the boy. The father had immediately called the police who in turn had called in Samantha to find more evidence on the home computer as to who this SK8BRDR person was.

Sam's job as an FBI computer forensics expert had been to find every possible IM and email on the computer. She'd found them and been disgusted by the blatant sexual messages. While she gathered the evidence from the computer, the police had arrived at the scene in time to rescue the boy from the thirty-six-year-old man who had duct tape and a knife in the trunk of his car.

Now, SK8BRDR was in custody, the boy was safe, and Sam was home. Watching the clock, longing for sleep, but still processing.

Fortunately, this potential victim had an astute dad who knew what to do. Unfortunately, a lot of Sam's cases didn't end so happily.

Drowsiness set in. Samantha felt herself relaxing. Finally. She looked at the clock.

Five-thirty already. Ugh. She considered taking a hot bath, but couldn't muster the energy necessary for the task. Instead, she shut her eyes praying to dream of a world where innocence was cherished, not stalked.

Just as her eyes closed, her phone rang.

"It's got to be the computers."

Connor slapped the IM fax down on the desk beside Andrew.

"What?"

Connor could barely contain his excitement. "The link. Somehow, the deaths of these three girls and the girls who are still missing are related to their computers."

"How do you figure?" Andrew frowned.

Connor pushed aside a mound of papers and edged his rear onto a corner of the desk while Andrew leaned back in his squeaky chair. "I had an idea, so I pulled all six files and compared the description of each girl's room and the layout of the house. Four out of the six had computers in their bedrooms. The three dead girls are three of the four who had the computer in the bedroom. The other two girls had access to a computer that was either in a family room or the den or whatnot."

"Yeah, but that doesn't mean anything. I mean we went over the computers in detail,

40

checking email accounts, files, documents, everything the girls did on those computers was examined thoroughly."

"Right, but we weren't looking for a link between the computers themselves, just between the victims. But what if their internet activity is related, like they visited the same websites, chatted with the same people? I think we need to pull in an expert and see if we can nail something that shows some kind of common denominator here."

"Guess we could talk to the captain about it."

"I already did. He said to go for it. Even gave me the name of an FBI agent who's supposed to be some kind of genius with computers. Samantha Cash."

Andrew raised a red-tinged brow and nodded. "Yeah, I know Samantha. She and her sister, Jamie, go to my church. Angie's done some ladies Bible studies with Samantha. So, what does the IM say?"

Connor laid it on the desk. "Jake said it was almost illegible. It had obviously been folded and unfolded numerous times, parts of it were torn. It was practically falling apart. Thanks to modern science, he was able to reconstruct it." His eyes followed the words as Andrew read aloud:

TIME4FUN: Aw. Come on send me a pic.

SEASANDS4EVER: 4 Real?

SEASANDS4EVER: Why?

TIME4FUN: Cuz, I know this guy that's hiring models and if you wanna break into the business, you gotta know people. And I know someone. IF you look as good as you say you do.

SEASANDS4EVER: I do. And I even have a portfolio already made up. Just haven't had any luck yet.

TIME4FUN: Well, Babe, that's where I come in. I act as your agent, see?

SEASANDS4EVER: Okay, hang on a sec.

SEASANDS4EVER: Okay, I sent it. You get it?

TIME4FUN: Got it. And yeah, you've got real potential. I think we can work something out. When do you want to meet?

SEASANDS4EVER: Are you serious?

TIME4FUN: Babe, I don't have time to play. Time is money. Of course I'm serious.

SEASANDS4EVER: I don't know. How do I know you're not some perv?

TIME4FUN: Ha. I guess you're just going to have to trust me on that one.

Okay, I'm going to give you a phone number. (864) 555-1234. Give me a call and we'll set something up. You can bring a friend with you if you're not comfortable meeting with me by yourself. We'll even meet in a public place the first time. Lots of people around and you can check me out.

SEASANDS4EVER: COOL!

"That's it?"

Connor nodded. "Yep. We called the number and it was a prepaid cell phone. Out of order now, of course. No way to trace it. No record of it. Whoever got it paid with cash."

"So now we see if we can get something else from the computers."

"Yeah." Connor sighed and rubbed his eyes. He needed a break.

Andrew said, "Oh, I went over and watched the video from the grocery store. It's not clear at all, but it does show Leslie being dumped by some guy draped in black."

"The black monster?"

"Obviously. And that homeless guy's no help. I tried to question him, but he's had some kind of psychotic break and is in the psychiatric hospital downtown."

"Great." Connor rubbed the back of his neck and stood.

Andrew stopped him with, "On a personal level — how's Jenna?"

"Hanging in there." He tapped the IM still enclosed in the plastic bag to protect it. "Andrew, you know I love my daughter, but we've got a killer to catch before someone else goes missing — and Jenna is a pretty teen, just the right age. It makes me extremely nervous. I know, in one way, I'm not being the kind of parent I need to be, but in another, I feel like I'm focused on getting this guy before he gets Jenna." Rubbing his eyes, he confessed, "Maybe that's crazy, but every time I see one of those dead girls, I see —" He forced down the sudden lump in his throat that always seemed to form when he thought about Jenna.

Andrew nodded, sympathy flashing.

"Anyway," Connor continued, "I'll be home in time to eat supper with her — or at least at my parents' home to eat. I asked my mother to pick her up this morning, take her to school, and pick her up later. She's going to be staying with them for the duration of this case. I don't like leaving her in the middle of the night. I don't like leaving her alone, period. Sixteen or not, she should have someone there."

Andrew held up a hand. "Hey, you don't have to justify it to me. There's a killer out there who's targeting girls like Jenna. I think you did the right thing. I do think you should call her. It's what . . . a little after four?"

Connor glanced at his watch. "Yeah, okay. I'll call her. Guess I can at least find out what we're having for supper, right?"

Andrew just shook his head as Connor pulled out his cell phone and dialed the number.

"Hello?"

"Hi, Mom, it's me."

"Hello, Connor. How are you?"

He winced at the tightly leashed disapproval coming over the line. "Fine, Mom. Just really busy trying to find out who's killing these girls."

"Any luck?" Genuine interest found its way into her voice. His mother may not approve of his parenting, but she did care about the teenagers and the progress of the case.

"Maybe. I've got a possible lead. We're getting ready to check it out."

"You sound exhausted. How much sleep have you had in the past forty-eight hours?"

"Not enough, that's for sure. But I'm okay. How's Jenna?"

Silence, then, "She's fine — I think. She's supposed to be working on her geometry homework. Would you like to speak to her?"

Connor heaved a sigh and rolled his eyes toward the ceiling. "Well, I guess the real question is, does she want to speak to me?"

"Jenna, your dad's on the phone." His mother's voice faded as she turned her head away from the mouthpiece.

"So?"

He heard that loud and clear.

"So? How about saying hello. You haven't seen him in a couple of days."

"Yeah? Well, whose fault is that?"

Connor had heard enough. "Um, Mom, it's okay. Forget it. I'll catch up with her later."

"Connor, you're going to have to do something about this disrespect. You can't let her get away with acting like this."

"I know, Mom. I know you're right, but what do I do? She's right too. It is my fault. Look, I'll be leaving here shortly. I'm just going to see if I can do a couple more things, then I'll be home hopefully in time to talk to her."

Connor hung up the phone and rubbed his blurring eyes. His mom was right, of course. He definitely had to do something about Jenna's insolence. But what? Ground

46

her, then wind up having to stick his mom
with enforcing it?

Somehow he had to come up with a plan
that would allow him to be both the dad he
needed to be and the cop he was born to
be.

4

By lunchtime Tuesday, Sam felt like a new person. When she'd answered her phone in the wee hours of yesterday morning, she'd refused to go in, knowing in her state of exhaustion, she wouldn't be good for anyone.

However, she promised to be available as soon as she completed the paperwork for the job she'd just finished and had a few hours of sleep. She'd had five, understanding the urgency of this new development in a case she'd been following.

Missing teenage girls who were turning up dead. Knowing how desperate the police were to find this sicko, she'd had a hard time sleeping, forcing herself to do so out of sheer physical necessity.

Now, she was ready to lend her expertise to the local police force. Their computer forensics guy was good, but Samantha was better and they knew it. Besides, they wanted to bring in the big guns for this case and Samantha's boss was happy to oblige them. He'd sent them the best.

She agreed to be down at the precinct by one o'clock in the afternoon to meet with the detectives working on the missing teens case. They thought somehow the vanishings and eventual deaths of the girls were linked to their computers.

Sam's job would be to find that link — if there was one. It had been a while since she'd been called in to work with the local police. As an FBI agent, it seemed like recently she'd spent her time and energy sitting in front of a computer, catching on-line predators. Now, she looked forward to being back out in the field, throwing all of her energy into nabbing this guy and getting him off the streets.

She parked in the visitor spot and made her way into the building. The front door faced downtown, and the traffic zipped past her, causing the breeze to tug at the strands of her casual ponytail.

Jeans, a hot pink T-shirt, and flip-flops completed her clothing ensemble. She didn't bother with makeup. It just got rubbed off within minutes, due to her habit of massaging her temples, cheeks, and eyes when she worked.

She paused at the entrance and put her hand on the door. "Okay, God. I'm here. Show me the way, use my skills, and let's get this guy off the streets, okay?"

Pulling open the door, she stepped inside and slid her sunglasses up to rest on the top of her head. Sam walked up to the glass-enclosed desk and rapped her knuckles on the protective barrier. The woman typing on the computer swiveled her chair around and offered a smile.

"Hey, Sam, it's been a while. How are ya?"

The woman's deep southern accent made Samantha grin back. "Oh, pretty good, Deb, how 'bout you?"

"I reckon I can't complain too much. Who're you looking for today?"

"Detective Connor Wolfe, a SLED agent. I haven't heard of him. Is he new?"

Deb shook her head. "Naw, not really. He's been in the business for a long time, a detective up in North Carolina, then joined up with SLED in Columbia about two years ago to be closer to his parents. The sheriff called them for help on this missing teens case about a year ago. Sheriff's getting kinda grumpy with them, though. Says they're taking up space and not showing much for the effort."

Sam grimaced at the thought of Sheriff

Chesterfield. A good man who did a good job, but was a bit territorial. She knew he'd only call SLED in as a last resort. "Detective Wolfe, huh? I wondered why I hadn't met him before. You guys haven't called me in a while."

"Don't know why not. It sure hasn't been quiet around here." Deb's fingers tapped on her keyboard, and the visitor's pass printed out. She handed it to Sam and said, "Okie dokie, you're all clear. When you get into the 'asylum' you'll just have to look for the name on his desk or ask someone. Good to see you again. Don't be a stranger, ya hear?"

A few clicks on the computer, and a buzz later, found Sam walking through the security door and down the hall.

Sam traced the familiar path to the "pit," a.k.a. the "asylum" according to Deb, where she entered the chaos she loved. Phones ringing off the hook, suspects being questioned and booked, perps exercising their right to one phone call. All in a day's work.

She wound her way around the desks, looking at nameplates, finally arriving at the third desk on the right.

Detective Connor Wolfe. A dark-haired, well-built gentleman leaned back in his chair with a phone pressed to his ear. He didn't look very happy. His next words

51

confirmed that initial impression.

"I said no, Jenna, and that's what I meant. No going out after dark. You understand? Girls are disappearing and turning up dead. I don't want you to be one of them. Clear?"

Despite his firm tone, the man looked bleary and tired. He rubbed his eyes, then squeezed the bridge of his nose — one that looked like it had been broken a time or two. "Yeah, yeah, sure. I'm sorry I'm ruining your social life. You'll thank me later. Look, Jenna . . ."

He stopped speaking, pulled the phone away from his ear only to slam it down. The glare he shot the handset should have melted it. He muttered, "She hung up on me."

"Excuse me. Connor Wolfe?"

He looked up. Blinked. Swallowed hard. Sam could have sworn his face lost a couple of shades of color as he gave her the once-over. "Huh?"

"Connor Wolfe?" she repeated.

Sam started to squirm under his avid scrutiny. Without taking his eyes from her face, he said, "Oh, yeah. That's me. Hang on a sec."

He looked over his shoulder at another detective one desk over who Sam recognized. "Hey, Andrew, when's that computer geek supposed to be here? Doesn't she realize we got murders to solve and kids to find?"

Computer geek? Samantha gaped at him.

Andrew choked on the sip of water he'd just taken, then sputtered, "Uh, Connor, when you pull your foot out of your mouth, you might want to use it to kick yourself in the rear before you introduce yourself to the computer geek."

Andrew pointed at her.

Samantha narrowed her eyes and gave Connor a tight smile. "Special Agent Samantha Cash. I was asked to come in and look at some computers?"

Connor stood, and Samantha was startled to see how tall he was. He dwarfed her five-feet-nine-inch height by at least five inches.

He held out his hand and had the grace to look slightly embarrassed; still his gaze never left her features. "Um, sorry about that. I'm a little frustrated at the moment, and I didn't realize . . . that is, I didn't know . . . aw, nuts, help me out here, huh?"

Samantha bit the inside of her cheek to keep from laughing as the man stuttered out his half apology, half excuse. She shook his hand and said, "One computer geek at your service."

■ ■ ■ ■

What was it with women and the careers they picked these days? First Serena, and now Samantha. She reminded Connor of a character on one of those cop shows he'd watched once or twice when he needed a good laugh at the thought of solving a case in the time frame of sixty minutes.

He swallowed hard, looked closer. She was also a dead ringer for —

Uh-uh. No way, not going there.

Straight blonde hair, blue eyes, no makeup, and just about perfect. Definitely not your typical computer geek. He really had to stop typecasting. Still, her resemblance to —

"Earth to Connor." Andrew whistled.

Connor blinked and rushed to cover the awkward moment. "Okay, now that I've got my foot out of my mouth, let's get started. Oh, by the way, that's my partner, Andrew West. I hear you two have met." He watched the two exchange nods.

"Yes, we've met. It was a missing kid, suspected online predator case, about two years ago. Andrew was the uniform on the scene. How's Angie?"

"She's great. Good to see you again."

Andrew's mirth still danced in his eyes. Connor shot him a warning look, mixed with a question Andrew would be answering later, before turning back to Samantha.

All business now, she asked him, "Okay, what do you have for me?"

Connor followed her lead. "Obviously you're aware of the missing teenagers case. We think it's the same guy doing it, and we think that somehow he's contacting them through the internet and getting them to meet him. None of the houses have been broken into, no forced entry, etc."

"Hmm, so what makes you think he's getting to them through the computer?"

"This." Connor handed her the IM. He reeled in his wandering thoughts again as he watched her read the note.

She set it down. "Okay, I'll say you're probably on the right track. Lead me to the computers and I'll see what I can dig up."

"We've got them all set up in a makeshift lab. Since my brainstorm several hours ago, I called in some reinforcements, so they're all hooked up and ready to go."

Samantha looked up at him and said, "Great."

He wondered what she was doing for dinner — then wondered what he was doing wondering that. Since Julia's death, he

hadn't even thought about other women —
at least not in terms of actually wondering
if she'd say yes if he asked her out. Was he
contemplating a date? With someone he just
met thirty seconds ago? Whoa! Back up,
buddy.

"I'm ready if you are."

Connor felt his face flush. He'd been
standing there like a fool, staring — again.
Clearing his throat, he turned without
another word and led her through the
crowded floor, down another hallway, then
left into what looked like a small computer
lab.

Connor stopped and said, "Make yourself
at home. Do you need anything to drink?"

"Yeah, some water would be great,
thanks."

"Sure, and could you start on the computers of the missing girls first? If there's
anything on there that could help us locate
them, I'd like to know it now. We can't help
the ones in the morgue, but there are still
three that we might be able to save."

"You got it. Which ones are they?"

"They're labeled with their names and
pictures posted on the monitors. The three
on this end are the ones we've found dead.
The three on that end are the ones still
missing — and hopefully still alive."

"Okay. I'll keep you updated."

"Great." Why was he finding it so hard to leave? Realizing he was going to make a fool of himself again if he kept stalling, he gave her a small salute and headed for the exit.

Sam grimaced as she watched Connor leave. She didn't want to admit it, but he was cute, if a bit awkward. At the ripe old age of thirty-eight, she'd given up on finding "the one" meant for her and wasn't quite sure she'd know what to do with him if she did find him. The attractive gray streaks in Connor's hair didn't make him look old, but rather distinguished. He'd recently shaved, but hadn't done a great job. He'd been in a hurry. Probably needed to slow down; realize he couldn't do it all alone. Sounded like he needed someone to —

Sam put the brakes on. Immediately. She'd ignore any attraction she might feel. She didn't date cops.

Period.

She booted up the first computer and started a simple routine search. She didn't expect to find anything immediately, but didn't want to skip any steps in the process just in case. She let her thoughts wander as she clicked through documents. She also checked the internet history to see where this girl went while online.

Then her thoughts returned to Connor.

While he was a very good-looking man, his eyes looked tired, weary. Like he'd lived a lifetime and managed to survive, but not without acquiring numerous battle scars.

He'd been talking to his daughter when Sam walked up earlier, which meant he was probably married. Or divorced. Or neither.

She tried to remember if he wore a wedding ring, but couldn't. Oh well, these days that didn't mean a thing. And it didn't matter to her one way or another. He was a cop. She wasn't interested.

Keep telling yourself that, Sam, and maybe you'll believe it.

She told herself to hush up and concentrate.

Click and search, click and search. She printed the internet history, but found nothing else interesting on the hard drive, so decided to move on to the next one. Getting up, she stretched a moment, then sat in the chair next to the one she just vacated.

She started her search procedure from the beginning with the new computer. Nothing, nada, zilch. Print the internet history.

She clicked a different combination and pulled up a document that had been hidden pretty well.

Interesting.

Sam sat up a little straighter. This one had a password. She looked at the picture of the young girl still missing. Sydney Carter. Fifteen years old with a mess of red hair, fair skin, and freckles. She looked like an older version of Annie.

Sam spoke to the girl's picture, "All right, Sydney, what would you use as a password?"

She sighed and ran her hand through her hair, catching her fingers in the ponytail. Oh well, password or no, most likely she'd get in without too much trouble.

Hearing the door open, she looked around to see Connor walk in with her water.

"Sorry it took me so long. I got sidetracked. Got anything yet?"

Sam took the water and thanked him. She looked at her watch and was surprised she'd been at it for about two hours. It didn't feel that long.

"Possibly. I just now found a document that was several layers deep on the computer, plus it's password protected. Give me a minute and I'll be in. Plus I'm printing out the internet history for each of the computers. Then we can compare sites the girls visited and see if any of them match up."

"Great job. How'd you find that document so quickly and our guy miss it?"

Sam shrugged, and ignored the warmth that the admiration in his voice stirred in her. "I just have a system of how I search. Think of it like an onion. I start peeling off the layers. One thing leads to another and sometimes it pays off. Like now, maybe. Plus, I've got a little more direction to go on than your guy had. I'm actually looking for a conversation from email or IM. Sometimes people will have an entire IM conversation, then save it as a document — like the one you found on Leslie."

"Okay, so how do you get into that document on this computer?"

Connor seemed like he was here to stay, so Sam told him, "Pull up a chair and I'll show you. Hopefully, it won't take but a minute."

"I've got however long it takes."

His resolution rang strong. He really wanted to catch this creep. Sam admired him for that. However, she wondered what it was costing him on the home front.

"What about your daughter? The one who hung up on you earlier?"

"Jenna, my one and only, sixteen-year-old. Since her mother's death, she's . . . *we've* . . . had a hard time. Two nights ago, I got home and she'd already locked herself in her room and said she was going to sleep."

Unwillingly, Samantha's heart hurt for him. Widowed. "I'm so sorry. Maybe she was really tired."

"It was seven o'clock. I was an hour later than I said I'd be and she was making me pay for it."

"Ouch."

He gave a shrug. "It's hard raising a teenager these days when you have two parents to tag team it, but raising one alone . . . some days I feel like all I do is make mistakes with her."

Samantha clicked and moved the mouse to click again. "That's tough. My parents felt the same way about my sister and me too, I'm sure. My church was such a blessing for us, I'm sure my parents would have been lost without it." She gave a little laugh. "And our youth pastor was awesome. He and his wife had an open door policy for us kids. We were always at their house or meeting them for some activity. I hate to think of the trouble we would have gotten into if not for the youth group."

Connor shook his head. "We don't really go to church. That was more my wife's thing, you know? I don't know, I guess every parent goes through phases and has those tough days."

Sam looked up from the keyboard. "Try years."

"Ugh, tell me about it. At first, after Julia died, we were both kind of in shock. Jenna was twelve years old when it happened, and my mom and dad kind of stepped in and took over. But then it was time for me to go back to work and Jenna to go back to school." He waved a hand. "We just haven't been able to reconnect; find some common ground. Since I needed so much help with her, we moved back here about two years ago to be closer to my parents."

Sam nodded sympathetically as she went back to work and clicked a series of keys.

Connor stood and asked, "You hungry?"

Once again she paused what she was doing and looked up . . . and up. My, he was tall. "No, thanks, I ate before I came."

"I'm going to go grab a sandwich and give Jenna a shout. She called me on her lunch break from school. It's after 3:30, so she should be on her way home. My mother would have picked her up by now."

"Jenna doesn't drive?"

Connor scowled. "No way I'd trust her behind the wheel of a car at this point. She's going to have to earn that privilege."

Sam nodded her understanding. "Okay,

I'll be right here."

Her hands resting on the keyboard, she listened to his receding footsteps, then focused on her task. Another minute and a few clicks and she had it up. She started reading.

"Oh no."

5

After Connor left Samantha to her search, he had gone back to his desk and called his parents' home. The machine picked up, so he left a message stating he was looking for Jenna, then he'd hung up and dialed her cell phone. When her voice mail came on, Connor swore. Frustration set in. Her phone had practically become an appendage. She'd probably looked at her caller ID and just didn't answer.

"Connor?"

He swiveled his chair around to see Samantha hurrying toward him. She held a piece of paper, waving it as she approached.

"What've you got?"

"Take a look at this."

Connor nabbed the paper. An email saved as a Word document. "Where's all the identifying information? There's no email or IP address for either party."

"I know. Before she deleted the email, she

must have copied it and pasted it into a Word document, then deleted all the identifying information."

Connor read it out loud. " 'Modern Models has an opening for you. Free portfolio, immediate gigs. Must be in excellent overall health, between the ages of fourteen and eighteen, get good grades in school, and be able to handle physical stress. Complete medical history required. $1,000 sign-on advance. Call 555-1234. Ask for Danny.' "

Sam tapped the paper. "Well, it's a name. A very common name, but it's a start, right?"

"Right. And it's the same prepaid number as the one listed on the IM we found on Leslie Sanders."

"Exactly, a link. So, now we get to track down every Danny in the modeling business. And see if we can find a company called Modern Models. And get the medical history for every girl who's disappeared. We need a search warrant."

Connor shook his head and called Andrew over to fill him in on what Samantha had found. "Check this out, partner."

Andrew gave a low whistle. "All right, Sam. Good job."

"Thanks, but I don't see how that's going to help much."

"It might help more than you know," Andrew muttered. " 'Complete medical history.' Why would they need that? That's kind of odd, isn't it?"

Connor brainstormed. "Well, models have to put up with a lot. Maybe they're covering their bases and making sure no one's going to drop dead on them, then have family turn around and sue them."

"I suppose, but it still seems weird to me. We need to check out this Modern Models company. See if it's real, but I'm betting it's bogus." Andrew handed the paper back to Connor, then grabbed the phone book. "M for Modern Models. M, m, m," he looked up. "Nope, not there. I told you. A fake."

"Maybe they have an unlisted number."

Andrew grunted. "I doubt it. Modeling agencies want to *attract* customers, don't they?"

Samantha nodded. "I would think. I googled Modern Models and did a pretty extensive search. I got nothing about any modeling agency, so I'm going to have to agree with you on that one, Andrew."

"You find anything else on any of the other computers?"

"Just one other thing. When I got onto the email servers to look for communication between the girls, there was another reference to a different modeling agency called The Runway. It was on Veronica Batson's email and I printed it off. Here." She handed Connor the copy. "I traced it back to a wireless internet provider, but it's probably some café where anyone can pick up a signal. You might find the place, but you probably won't be able to find the person."

Andrew grabbed up the phone book again and looked. "Nope, no Runway."

"No, and I did an internet search for that one too. Nothing. That was all I found. A few emails to friends, but nothing telling them what was going on. I got into the hard drive's 'slack space.' Most people think that when you empty your recycle bin, whatever you had in there is gone forever. But that's not the case. A lot of that information is still on the hard drive until the drive is reformatted or until new information is written over the old."

Connor and Andrew looked suitably impressed. She added, "Fortunately, most of these hard drives are relatively small and I was able to go through them pretty quick. I didn't see anything else on my initial search that would pertain to this case, but I want to keep at it, do a little more digging. Your guy was good too, so I might not find much more, but if it's there, I'll find it."

Connor waved the paper at her. "You're a genius in my book."

She flushed, and Connor found himself wanting to run a finger down her cheek.

She cleared her throat and said, "One more thing. Did you confiscate the cell phones?"

"Just their phone records, not the cell phones themselves. They disappeared with the girls. No GPS signals either. Whoever snatched the girls knew what to do to the phones to ensure they wouldn't be tracked."

"Then we need the text messages they've all sent."

"We've got them on file. When we looked at them originally, we really didn't know what we were looking for. Nothing really stood out, not even the texts from the day they disappeared. Even the texts that were from prepaid cells didn't give us much to go on."

"Also," Samantha handed over another sheet of paper, "here's a list of websites all the girls visited. It's interesting that four of the six girls visited several of the same chat rooms. You might want to log into these and keep track of what's going on in those sites. Could be our guy is getting to the girls through them." Tapping her chin, she sighed. "He probably has a dozen different screen names, because while I was able to get some of them off the hard drive, I can't tell if it's the same person. Most of the IP addresses are different, which only means he's using different wireless locations."

Connor knew he probably had a blank look on his face. He wasn't computer illiterate, but the forensics side baffled him.

"So, he's wireless location hopping?"

"Exactly." She smiled at him, a quirky little grin that said she knew he was stumped. "If you don't turn anything else up, see if your boss wants me to monitor those chat rooms. It takes a lot of time, though, and you might want to consider setting up a team specifically to watch those sites for any hits. Also, while I'm working this, I'll set it up so I can access the girls' computers from home."

"Really?"

"Sure, it's quite simple. It's called remote access. You want me to explain it?"

Connor nodded. "In basic English, please."

She laughed. "Okay, I type in a few codes on the girls' computers, use my computer from home to type in a few codes, and voilà . . . access with no problem. The Remote Access for Dummies explanation."

He looked at Andrew. "Did she just call

me a dummy?"

His partner grinned. "Definitely."

Samantha blushed — again. Narrowing her eyes, she pursed her lips, then gave a small smile.

Connor laughed and let her off the hook. "Simple enough and very cool. So, are you done for now?"

A shrug preceded her words. "For now. I've done what you called me to do. I'll work on what we've already talked about at home, but I need more information from you guys about what to look for next. I could go through every IM, every email, find every screen name used to log in, etc. These girls used the computer a lot and had a ton of contacts. I'm afraid that would take forever and wouldn't net you much viable information, most likely. So, until you can come up with some more specifics about what you want me to look for . . ." She gave another small shrug. "You might want to remember, too, that there could be absolutely nothing else on these girls' computers. They could have been communicating from any computer in the city if you think about it. And since there's so little information on their personal computers, it's entirely likely they used the library or school computers just in case they had nosey parents. Also, this is the age of texting. Who needs a home computer for communication these days when you can carry one in your pocket in the form of a phone?" Samantha stood. "I'll keep at it when I get home."

Connor momentarily panicked. He didn't want to say goodbye yet. He blurted, "Well, at least let me buy you dinner tonight."

Samantha blinked and Andrew covered a surprised snort by having a coughing fit. Connor wanted to punch him.

"Dinner?" she asked.

"Uh, sure. Oh, wait. I promised Jenna and Mom I'd be home in time to eat with them. Well, that settles it. Guess you'll just have to come home with me."

Connor thought Andrew was going to go into full-blown cardiac arrest.

He's a cop, Samantha! You just met this guy and you're not interested, remember? Hello? And you promised Jamie you'd come by to see her.

Sam slapped the steering wheel as she chastised her impulsiveness. She normally didn't do things like this. Especially when it came to her sister, Jamie. At least she didn't before tonight. *Well, it's not like it's a date,* she argued with herself. *You'll probably talk shop and eat well. Not a bad combination.*

How she found herself in her hot little red Miata following behind Connor's black Ford Mustang and heading down I-85 toward his parents' house, she had no idea.

Well, she had some idea. She liked the guy, found him interesting, not to mention extremely attractive. And he was taller than she. A major plus. But he was a cop. A major downer.

Poor guy. He'd looked so embarrassed after he'd blurted out the invitation that she just didn't have the heart to turn him down.

Yeah, right.

Now she headed west down Main Street, contemplating her impulsive acceptance and wondering what his mother and daughter would think. She had the feeling he didn't issue this kind of invitation very often — if at all. She grabbed her cell phone and punched in Jamie's number.

Two rings later, a hesitant voice answered. "Samantha?"

As always, there was an edge of timidity in her sister's voice that nearly killed Sam. And yet, Jamie didn't sound nearly as bad as she used to. Like she'd pass out in a dead faint if you just *thought* the word "boo" in her presence. She'd definitely made progress.

"Hey, Jamie, I've got some last-minute

plans. Can we reschedule?"

"Reschedule?"

Brake lights flashed, then his left turn signal came on. Samantha followed him into one of the nicer neighborhoods in town. Almost immediately, he turned right into a driveway. The garage door opened and he pulled his car in.

"Yeah, I've had something come up. I'll tell you all about it tomorrow, okay?"

"Um. Okay. Work related?"

"Yep."

"Then, I . . . think I'm going to walk down to the little café on the corner and grab a sandwich. I think. Maybe."

Disbelief nearly sent Sam careening into the mailbox. Automatically, she corrected her turn, but couldn't help the little screech that erupted from her. "What?"

Quickly, she reined in her shock. "Uh, well, yeah, sure. That sounds . . . great. Good. Call Tom and let him know, will you?"

"Sure. So, I'll, um . . . talk to you tomorrow, right?"

Sam parked in the drive behind him, turned off the engine, and released her seat belt. And just sat there. "You bet. Bye."

She clicked off, staring at the man approaching her.

What in the world are you doing, Sam? She didn't have an answer for her own question, so she took a deep breath and sent a prayer heavenward. *Lord, whatever I'm doing, let it be the right thing, please? Oh, and about Jamie? Thanks!*

The house stood magnificent with the sun setting behind it. The place Connor had once called home was a two-story red brick with white columns that ran the length of the front porch. Four white rockers swayed gently in the evening breeze. From what she could see of the lawn, professional landscapers had had a grand time.

He knocked on her window and she climbed out of the car. He asked, "You ready to meet the crew?"

"Ah, sure. I'm ready if you're ready."

"Come on in then. I'll just be blunt. I've never brought a woman home for dinner, so please don't hold me responsible for any embarrassing comments, okay?"

Poor thing, he really did look worried. Sam shut the car door. Patting him on the arm, she said lightly, "Don't worry about it. I have a sister who's ten years younger than I am. I'm used to embarrassment."

His brows furrowed tighter. "I've already explained that Jenna and I aren't on the best of terms lately, right? There's no telling what

74

she's going to say when she sees you."

"She's sixteen. I can handle her, I promise."

He raised his eyes and blew out a breath. "Okay, don't say I didn't warn you. And speaking of warning, I probably should tell you that you look . . ."

He stopped, indecision written on his face.

Curious about what he was going to say, but not wanting to push him into finishing the sentence if he didn't want to, Samantha ignored the flutter in her gut and grinned at him. "Come on, I'm hungry."

Connor walked up the driveway and opened the front door. "Mom? Jenna? We're here."

Samantha gasped at the beauty of the foyer. Marble graced the floor, and a gold and crystal chandelier lit up the entryway. Gorgeous polished hardwood steps wound upward to flow into the second floor. "Wow."

"Huh?" Connor looked at her with a puzzled expression.

"This house. Wow."

He shifted, obviously uncomfortable with the admiration. "Yeah, it's nice. Old money. Mom's money. Dad used to be a cop, but gave that up when he met Mom."

Something in his voice caught her attention, but she couldn't exactly put her finger on it.

"Connor?"

"Hi, Mom." Connor greeted a very stylish woman in her late sixties. The comfortable, yet obviously expensive, blue jumpsuit accentuated her blue eyes. The same eyes that peered from Connor's handsome face.

"Mom, I want you to meet someone who's helping with the case. This is Special Agent Samantha Cash, computer genius. Samantha, this is my mother, Amanda Wolfe."

"Hello, Mrs. Wolfe. It's nice to meet you." Samantha held out her hand.

The woman made no move to take it. She just stared open-mouthed at Samantha.

"Mom?" Connor prompted.

The woman snapped her mouth shut and reached slowly to clasp Samantha's hand in a warm, firm grip.

"Please, darling, call me Amanda. The pleasure is all mine."

Sam caught the questioning look she shot Connor. Nope, he didn't invite women home. But there was something else . . .

"Dad?"

The voice from the top of the stairs brought all three heads swiveling to look up.

Samantha met the gaze of a young girl.

This had to be Jenna. In a word, she was stunning, a female replica of her father. Samantha smiled, but when Jenna just stared, Sam let her smile slip and her puzzlement show.

The girl slowly walked down the steps until she was just a few feet away. Her colorless face had the stricken look of someone who's been delivered some bad, life-changing news. Sam's confusion blossomed into full-fledged shock when the girl whispered, "Mama?"

Samantha drew back in confusion. "What?" That was the last thing she'd expected to hear.

Connor nearly sucked all the air out of the room at his daughter's one-word question.

Samantha's head spun. *What in the world?*

Connor didn't seem able to come up with a response, so Samantha offered her hand to the pale girl. "No, I'm Samantha Cash. I was helping your dad with a case. Do I look like your mother or something?"

"Or something," Amanda Wolfe muttered. "Connor, what in heaven's name were you thinking bringing her here without some warning?"

"Mom . . ."

The woman ignored Connor's embarrassed plea, then turned to Samantha. "I'm so sorry. I didn't mean it to sound like you aren't welcome. It's just that . . . well . . . you're a dead ringer for Julia Wolfe, Jenna's mother."

"Ah . . . maybe I'd better go." Samantha backed toward door, ignoring the temptation to wring Connor's neck for putting her in this awkward situation.

"No," Connor protested, "look, I'm really sorry. I thought it was just me. I mean, yeah, I was shocked when I first saw you, but once I spent some time with you, it kind of wore off. Honestly. It's just the initial meeting. You really don't look that much like her."

"Really?"

"No, you do resemble her, but I do want you to stay."

"Yeah, please," Jenna asked. "Stay."

Samantha could have ignored Connor's invitation, but when she looked into Jenna's pleading eyes, she caved. "Okay, if you're sure."

"Definitely." Connor's mother took over then, all hesitation and shock seemingly forgotten. "Come on, everyone, let's go sit down and eat. Connor, will you take a tray up to your father? He just can't seem to kick that nasty cold he picked up somewhere."

"Sure, Mom, I'll be glad to."

Connor followed his mother into the kitchen, leaving Samantha and Jenna to bring up the rear. The girl still hadn't taken her eyes from Sam's face.

Samantha smiled, trying to ease the girl's shock. "Are you hungry?"

"Not really. And Dad's right. I can see the differences. But when I first saw you . . ." Jenna's eyes finally slid away and she stared at the floor.

"Well, I'm starved. Come on, let's grab some of that food that smells totally delicious." On impulse, Sam wrapped an arm around the girl's shoulders and gave her a slight squeeze.

Jenna responded by tearing up and whispering, "I miss my mom. When I saw you standing there beside Dad, I thought . . ."

Sam felt relieved when Connor interrupted the conversation by coming back down the steps from his dad's room.

"Hey, you guys coming? I'm hungry enough to eat the entire spread all by my lonesome."

"We're coming." Samantha let her arm drop, gave Jenna one more reassuring smile, and headed for the dining room.

Connor gestured toward two empty chairs, and Sam grabbed the nearest one. Jenna chose the one beside her.

Once seated, Connor's mother started passing the food. Jenna scooped a slice of roast on her plate, then asked, "So, what does your family think about you being a cop, Samantha?"

Sam looked at the girl, who kept her attention fully focused on the plate before her. "They're all right with it, I suppose. They worry about me sometimes, of course, but have accepted this is what I do, who I am."

Jenna shot her dad a look, one that Samantha couldn't interpret. Just as the girl opened her mouth to say something else, a loud beeping filled the air. Sam slapped at her side and pulled her phone out of its sling. She looked at the screen. Nothing. Huh?

"It's me." Connor looked grim and tight-lipped. "A text message. We've gotta go. Another girl's disappeared."

6

Jenna stared at the computer screen, the blinking cursor mocking her. Should she type it?

2COOL2BLV had just asked her to set up a time to meet him. Excitement trembled within her. But she trusted him, right? So, why did her finger hover over the ENTER key, hesitating?

Because another girl had disappeared and her dad was worried she might be next. Of course, if he was around more, he could make sure she was safe. So, if she met this guy and something happened to her, it would be her dad's fault, right? Just like if he'd been there that night her mom died, maybe her mom wouldn't have —

Jenna shut off those thoughts, twitched her finger to press ENTER . . . when her phone rang.

She jumped, heart pounding with excitement-induced adrenalin. Snatching up her cell phone, she slapped a hand over her racing heart and swallowed hard. "Hello?"

"Where are you?"

"Oh, hi, Patty. What do you mean? I'm at home on the computer. Where are you?" Music pounded in the background; she could barely hear her friend over the noise.

"Get your tail over to Mason's house. We've got a major party going on here."

Jenna shut her eyes. She could just imagine what her dad would have to say about that. But then again, he probably wouldn't even be coming back home tonight, so what did it matter?

"Give me a few to get ready. Can you come get me? I'm so not into the whole city bus thing."

An impatient sigh echoed in her ear. "You've *so* got to get your license. Your dad is the biggest loser."

Now that was uncalled for. She snapped, "Maybe so, but he's still my dad, so back off. Now come get me or forget it." She changed the subject. "Did you hear? There's another girl missing."

"No way. Who is it?"

"I don't know. Dad didn't say her name, just took off out of here. I've got something else to tell you about too." She twisted a strand of hair as she wondered whether she should tell Patty about the woman her dad had brought home for supper. But the words didn't form. Jenna couldn't even decide what she thought about Samantha.

She looked at her backpack in the corner. Six key chains dangled there. Key chains her mother had picked out especially for Jenna. She fingered one, a bright sun with extended rays. Underneath it said, "You are my sunshine."

Jenna missed her mom — a lot. But in just the few moments she'd spent with Samantha, she'd felt drawn to her.

Samantha. She rolled the name around in her head. A pretty name. And a woman who'd given her a flash of hope. Hope that her mother wasn't really dead, that it had all been a bad dream.

But it wasn't. Samantha wasn't her mom. Just a nice lady who kind of looked like Mom. No, her dad had stolen her mom away from her. Pain lanced her every time she remembered that night —

"What is it? Hello? Jenna, you there?" Patty had to yell over the music.

"Never mind. Look, can you ditch the party and come over here? I've got something I want you to see."

The cursor blinked on. Taunting her. Daring her.

"Aw, Jen, come on. Mason's been looking at me all night. I mean, I've been waiting for this forever, you know? And Bradley's here."

Her heart flipped. Bradley was there? "What's he doing there? I didn't think he was into that kind of thing."

"He came with Jeff and Stuart. I heard him arguing about wanting to go home, that they didn't have any business being here." She giggled. "I so don't know what you see in him other than the fact that he's drop-dead gorgeous."

Jenna looked at the screen.

Bradley or 2COOL?

She clicked off and grabbed up her brush. "Okay, come get me. I guess this other stuff can wait. I'll meet you around the corner. My grandparents are already upstairs in bed, so see you in a few."

"And this makes seven." Connor hitched a deep breath and approached the ranch-style brick house. Samantha accompanied him and he welcomed her presence. After all, she'd be the one to look at the computer.

Because he was sure there was a computer. Normally, he wouldn't be notified of a simple possible runaway, but he'd requested all young girl disappearances be put straight to him. He'd be relieved if it turned out to be nothing more than teen angst or a temper tantrum taken too far. Unfortunately, his gut told him not to hold his breath. Andrew pulled up to the curb and hopped out of his vintage Corvette to join them.

A sharp rap on the white-painted door summoned a haggard mother and worried father. The woman gushed, "Oh, thank God you're here. The sooner you start looking for her, the sooner she'll be home."

Hating to squelch the hope, Connor didn't bother to comment. As always, the thought of what he would be feeling if it were Jenna who were missing filled him . . . and compassion for the couple before him set in. "Hello, Mrs. Abrams, Mr. Abrams. I'm Connor Wolfe, my partner, Andrew West, and Special Agent Samantha Cash, our computer expert."

Mr. Abrams widened the door and gestured the trio inside. "Go on into the living room. We can talk in there. I'm Dennis and this is Maggie."

Connor motioned for Sam to precede him into the tastefully decorated formal area. Mrs. Adams twisted a much-used tissue between shaky fingers as she seated herself on the pristine white leather couch. Samantha and Connor took the matching love seat and Andrew helped himself to the wingbacked chair near the window while Dennis shoved his hands in his pockets and leaned against the fireplace mantel.

Connor pulled out a pad and pen. He looked at Mrs. Abrams. "All right, can you tell us when you last saw Miranda?"

"She was talking to her best friend, Alyssa Mabry, on the phone. They were trying to figure out how to get that thing called a webcam operating." She waved a hand as though she didn't understand the technology young people used these days.

Sam perked up. "After we finish getting the information from you, do you mind if I take a look at her computer?"

"Of course, if you think it'll help."

Connor made a notation on his pad, then looked back up.

Andrew stepped in to ask, "Do you have a picture of Miranda we could take with us?"

Dennis strode over to the piano tucked in the corner of the large room and pulled the five-by-seven photo from the top. He stood for a moment staring down at it, took a deep breath, and walked back over to Andrew and gave it to him. "That's her soccer picture. She loves sports and is well on her way to a soccer scholarship. Very athletic."

Connor had seen the picture when he entered but took another look when Andrew held it out to him. "Pretty too." Bright red hair pulled up into a ponytail with tendrils framing a heart-shaped face with full lips. Green eyes laughed at the camera, a smattering of freckles dotted her nose. One foot balanced on the soccer ball, hands on her hips, she had a carefree innocence about her that gripped Connor's heart with dread. Even if he found her, he was afraid that innocence would be stripped forever.

"Yes, but she didn't really care much about her looks until lately. Just recently she's gotten interested in modeling. Up until a few months ago, she was more interested in sports, school, and her friends . . ." The man couldn't continue as his voice cracked.

Andrew asked, "Did she seem troubled lately? Upset with anyone?"

Mrs. Abrams shook her head, fresh tears glinting at her husband's distress. "No, in fact, just the opposite. She seemed excited, energized." A flicker of a smile crossed her lips. "She doesn't get down often, doesn't really fight with her friends or us." A sigh slipped out. "Don't get me wrong. She isn't

87

perfect, but I'm not aware of any serious problems or issues she might be having. She was just so excited about getting that soccer scholarship —" Silent sobs finally choked off the woman's words and her husband moved to stand behind her, hands resting on her shoulders in a gesture of comfort.

Connor looked at Sam. She averted her gaze, but not before he caught the sheen of tears in her eyes. Softhearted, compassionate. His own heart clenched in sympathy.

Clearing his throat, he forced himself to focus. "Do you mind if we search her room?"

Miranda's father shook his head. "No, anything. Just find her."

While Connor and Andrew stood at the foot of the steps discussing the possible need to give Sheriff Chesterfield a call, Samantha made her way up the stairs to Miranda's room. She'd volunteered to take the pictures of the room. Since no crime had been committed here, they hadn't called in a forensics team, but Samantha still wanted to preserve the scene as it was.

Photographs dotted the ascending wall. Miranda as a newborn. Miranda about three years old, holding a baby in a blue blanket. Miranda graduating from kindergarten in her white cap and gown. And on they went, so that by the time Samantha reached the top of the steps, she had a pretty good outline of the teen's life — at least up until the age of sixteen.

Her phone buzzed. Stopping at the top of the stairs, she pulled it from the clip on her hip and looked at the number. Tom.

"Hello?"

"Hey there, where are you? Thought we were going over to Jamie's to grab a pizza?"

"Oh, Tom, sorry, I asked Jamie to call you. I guess she hasn't gotten around to it yet. I'm still working this case."

"The missing teens case?" He grunted his displeasure. "I have a bad feeling about that one. You be careful, okay? Have you found anything helpful?"

"I'm being careful. As for finding anything helpful, we'll see. Even if they used their phones for texting, it's kind of weird that the computers are as clean as they are." She didn't want to say too much since he wasn't an official on the case. "I'm sure I'll find what I need in due time." Worry niggled at her on a different front. "Do me a favor, will you? Check on Jamie for me. She was acting . . . weird."

"Weird? Weirder than . . . what?"

He had a point. But he didn't know the

reason behind her sister's odd behavior. A borderline agoraphobic, Jamie rarely left her small house when she had company, but definitely never went out alone.

"She said she was going up the street to the café to get a sandwich . . . by herself."

"Wow. That is weird. Want me to keep her company?"

Sam paused. "No, just go . . . spy on her a bit. Make sure she's okay, then call and let me know. Do you mind?"

"Nope, you and Jamie were my plans for the evening anyway."

"We'll do the original plan another time." Sam stepped into Miranda's room and looked around. "Gotta run, Tom. Thanks."

Classically elegant, it didn't fit the soccer player in the picture she'd seen downstairs. Apparently, Miranda had another side to her personality. Cool blues and lace graced the window. A matching bedspread and pillow shams gave the room a completed look. White wicker furniture, a memory board. A corner computer workstation sat to the left of the bed. Samantha pulled out her digital camera and snapped several pictures of the room.

Honing in on the board, she saw pictures of friends, reminders of specific dates, things to do, places to go, people to see.

The life of a teen. Miranda had a math quiz tomorrow.

"Hey, Samantha."

She turned at Connor's voice . . . and gulped. He sure filled the doorway nicely. Clearing her throat, she nodded to the memory board. "This might tell us something."

"Sure doesn't look like a teenager's room to me," she heard him mutter.

Chuckling a little under her breath, she said, "*Your* teenager, maybe. But it looks a lot like my room when I was growing up. I was a neat freak."

A tanned hand plucked a picture from the board. "Was?"

"Yeah, not so much now. I'm never home anyway, so it doesn't matter."

"Looks like this girl in the picture with Miranda might be the place to start."

"That's probably Alyssa, her best friend."

Shoving her camera under her arm, Sam snapped on a pair of latex-free gloves and opened the closet door. Then she pulled the camera from where she'd wedged it against her side and took note of the contents of the closet as she snapped picture after picture. You never knew what you would spot in a photo that you didn't see during an initial sweep.

About twenty pairs of flip-flops neatly lined the back wall. Two pairs of black dress shoes, boots. Samantha flipped through the clothes. Typical teen stuff. Jeans, shirts she would consider too small but were all the rage now. Dresses. Nice ones. A dress still in a hanging bag with a receipt attached.

Click went the camera, the flash lighting up the interior for a brief moment.

She pulled the bag out and unzipped it. "Hey, Connor, look at this." A black slinky dress spilled over her fingers. "Sexy. Expensive." She looked at the receipt from an upscale local boutique. "Six hundred dollars. Wow."

He let out a low whistle. "Where do you suppose she got the money for that?"

"Modeling?"

Connor raised a brow. "Paid for with cash?"

"Yep."

"Rats."

Sam nodded. "Of course. There's nothing about this guy that says he's stupid, just evil." Connor wrote the information down in his notebook. Samantha sighed. "You know, I was just thinking about something. That IM said to 'bring a friend.' Did any of the friends you talked to say anything about accompanying the missing girls to a meeting of any kind?"

"No, and we didn't specifically ask because we didn't have that information to ask about until today. I mean, we questioned friends and acquaintances, but none of them could really give us much. You can bet this will open up a whole new round of interviews. Bag that receipt and dress for evidence. We'll ask, but I'm willing to bet Mrs. Abrams didn't buy that dress. I'm calling in a buddy of mine who also works with the FBI. You might know him. Dakota Richards. I'm going to talk to the sheriff about getting that task force set up."

Samantha knew Connor didn't need the sheriff's permission to set it up. He was simply extending the man some professional courtesy. One more thing to like about Connor Wolfe.

Connor arrived home late, the case still heavy on his mind.

He'd been right. Neither Mr. nor Mrs. Abrams had known how Miranda would have been able to purchase a dress that expensive. Or why she would have wanted one. The only thing they could come up with was that it had something to do with a modeling gig.

But no one knew what the gig was, where

it was, or when it was.

So, now they had more questions and no more answers. Great, just what the governor wanted to hear. He looked at his phone. The man had called twice. Connor called him back, explained where they were in the case — refrained from venting his frustrations — and promised to keep the man posted.

Exhaustion pulled at him, but he knew he had to talk to Jenna. To apologize for having to leave the dinner table again.

And for not giving her fair warning about Samantha looking so much like Jenna's mom. He definitely should have called. The thing was, once he got over the initial jolt, the resemblance ended with some physical similarities.

His wife, Julia, had been demanding, sometimes downright nasty in the way she dealt with situations, with life — with him.

Opening the door, he spied his mother asleep in the recliner, the television still on, the Bible open in her lap. Picking up the remote, he clicked the power button. The television went black. His mother stirred, her blue eyes fluttering open.

Connor moved the Bible to the end table. "I guess Jenna's pretty ticked with me, huh?"

"So what else is new, Connor?" Awareness pushed aside any leftover fuzziness caused by her sleep. "She went to bed about an hour ago. You have to spend some time with her if you want to have a future with your daughter." Her hand reached out to touch the Bible. "And you need to get Jenna into church."

"Church is your thing, Mom, not mine."

"What happened, Connor? You used to go when you could, and Jenna loved the youth group."

"Julia happened. Every time we came home, she'd start in. She'd complain about what was wrong with people in the congregation or roll her eyes over the boring sermon. I rarely heard her say anything complimentary about anyone in the church other than the group she hung out with." He shrugged. "I got tired of listening to it."

"So you used work as an excuse to quit going."

"Yeah."

"Jenna needs you, son. You can't use work as an excuse not to spend time with her."

"I know, Mom. But I'm a cop. A good one. It's what I do, it's my job."

"It's your *life*."

He couldn't argue with that. "So what do I do? Quit?"

His mother sighed, rose from the recliner, and hugged him. "I don't have the answer. But I do know that unless something changes, you're going to lose that girl."

Connor hung his head. Nodded. "I know you're right." He sighed, too tired to delve into the subject any deeper. "I'm going to bed."

"See you in the morning."

She headed for the stairs and Connor spied the Bible his mother had been reading. Picking it up, he clutched it, flipped through it without reading a word. He looked at the ceiling and wondered if there was Someone else he needed to have a talk with.

Setting the book back on the end table, he turned to make his way up the stairs. Jenna's room was the first door on the right. Shut, of course.

He turned the knob, nudging it open, moving a pile of clothing with his efforts. A soft light, compliments of the moon, drifted across Jenna's face. His daughter lay on her stomach, arms wrapped around a pillow, the blanket crunched around her waist. Her dark curls spread haphazardly across the sheets, and he could detect a gentle snore.

Visions of her as a newborn flashed in his mind — red and wrinkled, the most precious bundle he'd ever held. Then she'd been a fearless toddler; an inquisitive six-year-old; a ten-year-old daddy's girl, laughing, squealing, carefree, running to jump in his arms so he could swing her around and around until they both collapsed to the ground, her giggles the sweetest music ever composed.

Then her mother died.

And she'd stopped laughing.

And it was his fault.

He sidestepped the booby-trapped floor to reach the side of her bed. Lightly, oh so softly, he touched her hair, wanting to pick her up and hug her to him, to rock her and tell her how much he loved her. In the quietest whisper, he told her, "I'm sorry. I do love you very much, baby."

Jenna heard the door click shut and she opened her eyes to stare through the dark at the opposite wall. She'd been to the party, found herself bored, wishing she were anywhere but there. Bradley had stayed for, like, two seconds before leaving with only a brief glance in her direction, so she'd told Patty she felt sick and needed to go home. Patty had been disgusted with her, but had grudgingly brought her home.

Jenna sighed and felt like she had a fifty-pound weight settled in the vicinity of her chest. Tears clogged her throat and her nose tingled with the effort to hold back the sobs.

"I love you too, Daddy," she whispered.

But it didn't matter. Nothing seemed to matter much anymore.

7

Samantha's phone had been unusually quiet. Devoting her time to one case severely cut down on her calls. Tom would continue to work solo, partnering up with another agent should he find himself in a situation that required it.

Last night, after Connor assured her there wasn't anything else she could do and had promised to keep her updated on any progress he made, she'd left, her mind humming with all the information she'd acquired in the last thirty-six hours.

Sydney's parents had found the girl's journal, hidden under her mattress, and brought it to the station. Andrew was going over it with a fine-tooth comb. So far he hadn't turned up anything pertinent. The warrant on the medical records had gone through, so those would be waiting for perusal today.

Miranda's computer would be waiting on

her downtown when Sam could get there. She'd given it a glance-through before she'd left, but hadn't found a thing. No hidden documents, no secret IMs, nothing. She'd look it over again today, but didn't really expect to find anything. Very weird. Completely unheard of. But she still had a few more tricks up her sleeve and she'd find something. There was always a trail, no matter how careful someone tried to be.

The slight stirring of excitement at the thought of going downtown again surprised her. She wanted to see Connor. He'd offered to pick her up, but she'd forced herself to refuse.

And then kicked herself. If it had been any other cop, she wouldn't have thought twice about accepting. But Connor made her feel things she wasn't interested in exploring.

Okay, she was. But . . .

First things first. Settling herself in the oversized recliner facing her one extravagance, her forty-six-inch flat screen television, she dialed her parents' number, sighing and mentally psyching herself up for the conversation. She glanced out the sliding glass door to her right. The balcony sat empty, forlorn. No plants, not even a plastic ficus tree to liven things up. At least she had the quiet woods beyond. After four rings the answering machine picked up. Sam glanced at the clock: 8:30. What was today?

Tuesday? No, Wednesday. Wednesday morning. Right. Felt like it should at least be Sunday. Of next week. Her parents would be doing their weekly grocery shopping this morning. She hung up. Oh well, she'd tried, right?

She picked up the remote and hit the power button. A commercial for some fast-food restaurant filled the screen, but her mind mulled over other things.

Tom had called just as she'd walked in the door last night to report Jamie was fine . . . and had indeed walked down to the café to get a sandwich and a cup of coffee. She'd made it safely back to her small house, eaten her sandwich, watched some TV, then went to bed.

Sam felt like crying. Ten years ago, when Jamie was eighteen years old, she'd been brutally assaulted, raped, and left for dead. The road to recovery had been a rocky one, with numerous ups and downs. One of the ups being, she'd moved into a small cottage-style house she managed to purchase while doing some contract work with the FBI. Samantha had roomed with her the first two years, then Jamie insisted she needed to learn to live alone. And so the recovery period continued. She'd finally gotten to the point that she was able to talk about the attack, but to Samantha's knowledge, had refused to leave her home by herself ever since she'd moved in. The fact that she'd ventured out on her own last night was . . . wow.

Thank you, God. Keep working on her spirit, her self-esteem. Help her conquer the fear. And help us catch the guy who did this to her. I know it's been ten years, but he's still out there, possibly still destroying lives. Let us get him, God, please.

Click. She changed channels. Glanced at the clock. Time to go downtown. To see Connor.

Movement to her right caught her attention. Setting the remote on the table, she looked out the glass doors to the trees beyond. A shadow? The sun changing positions. A cloud gliding past? She shrugged and turned.

Her sliding door exploded into a cloud of glass, an object missed her nose by a fraction of an inch. Sam released a scream and reacted instinctively, rolling to the floor, hands and arms covering her head.

Connor slapped the paper down on his desk

and gave a frustrated growl. Then glanced at the clock. She'd be here soon. His growl subsided at the thought.

"What's wrong, partner?"

Looking up, Connor watched Andrew sit down across from him, coffee cup balanced on a stack of files.

"Oh, hey. Morning."

"You look frustrated."

"To put it mildly. It's this case, of course."

"Yeah, it's stretching out too long."

"Way too long. I've been avoiding the governor. Not a good thing. Somehow, we've got to get this guy before any more girls go missing or turn up dead."

"The media's getting stirred up again. I noticed them on the steps when I came in this morning."

"I know. I had to barrel through myself. I guess they're hoping one of us will slip up and give them a juicy morsel."

"Ha. Not likely. I like my job too much."

"Yeah, well, listen to this." Connor picked up the paper he'd just thrown down. " 'In the last sixteen months, seven girls have disappeared. Three of those girls have been found dead. Is there a connection? With four girls still missing, what are the police doing? Why is it taking so long to apprehend this vicious killer? And when will another one go missing? The authorities have declined to comment. This reporter wants to know what they're doing to keep our teenage girls safe.' "

Andrew shook his head. "At least he doesn't have the fact that the three girls we do have were pregnant . . . and we don't know where the babies went. And," he added, "they don't have the IM information or text message stuff. Shoot, even we don't have that, yet. Unfortunately, it won't be long before they have those facts either. I wonder who they're bribing at this very moment. We've got to get this guy, Connor, and get him yesterday."

"Unfortunately, it's almost impossible to catch someone who covers his tracks so well. It's almost like he's . . ." Connor let his words trail off, not wanting to voice his horrid suspicion.

Andrew finished it for him. "Like he's a cop?"

Connor blew out a sigh. "Yeah."

"I know. I've thought it too. If so, that just means we've got to work extra hard and be extra smart."

"Smarter. I've got an idea, but want to run it by Tim." Tim Fields, a forensic psychiatrist, often worked with them on cases. He'd already profiled the killer of the teen girls. Now, Connor wanted to use that information in a rather unorthodox manner.

"What are you thinking?"

"What if we went public with the information Tim's profiled about this guy?"

"Like a news conference?" Andrew looked thoughtful, and Connor could almost see that the man's mind clicked along the same track as his.

He smiled. A partner like Andrew was a rare gift. They always seemed to be on the same page when it came to thinking things through. "Uh-huh."

"Draw the guy out. Take his focus off the girls."

"And put it on us."

"Whew." Andrew scrubbed a hand down a smooth-shaven cheek. "That could be dangerous."

"Yeah. I know. But it might be our only hope of stopping this guy. We'd have to wear vests practically 24/7 and even that's no guarantee."

"Have you run it by the captain?"

"No, I wanted to see what you thought first. If we make this guy mad enough, he might come after us. If you don't want to take that chance, then we'll figure something else out."

Andrew stood, walked to the watercooler, and drew a draft in the paper cup. He drank it, tossed the cup in the trash can beside the cooler. "You know, Angie and I eventually want to have kids. But with guys like this running around killing, all the evil in the world that we deal with every day, it's hard to think about bringing a child into this world."

"Thought you would trust God with that."

Surprise flickered in Andrew's green eyes. "Yes, of course, but as you know, it's an imperfect world. Just because I love the Lord doesn't mean he puts a bulletproof wall around me. Or around those I love. Bad stuff still happens."

"I know. I'm terrified every day for Jenna." Connor was a little shocked he'd admitted that out loud. But it was true.

Andrew sighed. "I worry about that girl myself. She needs you, Connor, more than ever now. I'd hate to be a teenager in this day and age. And Jenna . . ."

"What about her?"

"It's not just you she needs, my friend. She needs your guidance, she needs to see you going to church, to see you making the decision to spend time with her, to —"

"Right, look, Andrew, I appreciate your concern, but . . ." Connor sighed and punched a fist into an open palm. "Back to this. You game?"

"Yeah." Andrew let the topic slide. He'd made his point. "We can't let fear stop us from doing what's right." He nodded.

"Let me run it by the chief and pull Tim in on exactly what we need to say in the press conference." He changed the subject. "Now, want to go through the timeline again?"

"Sure, why not. Can't hurt, can it?"

The timeline, simply a whiteboard depicting the dates the teens went missing, the dates they were found, and the ones still missing, hung on the opposite wall, beginning with a date that started a little over a year ago. Connor pointed to the first one. "She disappeared May of last year, which means we're sixteen months into this case." He stopped, pursed his lips, and eyed the wall.

"What?" Andrew stared at him, confusion glittering in his green eyes.

"I think Samantha should be here for this."

Understanding replaced the confusion, along with a little smug smirk curling one corner of his mouth.

Connor held up a hand. "Don't even go there. I'm just thinking that she's helping us out on this case, so we should maybe wait for her to come on over and go through this with us."

"She's not done with the computers, is she?"

Connor shook his head. "No, and I promised her I'd keep her updated. She wants to stay involved. She should be here in a little bit, but I think I'll call her and tell her to get a move on." He picked up his cell phone and dialed her number, ignoring the excitement curling in his belly at the thought of seeing her again.

Glass rained down around her, nicking her arms and other exposed flesh. Samantha kicked over the coffee table and curled into a fetal position behind it. All she could think was that if the guy had another shot ready to fly, the wooden table wouldn't even slow it down.

She had to get to the hallway, her bedroom, and grab her gun. But did she dare move? Did she dare stay put?

Heart pounding, breath whistling through her nose, she shoved her left hand into her back pocket and pulled out her ringing Blackberry.

A shaking finger fumbled for the right button. "Connor! Get units to my apartment now. Someone's shooting it up!"

"What!" His shout nearly deafened her. "On the way. Stay on the phone with me!"

She looked over the edge of the coffee table at the disaster that was now her living room.

The silent stillness screamed in the aftermath.

Shaking, staring in disbelief, she finally realized Connor was shouting her name. "What? What? I'm here, yeah. I . . . I'm here. I'm okay."

She looked across to the opposite wall and gasped. "Oh my . . ."

"What is it? Come on, Sam, talk to me."

"Uh . . . I think you're going to have to see this to believe it."

A crossbow bolt was embedded in her wall above her kitchen table. And there was something on the shaft. A piece of paper?

Sirens sounded in the distance. "Is that you I hear?"

"That's me. I'm about thirty seconds away."

"Check the woods first. The bolt came from the trees across from my sliding glass door."

"Bolt?" he demanded.

Then she heard him speaking to someone in the car about a crime scene investigator, but her focus centered on the bolt protruding from her wall. Then she slid her gaze to the shattered door. Was he still out there?

Surely whoever had shot the bolt had heard the sirens and gotten away while he could.

A hard pounding on her door had her wading through the debris. She twisted the knob and Connor swept in, followed by four uniformed officers.

At the sight of her living area, they all pulled to a stop and stared.

Connor sucked in a deep breath. "Are you all right? You're cut."

The stinging of numerous cuts kicked in, burning the right side of her face, the back of her hands and arms. "Ow. Guess I've got a few nicks." Without thought, she reached up to comb her hair with her fingers, scattering pieces of the glass onto her floor — and adding a cut to the palm of her hand. "But other than that . . . yes, I think I'm okay."

He stepped toward her and she waved him off. "Don't worry about it, I'll take care of that later."

His gaze landed on her wall and he gaped. "Whoa. Is that a . . . ?"

"Uh-huh, a crossbow bolt."

He walked toward it reaching for his radio.

"Hey, Andrew, you see anything? You're looking for anything related to a crossbow."

Andrew's voice squawked back, "Nobody's here now. We're right across from her apartment. Ground's messed up, like someone was here for a good little while, though. Didn't leave anything obvious or helpful like cigarette butts with some DNA, but we'll get the crime scene guys working on it and see if they come up with anything."

"Good deal. You stay on that end, I'll cover this one."

Samantha watched him study the arrow. "There's a piece of paper wrapped around there."

"Yeah, I see it. As soon as we get the all clear, I'll let the crime scene guys do their stuff in here. They should be here soon."

No sooner had he spoken than his radio crackled again and Andrew came on. "We're good out here, Connor. Whoever this guy is, he's gone. I've already got a crime scene team going over the ground, but don't expect much."

A knock sounded. Samantha moved to get it. She opened the door to more uniforms. Connor turned to the two men entering. "Hey, Skip. Jake, glad you two caught this one."

Jake asked, "Where's the body?"

Samantha gave a choked laugh. "Alive and kicking, thank goodness. He missed and got the wall." She pointed.

Connor said, "Yeah, I want to know what's on that paper."

"Right." Jake stepped toward it, snapping his gloves in place as he tilted his head. With precise movements, he extracted the paper from the bolt and unfurled it. Connor peered over Jake's shoulder. Sam frowned, gave Connor a not-so-gentle nudge, and leaned in close to read it for herself.

He moved over a tad, but she couldn't help noticing the tangy scent of his after-shave, the warmth emanating from his body so close to hers. His hand came up to rest on her lower back.

Whoa! She shifted, moved away before she could see what was on the paper and headed toward the kitchen where she kept her first aid kit. "I'm going to take care of some of these cuts. Read it aloud, will you?"

Jake obliged. "BACK OFF OR NEXT TIME I WON'T MISS."

Adrenalin fired once again, then ebbed. The shakes set in. Weakness hit her knees and she gripped the edge of the sink to keep from falling. Warm male hands cupped her elbows, led her to the nearest chair.

She slumped into it and put her head

between her knees and waited for her world to stop spinning.

"Hey, it's going to be okay."

Sam pulled her head up and looked into his blue eyes. Concern, caring, stared back at her.

He cleared his throat. "Let me help you with those cuts."

Turning, he reached for the first aid kit she'd set on the counter. Swiveling back in front of her, he pulled out the ointment and gauze. Gentle fingers went to work on her face. He said, "I don't think you have any glass embedded. They're all small and look pretty superficial."

She nodded. "I'm fine. I really am. Just . . . a little shock settling in, I guess."

"Understandable. Someone must be really nervous that you've been called in on this."

"But how would anyone know?"

"Beats me, but this tells us one thing for sure."

"What's that?"

"Whoever sent this has done his home-work. He knows who you are, what you do, and he's scared about what you might find on those computers."

Andrew stood in the doorway.

Connor looked at him. "Looks like we

might not need that press conference after all."

"Too late. Chief's going on the news tonight at six."

8

At 5:25 that evening, Samantha pulled into her sister's driveway and cut the engine. Time to find out what was going on with Jamie, to focus on someone other than herself. The desire to get back to the computers tugged at her, but she had to prioritize. Right now, Jamie came first — and she'd brought her laptop with her.

Grabbing the bag of Krispy Kreme donuts and a small suitcase, she climbed out and walked up to the front door.

She knocked twice, paused, then rapped three more times. Her signal for Jamie that it was Samantha on her porch.

The door opened and Samantha gaped.

Jamie gave a little self-conscious laugh and touched her hair, then frowned, scrutinizing Samantha's face. "What happened to you? You look like you had a fight with Daddy's razor and lost."

"Thanks. Just a little incident with my

sliding glass door. I'll explain later. Let's talk about you. Your hair, it's . . ."

"It's what? What do you think?"

"It looks . . . awesome." And it did. Rather than the rat's nest in the ponytail she usually sported, Jamie's naturally curly blonde hair had been stylishly cut into long and short layers that looked beautiful. "Wow, when did someone come do that?"

"I . . . walked down to the salon near the little café up the street."

Samantha could only stare at the transformation the haircut had rendered in her sister.

Jamie laughed and gestured for Samantha to come inside. "Oh come on, it's not that big of a difference, is it?"

"Uh, well, it's not so much the haircut, although that looks great. I guess it's the fact that you went and had it done. You've left here twice" — she narrowed her eyes, drilling her sister with her gaze — "that I know of. What's going on?"

Jamie blushed, ducking her head, then she stood with clenched fists and the most beautiful expression Samantha had ever seen on her sister's face.

Determination.

Samantha sat on the couch and studied the woman before her. "Wow, I'm so impressed."

"Thanks. You brought your overnight bag."

"You should be a detective with those powers of observation." Samantha tried to ease a little humor into her situation. It fell flat. "I'm here to stay for a while if that's all right with you."

"Yes, of course. You know you're welcome here anytime."

"I do know and I appreciate it. Now tell me about you. Twice, Jamie?"

Jamie sat next to Sam. "I've left more than twice. A lot more, actually, if you count the times I've gone somewhere *with* someone. I'm going to get better. I'm going to have a life again. For ten years I've let him win. But I've been doing an online Bible study. The topic of this one was fear. I've learned so much about God now that I've stopped being mad at him."

Amazement set in. Ever since her sister had been rescued from her kidnapper, Samantha had thought of her as helpless, a poor, beaten victim who never seemed to recover from the trauma she'd endured.

Although she'd encouraged Jamie to seek professional help, to trust in God, to believe that she could get better, it stunned Samantha to realize that while she'd wanted Jamie

117

to heal, after all this time, she hadn't really believed she would. Ouch. Something to think — and pray — about later. "So, why haven't you shared all this with me?"

Jamie gave a small shrug. "Because, for a long time, I had a lot of anger. I was so full of anger." She crossed her arms in front of her and shook her head.

Samantha winced. She deserved Jamie's anger. A sibling tiff had ended in tragedy. She swallowed hard. "I'm so sorry, Jamie, I don't know what —"

Jamie held up a hand. "One thing I did come to understand is that you never meant for any of . . . what happened to happen. I don't blame you."

"I shouldn't have driven off. I'm ten years older, I should have been more mature, not reacted and been so . . . judgmental."

"Enough. I don't want to talk about that." She waved a hand in dismissal. "Like I said, I don't blame you anymore — or God. I blame . . . him." She reached out a hand and grabbed Samantha's, looking deep into her sister's eyes. "One day, I hope you can forgive yourself. I've forgiven you for driving off, I really have. I don't hold anyone responsible for what happened except the man who did this to me." She sucked in a deep breath and let go of Samantha's fingers.

"Anyway, I didn't want to say anything and wind up failing. I couldn't rely on you anymore. I can't depend on Mom and Dad or Tom or Casey." Casey was Jamie's best friend from childhood and had stood by her for the last ten years. "This was totally between God and me. Don't get me wrong, Sam, you've been incredible. Finding me that wonderful Christian counselor, talking me into getting my online college degree, getting me a part-time job with the FBI that allowed me to do all kinds of things from my home. But it's time for me to get out of my comfort zone."

"Can you really do it?"

Jamie shrugged. "I've been doing it." She gave a small laugh. "Now, I won't say I *like* it, exactly, but it's . . . freeing." Rubbing her hands together, she drew in a deep breath. "I finished all the classes I could take online and I've done all the labs. I'll be graduating soon."

"I'm stunned."

"I know. I am too. I can't believe I've actually done it. I didn't tell anyone because I was so afraid I'd fail. But I'm only twenty-eight years old, Sam. I want to meet someone, fall in love, have a family, go to the movies with friends. I don't want to be afraid anymore."

Samantha wondered where she'd been while all this was going on. She'd been a regular in her sister's life, visiting, calling. Sure she'd seen that Jamie had seemed to be improving, but this . . .

"How long has all this been going on? I mean, I knew you were staying busy, taking classes, working part-time, but . . ."

"I've been really working toward my PhD for about five years now. I told you when I got my degree in biology."

"Yeah, and you wouldn't even let us throw a party to celebrate," Samantha reminded her.

"Ha. Yes, well, I wasn't quite as mentally stable then as I am now. But, all those classes I kept taking, they kept my mind occupied. I studied day and night, falling asleep over my textbooks, only to wake up and start all over. You know I've always been fascinated with science. And after the . . . attack, I learned more about the human body than I ever thought I'd need. It was a natural thing to go into anthropology. And I chose forensics because . . ."

At the word "attack," Samantha had looked at the carpet. Attack wasn't near a strong enough word for what Jamie went through. "Because you still want to catch this guy."

"Yeah," Jamie whispered. "He's still out there, Sam. I want to work in a crime lab — or at least in some capacity that helps find the bad guys. I want to find *him* . . . somehow, someway because I have this awful feeling that he hasn't stopped doing —" She choked off the words.

"Aw, Jamie . . ."

"Anyway," Jamie ignored Samantha's teary sympathy, "all those classes eventually added up. I realized it wouldn't take much more than labs and rounds to get my PhD." She got up, paced to the window, and looked out. "But in order to do that, I had to be able to the leave the house. Maya's been a wonderful counselor. Either she or Casey made themselves available to go to the lab classes with me."

"Oh, wow. Jamie, I would have helped, I would have gone to classes with you . . ." She trailed off at Jamie's upraised hand.

"Sam, I . . ." She looked away, then back. "I didn't you want to. Don't get me wrong. I knew you'd arrange your life to do whatever I needed, but *I* needed to do this. On my own. Well, on my own with God and the people I asked to help me. You know? I just had to . . . figure it all out and just . . . do it. Does that make sense?"

"Yeah." And it did. She didn't know why she understood, but she did. She should have felt hurt, left out. Maybe even offended. But she didn't. Jamie had done what she'd needed to do.

Her sister gave a little laugh. "I even had one professor who came here to do an independent study with me. The university has made some special allowances for me." She shrugged. "I can't really explain how I worked through it after so many years of . . . incapacitating fear." Swallowing hard, she turned back to Samantha. "I have to give God the total credit for it. And I guess knowing Maya had been through some of what I experienced helped me talk about stuff I couldn't even think about before. It's definitely been one step at a time. Gathering the courage to just open the door. Then taking one step outside. Then another. Before I knew it, I was at the end of the driveway. Then a little farther each day with Maya at my side. Then venturing out alone. And I carry my Bible with me. I know it may seem silly, but it gives me comfort so I do it."

Tears flowed down Sam's cheeks. "Oh Jamie, I'm so proud of you."

Jamie's eyes filled too, but she blinked the

tears back. "I'm going to be okay, Sam. I really am."

The television caught Samantha's attention as she swiped her wet cheeks. Jamie got up to get some tissues and Sam grabbed the remote.

A press conference.

The sheriff was saying, ". . . a white male in his late twenties to early thirties. Probably a loner, yet able to fit into any social situation although he doesn't particularly like it. He functions better around those he considers weaker than himself. He has a very high opinion of himself, that he is powerful and in control, whereas in reality, he actually has very little power or control over his life, which causes him to act out, lash out at those who cross him. It is possible he is impotent and that's why he takes young, pretty girls in the hopes that they will 'cure' him."

Sam huffed in disbelief. What were the police doing? The guy had already taken a shot at removing her from the picture. Then realization sank into her, as well as a bit of anger at being left out of the loop.

They were drawing the killer out of hiding.

Connor sat outside his daughter's school Thursday afternoon, waiting for the final bell. He'd left work at three o'clock, a last-minute decision to pick Jenna up. She probably wouldn't be happy to see him, but Connor was determined to get back on the right foot with the girl.

There was nothing he could do right now with the investigation that couldn't wait for an hour. Nothing had turned up at Samantha's apartment. No prints on the bolt, nothing left at the location where the guy had launched his deadly weapon. Nothing. Not even a footprint, a hair, or an eyelash. Either the guy was very lucky or extremely good. Connor hoped it was the former. At least luck could run out.

Andrew was working on trying to figure out where the crossbow bolt came from. There were only a few specialty stores around Spartanburg that would carry that kind of weapon.

Of course, that didn't mean the guy who owned it had bought it in Spartanburg, but it was something that had to be checked out.

Three computer experts had worked the local library's computers and the school computer lab. And come up with zilch. Frustration didn't even begin to describe what everyone was feeling. Somehow it seemed like there were more dead ends than there were roads.

So far the press conference had produced over three hundred tips that also had to be followed up on. Fortunately, a specific team had been assigned those, leaving Connor and Andrew free to work the rest of the case.

And wait for the guy to come out of the woodwork.

Nothing like drawing a bull's-eye on the back of your head to keep you on your toes. But Connor couldn't let that stop him from doing his best to rebuild a relationship with his daughter.

And while he was anxious to question each of the missing girls' friends again and see if any of them remembered anything about meetings set up with Modern Models, this afternoon Jenna came first.

He heard the faint ringing of the bell signaling the end of another day for the students behind the double metal doors. Soon, those doors burst open and hundreds of feet clambered down the steps to waiting vehicles.

And then Jenna appeared, walking slowly, a couple of books propped in the crook of her arm, a backpack slung over her shoulder. She had her dark curls pulled up into a ponytail, her head tilted as she listened to something the girl to her left was saying.

Patty. Connor wondered at the influence the other teen had on Jenna. Then Jenna shook her head no, and Patty rolled her eyes, placed a hand on Jenna's upper arm, and said something else.

Jenna looked away, then back and nodded, but she didn't look happy. Connor had a bad feeling in his gut. Those two were up to something.

His phone rang just as Jenna caught sight of him. Her eyes flew open and puzzlement flashed across her features before she brought the ever-present shutters down.

Connor waved as he answered his phone. "Hello?"

"Hi, Connor, Samantha here."

His gut tightened at her voice. He *really* liked her. "Hey there, how are you?"

"I'm staying with my sister for a couple of days until my apartment is habitable again. I just wanted to call and see if you found anything about who might have shot up my home."

"Nothing yet. Hey, I'm picking up Jenna, you want to meet us up at Bruster's for some ice cream?"

"Ah, no. But thanks. I don't want to horn in on your time with Jenna."

"Trust me, it might be better to have you there. Come on. It'll be relaxing. Then after

126

Jenna makes her escape, we can talk about the case."

Jenna climbed in the car and slammed the door, eyes fixed straight ahead.

"Well, if you're sure . . ." Samantha still sounded hesitant.

"I'm sure."

"All right, see you in a few."

He hung up the phone and turned to Jenna. "So, how was your day?"

"Why are you so determined to ruin my life?" She laid her head back against the seat and closed her eyes.

Connor sighed. That went well.

Samantha left Jamie's house and headed for the Bruster's Ice Cream store. She needed a break from staring at the computer screen, but she wasn't so sure this was a good idea. From doughnuts to ice cream. Not exactly the best diet.

However, she couldn't resist the opportunity to see Connor again. Curiosity about what Jenna would say to her presence rippled through her. Would the girl resent her?

She turned into the parking lot and cut the engine. Connor pulled in a short five minutes later. He exited the car and the smile on his face sent her heart into overdrive. However, the scowl on Jenna's pretty features had Sam chewing the inside of her cheek. Uh-oh.

Jenna spotted her and stopped in her tracks. Gulped. The scowl faded to be replaced by a tentative smile. Relief eased the pressure in Sam's chest a bit. Jenna didn't mind her being there. In fact, the teen seemed to be drawn to her. Was it simply because she resembled Jenna's mother?

"Hey there," she called to the pair, noticing the similarities in their appearances. Jenna was a female version of Connor. Dark curly hair, wide blue eyes that saw everything — and matching stress lines between their brows.

"Hi." Jenna sounded young, eager to see her.

Samantha smiled at her. "Hi. Thanks for letting me join you." Then she looked at the man bringing up the rear. "Hello, Connor."

"Thanks for meeting us."

A shrug lifted her shoulders. "Sure, I love ice cream."

"No ill effects from yesterday?"

She grimaced. "No, but I'd really like to catch the guy playing target practice with my head."

"What happened?" Jenna stared at them.

"What happened to your face?"

"I was in the wrong place at the wrong time. Some flying glass caught me."

"From what?"

Connor shrugged and answered for Samantha. "Just this case, hon."

"Oh." They moved forward in the line. She was used to her dad not being able to talk about a case, so she didn't ask any more questions on that front. Instead, she looked back at him, studying him. "Who was the girl that went missing the other night?"

Discomfort crossed his face, and he hesitated as though he didn't want to say, then, "She went to your school. Her name is Miranda Abrams."

"Miranda Abrams!" Jenna went pasty white, shock widening her eyes.

Connor frowned. "Yes, you know her?"

Samantha leaned in and put her arm around the girl. "What do you know about Miranda?"

"She's in several of my classes. I noticed she hadn't been there for a couple of days, but I thought it was just because she was . . . um . . . you know . . . sick. She hadn't been feeling well for a while."

"Sick?" he asked.

Jenna averted her eyes, cluing Connor in, so he pushed. "How sick? Sick with what?"

129

The girl clamped her lips together, refusing to answer.

Samantha had a sinking feeling. She remembered what "sick" meant when she was in high school. "Was she pregnant?"

Jenna winced, then nodded slowly. "Yes, I think so. That was the rumor anyway the other night."

"The other night? What other night?"

Jenna gulped. He wouldn't have thought it possible, but her face went even whiter. "Um . . ."

"Don't lie to me, Jenna."

She snapped her lips together again.

Samantha broke in. "Look, you guys can figure that out in a minute. Jenna, what else do you know about Miranda?"

Connor watched relief spread across his daughter's face at the unexpected reprieve from having to answer to her whereabouts. He went along . . . for now. "How many days of school did she miss?" Connor knew he could get the information from the school, but if Jenna could fill them in . . .

Jenna screwed up her nose and looked up. "Um, today's Thursday. I think I saw her on Monday, don't remember her being in class Tuesday or yesterday."

Connor shifted. "Jenna, are you sure you didn't know any of the other girls who were missing? Three of them went to Stanton High and four went to Viking High School."

"No, Dad, you already asked me. I didn't hang out with them. I knew the Stanton High girls, their names, their faces, but that's it. I can't tell you anything more about them." Her eyes became clouds on a stormy day. "But Miranda I know."

Samantha asked, "Who was her best friend? Who did she hang out with?"

"The soccer players mostly. Other jocks. She and I talked in English class occasionally, but not about anything major."

Connor leaned in, intense blue eyes drilling his daughter. "Who would be the one person I should talk to in order to learn more about Miranda?"

They were at the window. Jenna shrugged. "Alyssa Mabry. They're pretty tight. Maybe Charlie Petroskie. They were an item for a while. Until she . . ."

"Found out she was pregnant?" Sam sighed as she asked.

"Yeah." She turned to the gum-snapping teen waiting to take their order. "I want a single scoop of New York Cheesecake on a waffle cone."

The Agent paced. His fury knew no limits. The audacity, the gall of the police to hold that press conference and say those kinds of things about him. They had no idea! His breathing grew ragged, echoing in his ears. He grabbed a glass lamp from the end table, threw it against the wall, and watched it shatter, pieces flying.

Boss said to let it go, not get so worked up about it.

But it wasn't Boss they'd insulted, questioned, called *powerless.* How dare they? Didn't they know he held the fate of all those girls in his hands?

Did they think he was really that stupid? Did they think that he didn't know they were doing it intentionally, that they wanted him to react? Of course he knew, and he hated the fact that he'd allowed them to draw him into a rage.

But they wouldn't win. They'd recant their spiteful, erroneous words or more people would die. It was as simple as that.

He took slow, measured breaths to begin to settle the anger, looking out his window at the large cottage-style house across the field.

Fists clenched so hard, his nails dug into his palms, drawing blood. He didn't care. The pain calmed him. His racing heart slowed. Sydney Carter's body still hadn't been found. Should he send them a note where to find her? But he didn't want her found. She didn't deserve to be found. She'd failed and therefore must be punished.

He allowed himself a cold smile. Let them wait, let them wonder what they were missing. He'd make sure the police got his reply to the blatant message they'd just sent him. But it would be his reply, and his own time and choosing. The only thing they would accomplish with the media would be to generate more false leads and confusing dead ends.

Oh yeah, he rubbed his hands together as the plan formed. He'd make those cops pay in the most painful way possible; he'd show the world who was powerless. And he'd give them more bodies to deal with.

And no leads as to who he was.

9

As a result of recent events, the mayor and the media buzzed louder than a nest of irritated hornets. The heat was on to arrest someone for the crimes being committed against the city's teenage girls.

By Friday morning, the task force had been assembled with Connor appointed as the head since he'd been working the case from the beginning. He had two FBI agents, several local officers, and Andrew.

Sam was recruited to head up the cyber task force. A team of three computer experts would continue to monitor the chat rooms and internet sites visited by the missing girls in hopes that they would log in. Sam had provided an extensive list of sites — and it might not even pay off, but they had to do it, couldn't take a chance on not covering all bases. If one of the girls logged in under any of the usernames Sam had extracted from their home computers, a task force member would be able to trace it.

Since there wasn't anything more forth-coming from the computers, Samantha agreed monitoring the sites would be the next step in determining what was going on.

At the downtown station, Connor sat next to her in the makeshift computer lab, fascinated beyond words as she manipulated the screens, flipped from one site to the next, signed in as a young female teen interested in meeting others.

"What are you doing now?"

"This is one of the chat rooms Sydney Carter visited. I'm letting the group on this site know that I'm pretty, smart, and a senior in high school. I'm also very much into modeling and want to get my career jump-started. I'm not interested in college, just modeling, and will basically do whatever it takes to get a contract with an agency."

"You think these girls are being targeted by men posing as modeling scouts?"

"That's what it's looking like, don't you think?"

"With two agencies that don't exist, it's looking more and more likely."

"Unfortunately, there's no telling how many screen names they're using. I pulled some off of each of the girls' computers, but there weren't any that were the same. I bet each time this guy contacts a new girl, he uses a different screen name."

Samantha clicked again and typed as:

WANNABAMODEL: I only weigh 115, but can lose 5 pounds if I need to.

2BPOISED: I'll ask my agent if he's interested in meeting another girl. What are your stats?

WANNABAMODEL: Blue eyes, long, thick blonde hair. I have freckles and a dimple in my left cheek. Really straight teeth too, compliments of my orthodontist.

2BPOISED: I'll check it out for you.

WANNABAMODEL: Don't you want me to send you a picture?

2BPOISED: Sure. If he's interested, I'll let you know. Hey, listen, I've got to run. Good luck.

"Hmm," she muttered. "I thought I was on to something. Guess I struck out there."

"You didn't send him your real picture, did you?"

"Of course not. Just a picture I dug up on the internet."

His discerning eyes swept her from head to toe. She probably weighed a hundred thirty, not the one-ten she claimed, but she wore it well; it matched her height.

"What?"

He jerked. "Huh?"

"You're staring at me."

"Oh." He felt the flush start in his chest and strike out for his face. "Sorry."

Her cheeks darkened a shade or two of red, and she looked back at the computer.

"How's it going, guys?"

Connor whipped his head toward the door, pulling his attention from the woman beside him. He smiled and stood, hand outstretched to the man entering the room. "Dakota Richards. I saw you in the meeting this morning, but didn't get a chance to talk. How are you?"

"Doing all right."

The Texas drawl made Connor smile. The Stetson on his friend's head made the smile stretch into a grin.

Dakota crossed his arms over his massive chest. "How about yourself?"

"Hanging in there. One day at a time. So, seems I still have some pull in the Charlotte office, huh? I call up there and they send me the best."

Dakota's grin grew, showing every one of his pearly whites. He shoved his hat back a little. "I heard you needed help and volunteered. Get over yourself."

Laughter spilled from Connor, and it felt good. "I've missed you, man."

"You want to introduce me?" Dakota nodded in Samantha's direction. A glint appeared in his eyes that hadn't been there when he'd been talking to Connor. The flame of jealousy singed Connor, taking him by surprise. Whoa. Where had that come from? He cleared his throat.

"Sure, um, this is Samantha Cash. She's with the FBI. I'm surprised you guys don't know each other. She's our computer forensics expert who's agreed to partner with us on the task force. Sam, meet an old buddy who used to be on the force with me, but then went with the FBI."

"Dakota Richards, special agent, at your service."

Samantha stood and held out her hand. Dakota shook it, holding it longer than Connor thought necessary.

Sam pulled away and said, "Nice to meet you. We need all the help we can get to find these other missing girls before they turn up in a dumpster somewhere."

Connor's phone rang. He excused himself and walked away, leaving Samantha and Dakota to talk for a minute. "Connor here."

"We've got another dead girl."

His heart sank to his toes. "Number four? Sydney Carter?"

"No, that's the strange thing. It's number seven. Miranda Abrams."

Miranda had washed up on the shore of one of the man-made lakes in a nearby neighborhood that boasted their share of half-a-million-dollar homes.

While he waited for the all clear from Serena, Connor glanced around, taking note of the time of day, the weather, the people.

Dakota said, "I'm going to go talk to some of those rubber-neckers. See if anyone saw anything."

Andrew blew out a sigh. "I'll help." He waved his camera. "Brought this too. Something tells me this guy is here somewhere, watching."

Samantha didn't say anything, just watched the process. The coroner's vehicle waited up the hill on a gravel path, patient, silent, knowing the inevitable would soon happen. Crime scene investigators in blue coveralls snapped photos from every possible angle.

Finally, Serena looked up and nodded to him. Connor led the way over to her and squatted on his heels to look over the body.

Revulsion filled him. How could anyone

do this to another person? Especially someone so young, just starting out, exploring
life and who she is. He understood ac-
cidents happened. People died. It was an
unfortunate part of life. But this, this was
deliberate and cruel, mean and just plain
evil. And for what? Why?

He knew the church answer. Because it
was a fallen world, a world that had allowed
sin to come into it and then turned its back
on God.

Like you, right?

Ignoring his inner sniping, he focused on
the scene before him. The body — no,
Miranda, he corrected, forcing himself to
think her name — lay faceup, skin bloated
and blue. With definite marks on her throat.
He looked up at Serena. "How long was she
in the water?"

"She disappeared between Tuesday night
and Wednesday morning, right?"

"Yeah."

"According to her liver temperature, she's
been dead at least a day."

"Cause of death?"

Serena looked up. "Probably drowning,
maybe strangulation, but again, I'll know
more in a little while."

"Right. Call me as soon as you know,
okay?"

"You got it."

Connor turned to see Samantha looking down at Miranda. Her expression unreadable, she dropped to her knees beside the girl. Fists clenched, breathing ragged, she simply stared. Connor shifted, unsure what to do. He glanced at Serena who shrugged.

"Is her computer still at the precinct?" Samantha suddenly asked.

The last thing he thought she'd be thinking of. "Yeah, it's there. Why?"

"I don't understand why I can't find more on them. In the age of IMs, there should be more."

"It's also the age of text messaging," Connor said slowly. "Jenna's always texting some friend or another. I had to go to the unlimited plan just to afford it."

Sam's eyes lifted to meet his, the dead, flat expression morphing into interest, almost excitement. She stood and faced him.

"It's got to be the cell phones. We need to go over Miranda's text messages, read between the lines. Instead of looking for something to stand out, look for something subtle, something that may be worded just so."

"We can sure give it a shot. We've got that subpoena in for Miranda's text messages, so right now it's a game of hurry up and wait."

Dakota and Andrew motioned they were ready when everyone else was.

Connor glanced back down at the girl now being zipped up into a black body bag. "Yeah. Let's see what we can do. And I've got to be home in time to have an overdue talk with my daughter."

The Agent watched. He'd heard on the radio that the body had been found. Excitement tingled through him. He liked the fact that he could watch the action, blend in, be one of the concerned neighbors. People clicked their tongues, furrowed their brows, turned to him and said how awful it was, wasn't it?

He agreed, nodding, murmuring that it was indeed a terrible loss. Inside, he smiled, thinking how simple they were to fool. Unsuspecting, unprotected. Welcoming him into their midst.

It was all just so simple.

But not everything had gone smoothly. He had messed up this time and Boss had been furious. With him and the girl.

Miranda had been sick when she'd arrived at the meeting, but The Agent hadn't realized it. When he brought her to meet Boss, she got out of the car and there was blood all over the seat. She stumbled, almost fell.

When he asked her what was wrong, she insisted she was fine. He grabbed her by the throat and gave her a good shake. He must have squeezed a little too hard, because she passed out. He carried her into the house, fresh blood staining his shirt, wetting the hand he had under her legs as he settled her on the couch.

He vomited and changed clothes. He hated blood, couldn't stand to have it on him. That's why he made sure to kill in a way that wouldn't leave any blood anywhere.

When he returned to check on her, she was awake, whispering she needed a doctor. He asked her why. When she explained, Boss ordered him to get rid of her.

The girl was too weak to realize what was happening as he rowed her out to the middle of the small lake. She was also too weak to swim to shore.

And he watched as she struggled.

She went under, back up, eyes wide as the water revived her enough to allow her to finally understand that she was going to die.

She flailed.

Kicked.

Tried to scream.

And then went under one more time.

To stay.

Until now. Now, there would be more questions, more media hype that got all the details wrong. The Agent shook his head. It didn't matter as long as he did his job, obeyed Boss. Because Boss had the money. Lots and lots of it.

He watched as the cameras clicked, the crime scene guys gathered what they thought was evidence. But they'd never catch him. Even if they compared photos from the different crime scenes. Disguises were a wonderful thing.

Then The Agent caught sight of someone he recognized. The cop from the dumpster. The tall one. The redheaded one must be his partner. The third man with the Stetson and boots puzzled him. Probably FBI. Then he saw the woman kneeling beside the body.

For the first time since his involvement in all this, he felt a touch of unease. He'd thought for sure the bolt through her door would have scared her off. But there she was. The unease shifted inside him.

Maybe the bolt had been a stupid move.

He pondered that thought. No, it had been the right move, but out of all of those investigating the case, she might be the biggest problem.

If she didn't scare easy, he'd just have to get rid of her like the girls.

It was as simple as that.

10

Before they returned to the office to check the text messages they'd obtained shortly after Miranda's death, Connor and Andrew made the drive over to Miranda's house to break the news to her parents. Dakota decided to head back to the precinct to work in the temporary task force office; a large storage closet had been cleaned out and was now equipped with two computers, a coffeemaker, and a half-empty box of donuts.

Samantha sat in the passenger seat, staring out the window. Connor had told her not to come, but she insisted. Andrew sat behind Connor, his head tilted back against the leather, eyes closed, lips subtly moving.

He was praying.

Admiration for Connor's partner darted through her. She sighed and mimicked Andrew's position. She dreaded the moment they would arrive, hated to think of the pain that this family would have to endure, the changes their lives would soon take. Never in a million years would she forget that night ten years ago when she'd opened the door to find two policemen standing on her parents' doorstep.

"Hey, Sam, what are you thinking about?"

She looked up. Connor's intriguing eyes stared back at her, revealing his concern — his interest.

"Nothing." She looked away, then started when his hand took hers. She met his eyes again.

"You don't have to do this, you know."

Shaking her head, she just pressed her lips together to fight the quiver — but didn't pull her hand away.

Pressure from Connor's squeeze brought a sigh from her. "Tell me," he insisted. "This is more than just Miranda."

"Ten years ago, two police officers came to my parents' house to tell us . . . about my sister."

"What?" A frown creased his forehead.

"She'd disappeared two months earlier. I'd been staying with my parents, praying for news, hoping against hope that she was still alive. Then one night, there was a knock on the door. She'd been found."

Sick dread crossed his face and his lips

tightened. "But?"

Sam's throat bobbed. As always, the horrors of what her sister had been through filleted her heart as though someone had taken a knife and physically stabbed her. "They thought she was dead at first. Her pulse was so faint, the person who checked her didn't feel anything. When the crime scene people flipped her over to take more photographs, she opened her eyes and screamed . . . then passed out again."

"Holy . . ."

"Yeah. They had the body bag waiting, the gurney on standby. And she was still alive. Barely." Sam closed her eyes, but no matter how often she tried to push the image of Jamie's battered body from her mind, she couldn't do it. "She had so many broken bones, all in various stages of healing — except for her right arm which she used to grab a tree limb that floated by. There'd been a storm the night she was found. The . . . um . . . water was rough, but when she hit it, she said she woke up and could see him sitting there. She let herself sink, said she wanted to die. She doesn't remember grabbing the limb or washing up to shore."

All color leached from Connor's face.

"And it was my fault," she whispered.

"How was it your fault?"

The tears came as they always did. She refused to let them fall. "We'd had a fight. A major one. Jamie was pretty intent on defying my parents at every turn. She'd snuck out of the house one night and I realized it. I tracked her down and forced her to get in the car to come home with me."

"Sounds like a loving sister action to me."

She gave a humorless laugh. "She started screaming at me that I was ruining her life, that I needed to mind my own business. She grabbed the wheel and the car started swerving out of control, so I stomped on the brakes."

"Let me guess, she jumped out of the car."

Surprise flickered. "Yeah."

"Sounds like something Jenna would do."

"Only instead of waiting for her to calm down and get back in, I left. We were only about a mile from home, just outside the neighborhood. I figured the walk would cool her off."

"Did it?"

Samantha shook her head. "I don't know. After waiting for about an hour for her to show up, I started feeling guilty, so I went looking for her. I never found her." A tear slipped down her cheek.

"Samantha . . ."

Suddenly, Sam regretted opening up. She'd never told anyone that story. Ever. Not even Tom, a man she considered one of her best friends. And here she was spilling her guts to the first man she found attractive. How pitiful.

"Are we there yet?"

Andrew. Sam sucked in a deep breath. She'd forgotten about him in the back. Had he heard? She turned in her seat and looked at him. His eyes said he hurt for her.

He'd heard. But she knew he'd be praying for her family from now on. She didn't know how she knew that, she just did. She looked at the man beside her. Did Connor ever pray?

Knowing God and church weren't exactly at the top of his list of favorite things to do on the weekend — or any other time for that matter — she hesitated, took a deep breath, then blurted, "Would you and Jenna come to church with me on Sunday?"

From the backseat, Samantha heard Andrew catch his breath. Connor looked at her, surprise written all over him. "Huh?"

"Church. Will you and Jenna come with me Sunday?"

Surprise fled, consternation took its place. "Um. Well, I, um, I don't know. I guess I'll have to ask Jenna if she wants to go."

"Good." She looked up. "We're here."

Connor sucked in a deep breath and stepped back into the car. That had not gone well. Miranda's parents were crushed, their world shattered by the gruesome death of their only child. Out of respect for their grief, he waited as they climbed into the car and headed to the morgue. Now it was up to him and the task force to find the killer.

"Do you think she was killed by the same guy killing these other girls?" Samantha asked.

She brushed away a tear that had escaped in spite of her valiant effort to hold it back. Connor's finger itched to do it for her. Molding his palm to the steering wheel, he focused on her question.

"I honestly don't know. Everything in my gut screams yes. And yet . . ." He shook his head and his phone buzzed. Cranking the car, he accepted the call. "Wolfe here."

"Hi, Connor, it's Serena."

"What do you know, Serena?"

Samantha's eyes shot to his. Andrew leaned forward from the backseat. Connor put the phone on speaker.

"She was definitely pregnant."

Sam winced. Andrew grunted.

Serena continued, "Cause of death is

drowning, but if she hadn't drowned, she'd have died from loss of blood."

"What? What about the strangulation marks around her neck?"

"I know. I would say someone probably grabbed her by the throat, but didn't squeeze hard enough to strangle her. I'm sure it hurt, but it didn't kill her. Whoever had his hands around her throat either stopped or *was* stopped."

"So, she almost bled out? From what?"

"A botched abortion."

"Whoa. Okay, thanks, Serena. Have you talked to her parents?"

A sigh echoed over the line. "They just walked in. Gotta go."

"Bye."

Connor hung up, resisting the urge to fling the device against something.

Andrew asked, "Want to go talk to the boyfriend?"

"Yeah, then I'm going to have to talk to Jenna before she hears this from someone else. I guess we should let the principal know, then I'll tell Jenna myself."

Sam laid a hand over his. "I'll help you tell her."

Warmth flooded him. Relief made him shudder. He wouldn't have to do it alone. "Thanks."

■ ■ ■ ■

Jenna spied Charlie Petroskie leaning against a locker talking to Beth Barry. Beth flipped her perfectly straight blonde hair over her shoulder and peered up at Charlie through heavily mascaraed lashes. A small grin curved pastel pink lips, and her tastefully jeweled pink shirt barely met the top of her jeans — and the dress code.

Disgust seized Jenna. Miranda had only been missing for a couple of days and already Charlie hunted for his next conquest like a shark in a school of feeder fish. He had the reputation for preying on the pretty and the innocent. Beth was both — an ugly duckling who'd blossomed into a swan over the summer thanks to a healthy diet and the local athletic club. The transformation had amazed even Jenna, who'd been around to watch it happen.

She forced a smile to her lips and stepped toward the flirting couple. "Hey, Beth." She cooled her tone. "Charlie."

Beth grinned revealing her newly whitened, orthodontically straightened teeth. "Hey, Jenna, haven't seen you around much."

Arching a brow, Jenna asked, "Who's fault

is that?"

A flush stained Beth's neck and she cut her eyes back at Charlie. "Sorry, life's been getting pretty interesting lately."

"So I hear." She turned to Charlie. "Have you heard anything from Miranda?"

It was his turn to be uncomfortable. "No," he clipped. "Why? Have you?"

"No. Last I heard, you'd knocked her up and she was desperately trying to find a way to have an abortion."

Beth blanched, sucked in a deep breath.

The color drained from Charlie's face. Then returned fire engine red. He took a step toward Jenna, fist clenched.

"Touch her and you'll have more problems on your hands than a pregnant girlfriend."

Jenna gasped and turned to see her dad standing three feet away; the look in his eye scared even her although he had it directed at Charlie. She gulped and moved back away from everyone. Samantha and Andrew stood in the background, silent, watching. Jenna met Samantha's eyes, and the look of compassion nearly sent her running into the woman's arms.

She stiffened her spine and looked away. She was a big girl, she could handle Charlie and whatever else came along. She didn't need to lean on anyone.

154

Just like her dad.

Charlie held his hands up in the universal symbol for surrender. "Hey, I wasn't going to do anything — except maybe yell at her for being such a —"

"Better watch your mouth, kid. That's his daughter." Samantha glowered at him.

Charlie flinched. "Oh."

The principal, Mr. Edward Harrington, stepped forward, motioning for his guests to lead the way.

Andrew blew out a sigh. "All righty, Mr. Petroskie, we need to see you in the principal's office."

A frown cut Charlie's forehead. "Why? I told you, I wasn't going to do anything."

"This is about Miranda Abrams," her dad said softly.

Jenna shot a look at him, one he avoided catching.

And she knew.

He only got that sad, defeated expression when one of his cases turned up dead. Sorrow and disbelief speared her.

Poor Miranda.

Willpower, self-control, don't snap the kid's neck. Connor repeated the mantra during the short walk to the office, his eyes boring holes into the back of the cocky teen's skull.

155

Principal Harrington opened the door and motioned everyone inside. "Help yourself. I need to go return a phone call, but will be available after that if you need me again."

Andrew shook the man's hand. "Thanks."

Samantha sat on the love seat, leaving the three chairs in front of the desk for the others.

Connor turned to Charlie. "Have a seat."

The boy crossed his arms, notched his chin up, and said, "I'll stand, thanks."

Andrew placed a hand on the boy's shoulder. "You'll sit." And shoved. Hard.

"Hey!"

"How old are you?"

"Just turned seventeen last week. Why?"

Connor let a thin grin stretch his lips. "Good, we don't have to call Mommy and Daddy."

Charlie huffed and leaned back. "Whatever. Can we just get this over with? I have a trig test I really don't feel like making up."

Desperately wanting to get in this guy's face, Connor deliberately shifted, putting some distance between them. No sense in being too close to someone you wanted to smash. "Your cooperation determines how long this takes. Totally up to you."

"All right, all right. What do you want to know?"

"Did you kill Miranda? Did you put your hands around her neck and choke her until she agreed to the abortion? Get her to have some quack get rid of the baby and then let her bleed to death?"

Sam's ferocious questioning came out of the blue. Connor frowned at her for interfering, but the intensity of her stare was directed at Charlie.

Whoa, she was mad. Furious and fuming.

The boy gaped, pure shock holding him silent and still for the first time since they'd met him.

He didn't kill her.

Finally, Charlie bolted to his feet and found his tongue. "What? No! What are you saying? She's dead?"

Andrew jumped in, shoving the kid once more back into his seat. "Yeah. It was you who got her pregnant, wasn't it?"

Shoulders slumping at the news, the teen bowed his head and gripped it with both hands. "I can't believe this."

"Wasn't it?" This time Andrew's voice rang through the room.

Charlie looked up. "Yes. Yes, she was pregnant, but I didn't kill her, I swear."

Sam wilted back against the couch. Connor caught her eye. She gave a defeated sigh and shook her head. He knew what she was

157

saying. The kid was telling the truth.

He tried another tack. "Do you know of anyone she might have been talking to online? A modeling agent? Anything like that?"

Eager to help now that he'd had the shock of his life, Charlie nodded. "Yeah. That's why she wanted the abortion. She said she was finally getting her big break, and a baby would send everything she was working for down the drain. She lived for soccer and modeling." He looked away for a minute, then stared up into Connor's eyes, honesty emanating from him. "I wanted her to keep the baby, but she wouldn't even talk about it."

"Let's talk about this modeling thing. How did she communicate with the guy?"

"Um, she met him in some chat room, then the guy only wanted to do text messaging. He said that way he could get in touch with her at the last minute if he needed her for a sudden job or something. He sent her some money, she bought a fancy dress and had some really nice pictures done."

Andrew and Connor exchanged a look. They'd been right. The text messages were the link. The dress a part of it.

Andrew leaned forward, hands clasped between his knees. "Did they ever exchange emails?"

"No, man, I told you. Text messages only. At least that's what Miranda said. And I think the guy even gave her a business phone to use."

"What was the guy's name?"

"David? Donny? No, Danny? Aw, I don't remember. She didn't tell me all that much about it, just that she was going to have some really big money soon and we could get married. She started spouting junk like that and I . . ." He swallowed hard.

"It scared you. Sent you running." Sam's no-nonsense tone told everyone what she thought about that. "You can sleep with her, but can't be man enough to handle the consequences, huh?"

Charlie recoiled, but anger glinted in his brown eyes. Before he could answer, Andrew slid in with, "Samantha, why don't you wait outside?"

Sam stood, stomped to the door. "That might be best."

Samantha didn't know whether she wanted to hit something or have a good cry. It was her opinion that while Charlie was a player and a jerk, he wasn't a killer. Somehow, in her gut, she knew that Miranda had fallen into the hands of the person . . . or people . . . killing teenage girls.

The fact that she'd had an abortion, however, interested Sam. Had she had the abortion before she'd been snatched? Or after? And then due to lack of medical care, bled to death? Thus surprising her kidnappers by dying on them so they'd dumped her body in the lake?

Several uniformed officers were in that subdivision still questioning the lakeside residents. Surely someone had seen something. A car. Or heard something. Like a splash.

A niggle of awareness tickled the back of her brain. If she could just bring it forward. What was she missing? What were they all missing?

Connor opened the door and stepped out. Sam bit her lip. "Sorry."

He nodded, eyes shuttered, hands shoved in his pockets. "Made you think about your sister?"

"Yes, but they all do. Every person who's a victim of brutality reminds me of her. I just can't let that get in the way of an investigation, though. I'm sorry."

"Apology accepted. You didn't do any damage. In fact, your blunt approach to the questioning may have helped. You shocked the mess out of him. That kid didn't have

160

any idea Miranda was dead."

"That's the impression I got. And now we know why you didn't find anything on the girls' text messages. He sends them a different phone. I bet when he snatches the girls, he just tosses the phones. No emails, no text messages, no trails, nothing to lead anyone back to him."

Connor sighed and swiped a hand over his jaw. He looked tired.

Andrew and Charlie finally exited the office. The teen gave Samantha a glare, but he kept his thoughts to himself. She met his gaze head-on, refusing to let him intimidate her.

Principal Harrington chose that moment to return. "Are we all done here?"

Charlie snorted, his earlier defiance back. "*I'm* done."

Connor nodded. "Thank you for your cooperation, Mr. Petroskie. We'll be in touch."

"I can't wait." With that, Charlie turned on his heel and stalked down the hall.

Samantha watched him go.

Jerk.

Connor shook the principal's hand. "Thank you for your help."

"No problem. I just hate things have turned out the way they have for these girls."

"Yeah."

On the way back out to the car, Sam mused, "You know, it's like these people don't care if the bodies are found. Unfortunately, there are ways to make a body disappear forever — or at least much longer than two days. Why throw Miranda in the lake? Why not bury her, cremate her, or whatever? I don't mean to sound gruesome, but it does cause me to wonder. It's like they're just tossing these dead girls out like yesterday's trash."

Connor looked at her, respect gleaming at her insight. "You're probably right. They just don't care."

"Not only does it seem like they don't care, they're being arrogant in the fact that they don't think they can get caught."

"We keep saying 'they,' " Sam said. "Are we under the assumption that more than one person is involved in this?"

Connor rubbed his chin. "Good question. I would say there would have to be more than one person involved. If this were a simple online predator, I think we could have caught him by now. This is different, has a different feel to it. And the baby angle. I honestly believe we're dealing with some kind of black market adoption ring or something along those lines."

Andrew nodded. "I've been thinking that

since we found Leslie Sanders. Two girls turning up dead, recently pregnant and missing babies, that's odd and suspect. But three girls . . . that's a whole different ball game."

"And now Miranda showing up dead," Sam muttered, not liking how this was all coming about. Too many dead girls, too many hurt families. Too much evil.

She sighed, then felt a tingle all the way up her arm when Connor placed a hand on her elbow to help her into the car, saying, "But she had an abortion and we don't know for sure if her disappearance is even related to the others."

"So how does all this fit together?"

"Dakota has been working with the FBI in the Behavioral Science Unit. Let's get his opinion on all this when we get back."

Sam shut her door and leaned her head back. Connor slipped into the driver's seat, Andrew once again claiming the driver's rear.

"Where to?"

"How about something to eat. I'm starving," Andrew begged.

"Right." Connor mocked. "So what else is new? What's the matter, Angie burn your breakfast this morning?"

Samantha managed a laugh as Andrew

kicked the driver's seat. "Watch what you say about my love."

Connor shot an amused look at Sam. "His *love* can't cook worth a darn."

"She's got other redeeming attributes," Andrew defended his bride.

"Yeah, she lets you keep that gas guzzler Corvette."

"And she's not even jealous. You should be glad I married the woman. She's consented to allowing you to be in the will."

Connor gave a chuckle and slid a glance at Samantha. "Only because she doesn't want the car. I get the Corvette when he kicks the bucket." Pure amusement danced in his eyes, the first time Samantha had seen them without the ever-present shadows. Wow. The humor may seem crass to those outside law enforcement, but she knew it was a coping mechanism, and it didn't bother her.

Connor insisted, "But she still can't cook."

Andrew warned, "You'd better not say anything about her cooking in front of her. She knows how to use my gun better than I do."

Connor and Samantha laughed harder than they needed to. But they all needed the release. Even through the laughter,

though, she wondered when the next tears
would fall.

11

The weekend slid in almost unnoticed, the change from Friday to Saturday subtle, ignored. Samantha knew it would be a working weekend. All except for three hours on Sunday morning when she would take time to worship. But after that . . .

There were still three missing girls and their days were numbered, if not already up. She sat in Jamie's living room eating a grape popsicle and staring at her laptop screen.

Wired into the girls' compuers, able to access any one of them from where she sat, she had an idea and wanted to go with it, but didn't want to live at the police station. Her sister's home was much more comfortable.

"Hey, whatcha working on?"

Samantha looked up and smiled. Her sister was finally coming out of her shell. Freshly showered, her hair clipped up into a curly blonde pile, a Panthers sweatshirt and jeans, she looked relaxed and . . . happy.

Sam nearly started crying at the sheer joy she felt run through her. "You painted your toes!"

"Just the nails, Sam." Jamie tossed her head, blonde curls dancing around her heart-shaped face. She gave a throaty laugh. Then chewed her lip. "They look okay, right?"

"Just . . . peachy." Tongue-in-cheek, she waited for Jamie's response.

Her sister grabbed the nearest throw pillow and lobbed it at Samantha's head. Loftily, Jamie told her, "It's Peachy Sunrise, thank you very much. Now, is Tom coming over or not?"

"He is. He just finished working some case and is on his way."

"He's been awfully busy lately."

"I know. He tracked a kid to Tokyo. The dad took him in the middle of the night four days ago, then logged in on the first computer he found, apparently. Tom was waiting on him, tracked him to Tokyo. A child recovery team is on the way."

"Tom didn't have to go?"

"Nope, not this time. He should be here soon."

Jamie smiled. "I'm going to go throw

together some food. You know he'll want to eat when he gets here."

Laughter spilled from both of them, and Sam sent up a silent thank-you prayer for the healing her sister was experiencing. Then her phone buzzed. She looked at the screen. Connor. Her heart quivered, but she refused to acknowledge that it was due to him being on the other end of the line. "Hello?"

"Hi, Samantha, Connor here."

"Hey there. How's your Saturday going?"

"Andrew, Dakota, and I've been putting a puzzle together."

"So what does the final picture look like?"

"Not sure yet. We've still got quite a few missing pieces. Are you free to go over some stuff? As part of the task force, we thought we'd keep you in the loop."

"Absolutely. Why don't you guys come on over here to my sister's house? Because of her contract computer work for them, she has FBI clearance. We can discuss the case in front of her. Also, my partner, Tom, is on the way over. He might be able to help us out."

"Let me see if I can get clearance for him to be in on the loop. We can use all the brains we can get on this case."

"Great."

She gave him the directions and hung up, gripping the phone for a solid minute before setting it on the table in front of her. *You're not interested. He's a cop.*

And he would be here in less than thirty minutes. Sam slapped a hand to her hair and looked down at the baggy sweats and hole-sporting T-shirt.

"Jamie? We're getting ready to have more company than just Tom! You might want to change into something else."

Sam trotted to the back guest bedroom where she'd stashed some of her things and pulled out a pair of clean jeans and another T-shirt. One without holes. Then she brushed her hair until it crackled. Eyeing the lip gloss on the dresser, she reminded herself, *You're not interested, remember? He's a cop.*

Right.

With a huff of disgust, she grabbed the lip gloss, applied it with a jerky hand, then bolted back to the den.

Jamie came out of the kitchen, sandwiches on a small tray and a pitcher of tea undulating in its plastic container. When she spied Sam, she stopped. Lifted a brow.

"Who is he?"

"Shut up."

Twenty-eight and a half minutes after he'd hung up with Samantha — not that he was counting or anything — Connor pulled into her sister's drive. Putting the car in park, he opened the door. Andrew and Dakota followed suit.

Samantha answered the door with a smile and a light in her eyes that made Connor's heart do stuff he didn't think it remembered how to do. "Hey, come on in. I had an idea I wanted to run by you guys."

Everyone trooped in, Connor bringing up the rear. Just before he entered the house, the nape of his neck tingled, like someone had just drawn a bead on it. The vest he wore wouldn't do much good if he got it in the head.

Samantha stood staring at him, waiting for him to enter so she could shut the door. He held up a finger. "I'll be right back. I want to have a look around."

A frown furrowed her brow. "Why?"

"Just go on inside. I'll be there in a minute."

"Connor —"

"Just . . ." He motioned for her to shut the door. She did and he turned back to scan the neighborhood. Should he let Dakota and Andrew in on his paranoia?

No, he would just take a little walk, seeing what he could see. He'd felt watched just as he'd been about to enter the door. Directly across the street another little cottage-style house sat, peaceful, still, with a neatly manicured lawn. Connor scanned the street, heard the door open behind him. Dakota stepped out, eyes alert, followed by Andrew who had his hand on his gun. Samantha must have said something.

Connor tilted his head to the left. Andrew went that way. Dakota motioned he'd go to the right. Connor walked across the street, panning his gaze from one house to the next, looking for anything, almost expecting to feel a bullet between his shoulder blades.

Nothing except normal Saturday morning activity. The scent of summer clinging, just before surrendering gracefully to the fall. Kids on bicycles, babies in strollers, dogs barking, lawn mowers growling.

Yet Connor couldn't let go of the feeling that someone had been watching them. Was still watching. Waiting. He wished he had a bulletproof helmet on.

Then he spied the tree house. A wooden structure, well-built and solid, it sat in the right-hand corner of the backyard. He looked back at Jamie's house. Back at the tree house. A small window cut into the side facing Connor provided a perfect view of Jamie's front door.

Jogging toward the thing, Connor stopped abruptly when a little boy about five years old opened the door and began climbing down the steps.

"Find anything?" Dakota asked, coming up behind Connor.

"Nope, guess my imagination is working overtime."

"I don't put much stock in imagination. You're a seasoned cop. If you felt something, you felt it."

"Maybe." Connor scanned the tree house once again. The door to the main house banged again, and the same little boy, juice box in hand, rushed back toward the steps to climb up them one handed, the drink clutched tightly in the other.

"Maybe not. Maybe my nerves are just strung too tight and I'm letting it get to me." He shook his head. "Come on, let's go see if Samantha can help us move forward in this thing. I feel like I'm pedaling backward out of control."

Dakota pushed his ever-present Stetson back on his head and nodded. "Just don't take your hands off the brakes."

■ ■ ■ ■

"I hope you like apple juice. It's all my mom had." The Agent took the proffered drink from the little guy. A cute fellow, he had curly blond hair and friendly green eyes.

Smiling, The Agent wondered what Boss would think about this little boy. Boss would like him, he decided. But wouldn't want to take him from his mother, not at this age. It was best to take them before they knew they were being taken. Otherwise they just cried a lot.

"I like apple juice. It's one of my favorites. Thanks."

"I already had one, so you don't have to share."

The Agent almost laughed. Then felt a pang of — what?

Longing?

Remorse?

No, allowing himself to feel those kinds of things would interfere with fulfilling his destiny. What he'd been born to do.

But — something. And that worried him.

His new little friend stared up at him, trust shining, taking gleeful joy in the new adventure that had disrupted his normal routine. "Is that a BB gun?"

173

What? Oh, he'd forgotten he held it. Look-ing out the small tree house window, he re-alized his chance was gone. This little guy had nearly surprised him into a heart at-tack. The Agent gave a small smile. He'd lost this opportunity so he'd wait for an-other. No hurry. And he'd enjoyed the banter with the child.

Dismantling the weapon, he slid the rifle into the case and smiled at the boy. "No, do you have a BB gun?"

"No, my big brother does. He's twelve. He won't let me touch it. Neither will my mom."

"If you keep it our little secret, I'll come back and teach you to shoot."

"You will?" Awestruck, the green-eyed urchin stared up at The Agent who had just become his new hero.

"Sure. Deal?"

"Deal." They shook on it. The Agent felt the warmth of the little boy's hand pressed against his own palm. Again, that pang. Again, he considered how easy it would be to take the boy. What would it be like to be a dad? To have the full responsibility of a young life like this one rest on his shoulders? His heart warmed at the thought. He'd be a good dad, patient, loving, not like —

But no. That wasn't why he was here.

He'd finish his job, follow his orders.

And he knew where the child lived should he change his mind.

The Agent pulled back the curtain covering the small window, saw his target walking back toward the house, giving up on whatever had sparked his interest. He frowned, wondering what he'd done to give himself away. How had the cop known he was being watched?

He told himself not to be stupid.

It was instinct. That survival instinct that came with being a cop. And it was strong.

He'd remember that. Never underestimate your opponent. Always be the strong one. The rich one. Weakness brought on bad things. Never again would he be weak. No, he was the strong one. The smart one. And he had Boss. Boss would never steer him wrong.

It was as simple as that.

Samantha watched from behind the window. When Connor had gone all cop on her, she'd sent in backup — Andrew and Dakota. She'd chosen to stay with Jamie just in case. Now they were returning en masse and she had questions.

Jamie looked afraid, chewing her bottom lip, and Sam prayed this didn't do irreparable damage to her sister's amazing progress in healing. Jamie sent her a small smile and a shrug. Relief oozed through Sam. Jamie was handling it.

Connor came through the door, followed by Andrew and Dakota.

"What is it?" she demanded.

"You'll think I'm crazy, but I felt like we were being watched."

"Why? By whom?"

"I don't know." Connor shook off the events by changing the subject. "Why don't I introduce everyone?"

"I'm Jamie."

Sam raised a brow as she realized her sister was staring at Dakota.

And Dakota was staring at Jamie.

"I'm Dakota Richards." He pushed his Stetson back and held out a hand.

Jamie hesitated, sucked in a deep breath, looked at the outstretched hand . . . and shook it. Samantha nearly fell over. Dakota Richards was the first male Jamie had touched — or allowed to touch her — in ten years. She hadn't even hugged their dad since the attack.

Connor finished the introductions, seeming not to notice the undercurrents zinging around the room. Jamie managed to drag her gaze from Dakota in order to smile at

Andrew and Connor.

But she didn't shake their hands.

Sam motioned for everyone to have a seat while Jamie disappeared back into the kitchen. Dakota looked like he might follow, but turned on his heel at the last minute and took a seat. Andrew stood beside the window, his gaze on the street beyond.

Samantha asked, "Any word back on the girls' medical records? The text messages?"

"Not yet." Connor shook his head at the slowness of the whole process. "Soon, I'm hoping. They know this could be a matter of life and death for these girls, so I know they're making it a priority."

A knock on the door sounded and Sam went to answer it. "Hey, Tom, come on in. We're having a regular crime-busters party."

Tom entered and smiled. "Can I do anything to help?"

"You can stop killing yourself. You have rings around your eyes. What on earth are you working on?"

"That missing kid from Tokyo kept me going through all hours. I'm just glad I didn't have to hop a plane."

"Did you get any sleep at all last night?"

He shrugged. "A few hours."

Samantha ushered him into the den and

made another round of introductions.

Connor spoke up. "Oh, I got him clearance to help with the case if he wants. Jamie's clearance still stands if she wants to help on this." He looked at Tom. "Your FBI status made that a no-brainer. We can use all the manpower we can get and if you're willing . . ."

"Sure. Be glad to." Tom settled on the couch.

Jamie came back into the room and Dakota shot to his feet. "Do you need any help with anything?"

A shy smile curved her full lips. "No, not right now, thanks. I decided to just order some pizzas."

"Smart woman." He rubbed his hands together. "All right, guys, we need to come up with a plan of action. Connor asked me to pitch in. So . . . the FBI's resources are at your disposal via me." He tapped his chest. "And our new buddy, Tom, here."

Tom piped in, "What do we have so far? Can someone fill me in?"

Connor turned serious. Andrew moved from the window where he'd been keeping an eye on things. Sam watched him and Connor have an entire conversation just with their eyes. Andrew communicated he'd seen nothing to cause alarm. Connor acknowledged that with a nod.

Wow. She tried to think if she'd ever had a connection like that with someone. And couldn't come up with one person. That saddened her, but she didn't have time to analyze this newly discovered longing.

Turning to Tom, she filled him in with the abridged version, then said, "We're waiting for the text messages from the girls' phones. We should have them any time now."

"Cool. What else?"

"Samantha's still working on the computers," Connor said. "She thinks she may have gotten everything off of them, but unfortunately there wasn't much to get. We've got several people checking the school computers and all the libraries within a thirty-mile radius. It's going to take forever, but we don't want to leave any stone unturned."

Tom rubbed a finger across his lips. "That's kind of weird. Teenagers use computers all the time. IM, email, seems like there would be more on their home computers. But if Sam couldn't find anything, then there wasn't anything there to find. She's the best."

Sam flushed at the praise. "Thanks, Tom. I have a feeling I'm not looking in the right place. I'm going to try something else."

"Like what?" Tom's raised brow expressed

his interest.

She looked at Connor. "You remember me telling you about remote access and how, if you had the right codes, you could gain entry to any computer?"

"Yep."

"I think this guy has done that somehow. Gained access to their computers from somewhere else, then erased his steps. It could be that the person who was after them knew what to tell the girls, to get rid of any trace on the computer, but I can't think of any way he could have done that without raising a red flag." Tom already knew this, but she explained in simple, non-computerese for the rest of the group. "Now, in comparing the Event Viewers from all of the computers, I'm able to see the record of when the machines were accessed and by whom. It's just a really tedious process. I'm sorry it's taking me so long."

"Do you want some help checking all the computers for a common denominator?" Tom offered.

"Maybe. I'll let you know. You need to get some rest."

Tom shrugged. "I'll be all right. Big brother's work is never done."

"Tom's putting his younger brother and sister through college, working two, sometimes three, jobs," Samantha said. "If he doesn't slow down, he's going to burn out."

"That's admirable," Connor said. "What're your other jobs?"

"Newspaper route when I'm in town, and I job share a security guard position at First National Bank."

"Whoa. That's a lot."

"Tell me about it. It's a shame I can't split myself down the middle and be in two places at once." He gave a wry chuckle. "Chelsea, my sister, after a rocky start, chose to be a nurse, thank goodness. Eventually that will pay her bills. She graduates in December. Ben's got two more years at the business college. Then I can relax."

"How is Chelsea?" Samantha knew the girl was having some issues related to a baby she'd given up for adoption two years ago. Waffling between wondering if she'd done the right thing or not.

"She's better. Doing great in school. I'm proud of her."

Connor's phone rang. Andrew got up to look out the window one more time. Dakota kept his eyes on Jamie, whose face flushed every time he looked at her.

"Text message reports are back. Do you have a fax machine?"

"Of course." She gave him the number and sat back to wait.

12

Connor scanned the reports. Miranda's text messages were available for the last six days. Today was Saturday; she'd disappeared Tuesday. There'd been six texts on Monday, twelve on Tuesday, and then they stopped. They'd been sent and received from a total of four different numbers.

Three of the numbers turned out to be high school friends. The other one was from a prepaid phone that was now disconnected, of course.

Connor read through the messages. One caught his interest. "Will meet U 2nite. Mall Food Court. 7:00. Bringing a friend."

The response: "Cool. I have ur pic. Will find u."

"C U then."

Dakota said, "That could be the one we need. Just looking at it doesn't cause me any great concern, but knowing that she's interested in modeling and the person has her picture . . . hmm." He looked at Connor. "We need to find the friend she took with her. We already know it wasn't the boyfriend. Mr. Petroskie has an airtight alibi for Tuesday night."

"Where was he?" Samantha wanted to know.

Andrew answered, "Church youth group. They were bowling. He's got about thirty witnesses who say he was there the whole time. I even got some pictures date and time stamped with him in them. He's a jerk, but he didn't have anything to do with Miranda's disappearance or death."

"One of the other phone numbers is in the name of a Mr. Vincent Mabry. I bet his daughter is Alyssa Mabry, the one Jenna mentioned."

Samantha picked up the phone. "One way to find out. What's the number?"

Jenna opened the door to let Patty into the house. Once again her father was out chasing the bad guys, her grandfather snored on the couch, and her gram had left to run errands. Patty's car keys dangled from her fingers, and Jenna felt a pang of envy shoot through her. When would her dad ever let her get her license? Part of her understood his reluctance. She would admit she hadn't been the easiest person to get along with in the last four years, but still . . .

"Hey, Jenna," Patty rapped knuckles against Jenna's forehead, "you in there?"

Jenna forced a laugh. "Sorry. Just wishing I could drive."

"Yeah, it would be nice."

"Come on upstairs, I want to show you something."

"I thought we were meeting the boys at the club." Some church had gotten together and built a place for teenagers to hang out. No alcohol, no smoking, but cool music and lots of video games, pool tables, a basketball court, volleyball area, and cheap "teen" food. It was a great place to meet — until the real fun began after dark.

"Just come upstairs for a minute."

Patty gave a loud sigh, but followed her up the stairs.

Jenna didn't bother telling Patty she had more fun at Teen Jam than she did at the parties that made her feel . . . like a piece of meat. Groping hands, ugly propositions, the alcohol she didn't like, the smoke that choked her and permeated her clothes and hair. Ugh.

But she put up with it because it made her somebody in school, one of the in crowd. Not the poor losers who walked the halls alone or were the butt of cruel practical jokes and taunting harassment. She shook her head. No way would she ever allow herself to be put in that situation.

Jenna went to the computer and pulled up the IM she'd been typing. "This is 2COOL2BLV."

Patty rolled her eyes. "Oh please, what kind of dumb screen name is that?"

"I know, but he's so nice. Look. Here's his picture." A few clicks later and the image of a young man filled the screen.

"Ooooh, he's yummy." Patty moved in closer. "How old is he?"

"Twenty-two."

"And he's interested in you?"

"Uh-huh."

"Have you used the webcam? Made sure it was really him?"

"No, he says he doesn't have a cam."

Patty flung herself across the twin bed, pushing Jenna's backpack out of the way. "Then I wouldn't talk to him anymore. He could be some really old guy, like thirty-five, fat and bald or something."

Jenna shrugged. "I don't get that vibe from him."

"Well, I sure wouldn't meet him anywhere."

"Well . . ."

Her friend bolted into a sitting position and eyed her, horrified. "Jenna, you wouldn't!"

"I don't know. I'm thinking about it. He's just so . . ."

"So what?"

"There."

" 'Scuze me?"

Jenna stood, paced from one end of her room to the other. "He gets me."

"And I don't?"

"You're my best *girl*friend. And I want a boyfriend, but I'm just not interested in any of the guys at school. They're so completely immature it's not funny." She looked back at the computer screen. "But he's not. He's real. We discuss Shakespeare, for crying out loud, the latest movies, the future."

"What about Bradley Fox?"

Jenna felt her face heat. "Yeah, I like him, but he won't give me the time of day."

"It's because he goes to church and all. We're not the kind of girls Bradley wants to hang around with. Our 'sinfulness' might rub off on him." Sarcasm dripped as she wiggled her fingers around the word.

Jenna frowned at her friend. "I don't get that impression. He speaks to me when we're in the hall, and when we were on that field trip, he sat with me on the bus. We had a good talk."

"Huh. Well, all I know is, he acts like I'm contagious or something."

Shrugging, Jenna kept her thoughts to herself. She slid a glance at her friend and nodded to the computer. "Anyway, this guy, he even said I have potential as a model."

That caught Patty's attention. "Wait a minute. That's my thing, not yours."

"I know, but you made it sound so fun. And if he thinks I might be able to do it . . ." She dug around in her dresser and pulled out a phone. "He even sent me my own phone so that we could stay in contact." She didn't tell Patty about the other envelope she'd received from him. She didn't want to tell anyone about that, yet.

"What's his name?"

"Danny."

13

Arms crossed, Connor leaned back in the pew as the preacher delivered his sermon. He still hadn't figured out how he'd managed to land here in this seat on this particular morning. He had a case to solve. And yet he'd agreed to come because Andrew had arranged for him to get up and talk to the teenagers about being extra careful, on their guard, both on the street and the internet. Now, he was finished and back in the pew, wondering if any of what he'd said had sunk in.

He squirmed again and Jenna shot him an aggravated look before turning her attention back to the preacher. Sitting to his left, Samantha cut him a questioning glance. Jamie, on the other side of Samantha, watched them all, bemusement written all over her.

Connor huffed and stilled. And tried to pay attention. How did Andrew suffer this week after week? His friend sat in front of him, arm around Angie who snuggled up under her new husband's shoulder. Envy speared him. Yet, what right did he have wishing for companionship when he didn't even make the time to spend with his own daughter? Shouldn't she come first?

He closed his eyes, mental fatigue gripped him. Think about something else. He focused his mind on the case, resisted the urge to wiggle into a more comfortable position . . . and thought.

Alyssa Mabry had been out of town on a school field trip eight hours away. They'd sent local law enforcement to pick her up, but due to car trouble, they'd been delayed. However, they'd just received word that she'd be back tonight. They would have to wait until then to see what she knew about who Miranda was meeting that day. In his mind, he outlined the questions he wanted to ask her.

Connor shifted subtly, then peeked. No one looked at him that time. He closed his eyes again.

How was he going to get this guy? What was his motive? Find pregnant teens, kidnap them, wait for the baby to be born, then kill the mother?

Then sell the babies.

Black market babies.

But what had happened with Miranda Abrams?

Serena had been specific that she'd died from blood loss due to a botched abortion. If they *wanted* pregnant girls, why would they have aborted her baby?

Unless she'd had the abortion before going to meet the killer, not realizing she was signing her own death warrant in more ways than one. If it truly was the babies they were after and she'd arrived at the meeting bleeding, sick, and needing a doctor because she'd gotten rid of it . . . and these sickos were furious at the loss . . .

However, the first two girls who'd been found dead hadn't been pregnant before they'd been snatched. At least there'd been nothing to indicate that they were. So that theory didn't make much sense.

Connor's eyes popped back open and scanned the middle section where the church's youth sat in a cluster. Dark heads, towheads, reds, blonds. All of them. Innocent. Unaware. Unexpecting. Never thinking that such tragedy could be right around their corner no matter how many times they were told, lectured to, about the evil that even right now stalked them.

It chilled him to realize his next call could

191

be for one of them. Shuddering at the thought, he looked at the front of the church. Straight at the empty cross hanging behind the preacher.

Empty.

As in not there anymore.

So where was he?

Andrew believed he was everywhere. Connor could quote the lines almost as well as Andrew did. That Christ had suffered, taken on the sins of the world, died as a sacrifice so others wouldn't have to spend eternity in a place called hell, and risen again, defeating death so all could have the opportunity to live in heaven.

Connor had heard it all before. He'd grown up in the church, hearing the stories about a loving God. His parents were strong believers. He got the impression Samantha believed the same. But his wife, Julia, had professed to be a Christian, she'd gone to church, yet she'd been a gossip, whining and complaining when she didn't get her way, bitter when she was not elected to some church committee she'd wanted to serve on. And yet, Samantha's words and actions matched up, even in the face of searching for a killer. She believed God was in charge, was with them, leading them.

Connor wondered a little bitterly if the

dead and missing girls had thought God was with them. Would somehow miraculously save them from their kidnapper/killer. Had they died with a plea on their lips, felt betrayed by him when they realized there was no escape? No hope? Or had they believed that he would protect them even to the very end?

As far as Connor was concerned, God had done a pretty lousy job all the way around.

The Agent watched from his perch across the street. Boss wasn't happy. They were getting too close even though they might not realize it, and Boss wanted them stopped.

And whatever Boss wanted, Boss got.

It was as simple as that.

The church service ended and the doors opened. People filed out and The Agent got ready, looking for his prey. The rifle felt natural, his position good. And no little kid to interrupt him this time.

He could see them, but they couldn't see him. Confusion would ensue at the first shot, allowing him time to get away.

Perfect. He pulled the butt of the gun up to his shoulder, lowered his head to look through the scope. Samantha Cash, Andrew West, Connor Wolfe.

Or . . . pretty little Jenna Wolfe? No, she might be useful later.

Or maybe someone totally unconnected to the case? A perfectly innocent bystander. The heavyset mom trying to keep up with the three rambunctious children circling her legs?

Yeah, that would get to them. They'd feel so guilty for putting someone else in the line of fire, they might back off.

Then again . . .

Sitting ducks. Pigeons just waiting to be picked off. Who would get the first bullet?

Eenie, meenie, miney, moe.

Samantha led the way from the church and realized how much she respected this intriguing man. He'd done a good job talking to the teens about taking extra care, explaining the need for caution, but he hadn't scared them to death.

Then he'd stepped down to sit in the pew to finish the service. The crossed arms and uncomfortable shifting didn't bode well for a good report on what he'd thought about the service. Jenna, on the other hand, after her initial reluctance to attend, had seemed to loosen up and enjoy it. She'd followed the words on the screen during the singing, taken notes on the sermon, and had intently focused on every part of what went on.

"Jenna!"

The group turned at the sound of the voice. Samantha recognized the girl coming their way as one of the student youth group leaders, Maria Delgado. A sharp dresser, an honor roll student, and comfortable with herself even though she was about forty pounds overweight. She exuded energy, friendliness, and the love of God.

"Jenna, wait."

Jenna eyed Maria, looking as though she'd like to crawl under a rock. Samantha just waited, not wanting to interfere, but neither would she let Jenna hurt Maria's feelings. Connor and Andrew walked to the bottom of the steps and immediately fell into a deep discussion. Jamie fidgeted as though she'd like everyone to hurry up.

Maria stopped in front of Jenna. "Hi, I was so glad to see you in church."

"Really? Why?" Jenna had her sarcasm reined in, and Samantha relaxed when she realized the teen wasn't being mean; she was genuinely curious.

Maria shrugged. "It's a fun place most of the time and I think you'd really enjoy it. Here —" she thrust a piece of paper into Jenna's reluctant grasp — "we're going camping next weekend. Why don't you come with us?"

"Camping? I don't think so." Her body language shouted her need to escape. Yet she stayed, kept the paper with the information between her thumb and forefinger.

"Well, think about it. If you want to come, just bring your stuff to the church Friday afternoon at five. You don't have to have a tent or anything. All that's provided."

"Well . . ."

"Why don't you come back inside with me and fill out the paperwork? That way you'll have a spot on the van if you decide to come."

Jenna looked at Sam as though asking permission.

Sam stuttered, "Uh . . . sure, your dad and Andrew are still talking and don't look like they're in a hurry. I'll wait here for you."

"Um . . . well . . ."

Maria wasn't taking no for an answer. She grabbed Jenna by the hand and led the way back into the church.

Samantha turned to walk over to the guys, heard the sound of a car backfire, then watched Andrew flinch and grab his chest.

14

Connor simply reacted. He snagged Andrew in a bear hug, pulling him, staggering under his buddy's dead weight, his only thought to get behind the parked car three feet away. Shock, horror, disbelief slugged him, one emotion after the other, over and over.

He ignored them all.

As he pulled Andrew behind the cover of the car, he forced his brain to work, to think — then he was in cop mode. Where was Jenna? Samantha?

"Samantha!"

His ears rang, his throat felt paralyzed, his breathing restricted. Had he screamed her name out loud? Yes, he must have. But she wasn't anywhere to be seen. Where was she?

"Get down!" he screamed at the confused and terrified parishioners. "Down!"

Connor looked down at Andrew, prayers falling from his lips. *Oh please, God, let him live, please, please, please.*

Andrew gasped, eyes open staring up at Connor, blinking rapidly. "Hurts," he whispered. The undeniable smell of fresh blood grabbed his nose. Andrew's blood.

Connor gagged, fear for his friend nearly strangling him.

"Hang on, partner. Don't you dare die on me." He yanked his shirt over his head and wadded it into padding, pressing it against the wound. He pulled his phone from the clip and punched in 911. He recognized the dispatcher. One he'd talked to several times and knew pretty well.

"I've got shots fired. East Henry and Main. New Life Community Church. Sniper across the street on the 2nd Northwest Bank building. Andrew's hit! I repeat, officer down. 10-33! Get EMS rolling."

"Connor?"

"Yeah, now get everyone rolling and seal off this area. Set up a perimeter and get me a chopper and a K-9 unit."

"Rolling now. Oh no, Connor . . . Andrew?" Her voice held a plea Connor had to ignore.

"Get me the Life Flight chopper now!"

Looking up, Connor scanned the still screaming crowd, he saw parents hovering behind cars, shielding their little ones.

Children, oh God, protect the children.

"Connor, Connor! What's Andrew's condition?"

He snapped the phone shut and pulled his gun.

A toddler about eighteen months old wandered into the open. Where was his mother? Father? Connor panned the area, watched the child bend down to pick up a white piece of paper. A bullet pinged about a foot in front of him. Bits of asphalt flew up and stung him, startling him into a mad cry, one pudgy hand swiping at the offending pain.

Terror for the child closing his throat, Connor looked down at Andrew, back over at the baby. Another bullet spit the ground behind the child.

No choice; no time to think. Heart pounding, blood rushing, he darted out, expecting to feel a bullet split his skull.

Another crack puffed up the cement in front of an elderly lady who dropped like a rock. Connor knew she'd just fainted. He hoped the gunman thought he'd hit her.

Snatching up the child, Connor swerved back to the covering offered by the car. Back to Andrew.

Where his partner lay dying.

More bullets pounded the wooden doors of the church, one after the other, chasing the parishioners, mocking their assumption that they should even try to find a safe haven inside the building.

They ducked and scattered like ashes in the wind — some taking cover behind cars, others running for the nearest building, a telephone pole, behind anything that might stop the next bullet. In between the pops and the screams, Connor thought he heard a raw voice calling a name, ending on a sob. The child's mother? Probably. She'd just have to wait.

The back of one man's head exploded. As he dropped, more screaming ensued.

"Jenna!" He didn't see her, wanted to yell at her to get inside the church. His heart pumped so hard he thought it might very well shatter the bones that protected it.

The child in his arms wailed, tears leaking down his now grimy cheeks. "Mama."

Connor wanted to join the toddler, raise his own voice in agonizing denial. Instead, he held it together, his training kicking in as he went on autopilot. "Everyone down! Get down!"

With one arm still around the baby, Connor raised his weapon, looking for the sniper. His finger itched to return fire. But if the person was on top of the bank where he'd figured him to be, his pistol wouldn't do much good. Grinding his teeth in frustration, he dropped to his knees beside Andrew, grabbing his friend's hand. Pressing it against the wound.

"Angie . . ." Andrew's grip slackened, his strength gone.

Connor looked down at him, saw the tears leaking down his friend's temples.

"Angie . . . tell . . . love her."

"Hang on, Andrew West, you hear me?" The child squirmed, kicking to get down. Connor tightened his grip and the boy sobbed louder.

Connor tuned it out.

"You gotta stop him . . . gotta find him." Andrew's breathing grew even more labored. He coughed and blood ran from his mouth.

Connor wiped it with his free hand, then swiped it against his khakis.

Sirens finally rent the air. It just sounded like more frantic screams to Connor's already tortured ears.

Next he noticed the stillness. The bullets had stopped. Only the sounds of the crying, sobbing, frantic parents looking for their children. The intense wailing of the woman whose husband had just had his brains literally blown away.

Jenna, please be safe, please. And Sam.

And Jamie. And Angie. Where were they?

Another hacking cough from Andrew, more dribbling blood from the corner of his mouth. A punctured lung?

"Get him, Connor. But . . . no . . . revenge . . . just . . . justice. Unnerstand?" Words slurring, Andrew's lids drooped, his breathing shallow, uneven, faltering. Then he forced his eyes open. "I'm going home, Connor. 'S my time. Don't be mad at God . . . love . . . him . . . tell Angie . . . love . . ."

"Noooo!"

Time to go. The dogs and the chopper would be here soon. That was fine, he'd made his point. The dogs would look to pick up a scent, but they wouldn't know which one to follow. It was hot, the sun beating down on the roof. That would evaporate his smell — and possibly the distractions he'd planted; nevertheless, he would escape. The CS powder would mess with the dogs' noses, too, and buy him even more time. Packing up the rifle with the skill of a longtime user, he was off the roof and through the door, carefully following his plan to the nth degree.

The shooting had started almost as soon as

Maria and Jenna had stepped back inside the church. Samantha had seen the bullet pierce the door beside Jenna's head and pulled her to the floor. Then Samantha had grabbed her gun and headed for the nearest window. One eye on the outside, she looked at Jenna, Maria, Angie, and Jamie huddled under the pews in the sanctuary.

Jamie looked shell-shocked and disoriented. Grief blasted Sam as she realized her sister would probably be emotionally back at the beginning of her journey.

Then Jamie reached out and pulled Jenna and Maria to her, holding them, her lips moving in a silent prayer. Samantha stopped, stared, and blew out a breath as a fission of pure relief flowed through her.

Then again, maybe Jamie would pull through this.

Just now, she realized Angie was weeping, deep, desperate sobs. She heard the woman's rasping breath hissing through her nose. Several others from the congregation had made it back inside and were now statues, prostate on the floor, listening for the pop of more bullets.

She heard none, just the sound of the aftershocks.

Chaos reigned. A rushing wave of emergency personnel dominated the scene.

Screams echoed, people hollered, babies cried.

The sanctuary doors flew open. Samantha tensed and swung her gun around, Angie whimpered. Jenna and Maria hugged Jamie close.

At the sight of uniformed officers coming in through the back, Sam released the breath she'd been holding and quickly flashed her badge. They nodded and called it in.

Connor. Andrew. *Oh Lord, please.*

But she knew Andrew had been shot. Visions of him flinching after the sound of what she now knew had been a gunshot, not a car backfiring, screeched across her memory. What about Connor? There'd been a whole lot more bullets after the one that had hit Andrew.

Angie bolted for the doors, only to be caught by an officer. "We need you to stay put, ma'am."

"Andrew. He was shot."

"The shooter's still out there somewhere. I can't let you leave."

Samantha raced to the woman and pulled her away. "He's right, you can't go out there."

Angie whimpered, fought a bit more, then

gave in, leaning against Samantha's shoulder.

Worry clawed her midsection as she walked Angie over to the others.

Jenna looked at her, fear darkening her eyes to stormy clouds. "Dad?" she whispered.

"I don't know, honey. I'm going to find out."

Angie's makeup looked 3D on her completely white face. She clutched her stomach and moaned. "Andrew."

Samantha gripped the woman's fingers and looked at Jamie, who bit her lip and swiped a hand through her ragged curls. "Are you okay?"

"I'm shaking so hard I might fall apart."

Sam held out a hand. It trembled as badly as Jamie's. Adrenaline. "I understand, but you have to keep it together, all right?"

Jamie nodded.

"I want to see my dad. Now." Jenna directed her words to the police officers standing guard just inside the door. His radio buzzed and he zeroed his attention in on that, listening to the voice in his ear. He looked at his partner as he spoke. "Shooter's on the run. This area's secure."

Jenna darted under the man's arm and

pressed the bar on the door, swinging it open.

"Hey," he shouted and grabbed for her.

The wiry girl slipped out the door. Sam raced after her, leaving the policeman cursing in their wake.

Once outside, Jenna plowed ahead. Samantha pulled to a stop, registering the carnage. A dead man; two wounded lying in the dirt, one clutching a shoulder, the other a leg. The woman who'd fainted groaned and sat up, only to cry out in agonized grief as reality hit her. Shocked parishioners did their best to help until the professional medical technicians could get through.

Someone yelled that the scene was secured, the shooter on the run.

Shattered vehicle windows littered the ground, shards of glass mingling with the blood, and an ambulance had stopped about thirty feet away, loading someone into the back. Connor stood, watching, clutching a child who'd — amazingly enough — fallen asleep on a broad shoulder.

Jenna ran toward him. "Dad! Are you okay?"

He never turned at the sound of his daughter calling him, just stared at the stretcher in front of him.

Fear clutched her. Andrew. Was he dead

or alive? Had the sheet been pulled all the way up covering his face or not? She couldn't remember.

"Andrew!"

The wail nearly pierced Sam's eardrum, then Angie raced past her for the ambulance.

Connor looked up and the shattered look in his eyes told Samantha that Angie was now a widow. Her world shifted, spun crazily about her. Muscles lost their strength and she sank to the asphalt, covered her face, and wept.

15

For some reason, God must hate him, want him to be as alone and as miserable as possible. Connor stared at Andrew's casket as it rolled past, wondering what he'd done to incur the Almighty's wrath.

Should he have quit the force like his wife wanted? Had begged him to do? Or at least changed jobs so he wasn't working all hours of the day and night? Or maybe it was because of the last fight with Julia. He'd gotten an emergency call in the middle of their fight. She'd been livid at his departure. Thirty minutes later he received another emergency call — the call that Julia had wrapped her car around a tree. That day he'd railed at God for leaving him alone with a child to raise. Or did it go back further than that? To the time when he'd flung his contempt for his father in the man's face? A fact Connor now regretted, but wasn't sure how to rectify.

The touch of a hand on his arm brought his head around to see Samantha's compassionate, tear-filled eyes silently asking him if he was all right. No, she knew he wasn't all right, she was saying she was there for him.

He shook his head, sighed, and turned away, rejecting her comfort. He didn't deserve it, didn't want it. He looked around the chapel. Somebody else's chapel. Because the church was still a crime scene and there'd been nowhere else to have Andrew's funeral.

Samantha didn't move from his side. He wondered why. He'd pushed her away so many times since the shooting two days ago — when all he really wanted to do was pull her close, bury his face in her shoulder, and sob. But he'd pushed everyone away, including Jenna and his mother.

"Connor . . ."

Everyone had left the church. Even Angie, sheltered beneath the loving care of her family, had walked past him, eyes blank with the disbelief of what she was living. They'd all gone to the burial.

"Not right now, Samantha."

"Yes, right now."

He heard the edge in her voice. Why didn't she just leave him alone?

But she said, "You've pushed everyone

who loves you away. Everyone who wants to be there for you, to support you. Andrew wouldn't want that for you."

Snakelike, he whipped his head around to spout, "Andrew wouldn't want any of this. He wouldn't want to be dead, leaving behind the people who loved him. And he sure as —" He swallowed the curse word. Even he couldn't bring himself to curse in God's house. "He sure wouldn't want to be remembered in a borrowed church. A church not even his own because some madman shot it up." His anger dissipated almost as quickly as it had risen, leaving him feeling that dead numbness he'd clung to for the last two days.

Samantha didn't even flinch at his outburst. Instead, she said, "Oh, I don't know. Andrew loved the Lord more than anything. I don't think he minds his funeral being held in a 'borrowed' chapel. Just one more thing he and Jesus have in common."

Connor swallowed twice. "What are you talking about?"

"After Jesus was taken down from the cross, he was buried in a borrowed tomb. The King of kings didn't even have his own grave. So —" she shrugged — "I wouldn't think Andrew would care one bit about where his funeral was held."

Connor simply stared at her. "But Jesus didn't stay there very long, did he? Andrew's not coming back."

Surprise darkened her eyes. "No, he didn't, and no, Andrew's not. But Andrew's not there either. Yes, his physical body is, but his spirit isn't, the part of what made Andrew, Andrew, isn't in that casket."

"God could have stopped it. He could have stopped it all, but he didn't. It's my fault. It was my idea, drawing the killer out. Even with a vest on, Andrew wouldn't have had a chance against that rifle, but it might have slowed the bullet somehow. Why didn't Andrew have his vest on? We agreed to wear vests. I never should have —"

Enough was enough.

"Don't make Andrew's death about you," Samantha told him, her tone gentle, her words scorching.

Confusion mingled with shock at what he probably thought was a harsh statement. "What do you mean?"

"God didn't do this to punish you or because he's mad at you, or whatever it is that's going through your mind right now. *He* didn't do it at all."

He jerked as if she'd slapped him. His eyes narrowed, slid from her face to the stained-glass window. Through clenched teeth, he ground out, "You don't know what you're talking about."

"Don't I?" Her hand covered his. He pulled away.

Samantha sighed. "Look, you don't own the market on grief, pain, and anger. I know you're hurt, you're mad, you're asking why. But for one thing, Andrew was a big boy, if he chose not to wear his vest . . ."

He turned on her, almost shouting the words in the stillness of the small chapel. "What do you know about it? Andrew was my best friend. The brother I never had. What do you know?" He folded his arms on the back of the pew in front of him, lowering his forehead to rest it on them. This time he whispered, "What do you know?"

Tears pricked behind her eyes. She wanted to cry for him, to hug him and tell him it would get better. But that wouldn't be fair. It *would* get better, but he'd also hurt for a long time. "I know, Connor, trust me, I know."

For a moment he didn't move, then he looked at her, really looked at her for the first time since the shooting. "Your sister."

"Yeah." She blew out a sigh and looked away from him, the memories edging her to the point of tears once again. "Yeah."

"But Andrew? Why him?"

"Better him than you."

"What a lousy thing to say!" He stood, ready to storm out.

She grabbed his hand, stopping him. "I didn't say that to be mean, Connor. Andrew's in heaven. Where would you be right now if that bullet had found you?"

His mouth worked, his Adam's apple bobbed. No words came out.

Samantha took pity on him. "Come on, let's go to the grave-side. I know you said you didn't want to see him buried, but I think you need to be there."

The Agent leaned back in the corner of the pew, hidden from sight by a large flower arrangement. The funeral had been — interesting. Filled to capacity, they'd had an overflow room set up with a large screen. Every officer from miles around had been there.

Cops, cops everywhere and not an arrest in sight.

He almost giggled at his silly thought.

He hadn't wanted to come to the funeral, but Boss had insisted. The last two mourners had just left. Samantha Cash and Connor Wolfe. Yes, he knew them. Knew everything about them. And had for a long time.

He figured the information would come in handy at some point, since they *were* the officers trying to catch him, to stop him from fulfilling his calling, his destiny.

The Agent wondered if he should go watch the casket be lowered to the ground, but decided against it. They'd be watching for him. Someone who was out of place, didn't fit in. He might even be recognized, his presence questioned.

No, that wouldn't do at all. He rose, stuck a hand in his pocket, and strolled to the small chapel's single door at the back. Satisfaction gripped him. He'd shown them he wasn't as powerless as they'd thought.

He hoped they got the message, that they now had a healthy respect for him.

Hmm. Well, if not, he could always kill them one by one.

Or, he could send another little message to Connor Wolfe. He rubbed his chin. Yes, one message after another until they gave up and realized they couldn't win. Then everything would get back to normal.

Yes, another message. That was the next step.

It was as simple as that.

Jenna slammed her body across her bed, using her backpack as a pillow; the key chains dug grooves into her check, but she didn't care. Restless, she flipped over and stared at her ceiling. Then looked at her computer sitting over by the wall. She hadn't been online for a couple of days. Not with the craziness of Andrew dying and the knowledge that she'd come very close to death at the hands of some crazed gunman. She expected to feel something more than just sad. Sad and . . . numb. Andrew had always been kind to her, and just a few months ago, she'd been a bridesmaid at their wedding because her dad was Andrew's best friend.

But she just felt . . . sad. And maybe a little angry.

And completely exhausted. Like she could sleep for years.

Weird.

She'd overheard her dad talking to Samantha. He thought the whole shooting thing had something to do with the case he was working on.

Why couldn't he just be a normal, nerdy accountant? Maybe then her mom would still be alive. Anger pulsed through her at the thought. Was it possible to hate someone and love him all at the same time?

Sometimes that's how she felt about her dad. She'd been scared to death when all that shooting had started and her dad had been outside. The relief she'd felt when she'd seen him standing there, handing over the baby to its mother, had made her knees go weak for a minute. She'd wanted to throw her arms around him and tell him she loved him so she'd run to him — and stopped, shuddering at the fury radiating from him.

He'd looked her in the eye and asked, "Are you all right?"

"Yes, are you?"

"I don't have any bullet holes." Then he'd watched the ambulance take off, his shoulder set, lips tight, eyes hard. He'd looked at Samantha. "Will you see she gets home safely?" Her grandmother had stayed home with her grandfather. Thank goodness they hadn't been there.

Sam had nodded, still stunned, seeming to be in some sort of limbo state.

Her dad hadn't said thanks, hadn't said he was glad she was okay. Hadn't hugged her.

Jenna looked at her computer once again, then got up to cross to the desk and plant herself in the chair. She moved the mouse, typed in her password, and saw she had a dozen IMs. Several from 2COOL2BLV. Three from Patty. One from Bradley. That was a surprise. Hmm.

Which one?

2COOL.

2COOL was always there when she needed him.

Samantha studied the screen before her. She couldn't sleep, couldn't eat, couldn't focus on anything but the case. Two days had passed in a blur. After the funeral, she watched Connor climb into his Mustang and pull away from the church, Jenna silent and still in the passenger seat.

Yesterday, she'd gone to see Angie. Her love for Andrew was strong. Her faith even stronger. She would survive. But she was terribly worried about Connor and Jenna. As was Samantha. It was Thursday morning and she'd heard nothing from Connor in the past two days. She'd called him and left him a message that had gone unanswered. There was nothing else she could do.

Except work. Study everything they had. Find every ounce of evidence on the computers and do one more desperate search to come up with something new.

And do all she could to help find Andrew's killer.

She wanted to know about those doctors' reports on the girls, and they still needed to talk to Alyssa Mabry. She had no doubt

Connor would be at work, buried to his eyeballs in paperwork, going over every scrap the crime scene guys had gotten from the church.

He wouldn't take a break, would work tirelessly, would focus on nothing but finding Andrew's killer.

And Jenna would be left alone to fend for herself once again — with a personal bodyguard, of course. It just wouldn't be her dad. Before Andrew had been killed, she'd seen progress in Connor and Jenna's relationship. Now that progress would come to a screeching halt. Unless Samantha did something about it.

But that really wasn't her place. Sure, she was very attracted to the man, and sure, she'd love to act on it in spite of the fact that he was a cop and she'd promised herself she wouldn't date a co-worker. But that was a moot point anyway. How could she take even a minute of Connor's time from Jenna when the girl needed him so much right now?

However, Samantha had the sneaking suspicion that Jenna was depressed but didn't feel like she could broach that with Connor any time soon.

Sighing, she tightened the band on her ever-present ponytail and looked around.

Repairs had been made to her sliding glass door, and now she had brand-new blinds that had stayed closed ever since she'd returned last night. After Andrew's funeral, she'd stayed one more night with Jamie. Then she'd run out of excuses. It was time to come home.

After four more hours of worthless digging into hard drives and slack space, resurrecting emails thought to be dead and gone from internet servers, and finding nothing related to the case, but plenty about the girls' lives, she shut down the computer and walked into her tiny kitchen to grab a bottle of water.

As she drank the cold liquid, she considered the fact that she could find nothing. Very strange. Strange enough to make her sit up and take notice. No teenager was that good with a computer.

Okay, maybe one or two, but all six of the girls? Savvy enough to wipe out practically everything they'd done on it? It was as if they'd been coached how to clean up a hard drive. How to erase emails, how to completely wipe the thing clean of any "footprints" they might have left behind.

Weird. She took another swig and considered everything. No, the more she studied the computers, the more she was sure that they'd all been accessed remotely. She'd compiled a list of IP addresses. Three of the six had a common one. But she wanted to know if the other computers had the same strange IP address.

She wondered if she should call Connor and ask him if he'd gotten the doctors' files on the girls and had he found anything. Or call Tom and see what he was up to and if there was anything he was working on she needed to know about. Or, call Jamie and see if she was interested in grabbing a bite to eat and then going back to her place to sleep for the night.

Because being alone in her apartment was downright creeping her out. She kept waiting for the explosion of glass, the thud of the bolt hitting her wall, the sting of shards piercing her skin.

Shuddering, she reached for the phone just as her doorbell rang and scared the daylights out of her.

Heart pounding, telling herself to relax for crying out loud, she stuck her eye up to the peephole and gasped.

Connor.

Gathering as much composure as she could, she opened the door. "Hi."

"Hi." He just stood there, looking at her like she was some specimen on a slide.

She shifted. "Um, you want to come in?"

He blinked. "Yes. If you don't mind."

So polite. So distant. So . . . un-Connor-like. What was going on?

Instead of asking, she backed up, pulling the door with her, making room for him to enter.

As he slipped past her, Samantha inhaled his freshly showered scent, watched his shirt stretch taut across finely tuned muscles. He worked out a lot, she knew. She'd wager he'd been spending a lot of time in the gym over the last couple of days.

Not necessarily just to work out, but to work *through*.

She hoped he'd been successful. But by the look of his eyes, he had a ways to go. He lowered himself on the couch and looked at her laptop, powered up, the notepad and pen. "Working?"

"Yes. I can't seem to focus on anything else."

He quirked her a sad smile. "I know what you mean."

"How's Jenna?"

He shrugged. "She's dealing, I think. I offered to let her talk to a counselor, but she just rolled her eyes and went to her room. She did tell me she was sorry about Andrew, but . . ." He cleared his throat and nodded toward her laptop. "So, did you find anything?"

Sam could take a hint. "Possibly. I have a hunch I'm working on. Here." She handed him the IP address. "I've got this IP address. I've put a trace on it. It was on three of the computers. I haven't had a chance to check the other three yet, but if they all have that in common, my guess is that this guy managed to get into their computers from a remote location."

"Great work, Samantha. Let me call it in and have someone else trace it, I want you to go with me." He picked up his phone and dialed, reciting the IP address to the person on the other end. He hung up and said, "Hopefully, we'll hear something soon."

"I was just getting ready to call you and ask if we could go talk to Alyssa Mabry. She's home now and we need to get over there and question her. I feel like she could give us some new insight into what was going on with Miranda. Maybe even give me a clue about going in a different direction with my search of her computer. Although, to be honest, I think I've found the biggest clue. This guy was accessing their computers from somewhere. Now, we just need to track down the location and see what we can turn up."

For the first time since Andrew's death, a little bit of life sparked in Connor's eyes. "That sounds like a good idea. I was going to have to track her down today anyway — now's as good a time as any. I've still got her parents' number in my phone. Let me give them a call."

Thirty minutes later, Connor pulled into the drive of a well-kept home. The L-shaped ranch sat on about an acre and a half. A huge Saint Bernard languished on the porch, lifting its head to stare inquisitively at the newcomers. Samantha exited the car and Connor followed. The front door opened as they approached to reveal a woman in her midforties, brown hair pulled up in a ponytail, wisps of gray peeking out every now and then.

Samantha wondered if the gray was a new development. The woman gave a tremulous smile and said, "Hello. I'm Bonnie Mabry. My husband's at work, but I know Alyssa will be glad to answer any questions you have. I called the school and asked them to release her early. She should be here shortly."

"Thank you, Mrs. Mabry, we appreciate that."

They stepped into the cool foyer, a blessed relief from the heat outside. Mrs. Mabry led them past a staircase and into an informal den area. "Would you care for anything to drink? I have bottled water or some tea."

"Nothing for me, thanks." Samantha smiled.

Connor accepted a bottle of water. The woman left to get it and Samantha eyed the picture on the mantel. The same one she'd seen in Miranda's bedroom on the memory board. The two girls stood, arm in arm in front of Mickey Mouse. They'd been to Disney World together and looked like they were having the time of their lives.

"Here you are."

"Thank you." Connor took the bottle and Samantha heard the back door open, then shut.

"Mom?"

One of the girls from the picture hurried into the den and slung an overfilled, heavy-looking backpack to the floor. "What's going on? Nobody at school would tell me anything except that I needed to come home and everyone in my family was fine and it wasn't an emergency and —" She caught sight of Sam and Connor on the sofa to her right. "Oh."

Mrs. Mabry motioned her in. "This is

Detective Wolfe and Special Agent Samantha Cash. They need to talk to you about Miranda."

Instantly, the big green eyes filled with tears. "I don't want to talk about her. It hurts too much."

Her mother slid an arm around the girl's shoulder. "I know, honey, but you've got to tell them anything you remember about Miranda's last moments with you. It might help them find her killer." A sheen covered the woman's eyes and she closed them for a moment. When she opened them, she looked at Connor. "Ask her what you need to, please. She'll cooperate." She looked back at Alyssa. "Right?"

"Right." Her chin quivered. "But I can't promise not to cry."

Samantha's heart hurt for the girl even as cold fury at the individual who was causing all this pain gripped her hard.

Connor asked, "Did you go with Miranda when she was supposed to meet with that guy from the modeling agency?"

Surprise lit Alyssa's eyes. "Yes, I did. How did you know she met with someone? I don't remember telling anyone that, because she didn't want her parents to find out. I mean it wasn't like she was doing anything wrong, but they thought the modeling stuff was dumb and wanted her to focus on school and . . ." She trailed off.

Samantha almost groaned out loud. Important information and the tight-lipped loyalty of a teen. A deadly combination in this instance.

If Connor had the same thought, he didn't show it. Eager now, he leaned forward. "Could you tell us what the guy looked like? The one that she met?"

"No, I'm sorry, but I never saw him."

"What? What do you mean? You just said you went with her."

"I did, but he was late. Miranda and I were sitting in the food court, eating, drinking, talking. Finally, I had to go to the bathroom. Miranda did too. But she didn't want to take a chance on missing the guy. So, I went by myself. When I came back, she was gone."

"And she didn't leave you a message or anything?"

"She texted me saying she was leaving for a little while and for me to go on home."

"She texted you? Did she use her own phone or a different one?"

A puzzled expression twisted Alyssa's pretty features. "A different one. One that he'd given her. But how did you know?"

"It doesn't matter. What happened next?"

"I texted her back a couple of times. She answered me once, saying she was fine, not to say anything to her parents and she would see me soon." She bit her lip. "But I was a little worried . . ." She didn't finish her sentence, her eyes darting toward her mother, then back to Connor.

Sam said gently, "You were worried because . . ."

"She . . . wasn't . . . um . . . feeling too well. She was really pale and said she felt a little sick."

"And do you know why she felt sick? Some bad food, maybe?"

Connor knew perfectly well why Miranda wasn't feeling well. The question was, did Alyssa know? Samantha's gut told her Alyssa had probably gone with Miranda to get the abortion. One didn't have to be an expert on body language to read the shifting feet, twisting fingers, flitting eyes. The girl was nervous and afraid, and she had a secret.

"Alyssa."

Sam's quiet voice had the desired effect. Alyssa looked at her and stilled.

"We know why Miranda wasn't feeling well. Now we need every detail."

16

She was good. Connor looked at Samantha in surprise, then didn't know why he was surprised. After all, she'd gone through the FBI training academy just as he had. But she was definitely a natural interrogator. Reading the person being questioned, picking up the verbal and nonverbal cues like a pro, honing in with the right tone of voice.

Alyssa dropped her head into her hands and started crying, quiet, massive sobs that shook her shoulders as she rocked back and forth. Her mother rushed to her and slipped her arms around her.

She looked at Connor, concern, fear, a little bit of anger mixed in her expression. "I think that's enough."

"Ma'am, your daughter is our only link right to the missing girls. Please, let her get her composure and permit us to continue talking to her. She may be the only hope these other girls have." He didn't need the woman's permission, but tried to phrase his words in a way that would make her feel more in control of the situation.

Mrs. Mabry swallowed hard, looked at her hiccuping child, and sighed. She leaned forward to touch Alyssa's head with her own. "Come on, Alyssa, darling. You've got to tell these people what you know. Miranda would want you to. It might mean saving another girl's life. Pull it together, sweetie."

A shuddering groan escaped Alyssa's throat, and Connor felt her anguish deep in him. Andrew would . . .

He almost groaned himself from the shaft of agony that ripped through him.

"She'd had an abortion," Alyssa finally ground out between clenched teeth. Ignoring her mother's horrified gasp, Alyssa went on. "That day. She'd found someone who would do it pretty cheap and she didn't have to have parental consent."

"Where?"

"A place just outside of town." She shuddered. "It was horrible. Just a little one-room place that didn't look like it had been there very long." Connor made a note to get directions from her and have that checked out right away. "I tried to talk her out of it, I promise, I really did. I told her she would get some kind of infection or disease. But she wouldn't listen. I . . . waited in the car, refused to go in, but I . . . couldn't just leave her there. And if I hadn't taken her, someone else would have. At least I could kind of keep an eye on her, but then . . ."

She pushed her palms down her jeans, then rubbed her hands together like they were cold. Taking a deep breath, she swiped a few stray tears. "When she came out, she was stumbling, weak. I had to help her into the car. I took her home, and when she got out of the car, there was some blood on the seat, not a lot, but enough to make me worry. I asked her if I could take her to the doctor, a *real* doctor. She said she just needed to lie down. I left, then about two hours later she called me and said she had to meet someone at the mall and would I go with her."

"How did she sound on the phone?"

"Weak, sick, but excited too. I told her no way, she needed to rest. I was worried she was going to bleed to death or something."

Connor flicked a look at Samantha. She bit her lip and closed her eyes, shaking her head. He turned back to Alyssa.

"Why didn't you tell anyone this after she was found?"

Alyssa looked to the ceiling. "I thought . . .

I didn't want to make it worse. She was dead and . . ." She shrugged. "What difference would telling that to someone make?"

"Wait a minute. Make what worse?"

She groaned and briefly closed her eyes. "Her reputation. All the kids at school were talking about her behind her back, laughing at her, calling her names. And Charlie, he was the father of the baby, he wanted Miranda to keep it, but said there was no way he was ruining his life with a kid. She was on her own. When he told her that, she made up her mind. And once she made up her mind, there wasn't much anyone could do to change it."

Connor's notebook was filling up fast. He flipped the page. "So, you took her to the mall. Went to the bathroom, came back, and she was gone." He looked at Samantha. "Are there any security cameras in that food court?"

"I'll check." She got up and walked into the kitchen to make the call.

"Okay, Alyssa, just a bit more. We found an IM on one of the girls' computers saying she needed to bring a complete medical history to the meeting. Do you know if Miranda got her medical records?"

Alyssa's eyes lit up. "Yes, I know she did because she was excited that they were ready that day. We actually swung by the office and picked them up before going to the mall to meet that guy."

Connor wrote down the name and address of the doctor's office. "Anything else you can tell me?"

Tears welled again. "Um . . . maybe. I don't know if this is important or not, but she was a little put out because she had to have a complete physical. Like a pap smear and everything. She wanted to know what that had to do with walking down the runway. Anyway, that's when she found out she was pregnant and got really scared. That was about a week before she . . . disappeared."

"Scared that if her parents found out, they'd be mad?"

"Yes, them and Charlie and what this was going to do for her modeling chances, her scholarship. Everything. But she made up her mind that she wasn't going to let that stop her. She'd have the abortion and get on with her life and career."

Well, they knew one thing. Miranda had the abortion before the meeting at the mall. "Thank you, Alyssa, you've been a big help."

"I'm really sorry I didn't tell you all this before."

"You've told us now and that's what

counts." Not really, but he wasn't going to let her carry that burden the rest of her life. She was a scared teen who'd just lost her best friend. Connor could relate. "Oh, one more question. Where did she get the money for the abortion?"

"From the modeling guy. He sent her a thousand dollars as a kind of down payment thing, I guess. He told her to use it to buy a dress for the photo shoot. She . . . um . . . used part of it for the abortion."

Connor sharpened his gaze. "Sent it to her? How?"

Alyssa shrugged. "Through the mail, I guess. The money came the day after the doctor's appointment, not the abortion appointment, but the first one she had. She was thrilled and scared all at the same time."

Samantha came back in the room. "Five cameras working, one not."

Relief flooded him. He made a note about that first doctor's appointment, then called in their location, their destination, and ordered a team out to the address where Miranda had gotten her abortion. Dakota would report back anything found there.

He looked at Samantha. "Let's go find out what this guy looks like."

The Agent sipped his coffee and turned the

page of the newspaper he had spread out in front of him. He'd made the front page again. And the article was so long it was continued on page three. A summary of the missing and dead girls read like a police report.

But no mention of the missing babies. At least that area seemed to be going well. Not that they didn't suspect a black market baby ring, but that's all they had. Suspicion.

Satisfaction filled him. He'd been careful. Covered his tracks. Thought of everything. He had nothing to be worried about, and yet . . .

That small niggle of uneasiness worked its way into his brain and no amount of rationalizing or trying to convince himself he hadn't left a traceable trail behind could silence it.

Another sip of coffee slid down. It was time. Under the table, he snapped on a rubber glove, rose, and started out of the restaurant. He bypassed several tables, stopping briefly to check his phone.

Then continued on his way.

Stopped to punch in a text message.

Then dropped the phone into the trash.

Message delivered.

The director of mall security pulled up the

surveillance video in question. Tuesday evening a week ago. "We have six cameras and keep these going all the time. They hold about seven days' worth of video. You're right on the edge here."

He clicked keys on the computer in front of him, scrolling through the days and time up to the point where Connor said, "Okay, stop there. Let's just watch it."

"Huh," the director said, "you got lucky."

Samantha watched the glass doors, waiting for a familiar face to appear. Finally. "There. That's Alyssa and Miranda." The two girls chatted as they walked through the seating area, carefully looking at each face as though searching for someone. As long as they didn't venture left or right, the camera would stay on them.

No such luck. They went left. The director punched a few more keys. This time the camera angled from in front of them.

Sam observed, "Miranda really doesn't look well. See the expression on her face?"

"Yeah. She looks ready to hurl."

Miranda grabbed Alyssa's arm and stumbled. Alyssa caught her, said something that brought a grimace to Miranda's face as she shook her head. Alyssa guided her friend to a chair and Miranda sank into it.

Alyssa said something else, pointed, and

Miranda nodded. Connor muttered, "Probably going to get something to eat for them."

A few minutes later she appeared on camera again.

"Right, here she comes with a tray."

For the next ten minutes, the girls talked and finished their meal with Miranda looking at her watch every few seconds, then glancing at the glass doors. "She's watching for him."

Connor grunted. "There goes Alyssa." The girl wandered across the food court and out of range of the camera. "To the restroom."

And here came the guy. Shoulders hunched, left arm in a sling, shaggy black hair sticking out from under a baseball cap.

Connor swore. "Can't see his face."

"Of course not," Samantha said softly. "He knows there are cameras all over the place. I bet that hair isn't real either."

"He's got on glasses."

"Clean shaven."

Three minutes passed. Miranda shook her head at something the guy said. He reached over with his good hand and touched hers in a comforting manner. He said something else. Miranda grinned, nodded, and pulled out her cell phone. Fingers flew over the numbers, then she snapped it closed.

Sam slapped the desk. "She's texting

Alyssa to let her know she's leaving."

"What's taking Alyssa so long?" Connor asked. "Does it really take that long to use the bathroom?"

Sam studied the two figures walking out of the food court. Miranda's gait, slow, unsteady, but determined. The food had helped — she seemed to have a bit more strength than she did when she'd first walked in. The guy kept his head bent toward Miranda, his face still hidden by the ball cap. "Alyssa got delayed."

"You think he sent someone to stall her? To give him time to get Miranda out of the place so Alyssa wouldn't see him?"

"Maybe, or something legitimate happened. As worried as she was about Miranda, I don't think she would have stayed in the bathroom that long without something keeping her in there."

Connor pulled out his cell, dialed a number, and waited. "This is Detective Wolfe, Mrs. Mabry. Is Alyssa still there? I have one more question for her, if you don't mind."

A pause. Then Connor said, "Hi, Alyssa. You said you went to the restroom, then when you came back out, Miranda was gone. How long were you in the restroom and did you talk to anyone while you were in there? Uh-huh. Okay. Right. Thanks. Bye."

Samantha didn't look away from the screen. "Look, there's Alyssa coming back to the table. She's looking around. See the puzzled look? She's wondering where Miranda went."

Then Alyssa pulled her cell phone from her pocket. Opened it. "She's reading the message Miranda sent her."

Fear crossed the girl's face. She sent an answer to the text immediately. Sat down and waited. While Alyssa sat, Connor explained the phone call. "Alyssa said a lady came in with a baby and a toddler. The toddler kept trying to get out the door while the mom was trying to change the diaper. Alyssa held on to the older one while the mom finished up."

"So, it was just a freak thing, or did our guy pay the mom to ask Alyssa to do that?"

"No telling. We probably won't ever know. As charming as this fellow seems to be, if he paid the mother, she probably thought it was all some kind of joke . . . or a surprise party, or whatever. And the arm in the sling was a good touch. Elicits sympathy."

"Yeah." Samantha knew he was right, but it was still frustrating all the same.

Five minutes went by. Alyssa finally stood

and walked to the glass doors. The director kept switching cameras to keep the girl in view just as he'd done moments earlier with Miranda and her kidnapper.

Alyssa went out the doors and Samantha sighed. "Just like Alyssa explained. And we still don't know what this guy looks like."

Sam's phone buzzed.

Tom. "Hello?"

"Hey, Sam. I got a call from the FBI. They've got a missing senator's kid. I'm going to need your help on this one."

Obligation to her buddy warred with the necessity to continue working the case she was already neck-deep in. "Tom, come on. You know I'm working this missing girls case. You're going to have to get someone else, my friend."

"No, you come on, Samantha. You've done what you were asked to do. The computer stuff. What's keeping you there?"

"I don't feel like I'm finished, Tom. And right now my boss hasn't released me from this case, so this is my priority, okay?"

"What about this missing kid?"

She didn't have an answer for that one. She sighed. "I'm sorry. You'll have to find another agent to help you handle it. It shouldn't be much longer, a few more days at most. I feel like we're closing in and I'm not really ready to give it up yet."

His answering sigh blew in her ear. "All right, I guess I can see if Bungee'll help me." Fred "Bungee" Kilpatrick was an avid bungee jumper, hence the nickname. Retired FBI, he also pitched in on an emergency basis when either Samantha or Tom needed help on a missing persons case.

"I'd appreciate it. And I promise, we'll be back working together soon. I just really want to catch this guy, Tom."

"Just make sure he doesn't catch you first."

His concern touched her. She had a feeling he was trying to get her to focus on something else because of the recent danger. "I'm being careful. And hopeful too. It means we're getting closer if he's scared enough to kill a cop."

Just saying the words sent grief spearing through her. She hoped Connor wasn't paying attention. Slicing him a glance, she relaxed as he still had his focus on the director.

Tom was still arguing with her. "I don't know. Just . . . be careful, you know?"

"I know."

"Have you talked to Jamie today?"

This time it was guilt that made its presence known. "Um. No, not today. When I talked to her day before yesterday, she was handling everything."

"I think I'll go by and see her."

"Good idea. Give her my love, will you?"

"Of course."

She hung up the phone and massaged her aching neck. Too much going on and not enough time to get to everything. Was she getting obsessed with this case?

Maybe.

They thanked the security director, shook his hand, and promised to let him know if they needed anything else.

Once back in the car, Connor said, "Those doctor reports are in. Let's go check them out. Dakota's waiting on us. Plus, I want to make a few phone calls about the girls receiving mail. I wonder if the parents have kept anything like that."

His phone buzzed and he sighed, pulling it out. Sam watched the color drain from his face. Every muscle in him seemed to go rigid as his throat worked.

"Connor? Connor, what's wrong?"

Connor felt like he couldn't breathe. Samantha's voice came from a distance, muffled, garbled, like she was underwater and trying to talk to him. He gasped for air and shoved the phone at her.

She took it.

"Oh no. Oh no. Connor, get to her school. She's in school, right?"

A picture of the African-American couple sitting at the restaurant eating, their faces sad. Together, yet separate, lost in their own thoughts, maybe memories of happier times or wondering when they'd find joy again. Sydney Carter's parents.

And a text message below.

DO YOU KNOW WHERE JENNA IS?

He shook, shuddered as he desperately tried to gain control. Fear for Jenna nearly strangled him.

"Connor! Get it together and let's go!"

He cranked the car. Fury sizzled through him. "If that creep so much as lays a finger on her . . ."

Samantha had her phone out, dialing.

"Is she answering?" He put his siren on. Swerved around the next curve.

"It's ringing."

"Why isn't she answering?" he shouted.

Samantha snapped her phone shut. "Voice mail."

He had to think. "Call the school. She . . . she won't answer her phone if she's in school. She'll have it on vibrate." Hope leaped within.

He yanked the steering wheel to careen around a car whose driver had slammed on the brakes.

Samantha grabbed the dash. He didn't care. All he could think about was Jenna in the hands of a psycho killer. He started praying.

Connor squealed into the parking lot of the school. Samantha had gotten the receptionist and asked her to get Jenna out of class immediately and have her waiting in the office. The woman agreed, but Samantha still didn't know if Jenna was actually at school. She could have left the campus without informing anyone.

Connor raced to the front door. Samantha pulled in close on his heels, catching the door as it started to close behind him.

The door led directly to the office. Two receptionists stood nearby, chatted and laughed while sipping coffee.

Slapping his badge on the counter, Connor demanded, "Where's Jenna Wolfe?"

The poor receptionist pedaled backward, no doubt petrified by the large scared and angry man in front of her. Coffee sloshed over the side of her cup and she winced at the sting.

Samantha stepped forward. The woman's name tag read Melody Mann. Samantha covered Connor's hand with her own and said, "I'm sorry. We just really need to see her. It's an emergency."

Flustered, but wanting to help, Ms. Mann went to her computer. "I called her to the office just a few minutes ago, but she hasn't shown up yet."

Connor threw his hands up, paced back toward the door, did a one-eighty, and stopped in front of the counter again. "What class does she have right now?"

The woman consulted her computer screen again. "Um. English."

"Where?" Connor barked.

"Room E310."

"And that's the room you just called her from?"

"Yes, sir."

"Call her again."

"But, I . . ." She stopped at his ferocious look and picked up the phone. "Mrs. Hayden? Please send Jenna to the office at once. Her father is here to pick her up." She listened. "Uh-huh. All right. Thank you." A troubled frown creased her forehead. "She's not in class right now."

"Then where is she?" Connor spoke in a very tight, extremely controlled voice.

"Well, I'm just not sure." She consulted the sign-out log. "But she hasn't signed out, so I'm sure she's here."

"Dad?"

Samantha and Connor turned as one at the young voice coming from the door behind them. Relief nearly knocked Samantha to her knees. Connor strode forward and grabbed Jenna by the arms.

"Are you okay?"

She shrugged him off. "Yeah, Dad, I'm fine. What's going on?"

Samantha watched Connor swallow hard.

"Where were you? Why weren't you in class?"

"Chill, Dad. I was with the new guidance counselor."

Connor swung back to the receptionist. "Mrs. Hayden couldn't have shared that information with us?"

Before the harried woman could answer, Jenna did it for her. "I never made it to Mrs. Hayden's class. He caught me in the hall just after the bell."

"Um, excuse me," Ms. Mann interrupted.

Everyone turned to look at her. She wrung her hands and said, "We don't have a new guidance counselor."

Connor narrowed his eyes and swung back to Jenna. "What was his name?"

The teen sighed and rolled her eyes. "I don't know. Um, I think he introduced himself as Daniel something."

Samantha froze. Connor did likewise.

Daniel. Danny.

His tone more gentle, he told Ms. Mann, "Get Principal Harrington in here and put this school on lockdown. Now!"

Alarm streaking her already stressed features, she nodded and got back on her phone.

"What did he look like, Jenna?"

"Um . . . dark hair, kind of curly. Green eyes, but I think they were contacts. He had an earring in his right ear that was kind of cool. I don't know." She shrugged. "He was taller than me, but shorter than you — and cute. Oh, and he looked like he worked out a lot."

Connor immediately got on the school intercom system. "This is Detective Connor Wolfe with SLED. We have a trespasser on campus. Be on the lookout for a white male, dark hair, green eyes, around six feet tall, and an earring in his right ear. This is not a drill. This man is dangerous. Do not approach him. Keep your doors locked until further notice."

He hung up the intercom and turned to Jenna.

Samantha watched father and daughter circle each other.

Tendons stood out on Connor's neck, his pulse beat at the base of his throat. A vein throbbed in his forehead. If they didn't catch this guy soon, Connor was going to rupture something. Jenna looked wary, not taking her eyes from her father.

Mr. Harrington sent notice that he was on his way.

Connor needed help to search the school. And he needed someone to find that cell phone he'd gotten the text from. But first, he needed to make sure the students were safe.

Find out if there was a killer on campus . . .

Doors slammed in the background. Students hurried into the nearest classrooms. Samantha took a seat, and Jenna dropped into the chair next to her. Poor kid. She looked like she wanted to crawl into a hole and hide.

Police vehicles were already turning into the parking lot. Samantha could see from her vantage point through the window behind the man's desk. The blades of a police helicopter thumped closer.

Principal Harrington entered his office, scanned the group of people who'd taken refuge there, and asked, "Detective Wolfe, what's going on? Why did you call for a lockdown?"

Connor looked at Samantha. She read the look. He didn't want Jenna to know that she'd been singled out by this guy. She'd have to get her out of the office, but into another safe area.

Samantha stood. "Jenna, come with me."

She pulled out her weapon and Jenna's eyes went wide, but she kept her mouth shut, following Samantha like a whipped puppy. The School Resource Officer entered the room with Connor and the principal and shut the door behind him.

Outside the office, Samantha looked left and right. Clear. She checked to make sure Jenna was behind her and made her way to the next office. It was empty, so she pulled Jenna inside and bolted the door shut.

"What's going on, Samantha?"

"We think the guy who's been killing the girls came on campus today."

"But —"

Sam held up a hand. "Your dad will have to fill you in, okay?"

The girl bit her lip and her eyes flashed, but she nodded. This office also had a window facing the parking lot, and Samantha walked to the window to watch the activity.

"What did the guidance counselor want to talk to you about?"

Jenna bit her lip. "He wasn't really a guidance counselor, was he?"

Hesitating, Sam finally decided she couldn't lie. "No. You heard the secretary. There aren't any new guidance counselors on campus. But it's okay, you're safe. Now tell me exactly what happened."

Rubbing her temples, Jenna drew in a deep breath then let it out slowly. "He stopped me in the hall and asked how I'd been doing since Andrew had been shot."

"Really?"

"Yeah. When I asked him who he was, he said he was new. Because he knew about Andrew, I figured he'd been reading my file and tracked me down." Jenna swallowed hard. "Is he the killer?"

Blowing out a frustrated breath, Samantha shook her head. "It's possible. That's what we're trying to figure out. What did he look like again?" She was going for consistency and to see if Jenna added anything useful to the description.

"Um . . . tall, slender, but not like a skinny basketball player, he was better built, stockier."

"What color was his hair?"

"Dark, curly, a little shaggy like he was trying to be in style. I didn't think the style fit him personally." Another shrug.

"His eyes?"

"Green! I already just told you this." She threw her hands up. "And he needed a shave, his face was all scruffy looking."

By the time Samantha had finished her gentle interrogation of Jenna, she was ready to climb the walls, but she knew she needed to stay put with the girl.

Then she noticed the emergency vehicles pulling out of the parking lot. He'd gotten away. Again.

A knock on the door brought her to her feet.

"Open up, Sam, it's me."

Samantha complied and Connor's frustration nearly slammed her back into the office.

"He got away, didn't he?"

"Yeah. We got a video of him talking to Jenna in the hall, but he very strategically had his back to the camera the whole time."

"Of course he did. The man's not stupid."

"No, but when I get my hands on him, he's going to wish he was dead. We also got video of him leaving the building. He crawled into a silver Camaro. We already ran the plates. It was stolen three hours ago."

Two hours later, Jenna had worked with a sketch artist and had her own personal bodyguard with numerous warnings about being careful, not going anywhere alone, and not ditching the bodyguard. The poor girl had been a bundle of nerves by the time they left. As much as Connor wanted to keep Jenna with him, he knew there was a good possibility that being in his presence would actually place her in more danger than if he simply hired someone to protect her.

As a precaution, Connor also sent someone to cover his home. The sheriff agreed the killer had gotten personal when he learned about the text message and Connor's family needed protection.

They were tracing the number now.

Connor bounced ideas off Samantha about what he should do with Jenna. Unfortunately, Samantha didn't have an answer for him.

While he pondered his options, they arrived back to the place they'd been before he'd gotten that text. They were on the way back to the precinct, and Connor got on the phone during the drive to see if he could nail down some answers.

He called the parents of each victim, asking them if they had any mail the girls may have received. Two said they would check and get back to him. He asked them to wear gloves before touching it. Probably a precaution that would be too late, but might as well try. Sydney Carter's mother asked him to hold on a moment.

Connor put the speakerphone on when she came back. "Detective, I have an envelope here with four one-hundred-dollar bills in it."

Excitement spiraled through him. Not that he expected the killer to leave his real address, but if he even left a PO box, it would be something to track. "What's the return address and name on it?"

"There's no return address, I'm sorry."

Another dead end. He thanked the woman and promised to have someone out to pick it up as soon as possible.

Back at the precinct, Samantha followed Connor to a small room with a table and eight chairs. Dakota was already waiting for them, papers spread in front of him.

He looked up when they entered. "Time to compare notes. I'll tell you about the abortion place in a minute. Fill me in on what you've got and I'll tell you what I've got."

Connor snagged a seat across from Dakota, and Sam planted herself in the one at the end so that the papers could be easily seen by all three of them.

"Your boss has added three more homicide detectives to the task force. This guy shooting up the church, killing Andrew . . ." Dakota's throat worked and he shook his head. He hadn't known Andrew long, but anytime a fellow officer fell, it hit hard. Connor appreciated the man's sense of comradeship. "And paying a visit to Jenna at the high school . . . not good. Our psychologist was right on the money in his assessment. This guy doesn't like to be thought of as powerless, or not in control, that's for sure. We've made him really mad, so everyone's going to have to be extremely careful."

"But he's not totally in control," Connor said quietly.

Sam looked at him. "What do you mean?"

"He shot up the church. He shot Andrew. Surely he knew that would get the entire police department, plus outside agencies, even more involved and determined to find him."

"But he didn't care," Dakota stated.

"Or he was so angry about that news conference, he just didn't think about it, acted impulsively. He lost control."

Dakota nodded slowly, thoughtfully. "And now that he's had time to think about it, he's going to be angry, not just with those of us working the case, but with himself. I would think he'd be even more careful, but going to the high school was a pretty bold move. He's made this case personal with you, Connor. In that respect, he's going to be even more careful. Because now he has something to prove, again, not just to us, but to himself. And anyone else who's involved with him."

"So let's get him before he strikes again. What do you have?" Connor gestured to the papers in front of Dakota.

"Each girl's medical record." He pulled the first one. "This one is Miranda Abrams. Let's start with her. She's the last to disappear, but the most recent to be found. I think if we can figure out who took her, we'll find the other girls."

Connor took the proffered file and opened it. He flipped pages and shrugged. "Looks like just a regular medical record to me."

"Yeah, that's what I thought too, until I compared all six. It took me a while. That's what I've been busy with while you all have been otherwise occupied."

Narrowing his eyes, Connor focused on what the man wasn't saying. "And what did you come up with?"

"They were all referred to the same doctor's office."

Confusion flickered. "But they all didn't have the same doctor. I specifically asked their parents who their daughter's doctor was. Two of them had the same one. The rest went to different ones."

"I know. After I got the records, I noticed a notation in each chart that kept jumping out at me." He leaned over and pointed to the fine print on one of the back pages. " 'Lecords requested by Physicians Associates of Greenville' and then the date it was faxed."

"And they all have this?" He gestured to the remaining files.

"Yes and if you compare the dates of the fax to the dates of the missing girls, you'll see it wasn't long after each doctor visit that each girl went missing."

Excitement stirred in Connor's chest. Finally. "Did you trace that fax?"

"Yes, it went to an office store. Business For All on East Main. Two detectives left to check it out as soon as I put the connection together. Oh, and that clinic where Miranda got her abortion? Closed down. Nothing left of it. Just a little one-room deal. I bet whoever did the abortion wasn't even a doctor, just some creep who takes advantage of girls in trouble. He probably saw the news about Miranda dying and got out of Dodge. I thought you might want to head over to Physicians Associates and see what the good docs have to say."

Connor looked at Sam. She was already on her feet. "You bet."

Dakota stood too. "They close at six."

Connor led the way. "Let's go."

17

Forty minutes west of Spartanburg, Physicians Associates sat up on a gently sloping hill, green sod grass neatly trimmed and hedged. Samantha walked up the sidewalk toward the front door. "Doesn't look like a crime scene, does it?"

"Nope. Unfortunately, appearances can be deceiving."

"Yeah. Let's hope we're here in time. It's getting close to six."

Connor held the door open for her, and she breathed a sigh of relief as the air-conditioning cooled the sweat beaded on her nose. It was hot today and she was ready for fall. Real fall. Not ninety-degree fall.

Approaching the desk, she watched Connor flash his badge and ask to speak to Dr. Josiah Pressley. "It'll just take a few minutes. Is there somewhere we can talk privately?"

The curious secretary nodded. "Sure, this way, please."

Samantha took note of the layout of the office. Each doctor had his or her own waiting area. Interesting. She passed a young mother reading to her child, a man with a bandage around his hand — and a teenage girl who looked to be about seventeen years old. She nudged Connor. "Look."

He spotted her. "Makes you wonder, doesn't it?"

"Big-time."

"You look like you're about her age. You want to see if you can get her name and figure out if she's a model wannabe while I talk to the doc?"

"Good idea." Samantha grinned at the thought that she could pass for seventeen or eighteen. Yeah, right.

She sat in the chair opposite the teen and picked up a magazine. She flipped through several pages, set it down, and picked up another. With a sigh, she dropped it on the stack, looked at the girl, and said, "You'd think they could at least provide some interesting reading material, like *Seventeen* magazine or *People*."

"I know. I've been sitting here for about thirty minutes. I'm going to start charging them for my time."

"Now that's a concept. Wonder what would happen if we sent them a bill. Think they'd realize we were poking fun at them or do you think they'd pay it?"

A thoughtful look crossed her pretty face. "I don't know. Want to try?"

"Margaret Addison?" A nurse stood in the hallway, holding a chart.

The teen rose. "That's me." She flashed a bright white smile. "It was nice talking to you."

Thinking fast, Samantha said, "You should be a model. You have a gorgeous smile."

Surprised, Margaret lifted a brow. "Well, thank you, but I'm not interested in modeling. I'm going into pediatrics."

"Oh, well, good luck." Sam didn't know whether to feel relieved or frustrated at the dead end. She watched Margaret walk down the hall and enter the room, then took off after Connor, wondering where he'd ended up.

Connor found himself in the office of Dr. Pressley, the leather seat across from the desk comfortable and welcoming. Although, he had a feeling his welcome was getting ready to run out.

Dr. Pressley seated himself behind his desk, resting his elbows on top, steepling his fingers. "How can I help you, Detective?"

"I'm sure you're aware of what's happening with these teenage girls disappearing."

"Of course." His brows met at the bridge of his nose. "But what's that got to do with me?"

"Your name came up in the investigation as a doctor who treated two of the girls."

The puzzlement never faded. "That's odd, because I've seen them on the news, and never did I think that any one of them looked familiar. Which ones did I treat?"

Connor consulted his notes. "Sydney Carter and Amanda Sheridan."

"I'm sorry, the names don't sound familiar."

"How about the faces?" Connor handed over the pictures that had been provided to him by the families.

Dr. Pressley studied the photos, looked up, and shook his head. "I don't remember them."

Was the man lying? Connor eyed the doctor, looking for any clue that he was uncomfortable or nervous. Not even a twitch.

"But you signed off the medical notes." He passed over the file.

Once again, the doctor studied what was in front of him. And once again, he shook his head. "If I only saw them once, I may not remember them. Do you know how many people I see in a week? The regulars,

I know, of course, but if I get a new person . . ." He shrugged. "That's my signature, but I don't know what else to tell you." He frowned. "It's kind of odd that I don't at least recognize their faces, but nothing's ringing a bell. I'm sorry."

Open, honest eyes stared back at him from behind the desk, and Connor realized he wasn't going to get anything more from this guy. His gut told him the man was telling the truth. Either he never saw the girls, or he just didn't remember them.

Time to move on to the next doctor. He rose and held out his hand. "Thank you for your time. If you think of anything more or remember anything, would you give me a call?" He pulled a card from his pocket and handed it over.

"Absolutely."

"Thanks."

Connor stepped out of the office to find Samantha sitting in a chair waiting on him. She popped up, a questioning look on her face.

"Nothing."

Crestfallen, she sighed. "Yeah, me neither. That girl wasn't even interested in modeling. I don't think she's here for the same reason our girls came."

"This isn't making any sense. Let's go talk

to all the doctors in the practice. There's a connection somewhere, we just have to find it."

"That's going to take a while."

"I've got the time."

An hour and a half later, his stomach grumbling its hunger, he and Samantha trudged out to the car, their questioning netting them zilch.

His cell phone buzzed and he propped it on his shoulder to listen while he shifted his paperwork. "Hello?"

Samantha took it from him and held it to his ear for him.

He stilled as he listened, shot his gaze to hers, and said "thanks" to the person on the other end.

Sam hung up the phone for him and asked, "What is it?"

"That text I got about Jenna?"

"Yeah."

"It came from Sydney Carter's cell phone."

"Sydney Carter's?"

"Uh-huh." Connor slammed the door and cranked the car. "They're tracking it down now. I'm not holding my breath that he still has it on him. I'm sure he's dumped it by now, probably tossed it the second he pressed SEND. But while we're waiting to hear about that, let's rehash what we learned inside."

"Or didn't learn."

"Right. I can't believe no one recognized those girls. Not even one of them."

Samantha shook her head in disbelief as Connor pulled out of the parking lot. "Somebody's lying. Has to be, but I swear, I don't have a clue as to which one."

"They all agreed the signatures on the physical form were their own. And none of them claimed the signature looked like it had been forged. Yet, they don't remember the girls."

"If they're forgeries, they're good."

"I guess we need to get a handwriting expert to tell us for sure. I'll get Dakota working on that one."

"This case is taking all kinds of crazy turns. I feel like I'm on a theme park ride. Spinning in circles while I go up one side then the other. And nothing makes any sense."

Connor actually laughed. A small one, but at least it was a chuckle. "An excellent analogy."

"Connor, I talked to Jenna, questioned her about the guy who stopped her in the hall. She said he tried to ask her about

Andrew, but she wasn't interested in saying much. How is she . . . really?"

Guilt coated his features. "I'm afraid I haven't seen her much since . . ."

Samantha didn't bother saying anything. She didn't have to.

Sighing, Connor flicked a glance in her direction, then looked away. "I don't know what to do. I'm scared to death for her right now. I know how to tell her to be careful, I can even put a guy on her to watch out for her, but on an emotional level . . . I'm just not sure how to reach her."

"Be there."

"How?" He went transparent and she saw his agony — the deep, gut-wrenching pain of being pulled between wanting to keep other girls from falling into a killer's hands and the knowledge that he was losing his daughter because the case consumed his every thought, his every waking moment.

"You have a task force. Let them do their jobs. You're so busy trying to cover every aspect of this case when you've got trained help waiting for orders. Let go a little."

"I'm delegating," he protested weakly.

"Not enough."

"Right." He paused, then said, "Okay. So, what do we know? Let's go through it."

Sam could take a hint. Change the subject.

Deal with it later. Or not. "Dakota went through Sydney's journal, right?"

"Right. And came up with nothing viable. She talked big about wanting to make it in modeling, but we've already figured out that this guy most likely has a slew of screen names and is pretending to be an agent or scout or whatever for a modeling agency. He's luring these girls in, convincing them he's legit."

Making a left at the next light, Connor tapped the wheel as he thought out loud. "You would think with all the girls who have gone missing and turned up dead, the teenagers around here would be a tad more cautious."

"He's promising them big bucks, fame, an awesome career. I guess they think it's worth the risk. The sheriff is going to do another press conference, explaining exactly how this guy is working and what to look for. And to ask parents to please monitor all computer activities, to call us with anything suspicious."

"You know, all of these girls had web pages, Facebook, a MySpace account, or something. It's possible this guy is cruising their pages before he initiates contact. I checked and all but one of the girls have a public page that accepts comments and friends from people they don't know."

"Huh?" Connor pulled into the parking lot of the police station and cut the engine before turning to face her.

Samantha shot him an amused look. "On MySpace and Face-book, you can choose to have only people in your network of friends have access to your page. It's called a private account. Or, you can allow anyone to look at it. All of these girls were open accounts. Meaning anyone had access to their pages."

He blinked. "Okay, I know what MySpace and Facebook are and everything, but why is this important?"

"I'm wondering if it's his way of getting to know them before he makes contact with them. His way of sneaking in the back door, so to speak. Unfortunately, teens put all kinds of personal information out there, and this guy could have figured out how to use it to get past defenses." She shrugged. "Just a theory."

"A real good one."

Admiration deepened his eyes, and she shivered at the look. As though he could see much more than she wanted him to. Then he shifted, looked away, and while she felt relief, she also realized she was disappointed. She wanted that connection with him. The fact that he was a cop almost didn't matter anymore. She found herself thinking about letting him in. Wondering what it would be like to open up and make herself vulnerable to him.

And that scared her. Because if he knew her deepest secret, her darkest guilt, he'd think she was a horrible person; he'd never look at her with admiration, respect, or in any other positive way ever again. Because she still hadn't dealt with the anger that still overtook her on occasion. Anger at Jamie for her being so defiant and impulsive back then and putting her family through what they'd experienced. Anger at the fact that she couldn't seem to stop the thought that maybe Jamie had deserved what happened to her. And then anger at herself for thinking it. Because mentally she knew it wasn't true. No one deserved that. And it was certainly something she'd never shared with Jamie. Or anyone for that matter. It was just something that she had to continue to take to God. Sadness invaded her. Regret. Sorrow.

"I wonder if Jenna has a MySpace or Facebook page," he muttered.

Shrugging off her dark thoughts, she told him, "It's easy enough to find out. All you have to do is type her name in the search box."

"Scary."

"Very."

"So what you're saying is that this guy does his homework."

"Absolutely."

"But why? What's his motive?"

"I think you're on the right track with the black market babies theory."

Connor blew out a breath. "So do I. I still say there's a link somewhere between that doctor's office and the missing girls. I find it mighty weird that none of the doctors remembered even one of them. Although, they were only there one time, just for that physical. But there has to be a reason they were referred to that office, and it's probably as plain as the nose on my face. Unfortunately, I can't see it."

"Somebody in that office is involved up to his or her eyebrows. How many people would you say work there?"

"A bunch. You've got twelve doctors, fourteen, fifteen nurses, lab techs, secretaries, janitorial staff. I'd say well over thirty or forty people."

"Could you delegate some of your task force to doing background checks on everyone employed there?"

He groaned. "It's scary how much we think alike. I was just considering that very thing. And to answer your question, it would take a long time."

Sam raised a brow and Connor reached for his phone, ready to do a little delegating. She led the way into the station, wondering how much longer they had before the next girl went missing.

The Agent watched from his car parked around the corner of the doctor's office. For the first time since he and Boss had started this little endeavor, he felt . . . nervous. A tad anxious. How had they found this doctor's office? What had he missed? Somehow, a clue had been left on one of the computers and Samantha Cash had found it. And that led them here.

But what? How much did they know? And who else besides them knew something? Probably everybody working on the case. He picked up the phone and hit the speed dial.

"Hello?"

"Did you see them?"

"Yes."

"Did they talk to you?"

A sigh. "Yes. They talked to every doctor and nurse here, showing everyone pictures of the girls. But they didn't learn anything."

"They learned something. They've got a connection now. Something that each of the girls had in common. They'll be doing background checks on everyone in that office. Will they find anything?"

"No, nothing criminal on me anyway. You know that as well as I do. But how did they know to come here?"

"I'm not sure, but I'll find out. Were you able to listen in on any of the conversations?"

"No, but I'm sure they were asking the same questions of everyone. They wanted to know if any of us recognized the dead girls. And they were asking about the signatures."

The Agent swore. "They got the medical records."

"What?"

"They compared all of the girls' medical records. There must have been a notation in there about this place when you requested them from each of the other offices. I should have figured out a way to cover that up."

Silence on the other end. "Is it safe to continue?"

"I think so. For now. I need that dark-haired girl you just saw. She's got the perfect shade of hair and eyes. We'll get at least a quarter million."

The person on the other end sucked in a deep breath. "I know, but I think it's too risky. I'd hold off on her. Don't contact her anymore."

"Maybe you're right. They're getting too close."

"We've got enough money to live like royalty for the rest of our lives."

"Or at least start over in another country. I'll talk to Boss, see what direction I need to take next."

"Whatever. I'm ready to cut all ties and get out of here. They're making me awfully nervous."

"Don't worry, I'll take care of them. Buy us some more time to get everything wrapped up before moving on. Yeah, just a little more time, a lot more money, then we disappear. It's as simple as that."

"Be careful. If they find you, they'll probably be able to find me."

"Have I let you down yet?"

The voice lowered. "Not yet, but I sure don't want there to be a first time."

"Go back to work. I'll talk to you tonight."

18

Friday morning, Jenna stared out the window, her geometry teacher once again droning on about the merits of angles and rays. Her mind drifted effortlessly. 2COOL had finally talked her into meeting him. Patty didn't know yet, and Jenna hadn't decided whether to tell her or not. She'd agreed, now she had to figure out if she was going to follow through and show up. Her father's warnings continued to echo in her mind whether she wanted them to or not.

And she couldn't discount the fact there was a guy in her town out there killing girls her age.

Then again, what were the chances that the guy she was going to meet would be that killer?

Of course, Miranda probably wondered the same thing. That thought chilled her enough to send goose bumps pimpling up her arms. She rubbed them, then bent to copy the diagram from the whiteboard. She'd have to study it later and see if she could figure out what it meant. Or maybe she could ask Bradley. But he seemed to be keeping his distance from her.

Then there was the matter of the sleepover thing tomorrow night with the church group. They'd changed it to Saturday so they could watch the sun come up one week after the shooting. Proof that hope exists, Maria had said, and they wanted to praise God for another Sunday.

Jenna wasn't so sure about praising a God who had allowed Andrew to be killed, but part of her was intensely curious about people who had the capacity to actually do that.

Maria had called her last night to tell her it was still on. They weren't going to let that gunman win, let him destroy their church. Jenna didn't know what to tell the girl. She'd avoided talking to her in the halls, afraid one of her friends would see her and demand to know what she was doing talking to a geek like that. Secretly, Jenna liked Maria, but wasn't willing to give up her coveted position of popularity to be friends with the girl publicly.

However, she kind of wanted to go on that sleepover. Just to do something different. To get away from everything. Just her and nature. No demanding friends, no crazy shooter trying to kill her, no dead cops, no funerals . . .

No quiet, grieving dad. Her eyes flicked to the doorway. No bodyguards. She hadn't seen anyone, but Jenna wondered if someone was watching her house too.

Most likely.

She doodled in her notebook. Danny. Bradley. 2COOL2BLV. Danny. Bradley. 2COOL.

Her gaze dropped to her book bag. He'd asked her not to IM him anymore. He'd said that his modeling agency was moving, and he wasn't sure when he'd be able to get to a computer since he didn't have one at home. But she could text message him if she needed him. She'd miss his online presence, though. He'd been quite funny, sending her sweet messages that said he "got" her, understood her. Every time she downloaded one, it would include a romantic card or just a thoughtful message. He made her smile.

But then he'd sent her the last message, asking her to meet him. He'd liked her pictures and wanted to do a portfolio for her. He even sent her money to buy a dress. Part of her was afraid to meet him. Oh, not because she was worried that he was a perv or something, but she was afraid of herself. Of ruining a friendship that she desperately needed. Of saying something stupid if she met him face-to-face. Online or with text messaging, she could take the time to think about her responses, be witty, funny, charming.

If she met him in person —

The bell rang, jarring her. She realized she'd totally zoned during the last half of the class. Gathering her books, she made her way toward the door. Her shadow stayed nearby.

Patty joined her in the hall and leaned over to whisper, "Hey, have you met that Danny guy yet?"

"No, why?"

Patty looked down, scuffed her toe, and shrugged. "Well, I was thinking I might like to see if he would be interested in representing me. You know . . . as a model. I really want to get into acting, and this might be the open door I need. To get my foot in and all."

"Really? I thought you were afraid he was old, bald, and fat."

Her friend grinned. "Doesn't matter what he looks like, I guess, as long as he has the right contacts."

Jenna shrugged. "Sure, I'll text him and ask him. He said they were moving the office, and he doesn't have a whole lot of computer access right now, but maybe if I decide to meet him, you could go with me."

Eyes bright, Patty nodded. "That sounds cool. Let me know when you set something up."

"Okay. I'm sure he'll want to. You're prettier than I am, and if he's interested in me, he'll sure be interested in you. I'll text him later and try to set up something for tomorrow."

Squealing, Patty hugged her. "You're the best friend a girl could ask for."

Jenna laughed. "Right. Just remember who to thank in your Oscar award acceptance speech."

Shared laughter felt good, and Jenna realized with a pang that she couldn't remember the last time she'd laughed out loud. Well, once she and Patty got their modeling contracts and she was making her own money, she could move out of the house of gloom and doom.

And laugh all the way to the bank.

Guilt eating her, Samantha rapped on Jamie's door. She'd been so busy she'd had to settle for phone calls to check on Jamie.

Finally, she had to visit in person to see how her sister was handling the aftermath of the shooting, not able to rely on Jamie's over-the-phone assurances that she was fine, not perfect, but not cowering in the corner either.

The door opened and Jamie cocked an eyebrow at her and waited.

Sam cleared her throat. "Well, you look fine."

"Told you I was okay."

"Had to see for myself."

"You coming in?"

Tears welled in Samantha's eyes and she grabbed her sister in a tight hug. "I was scared you wouldn't be," Sam finally managed to whisper.

"Sam, you really need to let go of your guilt."

Unable to find a suitable response to something she knew as well, she simply nodded and stepped inside. Just as Jamie shut the door, the bell rang.

"Are you expecting someone else?"

"Tom said he might stop by. He's been coming to check on me just about every day." Jamie pulled the door back open and froze.

Samantha smiled. "Hi, Dakota. What brings you by?" Like she had to ask.

"Oh." He swallowed. "I can come back later. I didn't realize Jamie had company. I mean I saw your car outside, but . . ."

"No, no, please come in." Samantha waved toward the den area and they made their way to the room.

Jamie, twisting her hands, backed toward the kitchen. "I . . . I'll just get us some drinks . . . or something."

Jamie disappeared. Sam turned to Dakota. "You like my sister, huh?"

Mr. FBI Man blushed.

Sam took pity on him. "Good. She could use someone like you in her life."

Surprise lit his eyes, then he smiled. "I don't know. There's just something about her."

"Yes, there is. Do you know anything about that 'something'?"

"What do you mean?" Dakota looked perplexed.

"Oh." He knew nothing. "Get to know her before you fall in love with her."

"Now that's a little presumptuous, isn't it?" He quirked a half smile.

Jamie reentered the room with three soda cans. "I hope you like diet."

"Diet's fine." Dakota took his.

Samantha grabbed hers and headed for the door. "I just thought of something I need to check into. You guys have a nice visit and I'll catch up with you later." She caught Dakota's eye and smiled at the twinkle. Yeah, yeah, he seemed to say, something to check into.

She wiggled her fingers, nearly giggled at Jamie's confused look, and headed to her car. Well, it wasn't a total lie. She did want to call Jenna and see how she felt about returning to the church where she'd nearly been killed. The repair guys had been working nonstop and had the church nearly finished and ready to resume services.

Just the thought of going back, knowing Andrew would never darken that door again, made her throat clog with tears. She hadn't really known Andrew that well until they'd started working this case, but she'd talked to Angie quite a bit at church, had done a ladies Bible study with her, and enjoyed her company. And now she was a widow.

As Sam shut off her thoughts, she pulled out her cell and dialed Connor's number.

"Hello?"

"Hey, I finished searching those computers. All of them had the same IP address. I'm even more sure now that the guy who snatched these girls found a way to access their computers remotely. Have you gotten a location on that IP address yet?"

As she pulled open her car door, Tom swung in the driveway beside her. Looking over the hood of her car, she watched as he got out of his vehicle and pocketed the keys. Samantha held up a finger to halt his progress. With a quizzical look, he stopped and leaned his forearms against the top of the passenger door of her car.

Connor was saying, "Yes, I just got it. Want to meet me there in about thirty minutes? I'm at my mother's house finishing up lunch. It's a little café two blocks from the police station."

"You're kidding."

"I know. Gall, huh?"

"And then some. Yes, I can meet you there. See you in a little bit."

She hung up and turned to greet Tom. "Jamie said you were coming by, but she's got company."

"Ah, the FBI guy?"

"Yeah, I think he likes her."

"Who wouldn't?"

Sam looked a little closer. And shock zipped through her. Did Tom feel something more for Jamie than just friendship? Before she could decide on an answer or just flat out ask him, he tilted his head and asked, "Where are you off to?"

A glance at her watch explained her growling stomach. "I'm going to grab a bite to eat and meet Connor to do a little investigating. I found a common IP address on the girls' computers, and it led back to this place near the police station. Wanna join me and we can discuss this case? It's making me crazier by the hour."

"Um . . ." Tom looked at the house, then back at Sam. "I really wanted to talk to Jamie, but, sure." He pulled his keys back out. "Come on and hop in, I'll drive."

"I need to run a couple of errands too. Let me drive and you come keep me company. You can give me an update on what's going on with your business. The missing senator's kid and everything. I've been so focused on this missing teens case, we haven't had a chance to catch up. So, climb in."

Hesitating, he heaved a sigh and glanced at the door to the house again. "I don't know. She really likes him, doesn't she?"

Samantha bit her lip and didn't answer.

Tom shook his head. "Look, why don't you just go on? I've got some stuff I need to work on. I'll give Jamie a call and tell her to call me when Dakota's gone and she can talk. I think I'll just go on home and curl up with my computer."

Concerned at her friend's despondency, she realized he did care for Jamie. And as more than a friend. Oh no. Not good. "Tom, get in the car. That's an order from one of your best friends and partner. We need to talk and we can do that on the way. Plus, we could use your help. Please?"

"Sam . . ." Another sigh. He shifted, touched the handle of the door, backed off, and looked at the house again. Gave another long-suffering sigh and said, "Oh, all right."

Tom pulled open her passenger door and settled himself on the seat, locking his seat belt into place.

"Great." Samantha slid into the driver's seat and slammed the door.

"Wait a minute. What was that?"

"What was what?" she asked as she inserted the key into the ignition.

"That clicking sound when you sat down." He put a hand over hers. "Don't crank it yet."

Sam paused. "Clicking sound? I didn't hear anything."

"Is someone still out to get you?"

"Possibly."

"Then I don't like the sound of what I just heard."

Sam gave a nervous laugh. "You're being paranoid, Tom."

"Too bad Andrew wasn't paranoid enough to wear his vest."

Hurt zinged. But the man had a point. "Okay, so what now?"

"I suggest calling in reinforcements to make sure we're not going to be blown to our eternal reward when you start the car or remove your weight from that seat."

Sweat beaded her forehead, slicked her palms. "All right. I guess paranoid for nothing is better than dead."

"My thoughts exactly."

"What if my phone is the right frequency and sets off the bomb?"

Tom blanched. "I would consider that the *wrong* frequency." A pause. "I don't see that we have any other choice. I think we have to try, don't you?"

"I could lay on the horn, get Jamie out here."

"What if it's rigged to the horn?"

She looked at him. "Phone?"

He closed his eyes and leaned his head back against the seat. "Well, I guess if we're wrong, we'll know in a minute. You got anyone on speed dial? Just press the redial button and hope for the best."

Connor hung up the phone, wiped the spaghetti sauce from his chin, and smiled at his mother. "Thanks, Mom. I'm glad I was able to get away and come over. How's Dad feeling?"

"Better. He's moving a little easier, the new medication seems to be helping his arthritis." She picked up the bowl of leftover meat sauce and walked it to the sink. "Connor, I had an ulterior motive for asking you to come over while Jenna was at school."

Dread consumed him. He'd wondered. "What is it?"

"You're absolutely going to have to do something about her."

"What's she done now?" He lowered his napkin to his plate, defenses rising up.

"She snuck out of the house last night. And I don't think it's the first time she's done it."

"Why didn't you call me?"

"I did! You didn't answer. I thought about calling 911, but . . ." She sighed. "I just didn't want to do that to her . . . or you, and I know you've got that man watching her. I decided if she wasn't home by 2:00, I'd call 911, but she slipped in around 1:30. You got here shortly after."

Great. Just what he needed. What was the point in staying at his parents' house for Jenna's safety when Jenna kept sneaking out? He had to push down the fear trampling him.

"Doesn't she realize there are girls going missing? That they're turning up dead and I'm not having much luck catching the guy who's doing this?" His voice built in volume so that by the last word, he was almost yelling.

His mother just looked at him.

He sighed, burying his face in his hands. What was he going to do? Send her away? The thought crept in. He pushed it away. It pushed back.

No, he couldn't do that. She'd never forgive him.

So, what was one more thing Jenna could hold against him? She already blamed him for her mother's death. At least if she was out of the city, she'd be safe.

"Next time, Mom, call 911 the minute she sneaks out. I don't have anyone on her at night. Just someone watching the house. If he didn't call me, then Jenna gave him the slip."

Her face paled. "Oh, I didn't realize, I thought he would be with her."

"I'm sorry." He scratched his chin and sighed. "I should have been more clear on his duties. But next time . . ." He stopped. "Somehow I have to make sure there isn't a next time," he muttered.

"What are you thinking about, Connor?"

"About how to keep Jenna safe, Mom."

"By doing what?"

"Something she'd probably not understand nor go along with willingly. Aunt Jasmine and Uncle Milton still live in Florida, don't they?"

"What? Of course. They've lived there forever."

"What if Jenna went to live with them for a while? Just until I catch this guy?"

"No! Connor, where is your head? I cannot believe you would completely destroy your relationship with your daughter over a case!"

Connor leaned back in shock. His mom hadn't raised her voice at him since . . . since . . . he couldn't remember since when. She went on, "You can't avoid this, you can't run away from it, and you can't *send* it away. Jenna needs you and she needs you now. Your father and I have done all we can do, but she doesn't respect us, she doesn't listen, and there aren't any real consequences for her behavior. Now do something before it's too late!"

She stormed from the kitchen, leaving Connor blinking, stunned . . . and thinking. Was he trying to avoid dealing with Jenna? Maybe, but his priority was to keep her safe, and this killer had made things personal. He'd killed Andrew. Who was to say he wouldn't come after him or Jenna? Or the rest of his family?

He went cold.

No, it was best if Jenna were gone. And he'd ask his parents to take her. Then once he had this killer behind bars, he could take some leave from the department and try to put his family back together. Build his relationship back with Jenna. Because he wanted to. Needed to.

Desperately.

His phone rang and he sighed. A glance at caller ID made him smile and grimace at the same time. Samantha.

"Hello?"

Her frantic voice came through. "I need a bomb squad ASAP."

Sam sat in her sister's driveway, not daring to move. If Tom was right and she'd planted herself on top of a bomb, they were all in big trouble. She'd been in tight spots before, some dangerous situations, but this one went straight to the top of the list for most dangerous.

She didn't like it.

About four minutes later, she heard sirens coming toward her, growing louder with each second.

Tom looked at her. "Don't blow us up, okay?"

"That's the plan, partner." Sweat slicked her palms, ran down her back. She even thought she felt her feet sweating. *Please, Jesus.*

Dare she reach under the seat and see if she could feel it? Right, Sam, brilliant idea. And flip the switch to detonate the thing. Actually, if it was the kind of bomb Tom thought it was, she'd already activated the switch, the initiator as it was called in bomb squad school. When she removed her weight, she'd trigger the explosion. And there was no way she could get out fast enough. She'd be blown right out of the seat.

"What do we do, Tom? You're the partner who went through the bomb squad training. I missed that class, remember?" She'd been sitting up nights with Jamie during one of her nightmare stints and had basically slept through the class. Somehow, she'd passed. Right now, she wished she could remember something from it. Anything.

"Sit tight. Just don't move, okay? Don't shift your weight. Don't. Do. Anything. Okay?"

"What if I start hyperventilating?"

"You'll probably blow us up."

Samantha closed her eyes, breathing in through her nose and out through her mouth. And praying hard. She wasn't afraid to die. She knew where she was going, but the crazy thought that kept going through her mind was that Connor would never be able to deal with it. *He doesn't know you yet, Lord. At least not like he needs to. If I die, I don't think he'll ever have anything to do with you again. Of course you know that better than I do, but . . . just please, get us out of this?*

And Tom . . . he wasn't a believer either, even though he tolerated her talking about God with him.

She opened her eyes and nearly screamed. Then realized the monster outside her window was a fully protected bomb squad member. He motioned for her to open her door.

Slowly, painstakingly, she eased it open, pushing, pausing, pushing some more until it stood wide open. She breathed a sigh when nothing went kaboom. Absently, she registered Tom's groan of relief.

Looking up into the bomb guy's alien eyes, she raised a brow. "Isn't there a robot for this kind of thing?"

"Yeah, with cameras and X-rays and

everything. But sometimes it's just easier to do things the old-fashioned way. I don't know if I could position him like we need to in this situation without causing more trouble than we want. I'm going to take a look under your seat. See what kind of bomb we've got here."

"If there is a bomb."

He bent down, moved her feet carefully out of the way. She let him do the shifting, keeping her rear planted securely, not wanting to lift a bit of her weight from the seat.

Alien eyes looked back up. "There's a bomb."

The air left her lungs. Terror set in. "My sister's in the house."

"We've already gotten her out and are evacuating the neighborhood. My name's Calvin and I'll be getting you two out of this safely. I've got to check the rest of the car to make sure I don't set off any little booby traps and I'll be back, all right?" He tapped the door lightly. "My daughter's birthday party's tonight and I don't plan to miss it."

His complete confidence eased her nerves — a little. "How old will she be?" Somehow, talking kept her mind from screaming, kept her from panicking.

Calvin paused. "Ten."

"What does she like? Her favorite food?"

"Animals and pizza — in that order."

She met his eyes — or where his eyes would be if she could see through the protective mask. "Thanks."

Tom spoke up. "How many of you are there?"

"Four. We've got our team leader, communications tech, equipment dude, and me. I'm the downrange tech, and like I said, I'm going to take care of this. Your job is to sit tight and do exactly what I say, got it?"

"Right. Got it."

He spoke into a microphone, but the words didn't register for Samantha. Now that the good guys were here, she was too busy praying to pay much attention.

Connor's brakes squealed as he pulled onto the right street. He'd had to flash his badge at the entrance to gain access to the neighborhood, but Samantha was in there, sitting on top of a bomb. Nothing would keep him away.

The intensity of his feelings shocked him, the fear crowding his throat choked him, but he didn't have time to even consider what it meant.

He stopped at the barricade. His phone rang. "Yeah."

"Connor, it's Dakota. Jamie's with me. Keep us up on what's going on with Samantha. I know there's a bomb in her car, but that's all I was able to pry out of the squad guy."

"As soon as I know anything, you'll know it."

"Thanks, I'll let Jamie know."

Connor hung up and climbed out of his car. Flashed his badge again and made his way over to the bomb squad van. He knew he couldn't go right up to the car like he wanted to in order to see for himself that she was still in one piece, but he'd be as close as they'd allow.

Connor entered the van, found the team leader, recited his credentials, and asked, "What do you have?"

"Looks like a couple of blocks of C-4. Standard military issue. You know anyone with access to that?"

"Easy enough to get that on the black market." Connor shuddered. "How big is it?"

"Looks like two one-and-a-quarter-pound blocks hooked together with wires."

"Holy . . ." His legs went weak. "If that blows . . ."

The leader's grim look told Connor his assessment was correct. If that bomb blew, it would be enough to blow the car and surrounding area sky-high.

Connor's hands shook. "So cut the wires and get it out of there."

"That's the plan."

19

Samantha waited, teeth clamped down on her lower lip. Hours seemed to have passed, but in reality it had only been about forty minutes since she'd hit the redial button to reach Connor. He'd been the last person she'd called and all she had to do was press the little green phone button to redial his number.

Calvin moved to the passenger side and repeated his assessment of Tom's situation. Carefully maneuvering his mirror out from under Tom's seat, he said, "All right, sir, you can get out. There's nothing under this seat."

"Will my moving set off her side? Because there's no way I'm doing that."

Sam appreciated Tom's willingness to put his neck on the line for her, but she insisted. "Get out while you can, Tom."

He hesitated, then nodded. "Right. But I'm not going far, got it?"

"Just stay safe." She looked at Calvin. "I'm beyond ready when you are."

"Coming your way."

Tom eased his way from the car, hand on the hood, pulling himself out. Everyone gave a collective sigh of relief as he moved to safety.

Sam closed her eyes, feeling the tension knot her shoulders into hard bricks. She heard Calvin back at her side of the vehicle.

"Okay," he breathed, "let's get you out of here."

"I'm good with that."

The Agent watched all the commotion going on, and while he was careful to keep an outward expression of concern, deep inside, he laughed silently to himself. They thought they were so smart.

If they only knew what was under their noses. His fingers tingled in remembrance of placing the bomb just so, watching the door to the house, knowing that he could be caught at any moment. And knowing he wouldn't be. He was too smart, too good at what he did. It had been a simple explosive device, very basic. Easy to rig, easy to disarm. He'd done it that way on purpose.

He glanced at his watch, then moved a hand to his pocket. He could just detonate the thing and watch the fireworks. But that would be counterproductive. Not the way the plan was supposed to go. So he'd wait, be patient, and see how it all went down. After all, the car might explode in spite of the bomb squad. Wouldn't that be a sight to see?

But then Boss would be upset with him if he did that. No, he'd wait. Be patient and let the bomb do its job. If the bomb squad tech was able to dismantle it, and The Agent had no doubt the man would, there'd be another time. Another place. Another opportunity.

It was as simple as that.

Tom was safe. Her sister was out of the house. Everyone she loved was fine. She was ready to join their ranks. "Any luck?" She couldn't resist asking.

"Yep. I didn't bother to tell you I was going to cut the wires. But I just finished." Calvin stood, hand pressed to the small of his back. "I'm getting too old for this."

"You already cut them?"

"Yep, you're good to go. Come on, let me help you out and I'll get that nasty little thing from under your seat. The rest of the car is clean."

Samantha pulled in some much needed

air. She'd been afraid to breathe anything more than slow, shallow breaths.

"Come on," Calvin reassured her, "you're fine."

"You're sure?" It never hurt to double-check things.

"As sure as I'll ever be," Calvin assured her.

Samantha looked at him in assessment. "I guess since you're still here working in the profession, you must have a pretty good track record." She tried to move and found herself stuck. Shocked, she gave a gasping laugh. "I don't think I can move. My muscles feel frozen." And they did. Like *they* didn't believe it was safe.

"A natural reaction. Here, let me give you a hand."

"I've got her."

Connor. He was here. Gladness filled her. *Oh, thank you, Lord. Thank you for another day, another chance, more time to bring Connor to you.*

She practically fell into his arms. And he pulled her close, burying his face in her sweat-drenched hair, not seeming to care that she desperately needed a shower.

After about thirty seconds, he helped her to the bomb squad van and with a grateful sigh, she sank into the back of it and took notice of the emergency personnel. Ambulance, police, fire trucks. All waiting in case they were needed.

Thank God they weren't.

Tom approached and gripped her hand. "Are you all right?"

"Yes, I'm fine. Or I will be. I need to let Jamie know everything's okay."

Connor squeezed her shoulder. "I've already taken care of it. The moment Calvin gave the all clear."

"Thank you." She leaned her head on his bicep for a brief moment, then stood. Anger flushed her cheeks. "I want this guy. I want to know why he's after me. Why me? Why Andrew?" A thought occurred to her. "Do you think he knows the members of the task force and has decided to take them out one by one?"

Connor shook his head. "Who knows?" He heaved a huge sigh. "I do know one thing. I'm going to have to stay away from my family for a while, I think. I can't take a chance on this nut job following me to my parents' house from work. I've been staying there almost constantly lately trying to be there for Jenna, but . . ."

He trailed off as a tall, athletically built black man approached them. "Told you I'd get you out of there." He smiled and Samantha stepped forward to give him a hug.

"Thank you, Calvin."

"Just doing my job, ma'am." He patted her back and turned to Tom who'd been sitting on the curb near the van. "Glad to see you in one piece." Tom stood, shook Calvin's hand, and expressed his thanks.

Calvin turned to go, but swung back to ask Samantha, "Just curious. What tipped you off there was a bomb under your seat?"

She answered, "Tom heard the click when I sat down. And after everything that's been going on lately, he decided to be a little paranoid."

Calvin looked at Tom and gave a little laugh. "Yeah. Guess paranoia can be a good thing when someone's after you."

Tom gave a short nod and turned to Samantha. "Hey, I'm going to pass on lunch today, if that's all right. I just want to go home and . . . process."

She gave him a sympathetic smile. "Sure, I understand."

Tom and Calvin left together.

Connor wrapped an arm around her and pulled her to him. She felt him press a kiss to the top of her head.

She shivered. "I need to see Jamie."

"Look behind you."

Samantha turned to see Jamie and Dakota

heading toward her. She caught Jamie's eyes and saw the worry and fear there, but a new strength that caught her by surprise. Gladly, she flung her arms around her sister and hugged her close.

Jamie clutched her and whispered, "I was so scared for you."

"Trust me, I was scared too. But I'm fine. We're all fine. And not a word of this to Mom and Dad, deal?"

Jamie gave a choked laugh. "Sure. Deal. They're getting ready to go on their annual two-week vacation. We wouldn't want to ruin it or anything. If we tell them about this, they might feel obligated to stay home . . . or something."

It was Samantha's turn to sputter a teary chuckle. "You're so bad." But she appreciated the attempt at levity. Now it was back to the real world.

She pulled away and looked at Connor who was deep in conversation with Dakota. They looked serious enough to cause her to wonder what they were up to.

Connor returned and filled her in. "We need to do a debriefing at the precinct, give a statement and all that fun stuff. Then I'm going to stop by the café and ask a few questions." He brushed her hair back from her eyes. "After that, I'm taking you out for dinner."

"You don't have to do this."

Samantha shot him a look that said "Shut up." Out loud she declared, "I'm fine. A little weak from the ebb of adrenalin, but fine. We need to catch this guy, and if he's using this place to do it, I want to know."

Connor shook his head. Stubborn woman. Admirable too. With his right hand, he pushed open the glass door and inhaled. Coffee, lattes, and cinnamon bread wafted up to greet him. His stomach rumbled in response. "We might not make it to dinner somewhere else."

"I thought you just finished lunch at your mother's."

"I did, but all that anxiety and gut-wrenching fear you just put me through ate through every single calorie I consumed at her house." He saw Samantha shudder at the mention of gut-wrenching fear.

She rubbed her stomach. "I still feel a little nauseous from all that. I've lost what little appetite I had. But you feel free to grab something if you want. Do you have the list of days and date stamps I gave you?"

Connor pulled it out and waved it at her. "Right here. Let's go figure this out."

Samantha began questioning the workers.

301

Connor took care of management. After an hour with no real luck, Connor wanted to howl his frustration.

"Hey, Connor, come here."

He looked up to see Samantha standing next to a uniformed worker. "What is it?"

"This is Ken. I've been asking him about the regulars. This is a wi-fi café so people are in and out all the time with their laptops. But he said there was one guy who comes in all the time. Stays a couple of hours, then leaves."

Connor's eyes sharpened, zeroed in on the young man. "Can you describe him?"

"Not really. He had on a ball cap most of the time. But he had kind of dirty blond hair that was curly. Long, like he needed a haircut. And he wore sunglasses a lot. Didn't talk to people much. I don't really know why I noticed him. He didn't really stand out, just seemed very — intense, I guess is the word."

"Try and help me out a little more. What about his age?"

"Um . . . maybe early to mid thirties?"

"Any scars? Tattoos? When was he last here?"

"No, he didn't have anything like that, and he was here, um . . . I think a couple of days ago."

"Did he make any phone calls? Or just sit in the booth?"

"He just sat there on his computer. No phone calls that I remember. But I mean, I wasn't really paying any attention to him. I was working."

"What about when he left? Did he get in a car? Did you see what direction he went?"

"No, sorry. I don't even really remember him leaving."

"Does he come here at a particular time during the day?"

"No." The guy shook his head. "Sometimes it's in the morning, sometimes evening up until we close. He doesn't have, like, a pattern, if that's what you're looking for."

"Do you mind coming down and talking to a sketch artist?"

"I guess not. Can it wait until my shift ends?"

Connor pursed his lips. "I'd rather not. We need this information pronto. A girl's life might depend on it, okay?"

"Sure, but will you explain it to my boss?"

"Absolutely."

Ten minutes later, with the young man on his way down to meet the sketch artist, Connor turned to Samantha. "There's really no way to track the guy from here, is there?"

"Not a chance, I'm afraid."

"Well, I'll get someone to stake this place out over the next several days and see if anyone with our description shows up. If so, we can nab him."

"Sounds good to me."

Disappointed, Connor led Samantha to his car. "I didn't eat. Where do you want to go for dinner?"

Spending time with Samantha reinforced the fact that his feelings for her weren't just a flash in the pan. The fear he'd felt today when she'd called asking for a bomb squad, seeing her silhouette behind the wheel of a car that could explode at any given moment, the knee-weakening relief when he realized she was going to be okay, all combined to send a dizzying rush of emotions through him.

He grabbed a soft drink from the refrigerator and slumped into a chair at the kitchen table. His parents were still out with friends, Jenna was in her room studying. Or at least she was supposed to be. Who knew what she was really doing.

He'd knocked on her door to let her know he was home, and she'd given him the brush-off. Studying. Yeah. Right. On a Friday night. He could only hope.

Samantha had been quiet at dinner, still processing the events of the day. She'd withdrawn into her thoughts, not yet ready to talk about what she was feeling. That was all right. Connor could relate.

Ah, Andrew, I wish you were here.

He stared at his soft drink and almost wished he were the type to use alcohol to dull the pain. But he wasn't. Had seen the effects on too many people to believe drowning his sorrows was the way to go.

The knock on the door startled him. He glanced at the clock on the microwave: 9:36. Who could that be? Was Jenna expecting someone? No, not this late.

Caution reared its head. Too many incidents had happened in the last week for him to just answer the door without taking care. Of course, the person wouldn't exactly knock on his door if he was going to kill him. Would he?

Paranoid's better than being dead.

His hand went to the gun at his waist and unclipped the strap that held it in place. Tension invaded him, bunching the muscles at the base of his neck. With a soft tread, he made his way to the front door and glanced out the full-length side window.

Angie? The tension seeped away leaving that aching, nagging, breath-stealing hole in the vicinity of his heart. Hiding his initial shock, he opened the door. "Hello, Angie."

"Connor."

He stood there a moment, staring. A thousand memories flashed through his mind. Angie and Andrew. He and Jenna. Fun times, hard times. And the funeral. He cleared his throat. "Um . . . sorry, come on in."

"Thanks." She carried a small bag in her left hand. Stepping over the threshold, she walked straight into the den area.

Connor followed. "How've you been?"

She plopped onto the sofa. "Lousy. How about you?"

"Yeah. The same." He lowered himself to the edge of the recliner.

She gave a small sad smile. "But God is good. He'll get me through this." She sent him a knowing look. "He'd get you through it too, if you'd let him."

Connor shrugged. "Maybe."

She raised a brow and he knew he'd shocked her that he hadn't outright negated the idea of God helping him. She didn't address it.

Instead, she sighed and leaned back. "I'm sorry it's so late. I've been meaning to come by, but we've been . . . tying things up. Fortunately, Andrew knew his . . . death —"

she bit her lip and closed her eyes, then sucked in a deep breath, blowing it out slowly — "that his death was a real possibility and was prepared. Everything was in order. He left some things for you."

Connor's throat clogged. He stood, walked to the window, and stared out into the night. "I don't want any *thing*. I want Andrew back."

He heard her breath hitch on a sob and the familiar feeling of guilt stabbed him. He wasn't making this any easier for her.

Crossing to her, he settled on the couch beside her and wrapped an arm around her shoulders. "Aw, Angie, I'm sorry. I'm sorry for everything. I want to make it better and I can't."

She leaned into his embrace for a minute, then pulled back with a sniff. "I know, Connor. It's not your fault. None of it is. Andrew should have had his vest on, but he just . . . walked out without it that morning. I'm not even sure why. He just . . . did. And to be honest, it wouldn't have mattered if he had it on. That bullet would have gone right through it. Maybe Andrew just figured, why bother?"

"Andrew marched to his own drummer, did things his way, the way he wanted to."

"Yeah." Angie nodded. "Which is why he

left you this." She rummaged in the bag. When she pulled her hand out, she had her fingers curled around into a fist which she held out toward Connor. "Here."

Confused, he held his hand out. Angie unfurled her fingers and dropped a key into his palm.

Grief nearly doubled him over. "Angie, no . . . I can't . . . it was just a joke . . . I . . . I . . . no . . ."

Her fingers stilled his lips. "It's fully paid for and all the paperwork is in the glove compartment. Along with something else he wanted you to have."

His throat worked, but he couldn't speak, couldn't make his lips form the words.

Angie's hand covering his jolted him. He lifted his gaze from the key to meet her eyes, not caring if she saw his own were filled with tears.

"I miss him," he whispered. "And I feel so selfish saying that, because I know your heart's been ripped out too."

Finally, she let the tears swimming in her eyes fall to drip a salty path down her cheeks. And Connor couldn't hold his back anymore either. Giving in, he touched his forehead to hers, his best friend's wife, and joined her in shared grief for the man they'd both loved and lost.

■ ■ ■ ■

Hidden on the steps, Jenna turned from the scene in her den to climb back up. She'd heard the knock on the door and thought it might be Patty. Coming downstairs to investigate, she'd heard Angie's voice and stopped to listen. Now, she wished she hadn't eavesdropped. Her dad's grief reached out to her all the way across the room.

Tears blurring her vision, and constricting her breathing, she entered her room and shut the door with a faint click. Her dad was really hurting. Wow. She'd known he was mad, furious with the man who'd shot Andrew, but the raw grief she'd just seen threw her. Of course, she'd known her dad was upset, grieving, but she hadn't realized exactly how *bad* he was hurting. And to see him actually cry . . .

Wow.

She slumped on her bed, wishing she could share his heartache. Just like she wished she could have poured out all of her grief on his strong shoulder after her mother died. All this pain. Would it ever end?

What if she ended it herself? Killed herself? It wasn't the first time she'd thought about it.

What would happen to her? Did she really have a soul? Did she believe all that stuff about heaven and hell? About a God who cared about her? Her grandparents did. Her grandmother was always reading the Bible, trying to get Jenna to listen to her, to make right decisions, she said, that would affect the rest of her life.

If she killed herself, that would certainly impact the rest of her life. Too afraid to think along those lines very long, she stuffed the hurt down deep and pressed the power button on her computer.

Sighing, she grabbed her cell phone off the dresser and sent a text to 2COOL asking him if he could talk. While waiting for his reply, she pulled open the drawer of her nightstand. The envelope sitting there mocked her. Addressed to her, it held ten one-hundred-dollar bills.

One thousand dollars. She felt so . . . grown up. Yet, sneaky too, even though she wasn't doing anything wrong. She'd already sent in her medical records and gone to have the physical at that doctor's office. And they paid her just for signing a contract saying she'd be available for whatever gig came up in the next twelve months.

All this without meeting anyone officially.

Everything had been done online, via telephone and text messaging. Danny said he would contact her soon, and they would meet and do her portfolio pictures. She was to use some of that money to buy herself the perfect outfit for the shoot.

Very cool. Yet, a touch of uneasiness whispered through her. Something seemed a little . . . off. Wishing she could put her finger on what it was that bothered her, she pulled out the contract. She'd asked for a copy and they'd mailed one to her. It all seemed straightforward to her, just two pages of stuff like they'd pay her this to do that and she agreed to follow their guidelines or she'd have to give the money back.

Sounded like a good deal to her.

A glance at her phone showed no response from 2COOL.

The door downstairs shut. Angie must have left. Her grandparents would be home soon and her dad would leave for his apartment. Maybe. Or maybe he was planning on staying here.

Jenna remembered her home in North Carolina. The place where her dad had lashed out and told her mother what a horrible person she was and what a bad influence she was being on Jenna. That had been where her mother had stormed out in anger,

311

climbed into the car, and then wrapped it around a tree.

No one knew if it was an accident or not. Jenna liked to believe her mother hadn't killed herself, but deep down doubts niggled.

Not that it mattered at this point. Her mother was dead and there was nothing that was going to change that.

But maybe she could do something to mend the rift between her father and herself. Maybe she could try to forgive him for driving her mother out of the house that night.

Possibly. Maybe then her dad would want to spend time with her. Would love her again.

Or maybe it was just too late.

20

Samantha closed her Bible, stood, and stretched out the kinks. Her kitchen table wasn't exactly the most comfortable spot in the house, but she'd started reading 1 Peter as she waited for her coffee to brew and hadn't been able to stop. Verse 8 in chapter 5 stopped her in her tracks. "Your enemy the devil prowls around like a roaring lion looking for someone to devour."

How true. How scary. How comforting to know God was on her side and she held power against that evil, could fight it not only with her profession, but with her prayers. And when it seemed like evil was winning, she just had to believe that God had everything in control.

Sometimes it was hard, though. Like today. Normally, she loved Saturday mornings, but with all the stress of trying to find a killer while staying out of his line of fire, she didn't exactly doubt God, but she sure did wonder why he continued to let it go on. The evil in the world. Wouldn't it be better to put them all out of their misery? To come back and dispense justice? To end the evil?

She supposed that's where faith came in to play. Faith and the fact that God wanted every person to have the opportunity to know him. What if he came back now? Where would Connor end up? Tom? She shuddered and decided she was glad she wasn't God.

Samantha picked up her phone and dialed Connor's cell number.

"Hello."

"Hi, Connor. How's your Saturday going?"

"Much better now that you're on the other end of the line."

Sam felt herself flush, a little disconcerted to realize she felt exactly the same. Clearing her throat, she said softly, "Yeah, I know how you feel."

Silence greeted her and she grinned to herself. She'd thrown him.

"We'll talk about that one later." The husky touch to his voice sent shivers down her spine. He continued, "I'm tracking down that receipt you found in Miranda's closet."

"The one from that fancy boutique downtown?"

"Yeah. Rene's."

"Did you find out anything?"

"The woman working remembers Miranda coming in. She came alone with a fistful of cash and bought that dress."

Sam poured herself a cup of the steaming brew. "Did Miranda tell her anything about what she was doing? Where she was going?" She took a sip and closed her eyes as she swallowed. Delicious.

"Unfortunately, no. But she said she'd had one other girl come in and do the same thing. One of the girls who's still missing."

"Which one?"

"Sydney Carter."

"So, do we need to be checking all the high-class dress shops and see if any of the other girls had cash to spend?"

"That's my next move. You'll be proud of me. I delegated."

Samantha gave a light chuckle. "You're right, I am proud of you. Good job."

"What are you up to?"

"I . . . wanted to ask you something. Something that might be really painful for you to do."

A pause. "All right."

"Would you be willing to bring Jenna and

come to church with me tomorrow?"

Another significant pause. "If Jenna wants to go, I'll let her. I'm not interested." Another pause. "Actually, I think she's going to go to that sleepover with the kids from the church, so . . ."

Sadness pierced her heart. If he absolutely refused to give God another try, she'd have to do something to distance herself from him. As much as she liked him, could easily see herself falling in love with him, she wouldn't — couldn't — tie herself to him. She needed a man who shared her faith, her love for God, and her need to worship that God. And if Connor wouldn't . . .

Samantha forced a smile into her voice. "So you haven't sent her off yet?"

He groaned. "No, but I haven't given up on the idea yet. I know she'll fight it with everything in her, and I . . . well, I don't really want her that far away from me unless it absolutely has to be that way."

"I understand and don't blame you a bit."

"I've warned her about taking extra precautions and being supercareful. I'll confess that I've got someone watching her during the time she's away from the house. I don't worry so much when she's at home."

"Ooh. Bet that went over well."

He cleared his throat. "I didn't exactly tell

her, but I don't expect it to be long before she notices. If Jenna decides not to go to the sleepover and agrees to go with you, just bring her back to Mom's when you're finished."

"You know, Connor, this could be time you spend with Jenna."

He didn't say anything at first, then, "I'll . . . think about it. I just don't know how I'll feel . . . going back there."

"I know. I have to admit, I'm struggling with that myself, but one of the reasons I think we all need to go back is to face the evil that happened there . . . and . . . and . . . *defeat it,* I guess is the right way to put it. I know there will be people who'll never set foot on that property again, but the majority of us want to. We don't want the 'bad guy' to win. It might help you to have a good experience there. One with your daughter."

"Like I said, I'll think about it."

"Okay, I'll quit pushing. I just . . . care about you and Jenna. I hate to see the two of you hurting."

His voice was husky when he thanked her and hung up.

Samantha looked heavenward. "Please help him, Lord. They both need you so much."

■ ■ ■ ■

Connor hung up. After hitting a dead end with the boutique, he'd stopped at a small café on Main street to order a latte and call Samantha, but she'd beat him to the call.

Staring at his phone, he thought about what she'd said. About going back to the church where Andrew had been killed. It wasn't the property's fault, it probably wasn't even God's fault. And that was hard to admit, because even as angry as Connor was at the way things were happening, he still believed in an all-powerful God. Which meant God *could* have stopped it all from going down the way it did.

Samantha had said not to make Andrew's death about him. He swallowed hard. She was right. That would be a pretty selfish thing to do. And yet . . . if God hadn't let Andrew die to punish Connor, why had it happened? Why had his wife died? Why was someone out there killing kids? Why was his relationship with Jenna slowly circling the drain?

Andrew's voice came back to him. "You're going to lose her." His mother's blunt words. "You'd better do something or you're going to lose her." Even Samantha's insight.

"I'm worried about you and Jenna."

He stood, reached into his pocket to grab some change for a tip. Tossing the coins on the table, he saw the Corvette key mixed in with them. The grief came out of nowhere, hitting him hard. Picking up the key, he studied it, remembered the joking and laughing with Andrew. Connor had given Andrew such a hard time about that car, making Andrew promise to will it to him.

Laughing about death seemed to keep it . . . distant, like it couldn't touch them if they mocked it. And now . . .

Pocketing the key, Connor walked from the café to climb in his black Ford Mustang. The car Jenna made him promise she could have when she started driving. He'd actually bought it with her in mind.

And then an idea started to form, and as he thought about it, for the first time in a long time, he felt anticipation. Excitement. And a way to spend some time with Jenna that not even she would say no to.

He dialed her number. "Hello?"

"Hey, I had an idea."

"What?"

Connor winced at the flat sound in her voice, but held steady. "Are you ready to learn to drive?" Complete silence echoed across the line. "Hey, you there?"

"Are you serious?" she blurted. Suppressed excitement shivered in her voice.

"Yep, it's Saturday. And . . . I . . . want to spend a few hours of it with you, teaching you to drive. That is, if you want. I know I haven't exactly —"

She cut him off. "When can you be here?"

"In about ten minutes."

"I'll be waiting."

"Oh, Jenna, Samantha called and wants to know if you want to go back to church with her tomorrow. I know it might be too soon, but she asked so I wanted to let you know."

"I . . . I don't know. That girl from the youth group, Maria, called me, too and asked me to come. I liked it up until . . ."

"Well, if you want to go, call Samantha." He rattled off her number. "And be ready to drive. See you in a few."

"Okay. And Dad?"

"Yeah?"

"Um . . . thanks."

Warmth centered in his heart. "You're welcome, darling." He hung up, a new purpose filling him. Maybe it wasn't too late after all.

Samantha hung up and grabbed her keys. It was still early and things were looking up.

Jamie wanted to meet for brunch, Jenna had decided to go on the sleepover and sounded excited about it. During the conversation with Jenna, Samantha had also learned that Connor's parents attended a small church not far from their home, but they didn't have much of a youth group, and Jenna refused to go, calling it the blue hair worship center.

However, she admitted she'd enjoyed meeting the kids her age last week at Samantha's church before the shooting. She was willing to give it another try when she returned from the sleepover.

And Jenna was beyond excited because her dad was on his way home to teach her how to drive. Satisfaction filled Samantha. Connor was trying, reaching out. *Keep working on him, Lord.*

Ten minutes later, she pulled into the parking lot of The Smooth Berry and walked inside to see Jamie sitting in a corner booth — facing the door, of course. She waved and grinned.

Tom sat beside her. Annoyance at his presence slid through Samantha. Not that she didn't like Tom, but she'd been looking forward to a little one-on-one sister time. Oh well. She kept the smile on her face and headed toward them.

"Hey, Tom, how are you doing?"

"Well, my nerves have finally settled down. How about you?" He plucked a chip from his bag. The rest of his food had yet to come.

"The same." She looked at Jamie. "Did you order for me?"

Jamie nodded. "Chicken Caesar salad, right?"

"Yep. I think I can handle one of those at 10:30 in the morning."

Jamie shook her head in amusement at her sister's eating preferences and Samantha kicked her under the table. They grinned at each other.

"Anything come back on that bomb?" Tom asked, immediately sobering the lighthearted mood.

"Nothing yet. I guess the lab guys are still going over everything."

"Come on, you guys, can we talk about something else?" Jamie looked ready to burst.

Samantha laughed. "Sure, what's on your mind?"

"I'm graduating. In December."

"What?!" Samantha squealed, jumping up to lean over and give her sister an awkward hug. "That's fantastic. I'm so proud of you." She settled back into her seat just as the food arrived.

"Jamie, that's great." Tom beamed at her, and Samantha once again saw more than just friendship in his eyes.

Hmm. Worry twinged her. She liked Tom, but she'd seen Jamie's interest piqued by a certain FBI man and didn't think Tom had a chance of capturing Jamie's attention while she was enjoying getting to know Dakota.

"Jamie, you'll be a doctor! I'll have to call you Dr. Cash. My sister, a forensic anthropologist. Oh my goodness, that's just crazy."

Jamie's face flushed at Samantha's praise, but she laughed, her eyes dancing with joy and pride in herself.

"Well, Dr. Cash, brunch is on —" Tom stopped midsentence, his eyes on the silent television screen mounted on the wall in front of him.

Samantha turned to see what had captured her friend's attention. The camera zoomed in on the smoldering remains of a house. "What happened?"

Closed captions ran across the bottom of the screen. She read aloud, ". . . a gas explosion happened last night, taking the lives of long-respected, veteran bomb squad member Calvin Calhoun and his nineteen-year-old son, Calvin Junior, better known as CJ."

Shock held her captive. Surprise, regret, dread filled her all at once. Along with a certain awful suspicion. "Calvin?"

Jamie covered her sister's hand. "Samantha, what's wrong?"

"That's Calvin, the man who saved our lives yesterday. He's dead?" Tears clogged her throat at the thought of the man's ten-year-old daughter. Oh no. How?

She tossed her napkin down on the table. "There's no way that's a coincidence."

Tom frowned. "What do you mean?"

"The guy who put that bomb in my car went after Calvin."

"What? But that's crazy. Why would you even suspect that?" Tom shook his head as he peppered Samantha with questions. "Why would he do that and how would he know which bomb squad member was involved? Come on, Sam, that's ridiculous."

Samantha threw her hands up. "Which question do I answer first? I don't know how I know, I just do. This guy we're after isn't sane. Who knows why he's doing the things he's doing? As for Calvin, maybe this guy went after him for revenge for diffusing the bomb and messing up his plans. Maybe it was just for kicks." She paused as a thought occurred to her. "Or maybe he's afraid Calvin saw something he shouldn't have. I don't know. All I know is that another good man is dead, and this guy has got to be stopped. And soon." She stood, turning to her sister. "Sorry, Jamie, but I've gotta run. I'll call you later."

Jamie smiled, a sad smile, but one that said she understood. "Bye."

The Agent watched her leave the restaurant. Her feet pounded the cement. Anger radiated from her. She would look even harder, work longer hours searching for answers, searching for him. But she wouldn't find him. Would never understand that which she desperately sought. Tapping his lip with a finger, he pondered what he ought to do. Should he call Boss and ask for direction? No, Boss would just tell him to get rid of the problem. Successfully this time. Many more failures and Boss would be ready to get rid of *him*.

He'd thought it would be simple. After all, he'd had no trouble killing before. Why was it so hard to get rid of Samantha Cash? Frustration rippled through him as he realized he'd made a mistake in not killing her when he'd had the chance. He should have blown the car the minute he could have done so without risk to himself. Now it looked like another opportunity might not present itself anytime soon.

He looked at her sister sitting there in the booth, innocent, oblivious to the danger surrounding her. Unfortunately, just being in Samantha's presence could be lethal for her. The Agent smiled at the thought.

If something happened to her sister, Samantha would be devastated. The Agent was nothing if not observant. He'd seen the interaction between the sisters. Especially the day he'd put the bomb in her car. If Jamie disappeared, maybe Samantha's focus would be diverted from her case, buying him a little more time to finish up his business, tie up any loose ends, and get out of town.

Once again he considered his options. No, Samantha and the cop were the ones who had to go. Samantha knew too much. Hmm. He took a sip from the Smooth Berry travel mug. Man, this place made good coffee.

So, about Samantha and the cop she seemed to be falling for.

He'd think on it and make the best decision.

Jenna pulled into the driveway, laughing at the stunned expression on her father's face. He unclipped his seat belt and turned to face her. "Where'd you learn to drive?"

She flushed a bright red. "I got my learner's permit a year ago."

"That's not what I asked."

"I don't want to tell you. You'll be really mad at me."

Great. He narrowed his eyes, saying nothing.

She sighed and mumbled, "Patty let me drive her car."

Horrified, Connor stared. "You're kidding."

"No, but never on the streets or anything like that," she hurried to assure him. "You know that deserted parking lot across town?"

Sweat beaded his forehead, and he nodded, feeling a fraction of relief that she hadn't been navigating the streets of town without a license.

"Well, she'd take me there after school and let me practice."

Connor rubbed his eyes. He should punish her, give her consequences for her actions. He looked at her and saw the misery reflected on her features. At least she'd been straight with him. "Do you realize the trouble you could have gotten into?"

"Yes." A simple admission. No buts. No trying to excuse her actions. She was waiting for the boon to fall.

"Okay, well, first thing after school on Monday, we're going to get your permanent license and there'll be no more driving illegally. Got it?"

Slowly her eyes lifted to his. Grateful surprise gazed back at him. "And?"

"And what?"

"And like, I'm grounded for a year? I can get my license, but my punishment is that I can't drive?"

"No."

"Um. Okay. Then could you put me out of my misery and let me in on what's going to happen?"

"Nothing." He reached over to stroke her hair. "I love you, Jenna. I forgive you."

This time he'd rendered her speechless. Her mouth worked, but no sound came out.

"Part of your problem is that I haven't been here for you. I know that. I also know you blame me for your mother's death and . . ." His throat closed up for a moment. He cleared it and said, "And maybe you have that right. I don't know. Maybe if I'd been more patient, less driven, had a different job . . ." He broke off again and shrugged. "Your mom had a temper and I set it off easier than anyone I know. Of course she had the same effect on me when she wanted to." He looked into Jenna's tear-filled eyes. "I'm sorry I didn't try harder. I'm sorry I got so caught up in my own grief I ignored yours. I'm . . . sorry. And I'm asking you to forgive me."

Jenna flung her arms around his neck and held on.

He wrapped his arms around her slender frame and cherished the moment. How long had it been since he'd hugged her? Too long.

"Thanks, Dad," she whispered in his ear. Then let go and pushed her way out of the car and ran into the house.

Connor sat back. She hadn't said she'd forgiven him. But they'd made progress. He'd give her time to process everything, then they'd talk again.

He watched Jenna's bodyguard take up his post once more, and Connor's anxiety level eased somewhat.

His phone rang and he pulled it out to look at it. Samantha. "Hello?"

"Did you see the news? He killed Calvin!"

21

The task force assembled. Papers rustled, laptops glowed. It was just after lunchtime and all was not well. Samantha paced the floor, wishing with all her heart she could figure out what was going on. How did this guy know their every move? Was it someone she *trusted?* The thought made her nauseated. *Please, God, not that.* Scanning the faces around the table, she wondered . . .

"Sam?"

Connor's voice jerked her around to stare at the dozen or so faces looking at her expectantly. "Oh, sorry, I was thinking. What'd I miss?"

"Any updates on the computers?" Dakota twisted a pen between his fingers and leaned back in his chair, booted feet propped up on the large desk that took up most of the room. He'd pushed his cowboy hat back on his head. The FBI agent next to him leaned forward and stared at Sam expectantly.

"Nothing more than what I've already given you. If I'd had the chance to get into the girls' network logs on their routers in a more timely manner, I might have found something more, but this guy is good, and I don't know if I would have found anything or not. As near as I can tell, I seriously suspect that he sent them an email with a 'payload.'"

Dakota looked up. "Huh?"

"Basically it's an email that allows him to take over the computer when the email is opened."

Dakota steepled his fingers and rested his chin on them. "Man, I'm going to stop opening emails."

Samantha smiled. "If you have a good firewall, it's not so simple. If you don't . . ." She shrugged and addressed the group. "All I'm saying is that this guy is as good as I am. Maybe better. I've got a call into the Abrams asking to let me hook into their router so I can look around in there again. I know what I'm looking for this time. But like I said, this guy knows what he's doing."

Connor slapped a folder on the table and stood. "Well, we do too. It's just a matter of time now."

The others nodded their agreement, and Connor placed his hands on the table in front of him. "All right, people, you know what to do. Let's find this guy, please?"

One by one, the law enforcement personnel filtered out of the room, leaving Connor, Dakota, and Samantha alone.

She looked at Connor, respect for the man seeping from her. "I don't know anyone who could be handling this case as well as you, Connor." Realizing she'd singled him out, she grinned at Dakota. "You too."

He raised a knowing eyebrow that nearly touched the brim of his Stetson. "Uh-huh. Right."

Connor flushed at her praise. "Aw shucks, ma'am, wasn't nothin'."

Dakota flipped his pen across the table, hitting Connor in the head. "Quit makin' fun of me."

The trio laughed, needing the break from the tension. The captain came in the door. "When y'all are done playing in here and are ready to get back to work, I need your attention."

Connor stood. "What is it, Cap?"

"Veronica Batson's mother just got a text message from her missing daughter."

How could she have made such a stupid mistake? The Agent's lips quivered with suppressed rage as he stared at the pregnant girl cowering in the corner, then turned his ire to the nurse who looked ready to flee at the least provocation.

The Agent took a deep breath. Closed his eyes. Calm. Reach for that inner peace that he always found when he needed it. Calm. Peace.

Opening his eyes, he looked at the woman who'd placed her cell phone on the counter and left the room for less than two minutes. And the girl on the table had slipped down to send a text message to her mother. He'd walked in just as she'd pressed the SEND button.

A two-minute mistake that could cost him everything. "Clean it up," he growled at the nurse.

"I . . . I'm so sorry. I can't believe she . . . I didn't even . . ."

"Think." The Agent ended the sentence for her. "You're right, you didn't. I chose you. I handpicked you because you were one of the best. The one who showed such great promise. And Boss had faith in you, brought you into our little group. I pay you way too much for this kind of stupidity. And now . . ." He took another deep breath. "We need to move."

"But where?" She looked around at the extensive lab, the medical equipment.

"How?"

"Believe it or not, I actually planned for this. In the event that this location was compromised, I have a backup plan. Now get everyone working and get it cleaned up. I'll have the truck backed up to the door. Start loading. Leave whatever isn't critically needed. I have work to do, things to take care of immediately. When I get back, it better look like a ghost town around here." He turned to the still trembling teen. "I'll deal with you later."

The slamming door echoed behind him. He fumed as he stomped down the hall. All of his hard work. So close. So very close. He pulled out his cell and punched in a number.

"We're packing it up. I don't know if they've located us yet, but they will."

A curse, a mutter, then, "What happened?"

"One of my nurses made a stupid mistake. One that could lead the cops right to this doorstep."

"Pack it up and follow Plan B. I'll have things ready for you when you get here."

"Working on it now."

"Yeah."

He felt a surly anger crowding out common sense. He sucked it back. Closed his eyes, tried to clear his head. It was imperative that he have his mind centered. "Okay, you get things moving on your end. I'm working on mine."

"We'll be ready for you."

The Agent hung up, threw papers and files into an open box. *Two more girls. Should have been three.* He cleaned out his desk drawers. *Was almost four.* He paused, thinking.

Actually, he could still add one more. He'd have a new location, a new setup. He was going to have to take the girls he had with him anyway. Right now, combined, they were worth over a quarter million dollars. There was no way he was missing out on all that money. He had a meeting set for tonight with Jenna. He planned to snatch her and hold her for insurance. The Agent threw open the door to his now empty office and scanned the area. He had to move fast. Stay one step ahead of them all.

It had better be as simple as that.

"Can you trace the text?"

"Working on it now." Dakota held the phone to his ear waiting for the information he desperately wanted.

"Sam, you got the computers? We got the

335

router." Connor spit the questions like bullets.

"Got it." She mimicked Dakota's previous posture, feet propped up on the table, laptop settled in snugly against her thighs. Her fingers flew over the keys.

"Cap, search warrant?"

"On the way. All we have to do is fill in the location Dakota gets us."

Samantha yelped. Her fingers froze over the keys. Connor strode to her side to look over her shoulder.

"I found it." She gave a breathless laugh. "I found another one."

He squeezed her shoulder. Excitement caused his stomach to turn flips. He felt almost hyper at the possibilities of what she'd discovered. "What?"

"Like I explained before, the home network accesses the internet through a router. I made myself at home in the network logs of Miranda again and found the IP address of the computer that accessed it from a remote location. It's a nonstandard IP address and it's different from the one we found on the other computers."

"Where?"

"I don't know where the IP address came from, but you can trace it just as easily as you did the other one."

She wrote it down on a piece of paper and Connor passed it to Dakota. Dakota grabbed another phone and made a call to his FBI contact. He was still holding for the nearest tower location of the phone that made the text. Now he was waiting for the location of the IP address.

Connor paced. Sam set the laptop on the table, stood and stretched. He turned his gaze from her lovely form. No time to think about how good she looked or how much he wanted uninterrupted time with her to explore their mutual feelings.

Dakota slapped the phone down with a triumphant expression. "The text came from a cell phone registered to a woman named Crystal Bennington. I've already got my guys on their way to her house." He looked at Samantha. "You should be getting a picture of this woman any minute on your email."

"What about the IP address?" she asked as she turned the laptop back toward her.

Dakota waved the other phone at him. "Still waiting."

Connor started pacing again. His cell phone rang. "Hi, Jenna, what's up, hon?"

"Are you going to be home anytime soon? I was planning on cooking for you before I left for the sleepover. Maria's mother said she'd pick me up, but . . ."

Connor closed his eyes, regret piercing him. "No, sweetheart, I'm sorry. We just got a break on this case and it's going to take up the rest of my evening, I'm afraid."

Silence on the other end.

"Jenna?"

"That's all right." Her voice sounded subdued. "It was a dumb idea anyway."

"No, no, it wasn't. It was a great idea and I . . . hey, will you cook it and put me a plate in the fridge so I can warm it up when I get there? I'm always starving when I get home. I'll look forward to it. Trust me, it'll be the highlight of my night."

She gave a sad chuckle. "You're laying it on a little thick, but sure, I'll do it. And . . . good luck catching whoever you're after."

Relief sang in his veins. They hadn't taken two steps back. "Thanks, Jenna. I really do appreciate it."

"Right. I'll see you later. Be careful."

"I will. And . . . lock the doors, will you? At least until you leave?"

This time a long-suffering sigh. "I always do, Dad."

"Bye."

"Bye."

He hung up, wishing with all his heart he could climb in his car and head home. But he had a bad guy to catch, and if that meant missing Jenna's supper, that's what it had to mean.

But he'd eat every bite the second he walked in the door. Whether he wanted it or not.

Samantha climbed in the car to join in the search at Crystal Bennington's home. Dakota received his answer about the IP address Sam had given him. It was a match to the internet address traced to Crystal Bennington. Dakota had also emailed a picture of the woman to Connor's phone. If he saw her, he'd know her.

Could it possibly be a woman behind all this? Samantha went through a mental checklist of what she knew about the perp, and a woman didn't fit the profile. Could she be that far off in her assessment?

"Turn that way," Samantha said, pointing left.

Dakota had headed for the judge to get the search warrant. He would meet them at the house.

Connor circled the block looking for the address.

"Right there." Samantha pointed. Chesapeake Avenue. A very nice part of town. "Not hurting for money, is she?"

"Doesn't look like it."

"What else do we have on her?"

"She was a nurse manager at the hospital up until about eighteen months ago. She quit and supposedly went into home health for a while." Connor pulled into the driveway and whistled through his teeth. "Sorry, but home health doesn't buy this. Neither does a nurse's salary." The sprawling house was at least five thousand square feet. Spanish stucco and arched doorways. "Nice."

"Rich husband?"

"Or old family money."

"Or a murderer for hire."

"Or that." Connor readied his gun.

Samantha slid her safety off. "You see any movement in the windows?"

"No, and the garage is closed. Looks like no one's home."

Connor's phone rang. Keeping his eye on the house, he answered it. "Hello?"

Senses on alert, Samantha watched the windows. Still nothing. The team would be here in short order, then they'd hit fast and hard.

The front door caught her eye. Was it cracked? It was hard to tell from her position in the car.

Connor hung up. "That was Dakota. He's about a minute away. The GPS signal

340

tracked the phone to here. But the text was originally sent from somewhere near Elizabeth Street off 56."

"That's farm country."

"Yeah. A great place to hide. I've got people pulling addresses of houses near there and names of their owners and any renters. Hopefully something will show up."

Samantha itched to get inside and see what they could find. Finally, Dakota pulled in next to the curb. Search warrant in hand, he nodded to Connor and pulled an MP5 from the back of his car. Eyes alert, protective gear donned, the trio waited.

Thirty seconds later, backup arrived in the form of six patrol cars and two unmarked. Officers divided up to surround the house. Connor, Samantha, and Dakota descended upon the front door.

She'd been right. It was open.

Connor banged on it with his fist and it swung open with a crash. "Police! Ms. Bennington?"

A SWAT member kicked the door in, and the team swarmed the house. Connor and Dakota quickly followed. Officers had already made their way to the back of the house. One reported in. "All clear back here."

Sam brought up the rear.

The house had an empty, hollow feeling. She doubted anyone was here, but wasn't taking any chances. Her Springfield Armory 1911-A1 pistol clutched in both hands, she looked at Connor and jutted her chin toward the kitchen. He nodded. Dakota took the stairs, another officer behind him.

Sam swung around the corner. Nothing. "Clear." Turning, she moved through the laundry room, the half bath, the dining room.

Connor covered her back. Then he swung into the dining room and she covered his. In a low voice, he growled, "Clear."

A crash followed by a curse came from the second floor and jerked her attention from the living area. Heart pounding, she looked at Connor; he took off for the stairs, bounding up them two at a time. Samantha did likewise, hearing several SWAT members coming after her.

They burst into the master bedroom to find one of the uniformed officers staring down at a broken lamp, an embarrassed flush scorching his ruddy cheeks.

Dakota stood next to the closet, disgust written on his features. "Rookie tripped over the cord."

Relief rolled off Connor's shoulders in almost visible waves, and Samantha knew he'd had visions of finding another one of his buddies covered in blood. "Right."

Two more officers met them in the bedroom. One holstered his weapon and said, "The place is clean. Literally. I gotta bring my wife over here and show her what clean looks like." Samantha raised a brow at the man and he shrugged. "It's no secret she hates housework."

Dakota swung his weapon around to rest on his back, the strap drawing a diagonal line across his chest from shoulder to hip. "All right, let's see what we can find. We've got to turn up something to justify this warrant, or the next time we ask for one, we're gonna get laughed at."

Connor slapped him on the shoulder. "I'll take the master bedroom. You guys spread out over the house. I don't know exactly what we're looking for, but you'll know it if you see it."

Samantha and Connor started going through dressers, closets, under the bed, under the mattress. Finally, he looked up in disgust. "Nothing here."

"Look at the walls." She walked over to look closer at the ocean scene. "See these pictures? She's an artist. She painted these pictures. There're gaps on the wall and a faint outline in certain spots. She took some of the smaller ones, probably her favorites." Samantha turned back to close a drawer that had been left open. "She's running and she's not planning on coming back."

He nodded. "I got that impression too. No jewelry box. Indention on the closet floor carpet from where a suitcase sat for a long time. Hangers on the floor like she pulled clothing off them in a hurry. Drawers not pushed back in. Pretty obvious."

"Single woman, big empty house. No pets. A few personal pictures." He looked around. "She was ready to run."

"Like she knew this could happen?"

"Yeah. And something spooked her. I'm even willing to bet she's got a first-rate new identity, passport, credit cards, etc." Connor pulled his phone out. "I'm putting a BOLO out on her anyway, get her description at every airport within a two-hour drive. I'll cover the trains and buses too, but again, I bet she's heading for the air."

"I would agree." Samantha went to the window and looked out. Yeah, they needed every available cop keeping their eyes peeled for this one. She wondered about the woman they'd hoped to find. Sam didn't blame her for running. If she was mixed up in whoever was killing the girls and she'd made him mad . . .

"Hey, Connor, come check this out!"

22

Dakota's shout came from the next bedroom. Connor and Samantha bolted over there to find the agent standing inside the closet.

"What'd you find?"

"Come here. You've got to see this."

Curious, Connor moved forward. Samantha trailed him. He could practically feel her excitement arching from her. "What is it?"

Dakota moved out of sight. A grunt echoed from the belly of the closet, then the sound of something sliding. "This. A small secret area. She didn't do a good job of closing it when she left, or I never would have spotted it. Clever."

Connor pushed aside what was left of some winter clothing and blinked when the light hit his eyes. About six by six by six, the room was a perfect little concealed area — when the door was closed right. A small filing cabinet was the only thing in the space. The bottom drawer jutted like a mouth with severe underbite. Cleaned out.

"Well, if we were going to find something, my guess is that it was probably in here." With a gloved hand, he reached out to pull open the top drawer, then stopped and looked up at Dakota. "This thing's not going to explode in my face, is it?"

"Naw, it's clean. I checked."

"Right." He grasped the handle and pulled. The drawer slid out easily. Empty.

"Well?"

The question came from Samantha. Connor smiled to himself in spite of his raging disappointment at coming up empty-handed. She'd stifled her impatience as long as she could stand it.

He called, "Come on back. Unfortunately, there's not much to see, but you can have a look."

Almost immediately, he felt her behind him. Her familiar scent wafted to him, and he inhaled as the desire to touch her caused his fingers to tingle. Curling them into a fist, he resisted. Then she was inside the little room and very close to Connor. He liked it.

Clearing his throat, he said, "This is it."

Disappointment that mirrored his made

347

her lip curl. "Rats."

"Yeah."

She pulled her gloves off. "Guess I don't need these. The guys finished the rest of the house."

"Let me guess. It's clean."

"Mr. Clean couldn't have done a better job himself."

"All right, well, we've still got our team out at the address where the text message came from. Let's head over there and see what they've come up with. The crime scene unit is on the way."

Dakota shifted the file cabinet. "I want to know if there are any other prints on here besides Ms. Bennington's."

Connor nodded. "Yep, I was just thinking that. Crime scene guys'll cover that and let us know. I want to get going." Connor stepped out of the closet and took a deep breath. Sam's vanilla scent lingered even here. Connor shook his head. He was finally ready to admit that he had it bad. Andrew would be thrilled. At that thought, a shaft of pain shot through him; he rubbed a hand through his hair as he waited for it to lessen in intensity.

Keep your mind on the case, Wolfe. Focus. You're not doing Andrew any good if you let yourself get distracted.

"Connor, come look at this." Excitement tinged Samantha's voice.

"What?" He turned and made his way back into the little room.

Samantha had slipped her gloves back on and now held a piece of paper. Dakota stood behind her, looking over her shoulder.

"What is it?" Connor stepped closer.

"A break. A lawyer's office receipt." She turned it over and looked closer. "Actually, it's a copy of a receipt."

"Where'd you find that?"

Dakota pointed. "Behind the cabinet. When I moved it, it slipped out. I'm guessing she stacked the papers on top of the cabinet as she was cleaning it out. One must have fallen from the stack and she didn't catch it."

"Fortunately for us."

"Let's bag that and pay a visit to . . ." He leaned over to read, "Jefferson Abbott, attorney-at-law."

Samantha slid the paper into the bag and labeled it.

A knock on the door brought Connor back out of the closet to find Jake and his team headed into the room. Connor extended his hand to shake his friend's. "Hey, Jake. Good luck with finding anything. Your best bet is probably that cabinet back there."

"We'll take care of it." Jake looked Connor in the eye and asked, "On a personal front, how are you doing?"

The pain returned with full intensity, but Connor forced a smile that probably looked more like a grimace. But he said, "I'm making it, Jake."

Jake nodded. "When are you going to let God help you make it?"

"Probably pretty soon."

Jake's eyes went wide at that. "Great." Then he saluted Connor and went to work.

Samantha and Dakota came from the closet, and Connor radioed to see how the task force was coming on locating a reasonable area to start searching for the text message's location. He got his answer and motioned for Samantha and Dakota to follow him down to the car. "Let's go."

Connor's phone buzzed again. "Wolfe here."

He listened and felt his gut clench. Turning to Samantha, he said, "Our nurse friend here works for Physicians Associates. She's actually a physician's assistant and she specialized in infertility treatments."

Samantha's eyes went wide and her mouth formed a perfect O.

Connor shook his head. "Our guys are also at an address off Highway 56. The place

350

was a rental. The renter's name was Danny Lucci."

Connor, Samantha, and Dakota headed out.

Barbed wire fence surrounded the twenty-six-acre farm. To the outside world, the place looked harmless, a peaceful haven. Horses grazed in the distant pasture. Two wrought iron gates remained firmly shut.

The house enclosed behind the fence was a white wooden structure that had been built in 1899. Black shutters and a red chimney gave it a hominess that Samantha envied. One day.

Right now, she just wanted to get in there and catch the bad guys, rescue the girls.

Samantha adjusted her earpiece, which would allow her to hear any conversation between the team, and took it all in — the scenery, the beautiful house, everything. "Do we have the right address?"

Connor nodded. "Yep, and we need to find a way in without tipping them off that we're here." He spoke into his microphone. "Johnson, you and Miller around the back?"

"Negative. Electric barbed wire fence encasing the entire property. We need the power shut off."

"Hold on."

Connor pulled his cell from his pocket and dialed his boss to explain the situation. He looked at Samantha and spoke again into his mic. "Captain said to give him ten minutes. I've got a SWAT team member ready to cut."

The tension was palpable, nerves stretched taut. Samantha itched to get in there, prayed the remaining girls were safe.

She shifted the gun to her right hand and swiped her palm down her jeans. The police chopper was on standby, the SWAT team ready. Everything was under control. She hoped.

The place looked deserted. A plethora of emotions raged inside her. Anticipation, healthy fear, impatience. The combination made her jittery; she wanted to move but held steady. Dakota held his submachine gun ready, fingers curled around it, knuckles white. Connor answered his vibrating cell phone. Listened and hung up.

"We're good to go." He motioned to the team member with the wire cutters. "Go."

The man darted across the street and began cutting. With heavily gloved hands, he pulled the wire back, creating a space large enough to drive a truck through.

All remained silent. Eerily quiet. Samantha kept waiting for the shooting to start.

Finished with his job, the man returned to his position.

"Pete, Janelle, check the front windows."

"Yes, sir." One voice echoed the other. One man and one woman broke from the SWAT team and ran at a crouch through the recently cut fence and up to the sides of the house. Samantha watched Pete ease up to the first window, look in, then ease back. He looked in their direction and made the sign for "all clear." His partner slid up to the twin window on the opposite side and repeated her buddy's actions. Nothing.

A gnawing feeling growing in her gut, Samantha felt a headache start behind her left eye. No one was there. They were too late. The girls had been moved. But there might still be evidence left behind. This time Connor motioned them forward, each person spreading out to cover the porch.

Connor rapped on the door. "Police! Open up!" He raised his foot and kicked it in. Surprisingly, the wood splintered easily. Heading the team, Connor broke right, Dakota went left, and Samantha entered the kitchen.

Just like at the Bennington house, more officers made their way up the steps, guns drawn, shoulders set.

"All clear up here," one yelled down.

"All clear here," Samantha reported, looking around the huge kitchen. Clean, but not sterile. It looked . . . comfortable. Like a family eating area. She could imagine a family happily sitting around the large oval oak table that seated twelve.

Connor came up behind her. "These places usually have a basement."

She nodded. "Yeah, and other buildings."

"I've got a team in the barn and the other outbuilding. All reported clean too." His jaw clenched. "We're too late."

Samantha holstered her weapon. "Look." She pointed to the drying rack over the sink.

"Baby bottles."

"For newborns."

"Hey, guys, come see this!" Dakota called from the east side of the house.

Samantha headed toward Dakota's voice with Connor nearly stepping on her heels as he followed her. They came upon an open door with stairs leading downward. Descending the steps, Samantha detected a decidedly hospital-type odor. On the last step, she halted and drew in a deep breath. Pulled her gun back out.

"Anyone down here?" She could feel Connor at her back. "Oh wow . . . ," she breathed.

"Clear!" someone called.

"What?" Connor stepped around her, gun ready, senses alert. "Oh my . . ."

"It's unbelievable."

"An underground mini medical office."

That had been torn up, dismantled, and left in pieces.

"Somebody left here in a hurry. It looks like Crystal Bennington's house."

Connor pulled in a deep breath, looked at his phone. "I've got a signal down here too. Weird. All right, people, find every scrap of evidence left." He walked away to start barking orders on his cell phone. Samantha caught something about a CSU team on the way.

She looked at him. "Connor, we need to get to that lawyer's office and have a long talk with him before he gets wind that things are falling apart. Because if he's involved in this like I think he is, he's going to be running too."

"I've already got guys watching his office and his house. But I agree with you. We need to talk to him and now. Those girls are running out of time. If our guy thinks he's caught, he might kill them, cut his losses, and disappear."

"This is a pretty elaborate operation. There's got to be someone out there who can tell us something."

"In here, people!"

The shout came from inside the examining room. Samantha pulled in a sharp breath and shot her gaze to Connor. Slipping his weapon back into his palm, he motioned for her to follow.

Connor entered the room, caution written all over him. Another sound, a gasping . . . gurgle. Samantha watched him round the examination table and stop. He dropped out of sight. She stepped around the other end and gasped. Connor and another SWAT member knelt over a young woman who'd had her throat slashed, a gaping wound that turned Samantha's stomach. Blood pooled on the white floor beneath her as she twitched.

Connor looked up at Samantha. "Call an ambulance." The sadness in his eyes told her he knew it would be too late, but he had to try.

Samantha finally looked into the woman's face.

Raising her eyes to Connor's, she said, "That's Crystal Bennington."

"You're sure there's nothing left there." The Agent paced his new office. He hated it. It was so different than what he'd left; his only consolation was that it was a temporary arrangement.

"Positive," Boss soothed. "Will you relax?"

The Agent snorted. "I'll relax when I'm in Mexico. They were so close. So very close. Crystal's dead by now. I need to know how soon before you can induce labor with the girl furthest along? Veronica."

"Not for a while. She's only thirty weeks."

He cursed. "This place isn't nearly as secure as the last one."

"But we won't need as much security as we used to. We've only got two girls now."

The Agent paced. "That's right, but I've got one more to take care of."

"What do you mean?" Anger coated Boss's tone. "I thought you agreed we needed to get out of here."

"We're taking these two. What's one more? I'll have her here tonight."

"No! Absolutely not. You're pushing it and it's not necessary."

"You're right about that. It's *not* necessary. It's *personal.* And it's as simple as that."

Jenna checked her text messages. Danny again. Pushing to meet her. Checking to make sure she wasn't backing out. Part of her really wanted to. But . . .

Insecurity ate at her.

Her phone vibrated once again. Flipping over on her back, she stared at the light fixture in her room. One lightbulb was out. Her life was like that. Part of it dark and hidden, the other part looking brighter, better. She'd actually had fun with her dad earlier today.

Sighing, she flipped open her phone and answered. "Hi, Patty."

"Whatcha doing?"

"Lying on my bed, staring at my ceiling, thinking about what I want to do."

"Hmm. Sounds completely fascinating. Now, come downstairs and let me in."

Jenna bolted into a sitting position. "What? You're here?"

"That would be why I need you to open the door."

"Very funny. I'm coming."

Jenna trotted down the steps. "Grandma? Grandpa?" They must be taking their mid-afternoon walk and had locked the door behind them. Her father's warnings echoed in her head, and for a brief moment she wondered if she should go after them and remind her grandparents that they might be safer inside.

But it wouldn't do any good. They were old and set in their ways. Too many cops in the family for them to be scared of much.

Although Andrew's death had shaken them up.

Not enough to stay inside, though.

Of course they had their own shadow who was probably walking somewhere behind them keeping an eye on things.

She flipped the lock and opened the door. "What are you doing here?"

"Wondering what you're doing hanging around this place on a Saturday when we could be having fun."

Patty stepped inside and shut the door behind her. Jenna could see her own protection sitting in the car parked next to the curb. Patty had clearance to come up to the house. Anyone without authorization would be stopped. And if Jenna left, she would be followed.

But there were ways around that.

"I'm . . . debating." Jenna turned to lead the way back up to her room.

"About?"

"Whether or not to go meet Danny tonight . . . or, um, do something else."

"What? You have a meeting set up with Danny?"

Jenna winced at the squealed question and wiggled a finger in her ear. "Chill, Patty."

"Why didn't you tell me?" Patty flung herself across Jenna's bed, dramatic flair oozing from her. "I'm your best friend and you tell me nothing. You're so not fair."

Jenna slapped her friend's leg. "Oh stop. I'm still trying to decide what to do. There's a psycho killer out there, remember?"

"Hmm. True. But what are the odds of this guy that you're meeting being the one killing girls?"

"Maybe higher odds than I'm willing to gamble with. Maybe I should ask my dad. See what he thinks. He might even be willing to go with me. Well, not tonight because of this stupid case, but maybe I could postpone it until he could, you know, check this guy out with me."

Patty burst out laughing. "Your dad? *Your* dad? Mr. Straight-laced, stick-in-the-mud, 'Jenna, if you leave this house you're grounded' dad?"

Anger pinched Jenna. "Careful, you might rupture something. And yes, my dad. He took me driving today and he's letting me get my license on Monday after school."

Sobering, Patty sat forward. "For real?"

"Yep."

"Oh. Wow. Well, that's great."

"Yeah, it is. Anyway, back to this meeting thing. I'm just going to text Danny and tell him I want to . . . postpone it until next week. I'll just tell him something came up unexpectedly and I can't meet him."

"You don't think you're blowing your big chance here?"

Jenna sighed. "I don't know." She walked to the window and looked out. "Maybe you're right. Maybe if I cancel, I'll be messing everything up."

"Well, it's up to you, but I want to meet this guy."

"Did you hear back from him?"

Patty gave a small pout. "No, that's why I want to go with you to see him. Maybe if he sees what he's missing out on, he'll give me a chance."

23

In the precinct conference room, Connor slapped the thick folder down on the table in front of him. "Crystal Bennington died in the ambulance. This is the background information for every person in the Physicians Associates office. I feel pretty sure Crystal was our connection, but we have to check the rest of them."

Dakota shook his head. Samantha sighed and wilted in her seat. The other three officers shifted, anticipation eating them.

"Pass it on over and we'll get started," a young female officer volunteered. The others nodded. Each one wanted to be responsible to find the clue that would bring this case to a satisfying conclusion.

Rubbing the back of his neck, Connor narrowed his eyes on the rest of them. "All right, people, we moved too slow. They got away. Didn't leave much evidence other than a dead body and the fact that something hinky is going on."

"You mean evil," Samantha spat. "They're selling babies. Custom-made babies, if you ask me."

Connor nodded. "That they are."

"They're using these girls, breeding them, then killing them like stray animals." She shuddered.

"This sicko needs to be stopped and stopped yesterday," Dakota stated, arms crossed in front of him, jaw tight, Stetson riding low on his forehead.

"Who owns that property again?" Connor asked.

Dakota looked at the file. "A guy by the name of Marshall Sykes."

"Did he have anything to say about the renters?" Sam shifted as Connor paced.

"Just that they were outstanding occupants. Paid the rent on time, never any disturbances, etc. Said there was a woman who took care of the horses and did most of the chores around there. Danny would come and go during all hours of the night and day, but Mr. Sykes thought that he was working swing shift and whatnot."

"Swing shift, right. More like the graveyard shift," she muttered.

"All right, I want to go talk to this lawyer and see what he's got to say about his client." Connor sighed, disgust written on his features at the miss. "We almost had him."

"I know." Samantha stood and laid a hand on his forearm. "We'll get him. He's leaving a trail to follow now. We're close enough to make him scared, to send him running. He's going to trip up somewhere, and when he does, we'll be there."

"Let's go."

Dakota handed a folder to Connor on his way out. "Here, I think you'll find this interesting reading."

Connor took it and led the way out of the office, down the steps to the car and doing a quick check-in with Jenna on the phone. She assured him she was fine and he made her promise to be careful once again.

"Da-a-ad . . ." She drew the word out into three syllables.

"What time are you leaving for the camp-out?"

"In a couple of hours."

"Where are Mom and Pop?"

"They went for a walk with their shadow. Now they're downstairs watching some stupid game show."

"Be nice."

"Bye, Dad. See you when I get back."

"Bye, Jenna." He hung up and shook his head.

"Sounds like things are a bit better between you guys," Samantha noted.

He gave a small smile. "Yeah, I think so. Not perfect by any means, but at least we're taking steps forward. She didn't hang up on me this time."

"I'm happy for you, Connor."

"Thanks." Her soft eyes lured him like a siren song. Tempted to say something, to express his growing admiration for her, he stopped short. Instead, he passed her the keys. "Here, you drive while I read."

He opened the passenger door and settled himself into the seat. Once Samantha had her belt fastened and the car started, he pushed aside personal feelings and said, "It's Saturday. I'm guessing our lawyer friend isn't in his office today."

"Probably not. What's his home address?"

He gave it to her and raised his brows. "Ve-e-ery nice."

Ten minutes later, Samantha understood what he meant by very nice. A white-columned, brick three-story house sat on an elevated hillside. The guard at the gated entrance had let them through once Connor flashed his badge.

"Wow."

"Well, he's a lawyer, I guess he can afford it."

"I guess. Anything on his background?"

"Not much, nothing criminal anyway." He slid her a look. "But get this, he handles most of the adoptions around here for affluent couples."

Samantha felt anticipation curl in her belly. "Now we're getting somewhere. Crystal was the fertility expert. She could do whatever necessary to make sure the girls got pregnant. She could also deliver the babies relatively easy. Mr. Abbott here would handle the rest. You think it's possible he could actually be involved in all this?"

She parked on the street and gazed up at the house, admiring the clean lines and manicured lawn.

Connor gave her a sardonic look. "I think we've got missing babies and a lawyer's name found in the house of a woman involved with our missing girls. I don't think assuming this guy's involved is a stretch."

"I agree."

"In fact, I'm going to see if I can get a search warrant on his files, home and office. You think between the two of us we can keep him talking long enough for Dakota to track down a judge and get a signature and a team over here?"

"Sure. He's getting Crystal Bennington's financial records and everything else. No reason he can't handle that too. Let me give him a quick call." She pulled out her phone and made the call. Dakota agreed to get on it and she hung up. "All right, let's see what we can do."

They climbed from the car and headed up the front walk. Samantha rapped on the door and waited. "What if he's not home?"

"He's home. I had a guy keeping an eye on him ever since we found that receipt."

Admiration for him bloomed. It was obvious that he loved his job even though he hated the reason for it. The same way Samantha felt about hers. However, he was also very, very good at what he did. She understood his drive, his dedication. She smiled to herself. Just something else they had in common.

"What?"

She'd been staring at him. Samantha blinked. "Oh, sorry, I was just thinking."

"About?"

"Tell you later."

Sounds from behind the door caught her attention. They waited. Finally, the door swung open. A classy lady in her late forties stood there. She raised a brow. "May I help you?"

"Detective Wolfe and Special Agent Cash. Are you Mrs. Abbott?"

Her chin lifted a notch. "I am."

"May we speak with your husband, please?"

She paused as though considering sending them on their way. Then she raised a professionally arched brow, drew in a deep breath, and stepped back, allowing them entry into her spectacular home.

Samantha looked around and couldn't help the thought that it was entirely possible blood money had bought the expensive oriental rug she now stood on. And everything else in the exquisite house.

Without another word, Mrs. Abbott turned and led them to a very tastefully decorated sitting room. "I'll get Jefferson. He's out by the pool."

"Thank you, ma'am," Connor said to her retreating back. He offered a shrug to Samantha who wrinkled her nose.

Five minutes later, Jefferson Abbott entered the room, a white robe thrown over his bathing suit. In his early fifties, a little on the heavy side, he had an aura of wealth around him. From the perfectly manicured nails to his freshly combed, professionally styled gray hair.

Holding out a hand to Connor, he said, "To what do I owe the pleasure of this visit?"

Samantha repressed the impulse to roll her eyes, then chastised herself. The man was innocent until proven guilty. She looked closer. He actually looked like a very nice man. Nothing slimy or anything that said "I'm a sleazebag."

Hmm.

She acquiesced to Connor taking the lead. He once again introduced the two of them and asked, "Do you mind if we ask you a few questions?"

"Certainly. Come, have a seat, and tell me what's going on."

Everyone sat, including Jefferson Abbott in his wet bathing suit. Of course the couch was leather, so she supposed it didn't matter. Samantha twisted her hands together and crossed her legs.

Connor leaned forward, elbows on his knees. "We're investigating the cases involving the missing girls. The ones who are turning up dead."

The man never flinched, although he did frown, an expression of sympathy crossing his face. Then he raised his brows. "What does that have to do with me?"

Connor reached into his shirt pocket and

pulled out a copy of the receipt they'd found at Crystal Bennington's house. "Does this look familiar?"

The lawyer studied the paper and frowned. "Yes, it does. I mean the receipt came from my office, obviously, but I can't imagine what it was for."

"Well, it was for $50,000. That's a pretty large amount of money. What do you do that costs that much?"

"I just told you, I don't know. Although it's pretty odd," he muttered as he narrowed his eyes on the piece of paper, "because on all of our receipts we reference what services the money is for in this column here. But this one doesn't have that. Just the amount owed and the name of the client."

"That's correct." Connor didn't say a whole lot, a tactic used to try to keep the man talking. See if he would trip himself up.

"I remember the couple, though. Mr. and Mrs. Michael Steadwell. They adopted a baby through our agency."

"We plan to talk to them next," Connor said as Mrs. Abbott reentered the room carrying a tray holding a coffee carafe and three mugs.

Jefferson smiled at his wife. "Thank you, dear." He poured the coffee as he talked.

"Nice people. They wanted a baby desperately, but couldn't conceive for various reasons. Within three months of them filling out the forms, I had a baby for them. Another happy ending. Something we try to specialize in." Satisfaction radiated from him.

Samantha shifted, but took the proffered coffee. Something was still off. "But that much money. What would it have been for?"

"Different things. Fees, hospital expenses for the birth mother. Possibly even some living expenses. It's not unheard of for adoptions to cost up to a hundred thousand dollars. We don't just wait for mothers wanting to give up their babies for adoption to come to us. We actively seek them out, recruit them, offer these women — sometimes young girls who've been kicked out of their homes — a safe place to live and a reason to choose adoption over abortion. Our clients are willing to pay for the proactive measures we take when it comes to locating a child for them. We do a very good service here."

"I'm not saying you don't." Samantha switched topics but couldn't help wondering if his proactive measures included kidnapping teen girls and forcing them into surrogate motherhood. "How do you know

Crystal Bennington?"

"I don't believe I recognize that name."

Samantha nearly ground her teeth in frustration, but kept a pleasant expression on her face as she stared into his eyes. No guile there. "Hmm. Well, this receipt was found in her house, and we'd really like to figure out how it got there."

"I'm sorry I'm not much help, but I don't know what else to tell you."

Connor sighed. The doorbell rang and Mrs. Abbott excused herself to answer it. Samantha figured that it was probably Dakota with the search warrant.

She turned back to Jefferson. Unfortunately, she halfway believed the smooth-talking lawyer. "Is there anyone else with access to those receipts?"

He laughed. "Sure, anyone in the office."

Great.

"Darling, there are more police here with a search warrant." She looked mildly irritated.

For the first time since they'd knocked on his door, anger showed on Mr. Abbott's face. "What's this? A search warrant? What for?"

"Your files, sir."

"All you had to do was ask."

"We figured you'd claim client confidentiality."

The man sighed and rubbed his neck. "Yes, I probably would have." Then he shrugged. "I don't have anything to hide, regardless. Here, follow me."

He led the way back to his office. Connor nodded and the search began. Samantha stepped back out of the way and watched the proceedings.

Jenna finished the text, shut her phone, and tossed it on the bed next to Patty. She was going camping. Getting away from it all. The fear, the depression, the constant worry about her dad. All of it. At least for the next twenty-four hours. She packed her backpack, grabbed her sleeping bag and a pillow, and ignored Patty's whining.

"Jenna, come on. Don't do this. Let's go meet this guy."

"I'm going camping, Patty. You can come too, you know."

Patty wrinkled a lightly freckled nose. "No way. That's so not my thing and you know it."

Jenna gave a little laugh. "Well, I can't say it's mine either, but I'm going."

"This is *so* not cool."

Rolling her eyes, Jenna wondered how

she'd put up with Patty this long. The girl was really starting to get on her nerves. "Patty, go home. Or wherever. I'm going to go chill out next to a fire and roast marshmallows, sing songs, or whatever they do at these things. I'm going to forget my life for a while. Now give me my phone."

She held her hand out. Patty had been messing with the device and Jenna wondered if she'd have to fix her screen saver back to the picture she'd snuck of Bradley. She looked at the screen. Nope. His gorgeous face peered back at her. The one guy at school she was interested in and he just didn't seem the least bit interested in her. How depressing. And she couldn't figure out why. Maybe she should just ask him. What would he do if she walked up to him bold as you please and asked. Jenna shuddered at the thought. No way.

She shoved the phone into the back pocket of her jeans. "I'll see you tomorrow night if you want. We can go get some ice cream or something."

"Fine," Patty huffed. "Go be with those losers. See if I care. I've got something better to do anyway."

"What?"

"None of your business."

"You're such a snot."

"Yeah, yeah. Call me if you get bored and I'll drive up to get you."

Jenna gave her friend a small smile. "So, you don't hate me?"

"Not much. A little maybe."

Laughing, she pushed Patty ahead of her out the bedroom door. "Come on and walk me down."

All laughter ceased as she watched Patty drive away. Jenna's reasons for wanting to go on this trip came rushing back double time as she once again caught sight of the man her father had hired to protect her, sitting in his car across the street.

Yes, she'd made the right decision to get away from it all. No doubt about it. Maria's mother waited in the driveway.

"Bye, Grandma, Grandpa, see you tomorrow."

Connor slammed the last drawer shut. "Nothing. It's clean."

"I told you I had nothing to hide. What is it you think I've done?"

"I'm sorry, Mr. Abbott, I can't share the details of that with you right now. We already have a team searching your office. If we don't find anything there, then I suppose we owe you a huge apology."

"All right" — the man bristled — "I really

must draw the line here. I've tried to be co-operative, answered your questions, put up no resistance to your search. But now, you're done."

Samantha eyed him. "Actually, we have a warrant for the office too. So, if you'll excuse us . . ."

"Victoria?" Mr. Abbott called to his wife.

She glided back into the room. "Yes?"

"I'll be down at the office. They have a search warrant for that too."

Expressionless, the woman nodded and returned to wherever she'd come from.

Jefferson Abbott led the way out the door and rode with Connor and Samantha. Fifteen minutes later, they'd acquired two uniformed officers and Dakota. Everyone followed the lawyer onto the elevator. At the third floor, they stepped off and headed left. Jefferson stopped at the second door on the right and swiped a card across the beam. Once inside, Samantha decided the office felt like a vacuum if you discounted the team ready to participate in the search. Empty and waiting, not the busy hive of activity she'd, for some reason, expected.

Samantha wondered out loud, "I thought lawyers put in weekend hours."

Jefferson quirked a small smile. "Not necessarily. Big law firms in bigger cities?

Sure. Here? Every once in a while. Come on in."

Neat, organized — plush. The office reeked of money. Samantha looked at Connor, who didn't seem fazed in the least. He went straight to the file cabinet and got to work.

Jefferson settled himself in the chair on the other side of the desk. "If you people would just tell me what you're looking for, I could probably save you a lot of time and energy."

Connor turned and sighed. "We need to see your adoption records for the last fifteen months."

The man laughed, but there was a definite lack of humor in the sound. "Are you kidding? Those records are closed."

"And my search warrant is the magic word to open them." He nodded. "Please?"

"Fine." The word came out through gritted teeth, but he complied.

Connor rubbed his face as the man gathered the files. "You don't keep this stuff on the computer?"

"Yes, but we also have hard copies. Sometimes we get reference letters, correspondence, medical records, and whatnot that we have to keep up with. Hence, the old-fashioned record keeping and the filing system."

"Right. Show me the Steadwell file, will you? That seems like the logical place to start."

Abbott handed it over.

Samantha peered over Connor's shoulder as he thumbed through it. "That receipt's not in there."

"I noticed." He turned to Jefferson. "Shouldn't a copy of that receipt be in the file?"

"Of course." He got up and took the file from Connor. Placing it on his desk, he methodically went through every paper in the folder. "I don't understand." Confusion crinkled his forehead. "We keep everything together. The one that you found, was it the original?"

"No, it was a copy."

"Then, the original should be in here." He shut the file and sat down. "I . . . I don't know what to tell you. I'm sorry."

Connor paced, thinking. Wondering where to go after this. He turned back to the officers still searching. "Keep working, people. Samantha, you coming with me? We've got a couple to interview." He looked at Dakota. "We're going to find the Steadwells."

"I've got this covered," Dakota said. "I'll

378

also see that Mr. Abbott gets home."

"Thanks."

Samantha followed Connor into the elevator and out the building. Connor was already on his cell working to get in touch with the Steadwells.

The Agent stood in the shadow of the plastic ficus tree, head bent, eyes watchful. Everything was spiraling out of control. He'd texted Jenna the address and time, but she had replied saying she wouldn't meet him tonight. She wanted to postpone it. Then almost immediately after that, she said she'd changed her mind. Yes, she would meet him.

He'd decided against the little café he enjoyed so much. Somewhere different. He'd had to find a new place since the one he normally frequented was now under surveillance. But he'd scoped this place out and it would do the trick. He also knew where the security cameras were and where to sit in order to minimize his exposure.

He thought about the other café where he'd ditched Sydney's cell phone. Sydney. One of the two girls who'd failed him. Sydney and Miranda. Miranda had been easy to dispose of. To kill. She'd aborted her own baby. Fury filled him at the thought, and he snorted, forced himself not to think of her. She hadn't earned the right to occupy a place in his thoughts.

But Sydney . . . she'd simply failed to fulfill her destiny. Failed to carry a child full term. She'd aborted almost as soon as she'd gotten pregnant. Three times. After the third time, he'd realized she wasn't one of the deserving ones.

As a result, she would be eternally punished. Never to be found. Never to be honored in death by those who loved her. He'd decided against sending a note to tell them where he'd hidden her. It was much more fun to watch them squirm in wonder and frustration as they struggled with their fruitless search.

And now Jenna.

He had special plans for her. That father of hers was proving quite annoying. Nothing seemed to scare him off. Not even having a killer show up at his kid's school had derailed the man from the case. And Samantha, she'd jumped right into the investigation. At first, he'd been a tad worried that she would be a problem, but had quickly come to the conclusion that while they both were causing him problems, the detective was the one that would cause him the most grief. And he was the one who needed to be taken care of. The solution to The Agent's problem should be walking through the glass door any moment now. He sighed and checked his watch. She'd better be on time.

The doors opened, and a family of four walked in. Restless energy suffused him. He really needed to get the girl and hurry back. But he forced himself to be still, to wait patiently, be invisible to those around him.

A dark-haired teen approached the restaurant. Ah, there she was. He straightened, pulled the ball cap lower around his ears. Time to throw out the line. And reel in his catch.

It was as simple as that.

24

Jenna stepped out of the church van and looked around. Beautiful. It wouldn't get dark until around nine o'clock. Plenty of time to drink in the vastness surrounding her. The campground held tents of various shapes and sizes. The RV park was within shouting distance. The showers and toilets resided behind the dark wooden structure to her left.

A pay phone captured her attention. She looked at her cell. Very low signal. She wondered if she could text from up here. Probably. Sometimes a text went through when a call itself would fail. But . . .

Who cared? She was here, she was free.

"So, what do you think? Glad you came?"

Jenna smiled at Maria. "Definitely. I needed this."

"I think we all did."

"True." But she wanted to say, "Not as bad as I did." But that would sound pretty selfish, so she kept her lips closed. The sound of a rushing river pulled her to the left. Maria followed.

"How's your father doing? With Andrew's death and all. I know they were partners."

Jenna closed her eyes and took a deep breath. "Look, Maria, I don't want to be rude, but I came on this trip to get away from all of that. I don't want to talk about my dad, Andrew, or any other icky or sad topic. I'm here to forget my life for the next few hours."

Maria lifted an eyebrow, then shrugged. "Sure."

Relief filled Jenna. "Thanks."

"Wanna go wading?"

"Definitely."

"Let's help get stuff set up so we can head down to the river."

The girls made their way back to help set up camp, but the four chaperones who'd accompanied them shooed the teenagers away. "Go enjoy yourself."

Jenna, Maria, a teen by the name of Spike, and the biggest surprise of the day, Bradley Fox, let out a cheer. "To the river!"

Jenna brought her backpack that held her towel, sunscreen, and a bottle of water. Her collection of key chains rattled as she walked, and she smiled at the racket. Her dad complained about the noise, but Jenna knew he didn't really care that she kept them. Her mother had given her every one of them.

"So, Bradley," she initiated conversation as they walked. "I didn't know you came to this church."

"I don't. I'm a friend of Spike's. His dad and mine work together and he invited me along. I didn't have anything better to do, so —" he shrugged — "here I am."

"I'm glad."

Bradley gave her a long, measured look, then he smiled. "Yeah, me too."

Jenna tossed her backpack to the ground and pulled out her water bottle. Then she slid out of her flip-flops and stepped into the river. The current flowed swift and hard. She almost lost her footing, but a strong hand on her arm kept her upright.

Turning, she smiled at Bradley. "Thanks."

"No problem." He helped her over to a large rock where they sat side by side, dangling their feet into the water. "So, how long have you been going to this church?"

"Hmm. I don't actually go there. I visited last week, then the shooting happened . . ."

"Yeah, I heard about that. I didn't realize you were there, though."

"My dad's the one investigating the case."

Realization lit his eyes. "Is that why you have a shadow following you everywhere at school?"

Cutting her eyes at him, she gave him a little grin. "Noticed that, did you?" She shrugged. "Yeah, but I haven't seen him lately. Maybe he decided nothing was going to happen up here in the boonies."

"Are you scared?"

Jenna looked down into the water. Was she? "No, not really. Not for me anyway. It's my dad he wants." She raised her eyes back to Bradley's. "That scares me. I've already lost my mom . . ."

She looked away again, unable to believe she was opening up to this guy like she was. Forcing a smile, she stood. "Come on, let's wade."

The next hour and a half passed in a blur of splashing and laughing. Jenna felt the weight of depression, sorrow, and worry fall from her shoulders as she frolicked like a little kid again.

Maria proved herself true and didn't bring up any touchy subjects. Instead, Jenna learned about the girl's background. That her parents were missionaries and Maria's goal was to follow in their footsteps. Her love of God touched something deep in the recesses of Jenna's heart. In fact, Maria reminded her of Samantha in that regard. Interesting.

Tired, yet relaxed in a way she hadn't been since before her mother died, she flopped onto her towel and laughed at the others' antics.

Out of habit, she pulled out her phone and checked it. She had two text messages. The first was from her dad asking if she was all right. She answered that she was fine.

The next text message made a liar out of her. She wasn't fine. Patty's text said, "Met Danny. He was mad you weren't here, but glad to meet me. Wants me to see his studio. Going with. C U later."

What? But she'd canceled that meeting.

And Patty had been playing with her phone before they left.

Jenna scrolled back through her SENT messages. And there it was. Patty, the little sneak, had sent a message saying Jenna had changed her mind and would meet him.

All of Jenna's tension rolled back onto her shoulders. She started to reply to Patty, to blast the girl for doing something so careless — never mind the fact that she herself had seriously considered it — when another text flashed back on her screen. Another one from Patty. This time nausea swirled. "Get help. Danny is a —"

She never finished the message. She'd hit the SEND button fast. Which meant her friend was in danger.

Jenna dialed her dad's number, but the call wouldn't go through. She jumped up, rustled up some change from the bottom of her backpack, and ran to the pay phone.

Fingers shaking, she dialed his number and got his voice mail. In a rush, she blurted, "Dad, Patty's in trouble. She's gone to meet a guy named Danny who she met online and I think she needs help. They were meeting at some coffee shop on Chester Street. I don't know if she's still there, but you've got to . . ." Jenna trailed off and sighed. Her dad was busy. He'd never stop what he was doing to find Patty. Not when he was busy looking for a killer.

Jenna hung up and dug out more change.

Connor heard his phone ringing from somewhere near the vicinity of his feet, but couldn't stop yet to grab it. He'd dropped it when he'd pulled into the Steadwells' drive practically on two wheels.

Absently, he noted the place looked deserted. Great. He opened his door, then knelt down to snatch the phone from the floorboard. Looked at it. An unknown number had called.

Samantha climbed out and headed for the front door. He listened to his voice mail and froze, heart thumping in sudden fear. At the end of the message, he immediately dialed the number Jenna had called from.

"Sam, get back in the car."

She looked back at him, a frown marring her forehead. Shrugging, she loped down the front steps and looked at him, questions churning in her steady blue gaze.

"Dad? Dad, is that you?"

Relief nearly sucked the strength from his knees. "Jenna, what's going on?"

"You've got to get over to that coffee shop on Chester Street."

Connor flipped the phone to speaker so Samantha could hear. They both climbed back into the car as Jenna continued.

"Patty's meeting this guy named Danny who she met online. And I think he's dangerous. She sent me a text message that said, 'Get help.' "

"Where's your bodyguard?"

"I don't know. I haven't seen him. He was sitting in front of the house when we left, but I don't remember seeing him behind the van driving up here. I just figured he decided I was safe with this group, but now . . ." They were about thirty minutes outside of the city. "I called a cab, Dad, I'm coming home."

"No!" Connor shouted as he headed toward Main Street. "You stay put."

"She's my friend, I'm coming."

Hearing the stubbornness in his daughter's voice, Connor wanted to swear. He knew she'd be in that cab the minute it arrived if he didn't do something. Then again, leaving Jenna up there with unsuspecting, innocent potential victims probably wasn't a good thing. If that guy decided to show up and grab Jenna and one of the church people tried to defend her . . .

"I'll send someone to pick you up. I don't want you alone." And that someone would make sure Jenna was nowhere near any of the trouble going on around here.

"Fine, I'll wait here, but just hurry, will you?"

Samantha looked at him. "I can call Tom."

Connor nodded. "Do it." He couldn't ask for better protection than a former fed.

Samantha got on her cell and made the arrangements, then nodded to Connor. "He was working his security guard job, but is getting off work immediately and will be on his way within minutes."

Samantha got back on her phone, trying to track down the Steadwells. She worked on the computer in the squad car, internet access compliments of the broadband card. "I've got two numbers for the Steadwells."

She rattled them off and Connor dialed as he drove. Again, he put the phone on speaker for Samantha's benefit. It rang four times, then went to voice mail. The next number did the same.

Connor growled and shut the phone. "What's his work number?"

Samantha clicked a few more keys and told him. Then said, "It's Saturday, I doubt he'll be there."

"Is it still Saturday? For some reason, I feel like I've lived a week in the last twelve hours."

"I know."

Connor dialed the number, pushed three more numbers when he was prompted to access the man's extension. They listened to his voice mail, then looked at each other in disbelief.

"He's out of town until next month." She could see Connor's disgust growing by leaps and bounds.

Samantha shook her head and muttered, "You've got to be kidding me."

"I wish. You heard what I did. He works for a pharmaceutical company, and apparently, he just left on an extended business trip. How convenient."

"And took his family with him. He was warned we were coming."

"I get the distinct impression that Jefferson Abbott didn't want us talking to the Stead-wells."

Samantha frowned as she thought. "But when would he have had time to call them? They would have needed quite a bit of time to get everything arranged to leave, and he was with us while they would have had to have been scurrying around making plans and leaving town."

Connor blew out a breath and turned into the parking lot of the small coffee shop. "I don't know, we'll have to come back to that. There's Patty's car. Here's a picture of her." He'd had her driver's license photo sent to his phone.

Samantha took a look. "Pretty girl."

Connor swung into a parking spot and they jumped out. Samantha hit the door first, Connor pulled up the rear.

Once inside, she scanned the nearest tables. "Do you see her?"

"Nope, keep going toward the back."

Samantha scooted around the tables, ignoring the looks she got from some of the customers. She glanced at each face, not finding the one she was searching for. Worry and concern ate at her. Not wanting to be an alarmist, Connor hadn't yet called Patty's parents. Samantha's gut clenched at the thought that that would be the next call he'd have to make.

Connor stepped around a corner. "She's not here."

"I've got Dakota tracking the GPS signal on her phone."

"I have a feeling that's not going to get us very far. Not if it's our killer."

"Yeah, and unfortunately, I'd be willing to place a bet that that's who we're dealing with." She sighed and tossed her ponytail over her shoulder.

Connor lifted his phone to his ear. "I need a tow." He gave the description of Patty's car and hung up. Turning to Samantha, he said, "We'll see if the crime scene guys get anything off the car. However, if she met him in here and left with him, there won't be anything. And of course, he picked a place that wasn't under surveillance."

"There are two cameras," Sam pointed out. "I'm sure this place was his idea, so we're not going to see his face."

"Come on, I need to check on Jenna. And we need to track the Steadwells. I want to know what flight they were on."

"Right." She thought for a moment. "We

need Jefferson Abbott's phone records too. Somehow he made a call and warned the Steadwells. Check with Dakota to see if the guy went to the bathroom or something before they took him home."

"I'll have his phone records pulled." He thought for a moment. "And his text messages."

Dakota made the arrangements on the drive back to his house. He wanted to know what was going on with the man who'd been assigned to watch Jenna, Rick Tremaine, and why he wasn't answering his phone.

Jenna paced back and forth in front of the entrance to the campsite. She'd already told the chaperones she'd be leaving as soon as her ride got there. One had asked to speak with her dad, so she'd had to call him back and have him explain what was going on.

"Where are you going?"

Jenna whirled to see Bradley, head cocked, eyes intent. She swallowed hard. He was so . . . something. Mature, yes, but a light emanated from him, from deep within him.

"Are you a Christian?" she blurted.

A slow smiled crossed his lips. "Yes."

A simple answer with a depth of meaning

she was only coming to understand. "I'm not."

Compassion softened his gaze even more. "I know." He gave a small chuckle. "But you can change that."

Impatience for her ride to arrive warred with the desire to stand here and talk to Bradley more. She looked at her watch.

He asked again, "Where are you going?"

"A friend of mine is in trouble."

"Patty?"

He'd not been as oblivious to her as she'd thought. Of course, it was a well-known fact around school that she and Patty were best friends. "Yes."

"What kind of trouble?"

"I'm . . . I'm not sure. She met someone on the internet and texted me that she was going to meet him in person and . . ."

His compassion morphed into deep concern. "That's not good."

"Tell me about it. I called my dad and he's sending someone to pick me up."

"Do you have a cell phone?"

"Of course."

"Store my number in it. Call me and let me know about Patty."

Her heart melted. He was so awesome. All of a sudden 2COOL/Danny didn't seem so wonderful anymore. Jenna realized that while she'd been attracted to Bradley's good looks, she'd also seen something else in him. Something she wanted in her own life. "Will you pray for us?"

"I've already started."

Whoa.

"And God isn't so hard to find, Jenna."

She felt her throat work and gave a slight nod. "I'm coming to see that. Thanks."

Another slow smile creased his cheeks revealing a dimple that winked at her. Her heart did that funny tripping thing again.

Bradley said, "Anytime you want to talk about him, let me know."

"I'll . . . do that." She hesitated, then asked, "Will you call to check on me? Make sure I'm all right in about an hour?"

"You bet."

"And if you don't get me, will you call my dad?"

He frowned. "Do you think something's going to happen to you?"

She forced a smile. "No, not really. It's just been a little crazy lately. And those missing girls are on my mind, and my dad has drilled safety and proactive measures in my head so much that I . . . ," she shrugged. "Oh never mind. I'm being silly."

"Give me your dad's number."

Jenna relaxed a tad and complied.

A dark, low-slung car pulled in next to them, and a voice called out, "Jenna Wolfe?"

"That's me." She turned back to Bradley. "Thank you."

"God loves you, Jenna. Don't forget that."

She opened her mouth to say something, then snapped it shut when she realized she didn't know what to say. She gave a short nod and crawled into the passenger seat, slamming the door behind her. "Thank you so much for picking me up. I'm really worried about my friend."

Tom gave her a smile. "Not a problem. When Samantha called, I was glad to help out."

Jenna raised a hand to wave goodbye to Bradley, who still stood in the same spot, his eyes still on her. He waved back, then turned to join the group. Wow. Excitement tingled inside her at the thought of something more happening with Bradley sometime in the near future.

Wow. Wow. Wow.

She finally turned her attention back to her chauffeur. "Don't you work with the FBI or something like that?"

Tom gave a nod. "Something like that."

Jenna twisted her hands as anxiety rose up in her again. "I know you're Samantha's friend, but are you working the case with the missing girls?"

"To a certain extent, yes."

"Oh." He didn't seem interested in talking that much. In fact, he made her a tad uneasy. She brushed aside that feeling. Her dad would only send the best. For a while, she simply watched the scenery as it flew past her window.

"So, where are we meeting my dad?"

"Don't worry. It's all arranged."

Jenna frowned. "Okay, good. So, where?"

Tom looked at her and frowned. "You're persistent, aren't you?"

"One of my more endearing traits." This guy was really starting to get on her nerves.

"Hmm. So, Patty's in trouble, is she?"

"Yeah."

Anxiety for her friend welled to new heights. She wanted to check her phone. But when he turned left off the road that would lead them back to town, she paused. "Hey, wait a minute. This isn't the right way. Where are you going?" she demanded.

"Taking you someplace safe. Just like your dad wanted." He grinned at her. "It's as simple as that."

25

Connor headed back to his parents' house. Rick should have answered his cell. Tom had Jenna, she was fine, but worry niggled at him. Where was her bodyguard? Rick should have been following Jenna all the way up to the campsite. He dialed his mom's number and it went to voice mail. The tiny worry turned to outright anxiety.

Finally, he came to his street, and he saw the tan Buick that Rick drove sitting in full view of the house. He flicked a glance at Sam. "This could be bad."

She had her hand on her gun. A shadow in the driver's seat was all he could make out. Connor slowed to a stop and opened his door. Samantha followed his lead.

Caution marking his steps, he made his way to the passenger side of the car . . . and stopped. Blood splattered against the window in front of him. "He's hurt!"

Samantha holstered her gun and hurried

to the driver's side. "Window's down."

The man's head rested against the steering wheel. Connor bolted around the front of the car to stand next to Samantha. He reached in to feel for a pulse. "He's still alive. Call for an ambulance. I'm going to check on my parents."

He left Rick in Samantha's care and hurried up the walkway to the front door.

Locked.

Shoving his hand into his right pocket, he pulled out a wad of keys. Found the right one. Inserted it and stepped inside.

Everything was quiet. Nothing out of place from his current vantage point. Keeping a hand on his gun, he turned right into the kitchen. Followed through to the den. The rest of the house was empty. Clean. Everything as it should be.

So where were his parents?

He dialed both cell phones, but didn't get an answer. Shocking. He rolled his eyes. Why they even bothered to have the devices was beyond him.

He took the stairs two at a time, examined the room he used when he stayed here, then stepped across the hall to Jenna's room. Everything looked normal. Her usual mess looked undisturbed. A pile of mail sat on her end table. Opened mail.

He stopped to think a minute. Jenna was safe. He had no reason to look at her mail.

And yet . . .

Memories of the poor unsuspecting parents flittered through his mind. He flipped through the envelopes. Mostly junk mail. Fashion catalogs.

A plain white envelope with a post office box as a return address. Connor's breath caught and he barely managed to restrain himself from snatching it up. Instead, he went into the bathroom and grabbed two plastic baggies from under the sink and a pair of tweezers. Returning to Jenna's room, he used one plastic bag as a makeshift glove on one hand. With the tweezers, he opened the envelope.

Looked inside.

Crisp one-hundred-dollar bills mocked his thinking that Jenna was safe. Dread crawled into his midsection and put down roots.

The killer had crossed his daughter's path, left his mark on her life. Still holding the envelope with the tweezers, he grabbed up the clean bag and slipped the evidence inside. His hand shook slightly and he knew he had to get a grip on his emotions.

He sealed the bag.

Connor went to the computer and wiggled the mouse.

Password protected.

It stunned him that he didn't have a clue what Jenna would use as a password. Heart pounding, he thought for a minute, slowly processing what his brain wanted to deny.

On a whim, he typed "Julia."

Password accepted.

He went straight to her email account, not really expecting to find anything. His expectations were met.

Frustrated, he stopped. He had no idea what he was doing. Samantha would do a much better job. On the surface there weren't any suspicious emails, but Connor didn't know anything about accessing the router and seeing where Jenna had been online.

But he did know one thing.

It seemed a killer was after his daughter.

And Connor might not have much time left to make sure she remained safe.

Evidence in hand, he bolted back downstairs and looked at the calendar by the phone. The Carsons were penciled in the small block. Relief nearly blistered him. His parents were out to eat with their close friends, the Carsons. They were fine. Jenna was with Tom. She was okay . . . for now. His family was secure.

Now he needed to get back out and see

how Rick was doing. He'd heard the ambulance pull up with more vehicles arriving a few short minutes later. The crime scene crew.

Samantha greeted him with a concerned look. "Everything okay?"

He knew she meant his family. "They're not home. Out having dinner with friends. Jenna's with Tom, so everything is cool on that front." He'd tell her about the envelope in a minute.

"Rick was shot in the head." Her anger simmered not too far below the surface.

"How's he still alive?"

"Our killer approached from the front and shot through the windshield. Probably didn't want to go up to the window and give Rick a chance to realize something was wrong. The bullet just grazed him and buried itself in the back of the car. Knocked him out and he's going to have a massive headache, but at least he'll be okay." She pointed. "He had the window down, his gun is still holstered."

"He knew the person who approached him?"

"Or at least wasn't alarmed at their presence. Probably thought the guy was coming up to the window and got the shock of his life when his windshield exploded."

The ambulance whirled off with a still unconscious Rick. Samantha and Connor left the crime scene guys to their work and climbed back in Connor's sedan. His phone rang.

"Hey, Dakota, please tell me you've got something for me?"

"Yeah, I checked Jefferson Abbott's cell and home phone records. Nothing on his cell, but a call was made to the Steadwells from his home about two minutes after everyone headed for Jefferson's office with the search warrant."

"The only other person at the house was Victoria Abbott."

"Has to be her."

"Can we get another warrant to search the house again?"

"I can try, but it might not be pretty. Besides, we didn't see any signs of criminal activity when we were there earlier."

"I want the blueprints of the place. Do they have a basement?"

"Not that we can tell, but if you'll give me a minute, I'll look it up." Clicks from the keyboard came over the line. Then Dakota said, "No, no basement."

"Great. I'm going to head back out there and see what I can find. Talk to Mrs. Abbott about why she called the Steadwells."

"I can meet you there if you think you need backup."

"Come on. I can use all the help I can get."

"See you in ten."

Connor hung up and looked at Samantha. She'd followed his end of the conversation. He filled her in on the rest.

She nodded. "I also want to know about Calvin. Have we got any word back about what really happened at his house?"

"Nope, it was ruled an accident. Someone left the gas stove on when they left for the birthday party. Calvin and his son left early while his wife and daughter stayed to say goodbye and clean up. They got home, flipped the light switch on . . . ," he shrugged and looked away. "Just a stupid accident."

"Do you really believe that?"

He looked at her. "No."

Jenna swallowed hard. They'd been driving about fifteen minutes and the hair on her arms quivered. Something wasn't right about this guy. Fed or no fed. She didn't like him. Something felt wrong.

"So, Jenna," he said, "did you like the cards I sent you?"

"Cards?"

"On the computer." A bit impatient, he

glanced at her.

It clicked. "Danny? You're not Tom, *you're* Danny!"

He grinned to reveal even, white teeth. "Very good, Jenna."

She blinked, his handsome features unnerving her. She looked past them and into the depths of his eyes. Emptiness stared back at her.

Fear hit her. "What have you done with Patty?"

"Patty's fine. For now."

She closed her eyes, desperate to control her panic. *Think, Jenna, think.*

All of her dad's warnings, lectures, pleas for her to be careful started clamoring in her head. Her breathing quickened, her heart pounded. She forced herself to ignore the smothering sensation pressing on her chest and sorted through the mess in her head to focus in on what he'd told her about the case. What did she know? What could she use as an advantage that the other girls didn't have?

Her cell phone.

Her dad had mentioned they'd never been able to track the girls through their cell phones because they'd been dismantled.

"What do you want with me?"

"You backed out on me tonight."

Keep him talking.

A curving part of the highway was coming up. She shifted the backpack between her feet and the key chains rattled.

"Be still."

"I am. I've gotta use the bathroom."

He laughed. "I bet you do."

In spite of the air-conditioning, she felt the sweat drip down to pool at the small of her back. She shifted once more, facing him more fully, taking in his handsome profile and feeling revulsion sweep through her.

"Why do you do it?" Her right hand crept toward the side pocket on her pack.

He glanced her way, then back at the road that required more concentration than just a straight highway. "Do what?"

"Kill." You creep, she wanted to add, but refrained.

He pulled in a deep breath just as his phone rang. He swore and took one hand from the wheel to pat at his pocket. He located his phone and barked, "What?"

Jenna watched him frown, heard him swear again. She inched her hand closer, waited until he spoke again, and pulled the side pocket open, praying his voice would cover the scratchy sound of Velcro opening.

He glanced at her, and she raised a hand to rub her head as though trying to erase a headache.

He glanced back at the road, saying, "I'll be there shortly. Don't worry. I have our insurance policy." He looked at her one more time.

She stared back in stony silence, wondering if he could see the fear raging through her.

In one smooth movement, she slipped the phone out of the pocket and dropped it to the floorboard, all without moving her body or taking her eyes from the killer beside her.

He hung up with another curse and muttered something under his breath.

"Problems?" she asked with a sideways, sardonic glance.

"Shut up."

She really should learn to keep her mouth shut. She didn't need his attention on her if it was focused elsewhere.

He turned back to her with a snarl. "And if you try to say a word or attract the attention of anyone, I'll make sure your dad gets a bullet in the brain. Understand?"

Jenna gulped and nodded. With a small shove of her heel, she managed to work the phone under the seat. She just wished she could remember if she had it on vibrate or not.

■ ■ ■ ■

Dakota was having a hard time getting the search warrant, seeing how they pretty much had nothing to go on. Jefferson Abbott had been released and was now on his way home.

The return address on Jenna's envelope was a post office box registered to a Daniel Lucci. No surprise there. Connor had shown Samantha the evidence and she'd been as horrified as he. "When was it delivered?"

"Two weeks ago according to the stamp." He paused, then said softly, "I let her keep the computer in her room."

"What?"

"How many times have we bashed parents for letting their teenager have a computer in their bedroom?"

"A lot."

"I should have moved it when she started spending so much time at my parents' house."

"Don't beat yourself up about it, Connor."

"It's hard. I hate . . ."

She placed a hand over his, curling her fingers around his. "Connor, stop. Don't let

408

the guilt eat you up. Your parents put the computer in that room. It was already there when Jenna started staying there. If you'd moved it, you might have sent her the wrong message. That you don't trust her."

"I don't. I didn't. But now . . ."

"But as far as you knew, she hadn't done anything to cause you to be suspicious to warrant removing the computer. Besides, you can't watch her 24/7. She could have gone to the local library and done anything she wanted and you'd never know it. She's practically an adult."

"I know that too. I do. I just . . ." He sighed. "You're right. Could you give Tom a call and make sure Jenna's all right? I just want to hear that she's okay."

Poor guy. She dialed Tom's number. It went to voice mail. "Hi, Tom, Samantha here. Could you have Jenna give Connor a call? Thanks."

"No answer, huh? Wonder what that means?"

"Nothing probably. He might be on the other line. He'll call when he gets the message."

"Right. Okay."

She could tell he was still worried. Samantha dialed Jenna's number, hoping the teen would answer.

■ ■ ■ ■

Jenna dragged in a deep breath as Danny pulled into the parking lot of a deserted warehouse. He pulled around to the back and into a covered garage. He looked at her and she shivered.

"Get out."

Her muscles felt paralyzed, the fear sweeping through her sucking every ounce of strength from her. *God? God? If you're there, I need you. I want my dad, God, please send me my dad.*

She must have hesitated too long because the next thing she knew, strong fingers wrapped around her upper arm and started pulling her from her seat toward the open driver's door.

"Wait!"

"Come on, now!"

Her phone.

She tried to pull away from the clamp on her arm with no success. He was way stronger than she. Her fingers groped blindly under the seat, but no luck.

Jenna felt herself being yanked toward the door. She flung out her hand and snatched her backpack. As she landed in the driver's seat, a grunt escaped her. "Hold on. Stop!"

He just pulled harder. Keeping a death grip on her backpack, she practically fell from the vehicle. A sudden yank on her right arm nearly took it from the socket. The backpack was caught on the gearshift, hooked by one of the key chains.

Another hard pull landed it beside her. She absently noted the strong smell of wood. When she finally looked up, she could see she was somewhere in the middle of nowhere. A large warehouse-type building loomed in front of her.

"Give me that." Danny gestured to her pack.

"No." She wrapped her arms around it, wondering why she was being so stubborn. There was no way she could beat this guy in a tug-of-war.

He proved her point by taking it from her with a rough jerk. "Where's your cell phone?"

"In my backpack." Shock, fear, adrenalin all had her shivering in the ninety degree heat. She felt like she was going to puke.

Danny snarled at her to stay put and then proceeded to tear the pack apart. He glared down at her. "It's not here."

"Then I must have left it back at the camp."

"Stand up."

"What?"

He grabbed her arm and propelled her into a standing position. Jenna cringed and pushed at his hands as he patted her down. Anger swept over her and she lashed out with a right hook, catching him on the chin. His head snapped back and ignoring her throbbing knuckles, she took off running for the front of the warehouse.

Rounding the corner, she pulled up short. The gun pointed in her direction said no one was playing games.

"Get back there. Now."

Somehow, the eyes behind the gun scared her more than the man who'd snatched her and brought her here. Jenna backed up slowly. A hand entangled itself in her curls. She winced as she was half directed, half dragged back to the little garage where Danny had parked the car.

"This wasn't the arrangement we had, Daniel."

Danny shuffled his feet and looked down. The grip on her hair loosened, and she glanced between the two. Jenna thought Danny suddenly seemed to shrink into himself.

"Sorry, Boss, but her dad's getting awfully close in finding out what's going on. I needed her for insurance."

"That's two girls we now have that we didn't plan on. I hope you've got it figured out how to move them. Soon. I want them off this property. If the cops come here —"

"Even with a search warrant, they won't find them. And besides, why would they come here? How would they even know about this place?"

Jenna watched the person called Boss sigh, then say, "Get her out of sight. And make sure you don't leave any sign of her anywhere."

"Right, Boss, no problem."

26

Connor pulled into the hospital parking lot. He needed to see how Rick was doing and if the man had regained consciousness. Questions needed answers, and so far Rick was the only person who'd lived after coming in face-to-face contact with the killer.

Samantha hurried along behind him. Dakota was keeping the crime lab to the grindstone. This case had taken top priority. All available personnel had been ordered to do whatever it took to find this killer.

The media had camped out at the precinct. Neither the governor nor the mayor could leave their offices without being hounded by the press.

They wanted this case closed — yesterday.

Connor watched Samantha punch another number in her phone and listen. Tension coiled around her so tight that he thought if he touched her, she'd snap. She was worried.

"Who do you keep calling?"

"Jenna and Tom."

"Not getting through, huh?"

"No and I don't like it. Tom almost always answers his cell phone when I call. This is really not like him and it's got me concerned."

"And that worries me." He strode to the information desk and flashed his badge. "I need to find Rick Tremaine, please."

The woman raised a brow and clicked a few keys on her computer. "He was brought into the ER, but it looks like he's being transferred to a room. I don't have a room number yet."

"Of course not," Sam muttered under her breath, "why would this be easy?"

Connor heard and silently agreed. "Is there any way to find him?"

"Go to the ER and they can tell you where he is. I only have the information available as it's updated."

"Thanks."

Samantha and Connor headed down the halls, following the signs to the emergency department. Connor noticed Samantha didn't even glance at them. It occurred to him she probably knew the layout of the hospital as well as her home. From what she'd told him about Jamie, her sister had spent a lot of time here following her rescue.

Connor caught the first person in a uniform that he came to. Flashed his badge again. "Where can I find a patient who's in the process of being transferred to a room?"

"That way. Stop at the desk and ask."

Five minutes later, they were allowed back to a room. Rick was still in the ER.

Connor looked at the doctor who followed them in. "How long before he regains consciousness?"

"Hard to tell. We've run quite a few tests already. He's suffered a pretty severe head trauma, but fortunately there's only minimal swelling on the brain. He should wake up in a few hours."

Connor groaned. "I don't know that we have a few hours. He may be the only witness we have to the killer who's running around our city."

"The missing teens case?"

"Yeah."

"Man, that's tough. If I could make him wake up, I would."

Samantha sighed and pushed redial on her phone. Jenna's rang four times, then went to voice mail. Tom's just went straight to voice mail. Had he turned the phone off or was the battery dead?

Connor handed the doctor his card and

said, "If he wakes up, will you call me immediately?"

"Absolutely." He pulled out his phone and placed the card behind it. "I won't lose it that way."

Samantha intervened. "We need to find Jenna and Tom. I'm really worried now."

They exited the room making the trek back through the maze of halls to the parking lot. Connor unlocked the car. "What if the guy shot Rick, then followed Jenna to the campsite?"

"And then was surprised when she got into Tom's car?"

"Yeah. What if he waited until they were halfway home on one of those little deserted roads and —" He broke off, swallowed hard.

"I know. That scenario's been going through my head too. Or at least one of a similar vein."

"He's lost control."

"What do you mean?"

"He's turned this case personal. I should have sent her away."

"If what you say is true, it wouldn't have mattered."

"You think?"

"He would have tracked her down one way or another."

"That doesn't help much."

"I know."

"I'm going to get Dakota to track her phone."

"Good idea."

Connor got back on his phone and called Dakota. The man answered with, "I don't have anything yet, Connor, I'm only one person in a lab full of criminalists who get mad when I invade their space."

"Can you put a GPS tracker on Jenna's phone? I'm worried about her."

"Does she have it turned on?"

"Yeah."

"Give me the number."

Connor obliged and Dakota promised to call him back shortly.

As soon as he hung up, Connor's phone rang again. He vaguely recognized the number. Then he realized it was the number that Jenna had called him from at the campsite. "Hello?"

"Detective Wolfe?"

"Speaking."

"I'm a friend of Jenna's. My name's Bradley Fox."

"What can I do for you, Bradley?"

"I'm at the campsite and she asked me to wait an hour, then call her. I did, but she's not answering."

"I know, I can't reach her either."

"She said to call you if she didn't answer her phone. It was like she thought something bad was going to happen to her."

Dread crawled through Connor's midsection. "But Tom picked her up, right?"

"If that was the dude she got into the car with, yeah. I didn't catch his name. Blond-haired, good-looking guy."

"Sounds like Tom. Thanks for calling, Bradley. I'll have Jenna call you when I find her."

Connor hung up and he looked at Samantha. "I'm feeling mighty worried right now."

Samantha grabbed his hand and squeezed.

Ah, Andrew, I need you, partner. I need to bounce things off of you, I need you tell me God's going to keep my baby safe.

"Hey."

Connor looked at the beautiful woman sitting beside him.

"Whether you believe it or not, God's got it under control."

He blinked. And almost believed her.

Jenna paced the large underground room. Her prison. She looked across at the other two girls. They stared back.

Patty lay on the cot near the door, unconscious. Jenna suspected she'd been drugged with something.

Her stomach hurt. She clasped her arms across it, gripping her elbows with her hands. She'd been here all of five minutes and already she felt like she was smothering.

"Who are you?" From the girl who looked about five months' pregnant.

Jenna recognized her picture from the news. Veronica Batson, a pretty black girl who looked like she needed to gain about twenty pounds. If it weren't for the basketball-sized stomach, she'd appear skeleton thin.

"Jenna Wolfe."

"Hey, I recognize your name. You go to Stanton High, don't you?"

"Yeah." Jenna uncrossed her arms and moved to sit on an empty cot. The room was about five hundred square feet and had six beds. An open door led to a full-sized bathroom at the back. The only door in or out of the room was at the top of a flight of stairs.

"I'm Julienna Harris."

"Are you pregnant too?"

The girl flinched and said bitterly, "I don't know, but it's not for a lack of trying on their part. In vitro."

Ew. Jenna grimaced.

"So are the other girls okay? We kept hoping that one of them would tell someone where we were. Only now, they've moved us, so the others wouldn't know where to tell anyone to look."

Jenna looked at them, the expectation on their faces piercing her. They didn't know. She swallowed hard. "Uh, no, no, they couldn't tell anyone where they'd been held." That was certainly true. There was no way she was telling them that the other girls were dead. "So you guys wanted to be models too and met Danny online, right?"

Twin nods of confirmation. Jenna pounded her thigh. "We've got to figure out a way to get out of here."

"There isn't a way." Julienna shook her head, defeat crossing her pretty dark features. "Up those stairs is it. Believe me, we've tried. I believe that door's made out of soundproof material. In fact, I'm pretty sure the whole room is soundproof."

At Jenna's questioning look, she said, "My dad's a professional musician. We have a soundproof basement."

"So what's the deal? You said they moved you."

"Yeah. Yesterday. Or maybe it was today." Veronica sighed and placed both hands on her lower back, pushing her belly out. "This is not how I envisioned having my first child." Tears welled and overflowed.

Jenna felt tears of her own surface. Ruthlessly she shoved them back. Tears wouldn't get her — them — out of this.

"Is this place bugged?"

"Huh?"

"You know. Do you think they listen in on your conversations?"

"Oh." Veronica shrugged. "I don't know. I hadn't thought about it."

Julienna grunted. "I wouldn't put it past them."

A groan from the cot by the door pulled Jenna's attention to her friend. "Patty." She rushed over to her side. "Are you all right?"

"What did I drink last night?" She held a hand to her head.

Grimly, Jenna responded, "A killer cocktail."

Connor couldn't help thinking that the lawyer was the link. "We can't get the warrant on the Abbott place again, can we?"

"We've got no proof that he's involved other than that weird receipt. And we don't have a viable reason to search the man's house again."

"So, how are we going to find more evidence if we can't access his house?"

"I know. It's a catch-22."

"We need to set up some kind of sting, but there's just no time." Connor put the binoculars in between the seats and looked at Samantha. "No suspicious activity going on. The mail was just delivered."

"Is Mrs. Abbott home?"

"Yeah, I think I saw her walk in front of one of the windows a few minutes ago. But I'm not sure. Could have been the house-keeper. I guess I could go knock and see who answers the door."

"And tip them off?"

"No." He glanced at the sky. "The sun's going to start going down in a couple of hours. I wish Dakota would call with something on Jenna."

"He will. As soon as he has something."

No sooner had the words left her mouth than his phone rang. He snatched it and put it on speaker. "Yeah."

"GPS tracked Jenna's phone coming from 55 Baker Street."

A cold feeling slid through him. A street full of abandoned warehouses, run-down businesses, druggies, and hookers. Nothing good happened there.

So, he had her. Connor looked at Samantha, who'd gone pale.

They'd been right. "He's got Jenna."

"And Tom."

"Looks like it might be a distinct possibility. But how? How would he know?" He spoke into the phone once again. "How soon can we get a team over there? I'm on the way." He cranked the car.

Dakota sucked in a breath. "Connor, just because her phone is there doesn't mean Jenna is. Don't do anything stupid like try to find her without backup."

"Where's the lawyer? Do we have someone on him?"

"Yeah. Looks like he caught a flight out of town. To give the man credit, the trip had been scheduled for almost two weeks, his ticket purchased way in advance."

"Was he with anyone?"

"No, he's on his way to a conference in New York where he's the guest speaker on handling adoptions."

"Great. Just great. And no one thought to stop him?"

"For what, Connor? We have no proof, nothing at all on the guy, just suspicions."

"And we still have four missing girls that he might know the whereabouts of."

"I know, it stinks, but it's the law."

Connor breathed out and looked at Sam. "I'm going to knock on the door and see who's in the house, then we're going to get over to that warehouse."

■ ■ ■ ■

The Agent grunted and tossed Jenna's backpack into the trunk of the car. He'd have to get rid of it later. Just like he'd have to get rid of Patty and Jenna. And if Julienna wasn't pregnant yet, she could go too.

Veronica, however, he'd have to be careful with. The clients buying her baby had already forked over some big bucks. If he didn't deliver, they would cause definite problems. But it shouldn't be too hard to hide one pregnant girl. After all, he'd hidden a lot more.

27

Jenna kicked at the door and grimaced at the shooting pain. That was dumb. The girls were right. There was no way out. If only she'd been able to grab her phone. The creep had even taken her backpack. She thumped back down the steps. "How often does he come down here?"

"Not often." Veronica got up and paced from one end of the room to the other.

"What do you *do* all day?"

"It's different here," Julienna said softly. "The other place had a game room type area plus a small television where we could watch some movies."

"I pray a lot."

"Yeah, we've been doing a lot of that."

Jenna studied them. Were they serious? "Pray? And has it helped? What good is that? You're still stuck here." She didn't mean to sound so sarcastic, it just came out that way.

Veronica shrugged, stuck out her chin. "Physically I may be trapped here, but he'll never have my spirit."

Jenna just looked at her. "Huh. So, can we not overpower him somehow? There's four of us." She looked at Patty who sat on the edge of the cot holding her head. She'd already lost the contents of her stomach twice. "Okay, three of us. Why can't we gang up on him and get out of here?"

"Because he'll kill a girl."

"What?"

"If I were to attack him, he might shoot you. Or Patty. Or Julienna. He made that very clear. Are you willing to risk that?"

"You mean if I jump him . . . or we jump him . . . he would shoot someone else?"

Veronica chewed her lower lip, then nodded. "Exactly."

"Whoa." She dropped onto the bed. "Does anyone else ever come down?"

"At the other place, there was a nurse. Her name's Crystal Bennington. I haven't seen her today, though." Veronica sat in the glider across from Jenna. "She was actually pretty nice. I think she got sucked into all this by accident — at least at first. She's the one who left her cell phone on the counter and walked out of the room. I managed to text my mom but don't know if she got it or

427

not. I would have called 911, but couldn't take a chance on them not answering right away or not understanding who I was."

"Wait, wait. Back up. What exactly is 'all this'?" Jenna wanted to know.

Veronica and Julienna looked at each other.

"Come on. I'm in this now. What?"

Veronica patted her bulge. "They're making and selling babies."

Jenna blew out a breath. "So that's what you meant by 'in vitro.' "

"Yep. As near as we can figure out, they 'take orders' from couples who can't conceive for some reason, then snatch girls who look like the couple. That way they have a pretty good chance of getting a kid that looks like them."

"But that's . . ."

"Crazy? You don't have to tell me that."

She studied the girls, wondering how they'd stayed sane in this completely whacked situation. Patty raised tear-filled eyes to Jenna's, sighed, turned her back to the room, and curled into a fetal position on the bed, escaping to another reality. She'd be no help.

"I can't just sit here and wait for him to come kill me. We've got to think of something."

"What do you mean? Wait for him to come kill you?"

Jenna stared at them. How did they not know what had happened to the girls who'd been snatched by this guy? But maybe they hadn't made the connection. After all, the average teen didn't really keep up with the news and junk. Jenna did simply because her dad was often a part of it. Plus, most of the information from the first girls who'd been reported missing hadn't come out until after these girls had disappeared.

Great. "You didn't get to watch the news, did you?"

At their blank looks, she changed the subject. "What I mean is, I don't like anyone keeping me locked in a room against my will. I mean I'm going to figure out how to get out of here."

The two girls exchanged another look. Jenna read it. They wondered if she was going to do something to cause their death.

She certainly didn't want to, but if getting out of this alive meant doing something risky, she'd take risky over certain death any day.

Connor climbed back into the car. "It's just the housekeeper. So, where's Mrs. Abbott?"

"No telling. I need to give Jamie a call

and let her know Tom and I aren't going to make it to her house tonight."

"You do that. It'll be about twenty minutes before we get to Warehouse Row."

Before calling Jamie, Samantha pulled the laptop out and called Dakota. He answered on the first ring. "Dakota, can you put Jenna's GPS signal through to the laptop?"

"Sure, hang on a second."

Samantha waited, city map pulled up on the screen. Then a little red dot appeared right where Dakota said it would. Warehouse Row.

"Thanks, Dakota."

"Welcome."

She hung up. If this guy really did have Jenna, he hadn't yet discovered her phone or he would have dismantled it and the GPS wouldn't still be getting a signal.

Keeping her eye on the dot, she dialed Jamie's number. When her sister answered, she sounded distracted.

"Hey, Jamie, what are you doing?"

"Oh, Sam. Sorry, I'm working on finalizing graduation requirements and all that fun stuff."

"Listen, Tom and I aren't going to be able to make it tonight. We're still working on this case."

"I hope you're making some headway. I

haven't been much help, have I?"

"Don't worry about it and yes, we're tracking a new angle." She paused. "Could you do serious praying for Jenna, Connor's daughter?"

"She's in trouble? I'll start now."

"Thanks, Jamie. I'll catch up with you later, okay?" She didn't want to mention Tom might possibly be in the hands of a killer. No need to say anything about that yet.

"Absolutely, I'll be praying. See you later."

Samantha hung up and said, "I can't believe how far she's come lately."

"I'm glad for her. For you too."

She smiled at him, then turned back to the computer. "He hasn't found her phone yet."

"I'm trying to think of what information Jenna might have overheard me talking about or what I might have said to her." He slapped a hand against the wheel in frustration. "I'm drawing a blank."

"You're worried."

"Scared spitless."

"Jamie's praying."

He looked at her. "I am too."

Pacing the floor, The Agent pondered his next move. He stood at the window and looked out. A car drove past. One he thought he recognized. What? Slowly, it turned into the deserted parking lot and around to the back.

Connor and Samantha! How had they found this place? Thank goodness he'd had the dumb luck to be standing in the window and spotted the car, otherwise . . .

A string of curses flew from his lips as he whirled from the window. They probably had a SWAT team on the way. He'd be trapped.

How in the —

Jenna's phone. She'd lied. Managed to hide it somewhere and they tracked it to here.

He thought. It wasn't in her backpack. It wasn't anywhere on her person.

Only one place it could be.

His car.

Clamoring down the steps, he raced into what had been renovated into a makeshift kitchen. *Think, think.*

He grabbed a knife from the wooden block. *Don't panic. You're in control.*

But he wasn't. For the first time since he'd gotten into this, he wasn't in control anymore. Placing both hands on the counter, he studied the knife.

A plan formed.

He had to get rid of the evidence. Fast.

Samantha curled her fingers around the butt of her gun and kept her eyes glued on the door in front of her. Movement sounded from the room behind it. Connor caught her eye and nodded.

They really should wait for backup, but Samantha knew Connor's thoughts were on Jenna, worry eating him from the inside out. On the other hand, if they walked into something beyond what the two of them could handle, it wouldn't do Jenna much good.

Samantha glanced at her watch. Backup should be here at any moment. Two steps farther in and she could see out the nearest window. Four police cars pulled in.

Before she or Connor had a chance to react, the door flew open and a bloodied figure stumbled out.

"Tom!"

She holstered her gun and ran to his side. She grabbed his arm to hold him up. "What happened to you?"

He weaved, leaning heavily on her. Connor slipped to the other side of the man and held on tight. "Where's Jenna?"

"I . . . I don't know. I lost her. Guy jumped me at a rest area. Stole my car. But

I grabbed a cab and managed to track Jenna's phone here. I called Marty at the FBI office, and she pulled up Jenna's phone on the GPS and directed me here. When I got here, they were in the kitchen. Guess I should have called for backup." He grimaced.

Samantha saw the color drain from Connor's face. "Marty didn't say anything about your call."

Tom shrugged, then groaned in obvious pain. "Oh, wait. It wasn't Marty. I don't remember who I talked to." He swayed, and Sam clung to his arm.

"Come on, we'll hash this all out after you've seen a doctor," she grunted. "We've got to get you some medical attention."

"Don't tell me. They're already gone," Connor said.

"Yeah. He got me with the knife." Tom raised a hand to his head. "I fell and cracked my head. Next thing I know, you're here."

Connor spoke into his radio. "Secure the area. We need an ambulance."

Tom protested. "No. I don't need an ambulance."

"I'll ride with you." Connor tossed Samantha his keys and went on like Tom hadn't spoken. "I'll also need a statement from you. Samantha, you can meet me at the hospital."

"You might as well go. He's not going to take no for an answer," Samantha told Tom as her cell phone rang.

Jamie. "Hey, what's up?"

"I just wanted to check in with you and see what was developing. I knew if you couldn't talk, you wouldn't answer. Is Jenna okay?"

"No, not really. Unfortunately, she's missing right now." Fear for the girl crowded her throat and she swallowed. "Tom's hurt and on the way to the hospital."

"What?!"

"Yeah, I'll fill you in later."

"Tell Tom I'll meet him there."

"I'm sure he'll appreciate that."

Sam hung up and watched the crime scene guys get to work.

Connor was beginning to believe that it was actually possible to go stark-raving mad from worry. Samantha had stayed at the scene. He went with Tom to the hospital. Once the guy was patched up, he wanted to be able to talk to him in minute detail about everything that had happened.

Hang on, Jenna, baby, I'm coming. Daddy's coming. Horrible visions clouded his mind, and it was all he could do not to scream.

He didn't want to be riding to the hospital, he wanted to be searching for Jenna. But Tom was the only person who'd come into contact with the guy killing girls and lived through it — except for the unconscious cop. Talking to Tom might net him that one clue that would lead him to his daughter.

And the killer.

He had to be patient, be smart.

At the hospital, Connor followed the gurney into the emergency department.

"Connor?"

He turned. "Jamie. Hey, how are you?"

"I'm all right, thanks. I've been praying for Jenna."

His throat worked. "Thank you."

"Is Tom in there?"

"Yeah, they're stitching him up."

"Do you think they'll keep him?"

Connor shrugged. "I don't know. It's possible. I know he conked his head and was unconscious for a while."

She grimaced. "Ouch."

"Detective Connor Wolfe?"

Connor stood. "Yeah, that's me."

The doctor walked over. "He's going to be spending the night. I want to keep an eye on him due to the head trauma. He'll be up in a room in about fifteen minutes if you want to meet him there. Room 525."

"Thank you."

Jamie popped up. "Do you mind if I come with you?"

"No, I'm sure Tom would be glad to see you."

They walked to the elevator and made their way up to the room to wait.

Samantha had a feeling they were missing something. They'd found Tom's car parked around the back in a small storage building. Jenna's phone along with her backpack had been recovered. The car had been impounded and any fingerprints found would be run through AFIS, the Automated Fingerprint Information System. Hopefully, there would be a match.

Before they could adequately finish the search of the area and the grounds surrounding it, the sun sank below the horizon, encasing her side of the world in darkness.

She wanted to get to the hospital, but before she left, she called Connor. "They're going to keep at it, but there's no way to make sure we've gotten everything, even with the artificial lights. We'll have to go over it again in the morning light too."

"I'll arrange to have third shift officers keep watch overnight. I don't want our guy coming back and trying anything funny."

"Fine, I'm on the way to the hospital."
But first she'd call the prayer chain at her
church.

Oh Lord, please keep Jenna safe.

Samantha was tired. A bone-deep weariness stalked her. When this case was resolved
and Jenna was safe, Sam planned to sleep
for a week.

Back to business.

She left the warehouse and crawled into
Connor's car to head to the hospital.

Jenna kept the scream from erupting by
sheer willpower. She'd never been a weak
person. According to her dad, from the time
she could talk, her favorite word was "no."

She used it now. No, she would not
scream. No, she would not pace. No, she
would not give in to the panic threatening
to consume her.

No, no, no, no . . .

"Do they bring you food?" Patty sat up
abruptly. "Or are we just going to be left
here to starve to death?"

Veronica's eye twitched. "Yes, they
brought us food, obviously. But here . . . I
don't know. We haven't been here long
enough for me to know what they're going
to do. But they planned this."

"What do mean? I thought they ran from

the other place not to get caught."

"They did, but this was no doubt their backup plan in case something went wrong with the original setup."

"And you know this . . . how?"

"The panic button."

"Come again?" Jenna wished the girl would just spit it out.

"Right there." She pointed to a red button on the wall by the foot of the stairs.

Jenna examined it. "What does that do?"

"It means one of the pregnant girls is in trouble or labor and it brings them running. But no one dares to push it without a good reason. He's already warned us of that."

"What would happen if I pushed it and no one was in trouble?"

"He'd punish someone."

"Who?"

"There's no way to know, but he'd cause someone a lot of pain. Most likely one of you three."

Great big tears filled Patty's eyes. "I don't want to stay here. I don't want to have a baby. I don't want to die. I want to leave!" She jumped up to race up the stairs and pound on the door.

Jenna sighed, heart clenching for her friend. Feeling partially responsible for her friend's predicament, she rose from her spot on the bed and went after her.

"Patty. Stop. You're wasting your energy. Stop."

She tried to put an arm around the girl, but she wasn't having it. Patty whirled so fast she nearly knocked Jenna back down the steps.

"Patty, watch it!"

"This is your fault," she sobbed. "All your fault."

Indignation welled up. "Hey, you're the one who messed with my phone and told Danny you'd meet him. So don't go blaming this on me."

She stomped back down the stairs, wanting to blister the air with curses. Instead, she clamped her teeth into her lower lip and held on to her fragile control.

Veronica and Julienna just sat there watching all the commotion.

Jenna stopped and asked, "How do you guys just . . . sit?"

"Not much choice. When you've been locked up as long as we have, you just kind of . . . make do. Adjust."

"I'd go insane."

"Or that."

Wondering if she was joking, Jenna looked into Veronica's eyes. She wasn't. "Who brings the meals?"

"Usually Danny. Occasionally, the nurse, Crystal. I've seen this other woman every once in a while, but don't know who she is."

Jenna paced, thinking. What would her dad do in this situation?

First of all, he wouldn't have been dumb enough to land in this situation, but if he did, what would he do?

Figure out how to get out of it. Patty came back down the steps and brushed past Jenna to fling herself across the nearest bed.

Jenna ignored her, thinking. "What would he do if I got sick? If I were bleeding or dying and needed medical attention?"

Veronica eyed her. "If it was beyond Crystal's ability to help you and you weren't pregnant yet — or you're an unplanned complication causing him trouble, he'd probably just let you die."

Lovely.

Jenna's gaze landed on Veronica's stomach.

"What?" Veronica asked, wariness oozing from her.

"What if it were you?"

The girl wasn't slow. "If it were beyond Crystal's expertise, he'd get me medical help. Somehow."

"Because he's got a lot of money riding

on Junior there, I'd bet."

Veronica nodded slowly, dark eyes flashing. "I hadn't thought about it. Actually have done everything not to think about it. But yeah, you're right."

"Okay, here's the plan."

28

By midnight, there'd been nothing new from any direction. Samantha paced as she took refuge in her apartment. They'd agreed to meet again at dawn. Connor had gone home to break the news to his parents about Jenna's disappearance.

Jamie decided to stay at the hospital and watch over Tom, who hadn't bothered to call his siblings to let them know what had happened. And had refused to allow anyone else to call them either.

"It's not a big deal. I've been hurt a lot worse."

Unfortunately, Tom hadn't had a lot to offer in the way of leads on his attacker. He'd been surprised from behind, yanked from the vehicle as he'd stopped to get gas, and tossed to the ground. The assailant had jumped into the idling vehicle and taken off — with the car and Tom's cell phone.

He explained that he managed to get to a

pay phone and call the FBI office to get a trace on Jenna's phone and a cab to get him back on the road. Once in the cab, he hadn't had time to stop and find a way to contact Samantha and Connor.

Tomorrow, Samantha and Connor would retrace Tom's steps to see if they could find someone who saw something. Until then, she might as well try to sleep.

Samantha's phone rang. She looked at the clock: 12:40.

This wouldn't be good.

With a sigh, she answered it.

"Hey, Jamie, what's up?"

Hesitantly, worried, Jamie answered. "I . . . I'm not sure. I need you to come by the hospital tomorrow when you can, all right?"

"Sure, you want to tell me what's wrong?"

"Well, that's the problem, I'm not sure anything is wrong. But there may be. I just need a little more time to figure out for sure."

"You know you're being aggravatingly vague here."

A small chuckle filtered through the line. "I know and I don't mean to, but I wanted to catch you and ask you to stop by sometime tomorrow."

"Not a problem. I'll probably head over

to the crime scene first, then come by. All right?"

"Thank you, Sam."

The Agent grunted as he shifted and thought about how to handle the coming morning. Boss had already taken care of the girls. And Boss had told him not to worry about anything but covering his tracks.

He glanced at his cell phone sitting on the end table. An FBI operative had brought one by to replace the one he'd tossed to ensure he didn't have it on him in case something went wrong. And boy, had something gone wrong. The only loose end was that he'd been stupid enough to say he'd called someone at the FBI to trace Jenna's phone. Hopefully, no one would check that out. And if they did . . . well, he'd be long gone before then.

Calling Boss might have been a mistake too, but it couldn't be helped. Too much money rode on this, and he needed Boss to care for the girls until he could get back there undetected.

Officers were guarding the warehouse while the CSU team searched it. He wracked his brain trying to think if there was any possible way someone could find the entrance to the underground room and locate the girls.

He didn't think so. It had been especially made for the purpose it was being used for. Plan B. Fury stirred within him at the fact that Plan A had been disrupted. Everything had been going along so nicely.

Until Crystal's betrayal.

But he'd taken care of her.

A scalpel to the throat had shut her up for good. He'd seen the news covering her death. But there'd been no mention of the basement in the house at the farm. No mention of her death being related to the missing girls. And no mention of her working at the doctor's office where she'd made sure the girls he'd snatched were appropriate for their needs.

And he knew they knew.

The authorities were playing with their cards held tight against their chests, not offering much in the way of information about the investigation, but warning parents to keep tabs on their kids and admonishing teens not to meet strangers over the internet.

The Agent smiled for the first time that day.

But they never listened.

Because it could never happen to them.

At least that's what they thought.

Until they met him.

And then he changed lives.

It was as simple as that.

Sunday morning, Samantha hated to skip church, but she had a case to solve. Her gut told her the end was in sight and she wanted to be there for Connor — however the ending played out.

She did take time to pause for about five minutes and have a heart to heart with God, asking for Jenna's safety and Connor's peace of mind. And that they would find the rest of the girls alive.

Then she slipped out the door into the still-dark morning, climbed in her car, and headed for the precinct. Jamie's comment about checking into something surfaced in Samantha's thoughts. She made a mental note to follow up on it — whatever it was, her sister had sounded worried.

Samantha made her way to the conference room where the task force would plan out the day. The crime scene guys should be on their way back to the scene to examine it more fully as soon as the sun made its appearance.

Entering the room, she pulled up short. Connor was already there, looking drawn and haggard. She doubted he'd slept the night before. Probably spent the wee hours of the morning going over all the evidence — or the lack thereof.

She laid a hand on his shoulder and he looked up. "How you doing?"

He released a sigh. "Hanging in there. Praying."

"Really?"

"Really."

"So you don't blame God for this? Feel like he's out to get you?"

He flinched. "No. For some reason I don't."

"God's grace is sufficient."

"What?"

"It means don't question it, just accept it, be thankful for it. He's there with Jenna no matter what. He wouldn't let her go through this alone. He won't let you either."

"That why he sent me you, huh?"

Shivers quivered through her. Not touching that one — yet. Later? Definitely worth exploring. The rest of the team filtered in and Samantha put her personal agenda on the back burner. "So, what's the plan?"

Dakota set a folder in front of him as he took a seat. "The warehouse is owned by a corporation called Steam Liners. The corporation went out of business about a year ago, and the warehouse has been empty since."

"Do you have the name of an individual?"

"Not yet. The information's been buried pretty deep. I've got a contact gradually peeling back the layers. He should have me the information within a couple of hours."

"Great." Connor stood. "Call me when you get it, will you?"

"Sure. You need some help at the scene?"

"All the help I can get. I just have a feeling we're missing something obvious."

"Then let's get out there and find it."

Twenty minutes later, they stood on the fringes watching the crime scene unit do their thing. Connor ducked under the tape and Dakota followed him.

Samantha walked over to the single garage where Tom's car had been found. Decidedly curious about what was bugging Jamie, she glanced at her watch. She considered pulling her phone out to call, then decided to give it a little more time. Jamie might not be up yet.

The car had already been moved to the lab, so she examined the area around it. The garage was small, not even really a garage, but more like a storage space that had been converted into a parking spot.

So, did that mean someone had come here often?

If so, what kind of business did that

someone have in an empty warehouse?

Nothing good, that was for sure.

The single bulb hanging from the ceiling didn't do much in the way of illumination, so she panned her flashlight over the walls. The floor.

Nothing.

Connor came up beside her. "Anything?" He added his light to hers.

"No. The car was here long enough to leak some oil." She indicated the fresh wet stain on the dirty concrete floor.

Connor sat on his haunches. "Jake called me earlier. Nothing was found in the car except DNA and fingerprints belonging to Jenna and Tom. I keep feeling like I'm missing something."

"I know. I'm right there with you on that one."

He swept the beam back to the edge of the wall and stood. "What's that?"

"What?"

"There. I caught a glint of something metal, I think."

Samantha stepped carefully, following him over to the other side of the garage. He stooped and she heard his swiftly indrawn breath.

"What is it?"

He pulled a pen out of his shirt pocket.

Using it to lift the object, he held it up for her to see.

She focused her flashlight on it. "A key chain."

"Not just any key chain. Jenna's."

"What's it doing here? She kept those on her backpack, right?"

"Yeah."

"Wasn't her backpack in the trunk of the car?"

"That's what they said."

"Then it was out of the car at one point." Connor studied the object, then said softly, "She fought him."

"Why do you say that?"

"The ring's bent."

"A tug-of-war over the pack?"

"Probably. Jenna's mom gave her those key chains. Keeping them with her was like keeping a part of her mother with her. She wouldn't have given them up easily."

"Let's keep searching."

The bathroom didn't inspire Jenna. Although dingy and musty, it was clean enough only because of the girls' efforts.

Think like your dad, Jenna.

All of his warnings, the six years of self-defense classes, games that included finding a weapon where none existed, came rolling through her mind in endless waves.

The towel rack.

The ceramic toilet bowl cover.

All possibilities. She'd slept last night in fits after dinner was delivered by the woman. Jenna hadn't recognized her, and she hadn't seen Danny since he'd dragged her down here. There'd been no sign of Crystal, the nurse the girls had told her about.

So, she'd curled up on one of the beds, forming plans and discarding them only to come back to the original idea she'd had earlier.

Soft music wafted from one of the other beds.

Veronica.

The girl had some pipes on her and sang constantly. Sang music about being rescued by her God, being saved by Jesus. Instead of mocking her, Jenna started listening. To the music, to the words, to the love. She thought about Samantha when Veronica sang. And Maria. And Bradley.

And her grandparents. Her heart ached at the thought of their suffering, wondering what happened to her. At her dad's agony. Losing one more person he loved.

And he did love her. She knew that.

Um, God? I know we haven't exactly been on good terms. And I guess that's my fault.

But do you think you could get us out of this so you and I could have a chance to get to know each other? Cuz I want to. Um, amen.

Patty had crawled into her mind somewhere and simply lay on her bed, staring at the ceiling, her eyes vacant, hopeless. Jenna shook her head. Not her. She'd fight to the bitter end.

The bed.

Another idea took shape.

Swinging her legs over the side of the bed, she wondered what time it was. She wanted this over with by breakfast.

One way or another.

Was she prepared to die?

For the first time, she seriously considered the fact that she might not make it. Might not live through this experience. Even in the car with Danny, she hadn't allowed her mind to think along those lines.

But now . . .

Julienna snored softly. Veronica continued to sing.

And Jenna went to work.

The Agent ate his breakfast with an outward appearance of calm. On the inside, impatience clawed at him. He needed to get to the girls, to check on Veronica, but couldn't get away from his current situation without raising eyebrows.

He had to play it low key.

Another bite of stiff eggs. Methodical chewing while he thought.

Boss was already telling him to get his act together and get his tail over to the warehouse. The cops were combing the place.

But it didn't matter. They wouldn't find the underground room. It was near the warehouse, true, but the way in was hidden from sight. However, Boss couldn't manage the girls alone. Now that Crystal was dead, The Agent needed to do even more, help out until he could find someone to replace Crystal. Because no one could find out who Boss was or everything would come crashing down.

The girls would just have to be patient.

"You'll never guess who the warehouse traced back to."

Still combing the garage for every last piece of evidence he could find, Connor looked up from Jenna's key chain to see Dakota at the entrance, blocking the sun, Stetson pulled low. His jeans rode low on his hips and his cell phone practically disappeared in the depths of his large hand.

"Who?"

"Our lawyer friend, Jefferson Abbott, who

is one of the founders of Steam Liners Corporation."

"Let's arrest this dude as soon as he steps off his plane."

"You're assuming he's coming back."

"He's coming back. He left too much here. I checked up on him again and the conference where he's speaking is definitely legit. And according to his secretary, he's also got several adoption cases that need to be wrapped up in the next few days. He's got a lot of money coming in over the next two weeks."

"All right. Let's nab him."

"I had his bank records and everything pulled. I gotta tell you, other than that warehouse and basically all the evidence pointing to him, this guy comes across clean."

Connor shot Dakota a dirty look. "That's helpful."

Dakota shrugged. "Sorry."

"It's not helping me find Jenna, though."

And although Connor was doing a pretty good job of keeping his focus on the case, keeping his cool on the outside, the worry, fear, and continuous mental pictures of finding his daughter killed by some psycho boiled within him.

"Just telling you what I know."

■ ■ ■ ■

It was time. Jenna's stomach told her it was breakfast time. The girls had agreed to the plan.

Well, most of them. Patty wasn't too keen on the idea, but once she realized Jenna was going to do it whether she helped or not, she pitched in her muscle.

Sweat stood out on Veronica's forehead, and she looked scared to death. That was okay. Jenna knew exactly how she felt. Patty paced and chewed all her fingernails down to the quick, reverting back to a childhood habit.

Hope and excitement stood out on Julienna's face.

Jenna couldn't believe no one had tried anything like this before. Wimps.

Then she felt bad. She was scared too.

"He killed Sydney, you know."

Veronica's soft voice filtered through the fog of Jenna's scrambling thoughts. With a final grunt, she gave the bed one more push.

Jenna stood and wiped the sweat from her neck. It was hot. She hadn't noticed the heat before. Ignoring Veronica's statement, she asked, "Hey, how does the air circulate in here?"

The girls looked at each other, then Juli-enna and Veronica shrugged.

Stupified, Jenna just stared at them. Did these girls not ever go to the movies? Read novels? What was the deal?

Whatever. She didn't have time to think about it.

Because the next person who came through that door was going to earn himself a bad headache.

29

Samantha pulled her phone out, ready to give Jamie a call, but a hand on her arm stopped her.

Connor.

Weariness and anxiety oozed from him, and she wished she could offer him some kind of comfort. However, she knew words wouldn't suffice. "You find anything?"

"No." He looked around. "I'm going to look outside the crime scene area. Look at the tape. It's wrapped around convenient stuff. That tree, the pole over there." He shook his head. "Sometimes you've got to think outside the box. Or in this case, look outside the tape."

"I'll help."

He raised a hand to her cheek for a brief moment before turning toward the tape and ducking under it.

Cheek tingling, she followed.

"See this path? It looks worn."

"True, but it could have been here for ages."

"I know." But he had to hope, had to feel like he was doing something to track down his daughter's kidnapper. "I wish Andrew were here."

His pain cut her. "He's here. In your heart. You're running a conversation about this whole case with him in your head, aren't you?"

His startled jump and shocked stare made her shrug.

"You're not so hard to read, Connor."

The key sounded in the lock. Jenna tensed. Veronica's eyes went wide with fear and Patty whimpered. Julienna trembled but held firm.

The door swung open. "All four of you where I can see you, now."

Dutifully, the girls lined up. The woman came down with the tray filled with grilled cheese sandwiches and fruit. The door snapped shut behind her.

Heart in her throat, Jenna waited. And waited.

"Remember, I've got someone waiting on me. Back up."

Jenna's lips thinned in anticipation. Just a little farther.

One more step.

Then Jenna pulled.

And the bed came crashing down, knocking into the woman. A howl of outrage and pain had Jenna and the other girls scrambling for the stairs.

Freedom. Jenna could practically taste it.

Patty reached the top first, threw open the door, and came face-to-face with a black gun.

The Agent stared at the girl backpedaling down the steps, practically taking the rest of them with her. Anger, fueled by a desperate need not to get caught, had his finger curling around the trigger.

With sheer force of will, he loosened it. Glared at the one he was sure had been in charge of this little escape attempt. Slowly, he made his way down the steps. Stepped over the woman. She was either dead or unconscious. He'd figure that out in a minute.

Wide, fearful eyes stared back at him. Veronica and Julienna looked scared yet resigned. They knew. They'd seen.

But these two. They didn't know. He'd have to teach them.

Through gritted teeth, he said, "Sit. Down."

They sat.

Jenna stared up at him, fear and defiance stamped clearly on her pretty face.

The Agent turned the gun to her. "It's time to teach you some obedience."

Fear overrode the defiance and she flinched. Then shot him a glare that should have singed him. She lifted her chin. "Fine. Whatever. It's better than being stuck here with you."

Sucking in a deep breath, The Agent clamped down on his fury. He'd teach the little brat a lesson if it's the last thing he did. An idea slowly formed. He'd seen the investigators processing the scene in the warehouse. Fortunately, this little bungalow was hidden away in a grove of trees surrounding it. The underground room perfect for a short-term stay for the girls. Just until he had another place ready. In another state, far away from here.

But for now, he had to take care of this mess. Jenna backed away. The Agent slowly stalked her. He watched her chest rise and fall. Good, she was scared. She should be.

But not for herself.

He placed the gun under her chin.

Patty squealed. Veronica clamped a hand over her mouth.

"Guess what, little girl?" he singsonged.

"Daddy's here."

Confusion flickered through the fear.

"Oh yeah, that's right. The big man himself is just about half a block away from here."

Hope brightened her eyes.

The Agent smiled. Now for the fun part. "And I'm going to sneak through these woods and shoot him in the head. Shoot him dead just like I killed Andrew."

Nostrils flared as he watched her reaction. Then something happened. The fear dissipated right in front of him. She relaxed, narrowed her eyes, then every muscle in her body went rigid as she clenched her fists and drew in a deep, controlled breath through her nose. He watched her anger build . . . and build.

And wondered if he'd finally met his match in one of the girls. One he couldn't intimidate or have cowering at his feet.

Huh. Interesting. Intrigued, he backed off a little, but growled, "I'll be back with Daddy's head on a platter. Give me about an hour."

She had to save her dad.

"You're going to kill us all!" Patty shrieked.

Jenna turned to her friend. "Then you'd

better hold that shower curtain a little tighter." Jaw clenched, Patty held it while Jenna taped it. She'd rummaged in the bathroom and found some painter's tape, pulled the shower curtain down, and formed another plan. This one she'd thought of after coming up with the "killer bed" idea, but had discarded it because she hadn't known if anyone would notice and she would've been taking the chance of burning the building down around them.

But now she knew her dad was out there. And close by.

"What are you doing?"

"Playing Indian." She grunted and ripped another strip of tape from the roll. She'd used a ragged edge of metal from one of the bed frames to tear the shower curtain plastic into a square, large enough to cover the air vent. Three sides were now taped up. She'd tape the fourth one after she had everything going.

After his threat to kill her dad, Danny had grabbed the woman on his way up the steps, lifted her head, examined her face, then let it drop. Had he assumed she was dead? The woman hadn't moved; the cut from her head was bleeding pretty bad. Jenna didn't care. She hoped she either woke up with the mother of all headaches or didn't wake up at all.

Wishing for some good old-fashioned gasoline, she twisted the cap on the bathroom cleaner. The label said, "Keep away from open flame." Hopefully that meant it would burn. She poured some on the sheets she'd ripped up and twisted into a rope.

Then she stood on the chair and stuffed them through the air vent. She'd managed to pull off the covering. It had been loose anyway, so all she'd had to do was grab it and pull. Her shoulder ached where she'd fallen off the chair when it had come loose, but she ignored the pain. If she didn't get out of here, she'd be feeling more than an aching shoulder, that she was sure of.

Next, she had to see if she had any skills left from her Girl Scout days. The beds were made of wood. Old dry, splintering wood. She stripped off several pieces.

"Now what are you doing?" Julienna asked, scared, but curiously hopeful at the same time.

Veronica just kept her lips pressed in a tight line. But she, too, couldn't hide the hope that Jenna would get them out of there before Danny came back.

"My dad is out there looking for me. I need to give him something to find."

"And burning down the building is a good

way to do that? So he can find our charred bones after the firemen get through putting out the fire?" Patty asked, sarcasm dripping.

"I'm actually hoping he gets here before all that."

Patty just groaned. "All right, what do you want me to do?"

"Thank you, Patty. I'm going to start a fire and I need you to hold that piece of sheet that I soaked in cleaner over the flame when I get it started. Then I'm going to burn the sheets in the air vent, praying like crazy some of the smoke makes it out whatever opening is allowing the air to come through to us."

Patty took up her spot and Jenna sat on the floor to get busy. She placed a piece of wood about the size of her palm on the floor, then grabbed up one of her longer pieces — a spindle that would hopefully work perfectly. Placing it on the block, she began rubbing it between her hands, creating as much friction as possible.

"How in the world is that going to start a fire?"

"It creates friction which generates heat which will soon give me the spark I need to catch this piece of cloth on fire." She hoped. "I'm going to need you guys to trade out with me. We need to take turns rubbing this, because it's going to take a while, and if I get tired, I'm going to slow down. Okay, Patty, put that cloth near the stick."

Patty did. And Jenna rubbed.

She'd been the only one in her troop to ever start a fire this way.

She just prayed she could do it again.

Connor kicked the brush away, going deeper into the woods. He stooped.

Samantha ran a hand through her hair and sighed. "You think we're doing any good here?"

"I think she's around here somewhere, Sam. He definitely brought her here. We tracked her phone pretty fast. He hasn't had time to move her."

"We've been over the building. The Heat-Seeker would have picked them up, but it didn't, just a few rats." If Jenna had been anywhere nearby, The AimShot HeatSeeker would have found them. Thermal imaging heat seekers, the latest in firefighting technology.

But nothing. That didn't bode well for Jenna.

Connor rubbed a hand over his jaw. "I know."

"Listen, I need to call Jamie. She's been waiting to discuss something . . ." Samantha stopped. Sniffed the air. "Do you smell that?"

"What?"

"Smoke?"

"Yeah, where's it coming from?"

"Over there. This isn't the time of year to build a fire to cozy up to, that's something else. Come on."

"Jake!" Connor hollered. The big man stopped what he was doing and looked up. Connor motioned for him to follow. A frown furrowing his brows, Jake said something to the woman with him and took off after Connor.

Finding where the smoke was coming from took a little doing, but he finally located the source. A small cabin set back in the woods.

"Who does this cabin belong to?" Connor demanded.

"I don't have any idea."

"I'm going in. There might be someone in there." Jenna might be in there. But with smoke coming from a house, he had every right to be concerned and enter the premises without waiting on a search warrant. Someone's life could be in danger.

Like Jenna's.

"I'm right behind you," Jake promised.

"I'm calling the fire department guys to

get back over here. And then I'm going to see if Dakota can find out who this place belongs to." Samantha grabbed her phone and started dialing.

Connor kicked the wooden door in and found himself in a kitchen that looked like it had been recently used.

"Police! We're here to help! Anyone here?"

The Agent wanted to scream, curse, and basically lose control. He wanted to kill them all. But he couldn't try it here. It was too risky, too many trees. And if he pulled the trigger, he needed the bullet to find its mark the first time.

Because there would be no second chances. Not with this man.

That brat had brought them to her. It wouldn't be long now and they'd find them and Boss. Should he have gotten her out? Pulled her from the room?

No.

The Agent had lost all respect for Boss. After all, she'd allowed the girls to almost escape. Would she give him away? He fingered the gun and considered whether he actually needed her anymore. He could wait until the police brought her up from the room, then pop her between the eyes.

Maybe.

Maybe not.

They'd figure out who he was shortly. He had no doubt Jenna would describe him down to every last detail. He grimaced. Great.

He gave a last, lingering look at the cops swarming Plan B. He gave in to the curses, beating the steering wheel until he'd bruised his hand. Finally, he calmed, breathing hard, but back in control.

He began to think again.

For now, he needed to find a hotel room. Then maybe he'd call his sister and see if she could put him up for a night or two. Just until he could figure out what to do next.

And then he'd have to figure out how to get Veronica away from the police. She had something that belonged to him, and there was no way he was letting her get away with keeping that baby. No, he'd get his hands on her one way or another.

And take care of Jenna and her dad in the meantime. And if Samantha got in the way, he'd kill her too.

Samantha pocketed her phone and pulled her gun from the holster. Jamie would just have to wait a little longer. Instead of following the gang inside, she walked the perimeter of the house, looking for an alternative entrance. The drive led up to the back of the house.

Empty.

Tire tracks, though, embedded in the mud beside the gravel. Whoever had pulled in had done so carelessly. Good. She pulled a crime scene tag from her pocket and dropped it onto the spot beside the track. Any cop coming this way would see it and avoid trampling the area.

Keeping her eyes open, she panned the wooded area. Nothing moved. Once she'd circled the house, she came back to the kitchen door. Entering, she made her way through to the small attached carport. The door swung open. Left by someone leaving in a hurry?

Smoke swirled, but it wasn't overwhelming. Recent footprints had stirred the dust on the floor.

The door slammed behind her and she whirled, lifting her weapon.

Connor stood just inside the carport door. He held his hands up, gun pointed toward the ceiling. "It's just me."

She lowered the gun, heart pounding. "You could give a girl some warning."

"Sorry, I didn't realize you were out here. I couldn't see you from the door."

"Did you find the source of the smoke?"

"No, and I didn't find anyone else either. The house is empty. It's been cleared. The fire squad's back going over it with a fine-tooth comb."

She nodded and pointed to another door sharing the wall with the main one that led back into the kitchen. "Wonder where that door goes? It looks a little out of place. Out of alignment with the house."

"Let's find out."

Sam stepped to the side, raising her gun, mimicking Connor's previous position right before he'd entered the carport area. Connor stood opposite her. With one hand, he reached out and twisted the knob.

Locked.

Raising a brow, he knocked on it.

Instantly someone banged from the other side.

Hope bloomed on his features.

"Jenna!"

Motioning for Samantha to step back, Connor raised his gun and blew the door-knob off. He punched the remaining part through the hole on the other side. Smoke drifted through the open space.

"Dad?" A faint voice came to them. "Dad!"

"Jenna! Stand back, I'm going to kick the

471

door in." To Samantha he said, "Hinges are on this side. I don't know if I'm going to be able to do much damage."

Samantha heard nothing. "You think it's soundproofed? Seems like we should be able to hear her a little better."

"Could be." He took a breath, then put his mouth to the hole and repeated his instructions. "Stand back!"

Several kicks later, he shook his head. "I need the ram. This is one strong door."

The battering ram. He called for one, and within seconds, the door was down, smoke billowing out.

"Jenna!"

"Dad!"

The stairs led directly down. Connor started to follow them, but stopped when his daughter appeared from the midst of the smoke and threw herself, coughing and gasping, into his waiting arms.

30

Back at the precinct, Connor watched happy parents gather their girls close. Veronica's mother and father had been shocked to see her extended belly, but it hadn't stopped them from yanking her into a never-ending hug.

Julienna's mom simply held her daughter and wept. Her father was flying in from California so it would take a while for him to get here.

Patty sat in one of the chairs, her legs drawn up tight to her chest. She stared at the commotion with empty eyes. Her parents were taking their own sweet time about getting here. Connor worried about that one.

Jenna seemed relieved. She'd clung to him like a leech for the first few minutes after coming up out of that room, but now seemed to be working through the experience. She was mad, furious, but he knew when that wore off she'd need to have a good cry.

And he'd be there to hold her.

He walked to the room next door and looked through the glass at the woman holding an ice pack to her battered head.

Victoria Abbott.

Who would have thought?

Connor shook his head and returned to the room he'd just vacated. Mrs. Abbott wasn't going anywhere. He'd let her stew for a bit.

The sketch artist worked with each girl individually.

It was Jenna's turn. Connor went with her ready to hang over her shoulder and watch the face materialize. He wanted to see this guy the minute the artist was done.

Samantha motioned that she would close up shop here with the families.

Then they would have to make plans how to catch the killer still on the loose.

Samantha sat back and swiped a few tears. She loved happy endings. However, she knew it wasn't finished yet. And she still had to call Jamie.

And get something to eat. She was starving.

While Connor and Jenna worked with the

sketch artist, Samantha pulled her phone out and dialed her sister's cell phone, assuming she'd still be at the hospital with Tom.

"Hello?"

"Jamie, hi, it's me. I'm sorry it's taken me so long to call, but we found the girls."

A gasp. "You're kidding!"

"Turn the television on. You and Tom can watch the celebration together."

"So, you caught the killer?" Confusion echoed in Jamie's voice.

"Um. No. We didn't. Not yet. But we've gotten the girls reunited with their families. All except Sydney Carter, and unfortunately, even though we haven't found her body yet, Veronica and Julienna say that Danny killed her."

A long pause.

"Jamie? Are you there?"

"I'm here. I'm just trying to figure out how to tell you something."

Wariness crept up Samantha's spine. "What? Just spit it out." Dread slipped through her. "Oh no, something's happened to Tom, hasn't it?"

"No, he's fine. But yes, it's something about Tom's wound."

"What about it?"

"I was here when the nurse came in to

change the bandage early this morning. When I saw it yesterday, it raised a red flag for me, but I didn't want to make a quick judgment. Now that I've had a better look, I'm pretty sure it's self-inflicted."

"Come again?"

Jamie sighed. "There's no way someone attacked him with a knife and cut his arm the way it's cut. Without going into great medical detail . . . well, just trust me when I say there's no way. I'm talking about the angle, the position on the arm, the depth, everything shouts that he did it to himself."

"But . . . but why?"

"I don't know, Samantha, but it worries me."

"Yeah. Me too. I've got to think about this. I'll call you later. Let me know when you get home."

"I'm home now. Tom checked himself out of the hospital a while ago."

Samantha hung up, her movements automatic as she mulled over Jamie's shocking news. Self-inflicted? Could . . . would Tom do that? And why?

Connor appeared in the doorway, his features haggard once again. Jenna stood by his side. She'd keep this phone call to herself. "Hey, did we get a picture of our guy?"

Connor and Jenna exchanged a frowning glance.

Samantha groaned. "Come on, guys, not more bad news, please?"

"Afraid so. We know who the killer is."

"But that's great! Why the long faces?"

Connor held up the paper, looked at it for a minute, then turned it around to face her.

And she gasped. Dark spots swirled before her eyes. It simply couldn't be.

"Are you sure?"

Jenna nodded. Connor sighed.

Samantha stood. Feeling like she was moving in slow motion, she crossed the space between the table and the door, took the picture from Connor's hand, and stared down at Tom Jackson's handsome face.

31

Monday morning, gray clouds and thunderstorms greeted Samantha. There'd been no word on Tom's location. It had been five weeks and no one had spotted him. Nothing had come of the latest news conference that aired last night asking for information on his whereabouts. The case was still being fully investigated. Tom Jackson's face appeared on television each night.

And still nothing. Which didn't really surprise Samantha. The man had a huge amount of resources at his disposal, including a multitude of disguises. Once they discovered it was Tom who was the perp, they'd gone back over the crime scene photos and she'd found him in almost every one.

He'd looked completely different each time. Even going so far as to use false teeth to change the shape of his mouth. She'd even found him dressed like a woman and wearing a wig with sunglasses in another.

Creepy.

She didn't like the feeling of having to constantly keep watch, looking over her shoulder. She had no doubt the man who had killed those girls wouldn't hesitate to kill her if she got in his way.

And she'd gotten in his way — big-time. Now she knew who she was on the lookout for. Thinking about Tom now still brought the same churning nausea to her stomach as it did when Connor had shown her the sketch artist picture.

He still had protection on his family. And Jamie didn't know it, but she had someone watching her too. Just in case. Dakota Richards had volunteered for that duty when he wasn't on the clock. Samantha smiled. She looked forward to seeing where that went.

Then she frowned again. Tom's sister and brother were devastated, of course, to learn the brother who'd worked so hard for them, sacrificed so much to take care of them, was such an evil person. They'd willingly offered up their home to be searched, but Tom wasn't there. It seemed he'd simply vanished.

Or was lying in wait.

In the meantime, Samantha kept tabs on the girls they'd found. Both Julienna and

Veronica were in some intense counseling. Jenna seemed to have dealt with the situation remarkably well. But she looked at it in the sense that she'd gotten her dad back because of everything that had happened, and while she still had some nightmares about being locked in the room, she was moving on. Bradley probably was at least partly responsible for the bright new smile on the girl's face.

Patty was still Patty and hung around Jenna as much as possible, even consenting to go to church occasionally.

Veronica was due to have her baby in a couple of weeks, and ironically, she'd decided to give it up for adoption. Samantha didn't blame the girl. She'd been through so much, it was amazing she'd come through it as well as she had.

She and Connor had put their feelings for each other on hold while he spent almost every spare moment with Jenna. He'd let the lease on his apartment go and had moved in with his parents who had decided to relocate into a local retirement community when a vacancy came up. Much to Connor's surprise, they were number one on the waiting list they'd signed over a year ago.

For now, Connor and Jenna would live in

the house, which was big enough for all four of them, but his parents had decided to move and that was that. Connor had decided to put in his resignation with SLED and stay in Spartanburg with the police department. They had an opening for a detective and he took it.

And so, here Samantha sat on a chilly November morning, staring out her window, lost in thought, wondering what she was missing.

Where was Tom? Where would he go? Who would he go to for help? Who would be dumb enough to help him?

A headache started in the base of her skull. Samantha rubbed the back of her head and thought — and prayed.

Then a chill slid through her at a sudden idea, and she stilled, sat up, and started to smile.

She reached for the phone.

Connor flipped through the file sitting on the desk before him. Technically, everything about this case was finished and he should be ready to move on.

Except a serial killer still roamed the streets. Maybe not the same streets he was on as of five weeks ago, but he was still out there.

So the case wasn't closed. Which was why Connor was still here.

His phone buzzed and he absently put it to his ear. Samantha's excited voice caught his full attention, and as he listened, his own excitement grew to match hers.

He slapped the folder shut and rose from his seat to head into the sheriff's office.

Samantha sat on Jamie's couch and switched channels. CNN was running the story that had caught the nation's attention. A reporter stood in front of Spartanburg Regional, microphone to her lips. "And now, an update on one of the girls who was snatched a little over ten months ago from her home here in Spartanburg, South Carolina."

A voice off camera asked, "What have you got for us, Lori?"

"Well, I've just learned that Veronica Batson is here at the hospital ready to give birth. She's five weeks early, so naturally precautions are being taken."

"Have you been able to talk to the family today?"

"I spoke with Mrs. Batson, Veronica's mother, just a few minutes ago, and she said Veronica was doing as well as could be expected. She'd been living practically in isolation since being found and rescued five weeks ago from the man, Tom Jackson, who kidnapped her."

"Any word on Tom Jackson and where he might be hiding out?"

"No, no word on that. The police continue their search for this man, but as you know, he's a former FBI agent and an expert with disguises. Unfortunately, he could be nearby and the police just don't recognize him. Which brings me to another point. Parents, you need to keep tabs on your teenage daughters at all times and monitor their internet activity as well as cell phone conversations. It may seem a bit extreme, but Tom Jackson is very clever and very dangerous. Please take every caution to protect your child."

"Thank you, Lori. Please keep us updated on Veronica's condition. Oh, do you know if she plans to keep this child who was fathered while she was held prisoner?"

"The word is that she plans to place the child, that we now know to be a little boy, up for adoption. The adoptive parents are here now, but have asked to remain anonymous."

"Certainly understandable in this bizarre situation. Again, thank you, Lori." The camera returned to the newsroom where the slick-looking man smiled and said, "Please stay with us. We'll have more after this."

Samantha clicked the television off and sighed. They'd been doing reports from the hospital since after lunch. She looked at her watch.

Time to go. "Jamie?"

Jamie looked up from her laptop. A couple of weeks away from graduation, she worked nonstop making sure everything was in order. "Yes?"

"I've got to go. Is Dakota coming over for dinner tonight?"

"He said he was. Why?"

"Just checking." She wiggled her brows. "So, how's that going?"

A dimple peeked at Samantha when Jamie flashed a grin. "It's going."

Emotion caught her by surprise and Samantha had to swallow twice before she could speak. "I'm glad."

Clouds appeared briefly in Jamie's eyes, then were swept away. "I . . . haven't told him anything yet."

Samantha strode to her sister's side. "And you don't have to. Not until you're ready."

"I feel like I should tell him . . . something. I think he suspects something anyway. I tend to be a little . . . jumpy around him."

Samantha gave Jamie a side hug. "In your own time, got it?"

"Got it."

"Is he . . ." She paused, not sure whether she should ask.

"What?"

"Well, is he a Christian?"

Softness covered Jamie's face. "Yes, he is. I think he's got his own burdens that he's carrying, but yes, he's a believer."

Relief swept Samantha. "I'm so glad." She glanced at her watch. "I've got to run."

"Where to?"

"To catch a killer."

32

Tom Jackson, aka The Agent, strode down the hall, his breathing even, anticipation sweet. The small suitcase stuffed with newspaper rolled silently along behind him.

He snarled. Stupid cops had traced everything attached to his name and had frozen all of his funds. He couldn't touch a dime of that money without them knowing it.

He needed this baby. Fortunately, the couple waiting to adopt little Veronica's bundle of joy had never seen his face. So, it was simply a matter of walking into Veronica's room, picking up the kid, getting out, meeting the couple, and grabbing his money. Of course he would have to deal with the little matter of the alarm on the brat's arm, but that wasn't anything a pair of scissors wouldn't take care of.

Tugging on the lapel of the white coat, he smoothed it down, then adjusted the stethoscope around his neck. One of the nurses to his left caught his eye and smiled.

Another doctor swept past him with a nod.

Tom kept walking; confidence oozed with every step.

He stopped at the nurses' desk. A well-built male looked up. "May I help you?"

"Veronica Batson's room, please."

The man narrowed his eyes. "And you are?"

"Dr. Ron Jessup. Since Veronica's baby is premature, I've been called in as backup, to do the initial observation. Preemies are my specialty."

Tom didn't even flinch as the nurse studied his name badge. He'd been planning this moment for the last five weeks.

"Veronica just delivered. She's in room 518."

"Is the baby in there or the nursery?"

"He's in the room with his mother."

"Thanks."

Tom rolled his suitcase behind him.

He stopped at room 518 and took a deep breath. He had no way of knowing how many people would be in the room. But he would ask them all to leave, take a break, whatever, while he examined the baby. Then he'd kill Veronica — she'd be an easy, weak victim of suffocation — put the child in the suitcase, and be on his way to collect his money.

He pushed open the door and stopped. The room was empty save the rolling crib on the far side of the bed, and a young girl in the bed with her back to the door. Jet black curls rested on the pillow. She had the sheet pulled up around her. She stirred, but didn't turn.

"Hello, Veronica."

The person in the bed turned toward him. "Hello, Tom."

Fury zipped through him.

"You set me up."

Samantha sat up, gun pointed at her ex-friend and occasional partner. She narrowed her eyes. "And enjoyed every minute of it."

Understanding crossed his face. "Everybody out there is a cop."

"Every last person on this wing."

"No babies."

"What?"

"I should have realized. All the way here, on the baby ward. I didn't see any babies."

"Actually, we had some people walking around carrying baby dolls. You must have missed them."

"So, this is it, huh?"

She let him see the pain he'd caused her.

"Just tell me why."

"Because it was my — destiny, I suppose you could say." A faraway look entered his eyes. "I gave those girls a higher purpose. Because of me, I gave their lives meaning."

Nausea swirled within her. "You're sick."

Anger flashed as he looked at her fully once again. "No, Samantha, not sick. Ambitious. I wanted the money too. Lots and lots of money."

"You killed those girls!"

"Of course I did. They'd seen my face without my disguises. And Boss — Victoria Abbott — insisted no one be left as witnesses. She was incredibly clever."

"Well, she's sitting in a jail cell now."

Disappointment crossed his handsome features. "I'm not sure what happened with her. She became weak in the end."

"No, she just met her match in Jenna Wolfe."

His jaw went tight, then he said, "Yes, that one didn't frighten easily."

"She's too much like her dad."

"Whatever." He drew in a deep breath. "I suppose you're recording this conversation."

"Of course."

"And the room will be swarmed as soon as you give the signal."

"Right again." She hauled in a gulp of air.

"Why did you kill Calvin, the bomb guy?"

"Yes, I figured you'd come up with that question."

"And?"

"Because as we were leaving the scene, he asked me how I knew the bomb was under the seat. I took a chance and told him I heard the click."

Understanding dawned within her. "There was no click, was there?"

"Nope. Not that kind of switch. It probably would have blown when you turned the first corner . . . when the chemicals mixed together, ignited, then hit the C-4."

"And Calvin pointed this out to you."

"No, he just looked at me funny and kept walking. But I knew he knew."

"So you killed him."

"Yep."

Sorrow grabbed her and held on. "He had a ten-year-old daughter, Tom. His nineteen-year-old son was killed too. Do you even have any kind of conscience left?"

"Not really, I guess, because I don't feel bad about the stuff I do. Makes me the perfect killer, doesn't it?" He shifted. "Tell Jamie she's the only one I ever really cared about."

Confusion hit her. "Why are you bringing up Jamie?"

"Just tell her."

His hand slid into the pocket of his white lab coat, and Samantha rolled to the floor, placing the bed between her and Tom. She hit the button on her radio, the signal for help as he pulled out his gun.

But he didn't fire, just stood there. "Tell her, Sam, okay?"

Then put the gun to his head and pulled the trigger.

33

The case was solved. Jenna was safe. A killer was dead, and parents would rest a little easier tonight. Connor knew he would. So now it was time to do what he'd put off for several weeks.

"Jenna, you ready?"

"I can't go, Dad."

"What? Why not?"

"Because I'm going to take you." Samantha's familiar voice had the same effect on him this time as it did the very first day he'd met her.

He turned from the steps to see her standing in his open front doorway. "You are?"

"Yeah. Is that okay?"

"More than okay."

Her smile flashed and singed his heart.

Connor followed her down the drive to the edge of the lawn where she'd parked her car. He climbed into the passenger seat and waited for her to slide behind the wheel of her Jeep.

She turned to say something and he acted on impulse. He leaned over and placed his lips on hers and wrapped his left hand around the base of her neck.

She froze for about a second, then accepted his kiss, eagerly returning it. He felt the electricity of attraction and passion with this incredible woman, and yet she also touched his vulnerable, gentle side too. He wanted to pull her close and never let her go.

Instead, he pulled away. Sat back and smiled as she slowly opened her eyes.

An answering smile crept across her face and she said, "Well, that was . . . unexpected."

"But?"

"But . . . nice."

"Nice?" He pretended to be wounded. "Nice? I guess I'm going to have to work on my technique."

Samantha threw back her head and laughed, then stared him down. "I'll be glad to give you plenty of opportunity to work on that." She reached up and cupped his cheek. "I need to tell you something."

He stopped her with a finger on her lips. "Tell me in a little while."

Her eyes said she understood, and she

cranked the car to head to the little storage
business about five miles up the street from
his neighborhood. She pulled through the
gate and around to the number he'd given
her.

"I'll wait here."

Already he could feel the knot in his throat
and wondered if he was ready for this. Her
hand covered his and he looked up, not
bothering to hide the tears that welled there.

"Go. God is with you. Lean on him. Cry
on his shoulder. Trust him."

Without a word, Connor opened the door
and stepped out. Punched in the code to
lift the garage door.

And there it was.

Andrew's sleek little red Corvette.

Connor fingered the key in his pocket and
pulled in a deep breath. Instead of going
around to the driver's door, he went to the
other side.

Pulling the door open, he slid in the pas-
senger seat and . . . inhaled. The scent of
Andrew's favorite aftershave assaulted him.
Tears flooded his eyes.

*Oh God, I can't do this! He was like my
brother, God. Why . . . Please . . .*

Deep breath.

Samantha's words came back to him. *God
is with you. Lean on him. Cry on his shoulder.*

Connor opened the glove compartment.

And saw the envelope sitting on top of the "About Your Car" book. Saw his name written in Andrew's neat, tight scrawl.

He reached out a hand and with trembling fingers picked up the envelope and opened it.

More of Andrew's handwriting filled the one page Connor pulled out.

"Dear Connor. I guess if you're reading this, I'm dead. I know you're probably missing me, but I have to be honest, I don't miss you a bit. I'm in heaven walking and talking with Jesus, so, sorry, buddy."

Connor gave a choked laugh and shook his head. "Ah, Andrew . . ."

He kept reading. "Anyway, in all seriousness, I know if I died during a case, you'd probably blame yourself in some way . . . or God. Connor, if that's what you're doing, you've got to stop that right now. You know better than anyone, with the exception of Angie, how much I love God. I'm home now. Don't blame God, don't blame yourself."

Connor leaned his head back against the headrest and swallowed hard. "I'm sorry, God. I didn't mean to blame you, but it was easier than blaming myself. And now . . . I guess I can't even do that after reading this.

I do blame Tom Jackson. I don't know why you don't take guys like that out before they're born, but I guess it's not for me to understand."

He went back to the letter. "Connor, God loves you so much. I hope one day you come to understand that. I think Samantha's kind of falling for you too."

He chuckled out loud. "I hope so, partner."

"Have faith, Connor. Faith in Samantha, faith in Jenna, faith in yourself. But most importantly, have faith in God. He won't let you down. I love you, my friend. I pray for you for peace that passes all understanding. I'd put in a good word for you up here, but it doesn't work that way. It's up to you, Connor. I love you, my friend. You've been the brother I never had. Thanks for looking after Angie as I know you will. Hang in there, partner, and give God the chance he deserves. I'll see you soon, as life on earth is a mere blink of the eye to the One who holds it all in his palm. Andrew."

But there was more. "P.S. Let Jenna drive the Vette. It's just a car. Material things don't mean squat compared to the spiritual stuff. Be sure to tell her to be careful, though."

Connor folded the letter, holding on to

his composure.

He felt a hand fall on his shoulder and looked up to see Samantha staring down at him. "Are you okay?"

He took a deep breath. "I don't know. Yes. I think so. Or at least I will be."

"Race you home?" She quirked a brow at him, and he laughed, stood and pulled her into his arms.

"I love you, Sam."

"I love you too, Connor."

"Andrew's watching all this and laughing his head off at me, you realize this, don't you?"

"Well, that's heaven for you. No tears or sorrow allowed."

He turned serious, but didn't let her go. "Yeah, that's heaven. But I have to admit, I think God's blessed me with a little slice of heaven on earth."

"You think?"

"Oh yeah." He leaned down and placed his lips against hers . . .

. . . and thanked God for loving him so much that he was willing to die for him . . .

. . . and to give him a woman like Samantha to live out the rest of his days with.

God is faithful.

EPILOGUE

The Hero snapped open the newspaper — and nearly choked on his chicken sandwich.

He pulled the paper closer to make sure his eyes weren't playing tricks on him.

They weren't.

She was alive.

What? How was that possible?

It wasn't. He knew that.

And yet — there she was. Smiling broadly and holding a diploma?

Sandwich forgotten, he scanned the article.

Jamie Cash, a doctor?

He tossed the paper aside and walked down to his basement. Bypassing the terrified young woman stretched out on the cot across the room, hands bound beneath her, he went straight to his safe. Her eyes never left him. He'd have to get rid of her tonight. If the newspaper article was true, he had pressing business to take care of.

Three twists later, he pulled out his most treasured possession.

The Book.

Opening it, he flipped through to number twelve.

And there she was.

He'd taken twelve pictures of her because she was number twelve.

He flicked a glance in the direction of his latest. She turned her head when he met her eyes — and screamed.

Number seventeen. He still needed six pictures of her.

Number twelve drew his attention back to The Book. She'd been his favorite. Out of all of them, she stood out in his memory the most. She'd fought him the hardest — and screamed the loudest.

And she'd lived even after he'd killed her.

Or thought he'd killed her.

Jamie Cash.

Beautiful Jamie.

Number twelve.

He slapped the book closed. Picked up the knife.

And cut his fun short.

Literally.

Holding the blade under the running water, he watched the red liquid swirl down the drain as he remembered back to the moment he met Jamie. Anticipation filled him as he slid the knife back into its proper place.

Slowly, methodically, he dried his hands.

Now, to find Jamie and finish what he'd started a little over ten years ago. He smiled.

Let the fun begin.

ACKNOWLEDGMENTS

Thank you to Jesus who answered my prayers and allowed my dreams to come true. I pray I always walk in accordance with the plans You have for me. I pray You are visible on each and every page.

Thanks to my agent, Tamela Murray, for all your wonderful, uplifting encouragement and hard work in seeing this book come to pass. Your faithfulness and integrity mean the world to me!

Thank you to my editor, Andrea Doering, who took a chance on a semi-newbie . . . LOL . . . and believed in the story and me. It's a pleasure to work with you!

Thanks to all the computer geniuses at crimescenewriter — you guys were never too busy to answer my computer questions. If anyone notices any errors in the computer stuff, it's totally my fault.

Thank you, Officer Jim Hall, fellow ACF-Wer and Carolina Christian Writer, for telling me how to get all my "cop stuff" right. I would have been sorely embarrassed if you hadn't fixed all my police procedural mistakes. I look forward to seeing your book in print one day because you've got a kickin' story — wish I'd thought of it!

Thank you to my family for putting up with me when I'm in writing mode — which is a lot of the time, I know! Thank you for your patience and understanding — and the willingness to eat out A LOT! And thank you to my parents, Lewis and Lou Jean Barker, and in-laws, Bill and Diane Eason, who provide kid care so I can write. I couldn't do it without you and I love you very much.

A special thank-you to my dear sweet husband who supports me 100 percent, but isn't sure he wants to read this book because one measly little chapter scared him. (You weren't supposed to read the end first!)

Thanks to my writing buddies, critique partners, and brainstormers! To the Brainstorming Authors: Camy Tang, Missy Tippens, Jennifer Hudson Taylor, Pammer James, and Cheryl Wyatt — and Ginny Aiken who was supposed to be there, but couldn't be. Thanks for your long-distance help! This book is the result of our weekend writers retreat up in the North Carolina mountains. Once I recovered from the altitude sickness, everything we discussed came together and actually made sense. You guys rock. Until next time . . .

Thank you, Dee Henderson, for the time you put into reading and critiquing the book. Thank you so much for your sweet endorsements of my writing. Your mentorship has been such a blessing and your friendship a gift from God. You've been a steadfast friend for ten years, and I appreciate you more than you know.

Thanks to Barb Barnes for her superior editing and to Michele Misiak for all of her help with marketing ideas, etc., and for keeping me updated on everything going on!

And a big thank-you to American Christian Fiction Writers and all of you who so helpfully answered research questions. I wish I could name you all.

ABOUT THE AUTHOR

Lynette Eason grew up in Greenville, South Carolina. She graduated from the University of South Carolina, Columbia, and then obtained her master's in education at Converse College. Author of eight inspirational romantic suspense books, she is also a member of American Christian Fiction Writers (ACFW) and Romance Writers of America (RWA). In 1998, Lynette married "the boy next door," and now she and her husband and two children make their home in Spartanburg, South Carolina.